W9-DEC-441

GUN IN
CHEEK

GUN IN CHEEK

A Study of
"Alternative"
Crime Fiction

By Bill Pronzini

COWARD, McCANN & GEOGHEGAN

Chapter 4, The Saga of the Risen Phoenix, appeared in different form
in *The Armchair Detective* for April 1977, under the title "The
Saga of the Phoenix that Probably Should Never Have Arisen."
Copyright © 1977 by Allen J. Hubin

Portions of Chapter 11, Don't Tell Me You've Got a Heater in Your
Girdle, Madam! appeared in different form in *The Armchair Detec-
tive* for Spring 1980, under the title "The Worst Mystery Novel of
All Time." Copyright © 1980 by The Mysterious Press.

Portions of Chapter 12, Ante-Bellem Days; or, "My Roscoe Sneezed:
Ka-Chee!" appeared under that title in *Clues*, edited by E. R. Hag-
emann and published by The Bowling Green University Popular
Press. Copyright © 1982 by Bill Pronzini.

Library of Congress Cataloging in Publication Data
Pronzini, Bill.
   Gun in cheek.

   Bibliography: p.
   Includes index.
   1. Detective and mystery stories, American—History
and criticism. 2. Detective and mystery stories,
English—History and criticism. 3. Crime and criminals
in literature. I. Title.
PS374.D4P7   1982   813'.0872'09   82-5172
ISBN 0-698-11180-X   AACR2

PRINTED IN THE UNITED STATES OF AMERICA

Acknowledgments

For their help and encouragement on this project, the author would like to thank the following writers, critics, and aficionados: Jeffrey Wallmann, Jon L. Breen, Francis M. Nevins, Douglas Greene, Ellen Nehr, Bill Blackbeard, Angelo Panagos, Art Scott, and Bruce Taylor.

Special thanks, for their faith and perseverance, to Clyde Taylor of Curtis Brown, Ltd., and Bill Thompson of Coward, McCann & Geoghegan.

For all those who love a mystery

Contents

Introduction

I think I know why Bill Pronzini asked me write an introduction to a book that really needs none. He *knows*. Not only does he know how to write good mystery novels, he also knows where to find all the *bad* ones, those he will soon define for you as "alternative classics." But more than that, he has an encyclopedic memory of the entire genre, and surely a man such as this *knows* that I myself wrote a few of these alternative classics, way back then when I was still struggling to learn my trade. Frankly, I feel a bit offended that some of my early masterpieces were passed over for consideration.

Who, for example, among any of the entrants Mr. Pronzini *has* chosen to include in his wonderful book could ever have written an exchange like:

"You're cute," she said. She was slightly looped, he thought, and her voice sounded deep and throaty even when she spoke. "I noticed you while I was singing, and I said to myself, He's cute. I was right."

She looked better close up, much better than she did on the bandstand. She had her hair pulled back tight over her ears, clipped at the back of her neck with an amber clasp, fanning out over her shoulders. The blouse she wore had a deep V sweeping down from her shoulders, terminating in a shadowed cleft between high breasts. He remembered staring at the soft whiteness of her skin as she leaned over the table.

"You're very cute," she repeated, and he said, "You're not bad yourself."

She blew smoke across the table. "Sparkling dialogue," she said dryly. "Refugees from a Grade-B stinkeroo."

"Pardon me. I'm not dressed for repartee."

I wrote those priceless lines. Yes, Mr. Pronzini.

Moreover, they were published.

But did this scrupulous scholar consider them worthy of inclusion in his otherwise impeccably researched and wittily informative book? I should say not. Or how about this?

And then I was falling.

I don't know what I thought as I fell. I know it seemed to take a long time, seemed to take forever, seemed never to end. I saw the ledge and the struggling figures on it, and the figures came closer, and below them I saw the twisted rocks of Hokus Pokus, waiting. I kept dropping, and there was a tight nausea in my throat, and a scream that never found voice. I closed my eyes, and I forced moisture from them, and I felt the wind ripping at me, and I was aware of the rope around my waist and the rush of air as I fell.

I hit. I hit with a wrenching pain that shot up the length of my leg. My body crushed onto my twisted foot, and a flash of yellow exploded inside my head. I heard someone scream, a hoarse curse that shattered the stillness of the mountain, an anguished cry of sheer, raw pain. And then I realized that my mouth was open, and the scream was coming from my own throat.

I wrote that, too.

And it, *too*, was published, Mr. Pronzini.

Or how about:

She snatched the knife from the table, and then she took a lithe step toward my chair, gripping my hair in one hand, pulling my head back, and then lifting the knife high over my throat, a tight grin on her face.

"Aren't you, darling?" she said through clenched teeth. "Aren't you quite helpless?"

Tarrance stood frozen. Yoshi, on the other side of the tea cart, had gone suddenly pale. I sat in the chair and looked up at the tip of the carving knife, and then Adrienne began laughing shrilly, tossing the knife down onto the terrace. Yoshi picked it up quickly.

"My wife has a keen sense of humor," I said coldly.

Now surely, if Mr. Pronzini had a decent bone in his body, he would have included at *least* this fine example of breathless suspense among those he winnowed out for honors. What else *did* one have to write to be considered a nominee? Was he looking for something a bit more literary? In which case, I offer the following:

The sky hung overhead like a moth-eaten gray shawl, and the flakes spilled down from it like a loose dandruff at first, lazy and slow.

I could go on. And on. (Oh, how I *did* go on and on in those days.) The point, of course, is that Mr. Pronzini surely *knew* about these gems when he was preparing his brief. He has obviously read and digested everything ever written in the genre by anyone anywhere. But even giving him the benefit of the doubt, even assuming he somehow missed these published morsels, doesn't the man ever go to the *movies*? Didn't he see the film *The Birds*, for which I wrote the screenplay? Does he *truly* not remember (or is his forgetfulness just a clever ploy to avoid giving me my rightful due?) the birthday party scene? Where all the birds swoop down and break balloons and knock over tables and whatnot? Did Mr. Pronzini *truly* not witness the touching scene afterward, in which the hero expresses his concern for the heroine? A scene Hitch desperately tried to excise from the film but couldn't because the camera was in tight on his stars talking, and he had no covering footage? Has Mr. Pronzini honestly forgotten those immortal lines?

MITCH: Look, do you have to go back to Annie's?

MELANIE: No, I have my things in the car.

MITCH: Then stay and have something to eat before you start back. I'd feel a lot better.

I rest my case.

Mr. Pronzini asked me to write this introduction only because he knew samples of my work *should* have been included in this book and *weren't*. As simple as that. I am properly insulted.

So I'll leave now.

—Ed McBain
(Evan Hunter)

Without Malice,
A Forethought

In recent years, those of us who love the mystery have been pleased to note the publication of an increasing number of critical works devoted to the genre and its writers. These include general histories (Julian Symons's *Mortal Consequences*); social histories (Colin Watson's *Snobbery With Violence*); biographies (Frank McShane's *The Life of Raymond Chandler*, John McAleer's *Rex Stout: A Biography*); collections of critical essays and commentary (Barzun and Taylor's *A Catalogue of Crime*); appreciations (Leroy Panek's *Watteau's Shepherds*, Robert Barnard's *A Talent to Deceive*); and bibliographic and encyclopedic reference works (Allen Hubin's *The Bibliography of Crime Fiction, 1749–1975*, Otto Penzler's and Chris Steinbrunner's *The Encyclopedia of Mystery and Detection*, and the recent *Twentieth Century Crime and Mystery Writers*, edited by John Reilly).

Without exception, these and other critical works have focused on the positive side of crime fiction. That is, they dwell on its technical and/or artistic qualities. They offer in-depth studies of its best writers, its best books. They laud, applaud, dissect, gently chastise, and sometimes canonize the great and the near-great of mysterydom.

Which is all fine, of course; no one could be more delighted

than I at this passionate interest in the field in which I publish
the bulk of my fiction. And yet the absolute emphasis on the
good strikes me as unfair. The good mystery gets all the credit,
all the attention. So does the good writer.

But what about the *bad* mystery?

What about the *bad* writer?

The amount of (critically) inferior crime fiction published
during this century far exceeds that of the superior, after all;
there have been hundreds, if not thousands, of works of all
types and description. Most of these are of average badness, to
be sure. Yet several stand out as unique and in their own way
are every bit as memorable as any of the classic good ones. Or
would be if enough people knew of their existence.

The "alternative classics" and their authors, however, have
been neglected to the point of invisibility. Much has been written about the contributions of Doyle, Christie, Hammett,
Chandler, Stout. But how many readers—indeed, how many
aficionados—are aware of the contributions of Michael Morgan, Tom Roan, Eric Heath, James O'Hanlon, Sydney Horler,
Michael Avallone, Robert Leslie Bellem, Milton M. Raison, and
Joseph Rosenberger? Everyone has heard of *The Hound of the
Baskervilles, The Maltese Falcon, The Murder of Roger
Ackroyd, The Big Sleep.* But how many know the joys to be
found in *Decoy, The Dragon Strikes Back, Murder of a Mystery
Writer, Murder at Horsethief, Lord of Terror, Bride of Terror,*
and *The Bat?*

The purpose of this book is threefold: first, to rectify the
neglect of these writers and their works, to give them the critical attention they deserve; second, to provide a different historical perspective on crime fiction—its detectives, its sub-
genres, its publishers—and on the social attitudes it reflects
(which are often more pronounced in the bad mystery than in
the good one); and third, to add a few chuckles—perhaps even a
guffaw or two—to the heretofore sobersided field of mystery
criticism. It is all well and good to take the genre seriously; as a
mystery writer, I take it (and this book) rather seriously
myself. But it is not hallowed ground, as some would have us
believe. Nor should it be so snooty in its newfound position as a
"legitimate" literary art form to want to bury its so-called
black sheep or refuse to give itself an old-fashioned horse laugh

now and then.* The ability to laugh at oneself or one's own, it has been said, is the sign of a healthy organism. And the mystery, one hopes, is a *very* healthy organism.

As to my qualifications for undertaking such a project, I submit the following credentials: mystery novelist, short-story writer, anthologist, and essayist; collector and student of mystery criticism, biography, bibliography, history, and ephemera; owner of several thousand mystery novels, collections, anthologies, and pulp and digest magazines, a good many of which are quite bad. I also submit the following sentence from my novel, *The Stalker:* "When would this phantasmagoria that was all too real reality end? he asked himself."

Can there be anyone better suited to write a tribute to the alternative classics of crime fiction than the author of *that* immortal line?

---

*Academics consider it "legitimate" nowadays, anyhow. The self-styled "literary establishment" considers any prose that has a plot, makes a linear kind of sense throughout, and does not involve suburban sexual angst to be trash, or at best subliterary.

1. "Wanna Woo-woo?"

" . . . I have a plot for a book that I intend to write some day that I believe gets over the perfect murder most adequately. . . . In that book I shall show that the police and detectives are utterly baffled and that at last the murderer himself has to come forward and tell how he committed the crime. I will have him to do this out of a pure sense of bravado and love of the dramatic, or possibly motivate it by showing that he is suffering from an incurable disease and is going to die soon anyway."

"Sounds like a lot of baloney to me," snorted Lang.

—Eric Heath,
Murder of a Mystery Writer

"Fire's a damned sight worse," he muttered. "Cripes, my head's like a pumpkin! It's always at the back of my mind."

—Ellery Queen,
The Siamese Twin Mystery

The amateur detective, or AD as he is affectionately known to insiders, is the most popular crime-solving creation among the writers of detective fiction. Beginning with Jacques Futrelle's Professor F. X. Van Duesen, "The Thinking Machine," in this country, and, somewhat later, Chesterton's Father Brown in England, the AD has seen more bloodletting, faced more peril, and unraveled more mysteries than all professional detectives, public and private, combined.

The AD can be of either sex, of any age; can possess any quirk or specialized knowledge and be of any profession (or no profession at all). The AD roster includes doctors, lawyers, merchants, thieves; little old ladies with a homicidal eye and fusty professors with very large brains; bored young men of wealth and breeding, and derelicts on Skid Row; newspaper reporters, poets, playwrights, fiction writers, nonfiction writers, unpublished writers, songwriters, and insurance underwriters; salesmen, bankers, Indians, artists, magicians, priests, nuns, gamblers, teachers, scientists, sports figures, photographers, publicans—and a hundred more. The AD can be hard-boiled, soft-boiled, half-baked, well-pickled, or sugar-coated. He/she can use fists, guns, wits, half-wits, innocence, guile, luck, pluck, deduction, guesswork, or any combination of these to solve a case and bring an evildoer to justice.

What the most enduring of the amateur detectives seem to have in common is an abiding interest in criminology, an encyclopedic knowledge of trivial and/or esoteric facts, a Sherlockian intelligence, a penchant for withholding evidence from the police (but never from the reader, no matter how obliquely it is couched), and such endearing qualities as the enigmatic smile, the gimlet eye, the curled lip, the disarming grin, the sharp retort, the clever pun, the cryptic remark, and the perfect squelch. Consider the great ADs of mystery fiction: Father Brown, Dr. Fell, Ellery Queen, Lord Peter Wimsey, Reggie Fortune, The Great Merlini, Miss Marple, Perry Mason, John J. Malone, "The Old Man in the Corner," Mr. and Mrs. North, Miss Hildegarde Withers. When these ladies and gentlemen embark on a case, it is bound to be a memorable one.

The same is true of the great ADs on the other side of the qualitative coin.

The earliest of these is Joseph Rouletabille, a Parisian reporter who solves a number of cases in the early 1900s narrated by his Watson, Sainclair, and created by French writer Gaston Leroux. The first, *The Mystery of the Yellow Room* (1907), is well known and also considered by some—John Dickson Carr, the grand master of the "impossible crime" story, was one—to be among the finest "locked-room" mysteries ever penned. This may be true, if one reckons solely on ingenuity of plot; but if one takes into account stilted writing, nonexistent characterization, incredible coincidences, and a welter of disguises, aliases, and red herrings—plus such other implausibilities as the fact that Rouletabille, already a successful journalist, is not much older than sixteen when he solves the mystery of the yellow room—Leroux might seem better placed, or at least equally well placed, at the opposite end of the mystery spectrum.

From this standpoint, his most (or least) accomplished work is the second of the Rouletabille cases, *The Perfume of the Lady in Black* (1909). Chief among its noteworthy aspects is a preposterous plot in which the villain of *The Mystery of the Yellow Room,* a brilliant former detective named Frédéric Larsan, who was supposedly killed off in that book, returns alive and in disguise (à la Sherlock Holmes) to commit a new locked-room murder, this one involving the use of false-face and a tricked-up wardrobe. There are also more aliases, red herrings, and coincidences, some crudely worked out motivations, a final "revelation" that Rouletabille is the illegitimate son of Larsan, and such artful prose as:

> He rushed to the canal, sobbing, and, with a prayer, uttered as much to the Lady in Black as to God Himself, threw himself into the water. Happily, in his despair, the poor child had forgotten that he knew how to swim.

> He had mocked her, even while the tears had streamed down his cheeks. I could never have believed that Rouletabille could have been so cruel or so heartless—or, even, so ill-bred!

The first of the notable ADs on the American front is Professor Herman Brierly, who appears in four novels by Will Levinrew published in the late twenties and early thirties. Brierly is an elderly research scientist of the following description: "small, exquisitely formed body, not over five feet tall; tiny hands and feet, bushy, snow-white hair, bushy black brows over dark blue eyes so deeply sunken in their sockets as to seem jet black; high, fresh complexion rarely found except in infancy." Brierly is also a superintellect of a crabby, somewhat egotistical nature that puts him in a class with his obvious role model, Philo Vance. His stock-in-trade is solving crimes through "scientific deduction," which is a masking euphemism for the fact that he unravels the most convoluted, Van Dineish plots with a minimum of detection and a maximum of obscure textbook science and pathology.

The most interesting of his cases is *Murder on the Palisades* (1930), in which a number of people are murdered in a gloomy old mansion on the New Jersey Palisades, across the Hudson River from New York City. Because Levinrew was a devotee of Van Dine, this novel, like his others, is chock full of footnotes, interminable question-and-answer sessions, befuddled cops, bizarre occurrences, and clues of the esoteric variety (the first few letters of the Hebrew alphabet, for example, play an important, if rather unbelievable, part in the plot). But it is none of these things that distinguishes *Murder on the Palisades*; rather it is the sheer number of exotic methods of murder and attempted murder—certainly more than in any other mystery novel in the genre's history—and the identity of the "instrument" used in perpetrating most of the crimes.

Characters are murdered, or almost murdered, by the injection of microorganisms to cause spinal meningitis; by mixing a quantity of ergotized (ergot is a poisonous grain fungus) flour with whole-wheat flour and baking it into a loaf of bread; by poisoning some chocolate-coated almonds with almond-tasting nitrobenzol; by injecting a drug called phlorizin, which causes diabetes, so that the person can then be given too large a dose of insulin, which will send him into fatal insulin shock; and by scratching a man's hand with a match that has been dipped into a jar of hydrophobia germs. But the crowning method is a locked-room murder in which a missile, presumably a stone, is hurled through a window to crush a man's skull but then "disappears" before the police arrive on the scene seconds later. The explanation for this one is demonstrated as follows by Professor Brierly:

> [They] suddenly saw an object, at the end of a rope, rise above the roof with incredible velocity. This

object described a giant arc, and continued describing the arc, limited by the rope with undiminished speed. . . .

The rope flattened out on the roof; the object at its free end continued with undiminished speed outward and downward, the rope flattened out against the rear of the building and the object at the end of this gigantic lash whipped through the closed window with a crash, shortly to reappear hanging taut at the end of the rope, oscillating gently.

According to the professor, this device—a large catapult affixed to the roof by bolts, with a rope stretching to it from a staple—works in the following manner:

"This rope is taut. I have at the end of it in the toe of this stocking a stone a little larger than a baseball. I tied a piece of string around the stocking above the stone, although hardly necessary. I now put it into the catapult which is aimed upward in the direction of the garage door, in perfect line with the window. The force of the catapult will shoot it almost straight upward, but the pull of the rope on that staple will prevent it from going straight upward. Also, it will not jerk as it would if I propelled it straight upward or straight outward from the staple. No, this counterforce will make it describe the arc you saw. Whirl a watch-chain and see the undiminished speed with which it will wind itself around your finger, to the very end. Same principle involved here. The initial impetus on the end of the watch chain is not *around* the finger, but straight ahead or upward as it is here. This staple acts like the finger on the chain."

The person responsible for most of these fanciful acts is an embittered member of the household, the wife of one of the victims, who has been confined to a wheelchair since suffering a paralyzing attack of poliomyelitis. It was she who worked the catapult from the roof, we are told, but since she couldn't get around to commit the other crimes, she hypnotized her twelve-year-old son, who is suffering from a form of dementia praecox, and ordered *him* to commit them in her stead. When Brierly has the boy hypnotized as part of his reconstruction of events and instructs him to reenact his crimes, the youth becomes "all evil, the personification of murderous desire," and the sight of him causes a hardened newspaperman to tremble "as if with the ague" and a hard-boiled cop, "inured to hardships in himself and others, familiar with ugly sights and scenes, exponent of the third degree with recalcitrant prisoners," almost to faint dead away. Brierly, however, is unmoved. Nothing much bothers the true scientist—and the true AD—in his never-ending pursuit of truth, justice, and the American way.

A considerably different, if no less notable, amateur detective is Tony Woolrich, a New York drama critic fathered in the forties by Milton M. Raison. Woolrich's greatest case is *Murder in a Lighter Vein* (1947), about which Anthony Boucher wrote in the San Francisco *Chronicle:* "This latest exploit of Tony Woolrich . . . is in plot and writing simply down to Mr. Raison's standard. I list it only to warn you that this (to quote the jacket) 'intimate, behind-the-scenes tale of big-time radio' does not even have the virtue of reasonable accuracy in depicting the industry."

Murder in a Lighter Vein is set in Hollywood, to which city Woolrich has come to write a series of articles on its "little theaters." (Why anyone in New York would be interested in Hollywood's little theaters is not specified.) The first theater group with which he becomes involved is the Dramatic Arts Guild, a serious bunch that has selected for its first production Edmond Rostand's verse play, *Cyrano de Bergerac.*

The group is so serious, in fact, that they have picked up a sponsor to air a radio adaptation of the play and persuaded a stand-up radio comic of uncouth reputation to play Cyrano. The rationale for this decision is that the comic, Artie Aragon, has a very high Hooper rating—the radio equivalent of the Nielsen TV ratings—and it is felt Artie will pull a large audience and thereby launch the Dramatic Arts Guild into the big time. If the logic of this seems dubious, it is because Raison was a master of dubious logic—an art perhaps learned while practicing his alternate career of scripting screen potboilers.

Problems begin to develop when Artie decides he doesn't like the *Cyrano* script. It's not right for him and his image, he says. It doesn't have any boffo laughs. Worst of all, it doesn't have any "Wanna woo-woos?"

* * *

"Maybe I might look at a rough scrip'," hedged Artie. He turned to the Worths. "Get writin'. Fix up somethin' good. Put that dame [an actress named Sara] in lots of scenes with me. And don't forget to put in a couple 'wanna woo-woos.' "

There was dead silence as Rostand whirled in his grave like a dervish.

Parmalee finally cleared his throat and asked almost timidly, "A couple of what?"

"Woo-woos," said Artie impatiently, as though he was explaining something to an idiot. . . . "There's a reason for it in all my scrip's. Wanna woo-woo made me what I am today."

"Wanna woo-woo?", you see, is Artie's big catch phrase, in the mode of Lou Costello's "I'm a baaaaaaaaaaaddd boy!" or Joe Penner's "Wanna buy a duck?" At some point in each of his radio shows, Artie looks at one of the female cast members, leers obscenely, grabs the microphone as if it were the woman, and says, "Wanna woo-woo?" For some reason, this is deemed hilarious by one and all, and the audience topples out of its collective seat and rolls in the aisle.

The various members of the Dramatic Arts Guild are shocked; they are artists, after all, and can't bear to see a wonderful play like *Cyrano* ruined with one-liners and "Wanna woo-woos?" They all hate Artie; so do his drunken wife, his well-endowed mistress, and his two "scrip' " writers. And so does Woolrich, who has a professed fondness for fine art. Of course, Tony also has a fondness for such fine art as one of the actresses, Sara, and is too busily engaged in making a play for her to worry about somebody knocking off Artie.

(You should not get the impression, however, that Tony is a playboy. Nor should you get the impression that he is suave, sophisticated, or has a scintillating wit. The best word to describe him might be "virginal." He blushes quite a bit, particularly when someone makes a sexual reference, and says things like "the moon fell on my head and burst into a million rose-colored bubbles" after an evening with Sara.)

Comes the night of the big broadcast. Artie's role in *Cyrano* has been completely rewritten to include plenty of boffo laughs and "Wanna woo-woos?" The audience, we are told, topples out

of its collective seat and rolls in the aisle. The cast grimaces.
Woolrich grimaces. Then, near the climax, Artie grabs the
microphone in both hands, gives Sara a magnificent leer, and
says his most obscene "Wanna woo-woo?" ever. Whereupon he
falls down dead. No fanfare, no histrionics. He simply says
"Wanna woo-woo?" and falls down dead.

Joe Holden, of the "downtown Homicide Squad," is called in.
A preliminary examination of the body reveals no marks or
signs of violence; could Artie have succumbed to a heart attack?
Joe, who has the IQ of a house plant, conducts a superficial
investigation, becomes frustrated, and turns to Woolrich for
assistance; it seems he is in awe of Tony's AD abilities, having
worked with him once before on a case. He asks the county
sheriff to swear Woolrich in as a special deputy, complete with
badge and gun and a salary of ten dollars a day.

Tony is overwhelmed by this. "Imagine," he says, "an undercover deputy at my age? It's like a bad B picture!"

Yes, indeed.

Joe and Tony do a considerable amount of running around,
questioning and also bantering with suspects. Raison's long suit
is sparkling repartee, as may be seen from the following two
examples:

> "Been having your tea-leaves read?" asked Tony.
> "No. I guess I've had my intuition simonized."

> "I've been wondering about you, Joe."
> "Well, here I am, sister. If they kick me off the
> force, maybe you can make me a radio writer."
> "Radio writers are not made; they're unearthed,"
> she answered.
> "You're a pretty good-looking corpse yourself, Bet-
> ty," said Joe.

What seems like a long time later, inspiration strikes Tony.
Despite the fact that the coroner has carved up Artie's remains
and discovered no internal evidence of violence, Tony is convinced Artie *was* murdered. And he knows who did it and how
it was done! He does some checking at the studio where *Cyrano*
was broadcast, after which he has all the suspects assembled
there in traditional AD fashion. Then he begins his reconstruction of the crime.

The killer, who turns out to be one of Artie's writers, a man who "had obviously overeaten since leaving the Navy, for his stomach bulged suddenly," happens to have had electrical training from Uncle Sam during the war. After deciding to murder Artie—Artie had been having a secret affair with the writer's wife—he rigged an "electric ear": an electromagnetic relay connected to a "hot" 220-volt circuit attached to the base of Artie's microphone. This relay was activated by a photocell designed to respond to Artie's speech pattern when the comic spoke a specific phrase. As the culprit explains:

> "In order for Artie to kill himself . . . he had to grab both the mike and the stand to complete the circuit the moment he said 'Wanna woo-woo?' Well, there wasn't much chance that Artie wouldn't do that. It was part of the act. I was really playing safe because I knew that he would at least once—in the many times he said that poisonous gag—say it at the precise moment he grabbed the mike and stand and made love to it. . . ."

The reason, if Artie was electrocuted, that there were no burn marks on the body and none of the internal organs was damaged? Simple. "Amps, the strength of electricity, [can] cause death even with *low* voltage . . . since *low* voltage would leave no burns!"

Exit Tony Woolrich.

The AD of the fifties, by a wide margin—and perhaps the greatest of all alternative ADs—is Dr. Wade Anthony, the creation of Eric Heath, a writer with talents that can only be described as awesome. Psychiatrist, amateur criminologist, writer, and inventor of the motion-picture theory of crime detection and prevention, Dr. Anthony uses observation, ratiocination, the motion-picture theory of crime detection and prevention, and plenty of sneaky help from the author to solve his cases. He is a lean Dr. Fell, an American Peter Wimsey, a male Miss Marple—truly, an AD among ADs.

Murder of a Mystery Writer (1955) is his finest performance. It is one of those rare books that must be read two or three times to be fully savored and appreciated. On each rereading, new subtleties and nuances reveal themselves, much as is the case with Chandler, Hammett, and other masters.

The novel opens with Dr. Anthony and his beautiful secretary, Penny Lake, arriving at a place called Mystery Lodge in the snow-covered Sierras. Attached to their car is a large trailer containing Anthony's portable crime lab, darkroom, and equipment for the perpetuation of his motion-picture theory of crime detection and prevention. But their purpose in coming to Mystery Lodge is not crime; it is for a few weeks of peace and quiet so that the doctor can dictate a treatise on psychiatry and crime.

What he and Penny find at Mystery Lodge is anything but an atmosphere of peace and quiet, however. They find Egyptian sarcophagi, rugs bearing mystic designs, chandeliers fashioned to resemble "long silver tentacles holding in place a great hoop of brass, dangling from which were a number of half coiled snakes, each one holding a light globe between open fangs," light bulbs set in human skulls inside wall niches, a painting of a bloodstained man wielding a dagger, another painting of Satan gloating down at a bunch of pleading faces in a smoldering lake of lava (" 'Isn't it beautiful! A masterpiece! It has so much depth of feeling!' "), drawer keyholes painted to look like great hypnotic eyes with gleaming white eyeballs, a Mephistophelian dummy brandishing a revolver and hidden away inside a closet, and a lifelike statue of a huge black cat in the dining room. They also find a Brazilian parrot, a dwarf named Gargoyle, assorted Chinese servants, six vacationing members of the Mystery Writers Guild, and an artist who sketches portraits of murderers and whose other hobby is the ruination of young girls. They also find Antrim Zarzour, the owner of Mystery Lodge, who looks like a cross between John Carradine and Don Rickles, and his lovely but strange wife Sonia, who looks like something out of Charles Addams. They also find "a grotesque, ferocious-looking animal [with] a scaly, fish-like body and a head which was part human and part wolf; gleaming fangs protruded from its mouth and its eyes were two circles of phosphorous." Penny, upon seeing this apparition, screeches in terror. "Don't be frightened, Miss Lake," Zarzour tells her. "It's just my pet cat made up in a way that is a little frightening."

The pet cat's name turns out to be Balzac. The reason for that, Zarzour says, is "because the more you study him, the less you can understand him."

Zarzour also explains that the horrific trappings have been

carefully manufactured to make the lodge live up to its name, to give it "a charming atmosphere of mystery—something different." He has also had a lifelong love affair with the macabre, he says, and is a great fan of mystery stories. That is why he invited the six members of the Mystery Writers Guild to hold their annual meeting at Mystery Lodge.

After Penny and Dr. Anthony are shown to their respective rooms, they get together again to discuss Anthony's motion-picture theory of crime detection and prevention. "I would like to see every suspect in a murder case," Wade says, "questioned with a microphone in front of him and a motion picture camera photographing him—in other words, have a sound motion picture made of each suspect as he tells his story or makes a confession." He also thinks pictures ought to be taken of "bits of evidence, such as weapons used to commit murders, bullets taken from guns, pieces of pipe, vials of poison, and the like."

Penny thinks the doctor's motion-picture theory of crime detection and prevention is a wonderful theory. "It [the film] could even be run off in a courtroom for the judge and jury, district attorney and others," she says. "They would all have every aspect of the case right before their eyes. It would simplify the procedure, save time . . ." Penny is no dummy, either. She even comes up with a suggestion Anthony admits he hadn't thought of himself and which he finds splendid: "Couldn't sound pictures also be used for identification purposes? Why not take motion pictures of every major criminal arrested, showing him moving around and talking? Wouldn't that give detectives a much better idea of his appearance and personality, voice and distinguishing characteristics—a splendid adjunct to fingerprints and the regular rogues gallery snapshot?"

Later, at dinner, while a storm rages outside, Penny and the doctor are introduced to some of the vacationing mystery writers, including an obnoxious sort named Ferdinard Lang and one Merrill Atwell, author of "those corny Chet Huntley yarns." There is a good deal of shoptalk, and the topic of conversation naturally turns to murder in general and the perfect murder in particular. Zarzour says he has always been fascinated by the perfect crime. Lang asks him how he would commit one if, say, Lang were in love with Zarzour's wife and Zarzour wanted to get rid of him. Zarzour gives this some thought. Then he says, "Suppose you were right where you are seated now, Mr. Lang. Let us say that the lights go out, which the storm might bring about. A shot is heard. When the room is again illuminated, you are found to be dead, with a bullet in your head. Everyone in the room is searched. No revolver is found in the room. No one apparently had moved from his seat at the table. Just how would you say the murder was committed?"

Lang has no answer for that. Neither does Zarzour; he is called away to the telephone. When he returns, he informs his guests that they are completely "marooned" at Mystery Lodge by the storm and may be so for days.

You might expect something terrible to happen at that very moment, or at least that very night. But no. Instead, Heath introduces the artist and ruiner of young girls, whose name is Jorgenson and who has gotten himself caught in the blizzard; he is not only suffering from "severe exposure" but has an injury at the base of his skull, evidently from a fall, which seems to have resulted in temporary amnesia. As soon as Jorgenson's name is mentioned another of the mystery writers, Otto Oswald, becomes very upset and says that the artist "should be consigned to hell and appointed illustrator for the Devil!" The reason for this outburst is that one of the young girls whom Jorgenson ruined, back in wicked old New York, was Oswald's sixteen-year-old sister.

After the furor over this dies down, everyone retires for the evening. We are not told whether Penny and Dr. Anthony retire alone to their separate bedrooms or whether they decide to share a bed for the night; the precise nature of their relationship is never divulged. We can presume, however, that they are not now nor have they ever been intimate. Penny might wish it otherwise; she is constantly dropping little hints about not wanting to sleep alone in her bed, what with all the horrible things around. But Dr. Anthony ignores her.

Still and all, the next morning he *does* make an unintentional pass at Penny. He comes to her boudoir and asks if she minds having breakfast with a man in her room. She says it all depends on the man, but "inasmuch as it is you, boss, and as you are vouched for by my Puritanical aunt as about the only safe member extant of the male sex, beautiful me is willing to take a chance and allow you to enter." She's being coy, you see. Anthony sits down to breakfast with her, poises a piece of toast over his coffee cup, looks Penny in the eye, and says, "Have I your permission to dunk? I generally do it strictly in private." Penny, who knows a double entendre when she hears one, tells the good doctor that he can dunk all he wants. But Anthony, who wouldn't know a double entendre if it smacked him in the eye, still refuses to take the hint and instead begins rhapsodizing about his motion-picture theory of crime detection and prevention.

That night, everyone is again seated at the table in the dining room (except Jorgenson the seducer, who is confined to one of the guest cottages). The only female member of the mystery writers, curmudgeonly Cora Courtwright, appears for the first time—she was offstage with a headache the previous night—and immediately begins to make pithy comments. When the talk once more shifts to murder, and Zarzour alludes to her authorial talents by calling her "a superbly vicarious murderess," she says:

> "I don't know whether that is a compliment or an intimation that I am a murderess at heart," chortled Cora. "And yet you may have something there, Zarzour. I will give my friend, Lang . . . a thought to mull over. Could it be true, Lang, that every good mystery writer is giving vent to a repressed desire to commit murder—or to put it more plainly, is every mystery writer a killer at heart? If he had not turned to writing mystery fiction, would he have developed into a gangster?"

In spite of such speculation, it is not Cora Courtwright who is murdered a short while later. It is, to no one's surprise, the other obnoxious one, Ferdinand Lang. The murder takes place in more or less the same way as postulated by Zarzour the previous evening: all the lights suddenly go out, and when they come back on, Lang is lying dead across the table with a bullet in his heart; no one has moved from his chair during the blackout; a subsequent search reveals that there is no gun on any of the suspects or anywhere else in the room. Nobody heard the shot, either. Is it because a Wagnerian opus was playing on the phonograph? Is it because the Brazilian parrot let out a "guttural squawk"? Or is there another reason?

Dr. Anthony immediately assumes command, over protests from the others as to his qualifications. Cora Courtwright has the last word on the matter; when Zarzour makes grumbling noises, she says, "You'd better sit down and cool your gum shoes, Zarzour. You are only a reader of mystery fiction, and we are only the writers of such popular tripe. Therefore, the famous Doctor Anthony is in complete command of this snow-bound murder castle."

Anthony proceeds to question everyone, without learning much. The mystery writers, meanwhile, argue over which of them is going to write up Lang's murder in fictional form; each wants to do so and each under the title *Murder of a Mystery Writer*. Nobody pays much attention to the corpse.

Suspicion falls on the dwarf, Gargoyle, when Zarzour claims to have found the murder weapon in Gargoyle's possession. (He also found a Maxim silencer, and *that's* why nobody heard the shot that killed Lang.) The dwarf proclaims his innocence. He doesn't know how the gun and silencer got into his coat pocket, he says, which is where he discovered them when he returned to his room after the shooting. Anthony's sharp questioning reveals that Gargoyle had once spilled a glass of water in Lang's lap and Lang had cursed him for his clumsiness. Every-one thinks this is a very damning motive for murder. Cora is particularly pithy in her condemnation: "Does anybody know whether cretinism causes people to see better in the dark than normally built people?"

Dr. Anthony isn't so sure of Gargoyle's guilt, though. As he confides to Penny later, "I'm inclined to think that there is a much deeper psychological basis for this crime than a dwarf committing murder to avenge a personal insult."

Another startling development occurs the following morn-ing, when Jorgenson is found stabbed to death in his cottage. Anthony and Penny immediately rush to the scene, where the doctor soon discovers that the artist did not die instantly from his wounds. He had time to crawl to a desk, on which was a sketch pad, and to draw three Indian symbols—eagle feathers, a snake, and a tepee. Anthony decides these must be a clue to the identity of the murderer, so he carts the note off to his por-table laboratory for further study. He also carts the corpse off to the portable lab for a quick autopsy—a medical talent sorely lacking in most other ADs.

Some time later, while Anthony is preparing his equipment so that he can put his motion-picture theory of crime detection and prevention into its first practical use, Sonia Zarzour appears and tells the doctor and Penny that she has something to show them in the cellar. The something turns out to be a ladder and a trapdoor in the ceiling. "That opening," she says, "allows a person to enter into the hollow body of the statue of the black cat in the dining room. If you will climb up the ladder, Doctor, you will find that you can enter the interior of the black cat and look through its open mouth into the dining room."

Anthony makes an immediate deduction: "Now we know how the murder of Mr. Lang could have been committed. Someone standing inside the body of the black cat would be able to fire a revolver through its mouth!" And when Mrs. Zarzour proceeds to tell them that Gargoyle used to climb up inside the cat and make ghostly noises to frighten the guests, as part of her husband's Mystery Lodge trappings, Penny remarks, "That makes the case against Gargoyle bulletproof, doesn't it?"

While the doctor hurries off to his room to do some more work on the motion-picture theory of crime detection and prevention, Penny searches the cellar for clues. And finds one, "a bit of metal formed into two cylinders," which she takes straightaway to Anthony. He identifies it as "a child's whistle, or a tuning pipe," and promptly records it on film.

All sorts of other clues and things are also recorded on film, with Penny acting as "camera woman." Then, after Anthony has processed the film in his portable crime lab and morgue, all the suspects are gathered together in the drawing room. There they are shown film clips of the revolver and Maxim silencer, of the whistle, of the statue of the black cat; and filmed interviews with Gargoyle, with one of the Chinese servants, with Oswald, and finally with Zarzour. At the end of each interview, the interviewees are depicted stabbing the dummy with overhand downward thrusts. All except Zarzour, that is. *He* starts to stab the dummy with an underhand upward thrust and only at the last instant changes it to an overhand downward thrust.

Zarzour, therefore, is the murderer.

And it has been proven by the motion-picture theory of crime detection and prevention!

For Jorgenson had been stabbed in the back with an under-hand upward thrust, not an overhand downward thrust, and Zarzour is the only one present who stabs dummies (or people) that way. His motive? It seems that Zarzour was confined to an asylum in New York after having been convicted of some sort of heinous crime, and that Jorgenson had once sketched Zar-zour as part of his series of murderer portraits. Zarzour was afraid that Jorgenson would recover from his amnesia and rec-ognize him (in spite of the fact that, we subsequently learn, Zarzour has had plastic surgery, which altered his appearance from handsome to Carradine/Rickles). So killing the ruiner of young girls was imperative. Besides which, he had also killed Lang and murder was old hat to him by that time.

As for the Indian symbols Jorgenson drew before he died, and which Anthony also shows on film, the explanation is thus:

> "I spent some time in Mr. Zarzour's excellent libra-ry before I was able to translate them. Among the Indian tribes of New Mexico such sign language was their only means of written communication . . . These eagle feathers mean *Big Chief.* This snake is a symbol meaning *evil,* or an evil person. And the final sketch, which you will all recognize, is an Indian tepee, denoting *home.*"
>
> Wade paused so everyone would have time to study the drawings and digest what he had said. Then he went on, "The meaning, therefore, as I interpret the symbols, is that the person who stabbed Jorgenson was the Big Chief or Master of a home or house, and that he was an evil person. *That, Mr. Zarzour, could hardly be anyone but you!*"

Zarzour doesn't have anything to say, although "a movement of his cheeks indicated that he was moving his jaw-bones up and down, and his attitude had become obviously tense."

Anthony proceeds to explain how the murder of Lang was accomplished. The lights did not go out accidentally that night, he says; they went out when Zarzour blew into one of the tubes of the whistle Penny found in the cellar. It is a supersonic receiving set mounted inside the black-cat statue and connected to the main light switch. The second tube, of course, activated "a tiny motor, when the tonal vibrations are transmitted to an electromagnet and the infinitesimal power generated is stepped up by means of a series of amplifying tubes," thereby turning a wheel with a string or wire attached to the trigger of the revolver, which is also mounted inside the black cat. As soon as the gun discharged, Zarzour dropped the whistle down the cat's gullet and through the trapdoor into the cellar. (Why he left it lying on the cellar floor for Penny to find is never explained. Nor is it ever explained how he managed to mount the gun inside the mouth of a ceramic statue. On the other hand, it *is* explained how Zarzour could be sure the mounted gun was aimed at Lang's heart: he had bolted that particular chair to the floor.)

Anthony continues: "After you were searched you had an opportunity to leave the dining room and go down to the basement. You had to do that in order to close the trap-door and remove the supersonic receiving sets. . . . As stated, one of the supersonic sound receiving devices operated under certain high frequency vibrations given out by blowing on one tube of this whistle. The other device was acted upon by different vibrations given out by blowing on the second tube."

But what about the gun? "While you were inspecting the body of Lang," Zarzour confesses, "I had a chance to take out the revolver with the silencer from the opening in the head of the statue. . . . My only chance was to slip the revolver and silencer into Gargoyle's pocket . . .."

Zarzour's motive for killing Lang has nothing to do with the writer having an affair with Mrs. Zarzour. It was simply that he has always been obsessed with committing the perfect crime, as Sonia notes after pushing her way to his side. "Antrim," she says, "I don't know what you've done, but I forgive you. I've known for a long time that you were in an asylum back East before we were married, paying the penalty for your first attempt at a perfect murder!"

But Zarzour isn't about to be shut away in another asylum. When his jawbones were working up and down, he had "taken something to destroy myself—something that I really believe will leave you completely baffled." (Not so. Following Zarzour's death, Anthony uses the facilities in his portable laboratory, as well as his autopsy-surgeon's knife, to discover that the red and white corpuscles in Zarzour's bloodstream were almost totally destroyed—the result of gulping down a large dose of irradiated phosphorus. "A most unusual manner of committing suicide," Anthony observes.)

As everyone prepares to leave Mystery Lodge, the remaining members of the Mystery Writers Guild heap praise on Dr. Anthony for his AD abilities in general and his motion-picture theory of crime detection and prevention in particular. One of them, Martenson, also notes that "Zarzour *looked* like a murderer—he *acted* like one—and he kept talking about committing the perfect crime. Now according to every precept of mystery fiction, he definitely should *not* have been the actual killer!"

Anthony smiles at this. And just before he and Penny drive off into the sunset (the storm has ended and the sun has come out), he leans out of the car window and says, "Don't forget, Martenson, that you are supposed to fool your readers. Maybe it pays to be original once in a while."

Maybe it does. And *Murder of a Mystery Writer* most definitely *is* an original. Not as original as the motion-picture theory of crime detection and prevention, perhaps, but pretty original just the same.

In the past two decades, the foremost addition to the AD ranks has been that of the real person no longer alive—and, in particular, the real mystery writer no longer alive—who is placed within a fictional framework in order to solve a fictional crime. Joe Gores's *Hammett* (1976) was the first of these, with its time frame of 1929 and its San Francisco setting; another of note, despite some rather nasty speculation and innuendo, is Kathleen Tynan's *Agatha,* in which Agatha Christie becomes involved in murder and intrigue during her now-famous disappearance in 1926. This sort of fictionalizing is acceptable so long as the author treats his real-life character with intelligence and insight, makes a serious effort to portray accurately the life and times of the individual, and concocts a plot worthy of that person's abilities. In the case of an item called *Chandler* (1977), by someone named William Denbow, none of the foregoing applies.

Chandler is a rather obvious attempt to capitalize on the modest success of the Gores novel—one of those quickie paperback exploitations that hack writers disgorge in a few days, utilizing no more research than a bottle of Scotch. It purports to tell the story of how Raymond Chandler, during a visit to New York, saves Dashiell Hammett, who is also on a visit to New York, from some vengeful "wop" gangsters. To anyone who knows anything at all about either Chandler or Hammett, however, the characters in this novel are instantly recognizable as imposters.

The number and magnitude of the gaffes that permeate *Chandler* are staggering. The novel appears to take place in 1936, owing to the statement that "a few years had passed since Repeal," and owing to the fact that one of the characters, who was born in 1896, is forty years old; yet Hammett is said to have just published *Red Harvest* in book form (it first appeared thus in 1929) and to still be turning out pulp stories for *Black Mask* (his last appearance in that magazine was in November 1931 with a story called "Death and Company"). "Hammett" repeatedly refers to San Francisco as Frisco, something no long-standing resident of that city, as the real Hammett was, would ever think of doing. He is depicted as an alcoholic so cynically and hopelessly besotted that he can barely write or otherwise function without first taking a drink; we are also informed that Joseph T. "Cap" Shaw, the pioneering editor of *Black Mask,* has been either rejecting outright Hammett's most recent submissions or returning them for extensive revisions. Hammett's days as a Pinkerton operative are described as if he himself had been a tough pulp hero—kicking down doors, shooting and arresting gangsters, watching out that "you didn't catch a bullet from some hophead with three guns on his emaciated person." The claim is also made that Hammett was a puking drunk during his Pinkerton stint and that he had to take "a sneaky drink now and then" to steady his nerves and give him Dutch courage.

Chandler, too, is portrayed as an alcoholic, though not quite of the same whiskey-soaked variety as Hammett. He has come to New York, he tells Cap Shaw, to buy some books he has been wanting to read; when Shaw asks him if they didn't have bookshops in Los Angeles, Chandler answers that they do but "not like the bookshops on Fourth Avenue." On some occasions Chandler is made to speak in stilted Britishisms, and on others like Philip Marlowe, and on still others like a pulp hoodlum. No mention is made anywhere of his elderly wife Cissy, who was far more important to him than either alcohol or his writing, or of any other aspect of his life in southern California. (Similarly, no mention is made of Hammett's relationship with Lillian Hellman, his Hollywood connections, his Communist affiliation, or of anybody or anything else that shaped and controlled his life in the thirties.)

In a drunken scene with Hammett, who has refused to meet with Chandler unless he agrees to bring a quart of Jack Daniel's to his hotel room, Chandler is told that he'll never make the big time unless he changes the name of his detective character from Carmady (only three of Chandler's several *Black Mask* stories feature a detective named Carmady) to something classier. "Let's give the mick a limey name for a change," Hammett says. "More class. I always liked Christopher Marlowe because he was some kind of secret agent. This isn't gumshoe exactly but it'll do. That's it, chum, we'll rename Carmady Chris Marlowe." And when Chandler protests that he doesn't like the name Chris because it's "too pansy," Hammett says, "I had a hound dog once, back in Maryland when I was a kid. We called him Phil. Phil was a good old dog, one hell of a good *ole* dog. Why don't we call your gumshoe *Philip Marlowe*?"

This sort of mind-boggling dialogue continues throughout. Another example:

> "You don't look so good," Chandler said and wished he hadn't said it.
> Knocking back the rest of his drink, Hammett snapped, "You don't look so great yourself, chum. You look like a guy who's pretending not to have a hangover."
> "It's just a little hangover."
> "They'll get bigger as time goes on. You say no but I say yes. I know whereof I speak, chum."
> "I didn't say anything," Chandler said.
> "I thought you were an American," Hammett said, looking sour and argumentative.
> "As the Fourth of July," Chandler said. . . .
> "Then why the hell do you speak like a God damned limey? Next thing you'll be telling me you come from Boston. That won't wash with me, chum. I been to Boston lots of times when I was with the Pinks. They like to think they sound like limeys in Boston, for

whatever God damned reason I can't imagine, but they don't."

Chandler said he'd been born in Chicago.

"That's better," Hammett, mellowing slightly as the sour mash took the edge off his frightful hangover [sic]. "Chicago is a tough town, a good tough town. You don't catch much shit flying in Chicago."

And here is Cap Shaw philosophizing about writers and writing to Chandler at the *Black Mask* offices:

"That blasted fool Hammett! There you have a man who could become one of the greatest American writers, but instead of taking hold of himself he's pissing his talent away, rotting his brain with liquor. Ah," he said—the compleat martinet—"if I could only lock you fellows up somewhere. Chain you to your typewriters and let you get drunk just once a year, on Christmas day. Then you'd see some worthwhile writing."

The plot, such as it may be, concerns the efforts of a New York gangster named Salvatore Tenuto to wreak vengeance on Hammett because Hammett, while working for the Pinks, locked Tenuto up in a Mexican jail on a charge of "running Mexican girls—kids—across the border into L.A. for the whorehouse trade, for the guys that like their meat . . . to be real young and fresh." When Chandler gets wind that somebody is after Hammett, he sets out to foil the attempt. And of course succeeds, with some help from the obligatory cop friend, a sergeant on the New York Homicide Squad whom Chandler had known "for ten years, ever since they both worked together for a failed oil company."

The climax takes place in Hammett's hotel room, where he has been drugged and tied up by two of Tenuto's hoods. When the hoods return, bringing with them a thirteen-year-old girl so they can rape her and frame Hammett for it, Chandler and the police sergeant are waiting for them.

Chandler came out of the closet with the automatic in his hand. This was the real thing, but he wasn't afraid. He was too angry to be afraid. His voice was quiet and cool but there was real menace in it. "Hit that kid and I'll blow your fucking head off," he said. "Put your hands behind your heads and lean against the wall. Don't drop your guns, don't do anything."

"What the fuck!" Joey blurted out in astonishment. Charlie the Dasher's hand started to streak inside his coat. He stopped when the muzzle of the Browning lined up with his heart. "Go on, do it," Chandler said, shaking with the urge to kill the evil bastard while the automatic remained steady in his hand. "Go to it, you wop bastard, you stinking greaseball. Put your hands behind your head or I'll drop you right now. You too, moron."

Sic transit gloria AD.

2. The Eyes Have It

> He poured himself a drink and counted the money.
> It came to ten thousand even, mostly in fifties and
> twenty-fives.
>
> —Brett Halliday,
> *The Violent World of*
> *Michael Shayne*

> She was as lovely as a girl could be without blud-
> geoning your endocrines.
>
> —Stephen Marlowe,
> *Killers Are My Meat*

> The sun [was] shining its ass off . . .
> —Robert B. Parker,
> *Looking for Rachel Wallace*

The private eye as we know and love him today was not born in
the pages of twentieth-century pulp magazines, as some people
seem to believe. He was not fathered by Dashiell Hammett or
Carroll John Daly; they toughened him, taught him to shoot
and to fight and to make love to beautiful women, adapted him
to the violent American milieu of the twenties and thirties—

but they did not create him. He is a hundred years old, not fifty, and his heritage is only half-American, only half-fictional. The fictional half, in fact, is British, and the milieu Victorian England.

The eye's British parent, of course, is Sir Arthur Conan Doyle. Sherlock Holmes was a private investigator; people came to him with problems, and he proceeded to investigate and to solve them. The focal points of his phenomenal success were certainly his power of observation and his deductive ability, but there is no question that some readers and writers equated his talents with his profession. The self-reliant loner, the white knight, the indefatigable crime fighter with abilities greater and methods less restricted than those of the police—these Holmesian characteristics became a central part of the budding mystique of the private detective.

The eye's American parent was Allan Pinkerton, the transplanted Scot who opened the first private investigative agency in Chicago in the 1850s, was a paid Union spy during the Civil War, and achieved something of an international reputation in the late 1800s for his well-publicized battles with train robbers and other Western outlaws. The famous Pinkerton symbol—a wide-open eye, with the words "We Never Sleep" below it—appeared on a number of ghostwritten "case histories" in the 1870s, bearing such titles as *The Expressman and the Detective* and *The Detective and the Somnambulist*. These were actually more sensational fiction than fact and contained a number of dubious observations:

> We often find that persons who have committed grave offenses will fly to the moors, or to the prairies, or to the vast solitudes of almost impenetrable forests, and there give vent to their feelings. I instanced the case of Eugene Aram, who took up his abode on the bleak and solitary moor, and, removed from the society of his fellowmen, tried to maintain his secret by devoting himself to astronomical observations and musings with nature, but who, nevertheless, felt compelled to relieve his overburdened mind by muttering to himself details of the murder while taking long and dreary walks on the moor. (*The Expressman and the Detective*)

* * *

Pinkerton's books proved enormously popular, went into numerous reprintings, and inspired the dime novelists of the day to invent such Pinkerton-modeled characters as Old Sleuth and Nick Carter. With their talents for disguise, their feats of derring-do, and their continual assault on the organized forces of evil, these fictional operatives added yet another dimension to the mystique and carried it on a new popular wave into the twentieth century.

The heir apparent to the dime-novel sleuths was Fleming Stone, the primary creation of Carolyn Wells—novelist, playwright, poet, anthologist, writer of juveniles and short stories, and author of the genre's first nonfiction work, a combination of how-to and historical overview called *The Technique of the Mystery Story* (1913). Stone is what Miss Wells describes in *Technique* as a "transcendant detective"; that is, a detective larger than life, omniscient; a creature of fiction rather than fact. And indeed, Fleming Stone is as unreal an investigator as any of his dime-novel predecessors. In not one of his fifty-seven recorded cases does he come alive as a human being, or as anything more than a two-dimensional silhouette with a penchant for pulling murderers out of hats on the flimsiest of clues and evidence.

Many of Stone's cases are of the "impossible crime" variety. Carolyn Wells had an inordinate fondness for this type of story and so perpetrated more than a score of them during her career. In *The Technique of the Mystery Story,* she warns beginning writers to plan their stories with absolute logic and sequence; this is sound advice, which, unfortunately, she seemed disinclined to follow in her own work. Some critics have allowed that she was expert at constructing a mystery, and this may be true; but when it came to constructing a *plausible* mystery, she was every bit as helpless as Gaston Leroux. It may be said, without fear of contradiction, that she produced the definitive "don't" list of impossible crime plots—that is, everyone's list of unbelievable plot gimmicks that every mystery writer who wishes to write a salable locked-room story should avoid at all cost.

Hidden panels and secret exits were far and away her favorites. Among her impossible-crime novels are ones in which the solution depends on a hidden sliding panel in a closet, a secret exit behind a sliding panel, a secret passage beneath the floor, a secret entrance into a room through a chimney, a hidden door frame with concealed hinges and lock, a secret elevator, a secret subterranean passage, and a shaft between a chimney and an external wall. Other of her "impossible" solutions include a victim stabbing himself with an icicle which melts before the body is discovered, a victim licking a postage stamp coated with poison, and a door locked from the outside with a duplicate key and inner bolts drawn by means of a thread.

Fleming Stone's two greatest cases are *The Broken O* (1933) and *The Wooden Indian* (1935). In the former, a strange death by poison occurs in a locked room, with the subsequent investigation uncovering no apparent means by which the poison could have been induced. Stone deduces that the murderer, a surgeon, implanted a tiny glass bulb into the heart of the victim; inside the bulb was a poisonous gas that slowly destroyed the surrounding tissues, thereby causing sudden death in the locked room more than twenty-four hours later. In *The Wooden Indian,* a collector of Indian artifacts is found shot to death with an arrow inside a locked room, the arrow having come from a wooden Indian kept inside the room. This was not the result of an accidental discharge, as everyone is supposed to believe, but through the machinations of a typical Wells murderer: while he was a guest in the victim's house some time earlier, the culprit manufactured a trapdoor leading from the attic into a grilled cabinet inside the Indian room; this enabled him to let himself down into the cabinet by means of a rope, from where, being an expert archer, he fired the fatal arrow through one of the grill openings. That the cabinet in question is barely large enough for a man to fit in, and that a considerable amount of space is required to maneuver a bow and arrow, are conveniently ignored by both the author and Fleming Stone.

Miss Wells also created another private detective of note, one Pennington "Penny" Wise, who appears in seven novels, foremost among them *The Man Who Fell Through the Earth* (1919). Although one of the characters in this book says that Penny Wise is not "the usual Smarty-Cat detective" and has "none of the earmarks of the Transcendental Detective of the story-books," he is and he does. Under all but the closest scrutiny, he appears indistinguishable from Fleming Stone.

The Man Who Fell Through the Earth is concerned with a double disappearance from a locked New York office. One of the men exited the office by means of a secret elevator; the other walked out in front of a not very reliable witness, only to vanish again during a howling blizzard outside. The second man is subsequently found alive in the icy East River, having "fallen through the earth, perhaps all the way from the Arctic." Or so he claims at first, in his delirium. What really happened is this:

> "And as I took a step—I went down an open manhole into the sewer.
> ". . . I fell and fell—down, down,—it seemed for miles; I was whirled dizzily about—but still I fell—on and on—interminably. I felt my consciousness going—at first, abnormally acute, my senses became dulled, and I had only a sensation of falling—ever falling—through the earth!
> "There my memory ceases. . . . My realization of falling only lasted until I struck the water in the sewer. That, doubtless, knocked me out for good and all—mentally, I mean. I have to thank my wonderful vitality and strong constitution for the fact that I really lived through the catastrophe. Think what it means! Hurtled through that rushing torrent of a sewer half filled with melted snow and water—flung out into the river, dashed about among the floating cakes of ice, and all with sufficient force to tear off my clothing—and yet to live through it!"

While Fleming Stone and Penny Wise were engaged in such goings-on, the hard-boiled detective as defined by Hammett and Carroll John Daly was beginning to prosper in the pages of *Black Mask* in the 1920s. Hammett's Continental Op was based on his own experiences with the Pinkerton agency and his intimate knowledge of how twentieth-century private detectives went about their business; and it was his genius that gave the American fictional investigator the one vital element he had been lacking: realism. And it was realism, or the illusion of it, that completed and cemented the mystique of the private eye.

Yet although Hammett is the acknowledged patriarch of the

modern tough-detective school, in truth he must share that distinction with Daly. Daly's rough-and-tumble, somewhat sadistic shamus Race Williams first appeared in "Knights of the Open Palm" in the June 1, 1923, issue of *Black Mask,* five months before Hammett's initial Continental Op story was published. (Daly's first story, "The False Burton Combs," a hardboiled tale about a "gentleman adventurer" who makes his living battling lawbreakers, appeared in *Black Mask* in 1922; and two weeks before Race Williams made his debut, another Daly private eye, Terry Mack, began shooting folks in a novelette called "Three Gun Terry." Also, Daly's first Race Williams novel, *The Snarl of the Beast,* was published in 1927, two years prior to the book publication of *Red Harvest* and *The Dain Curse* and to Hammett's invention of Sam Spade and *The Maltese Falcon.*)

If Hammett's work can be said to have inspired Raymond Chandler, Ross Macdonald, and other of the best practitioners of the private-eye story, then Daly's work can be said to have inspired a number of writers who produced alternative classics. It is in his footsteps and those of Race Williams that Mickey Spillane (a confessed admirer of Daly) and Mike Hammer, Richard S. Prather and Shell Scott, and dozens of other writer-detective teams have walked over the past fifty years.

Both Daly and Williams were amazingly popular during the twenties and early thirties, in particular among the readers of *Black Mask.* In a poll conducted by editor Shaw in 1930, Daly was judged the magazine's favorite writer; Erle Stanley Gardner was the runner-up, with Hammett a somewhat distant third in the voting. The reason for Williams's popularity, it may be supposed, is that he was a man of action, with no compunctions and no real vulnerabilities (not even women, whose company he eschewed in favor of his own pair of .44s). He didn't mind killing people if it was in the public interest; in fact, he rather enjoyed it. He was the classic fantasy figure of that type of individual who believes violence is best fought with violence—the Charles Bronson figure in the film version of Brian Garfield's *Death Wish,* the kind of "hero" such a person would be himself if only he had the courage. Besides which, Williams was forever taking the reader into his confidence, talking to him in personal asides, as if the two of them were confidants. This is Race Williams:

* * *

For once my control of myself seemed to desert me.
I tried to sleep—but I couldn't. I just lay there and
planned, while Gregory smoked and watched me. But
all my plans were grim and strange. There was the
burning desire to strike and maim—and kill. Kill!
That was it. I never felt like that before. (*The Tag
Murders*)

I'm not much on the sex stuff, nor the lithe slender-
ness and gracefulness of women. Still, there was a
suppleness to her body that made her seem to creep in
and out of my arms without actually ever doing it.
Get what I mean? The best way I can describe it is,
that she clung to me like a wet sock. (*The Tag Murders*)

. . . The Flame had many admirers. Many men
had loved her. Some there were who had held her in
their arms. And—those men were dead—even to the
last one.
I'm not saying that The Flame had anything to do
with it. I'm not even trying to judge her. But there is
no discounting the fact that they were dead. With
me, then, although I've always denied I had any, but
I guess it was just plain superstition. Ashamed of it?
Of course I am. But it was there, just the same. I had
an overpowering belief—almost an obsession—that
to hold The Flame in my arms—that to crush that
wondrous, beautiful body to me spelled death. Yes—
laugh if you want. We all have our weaknesses, I
suppose. That was one of mine. To love The Flame
meant my death. And that's that. Foolish! Childish!
Ridiculous! Sure, but truth is truth, just the same.
(*Tainted Power*)

"You're Williams?" he chirped, through the side of
his mouth as he spat on my new rug. I frowned slightly. I felt that we were not going to get along—
decidedly, I did not get that psychological impression
that here was the beginning of a lifelong friend-
ship.
"Name of Little—Paul Little." He pounded himself

on the chest. "From Chi—want to know more?". . .
I leaned back slightly and laughed. An ordinary
gunman, this. Real cheap stuff. . . .
"Ya needn't laugh it off." Thick lips curled.
"You've bluffed it out with the New York boys,
maybe—but I'm a different lad again. I ain't aimin'
to harm ya none, and perhaps I'll even slip ya a little
change—though that part weren't my thought.
But—you raise one hand . . . an' I'll cop ya through
the noodle." (*The Tag Murders*)

Nearly all Daly's novels and short stories deal with bootleg-
ging, gang warfare, crooked politics, blackmail and mayhem
among the corrupt upper classes, and lunatics bent on domination of organizations, cities, and, in one instance, the world (the
villain in *Murder from the East* is a Eurasian megalomaniac of
Fu Manchu dimensions). Daly's one obsessive theme is the evil
wrought by a lust for power. In *Tainted Power* (1931), Williams himself almost succumbs to this lust when, after wiping
out a blackmail ring and coming into possession of all its doc-
umentation, he is tempted by The Flame, "the Girl with the
Criminal Mind," to join in the foundation of a criminal empire.
Williams, however, comes to his senses just in time: "Let's be
charitable, even to ourselves. Maybe my brain cleared then,
and I was a sane man again. Maybe it had been greed. Maybe it
was only loss of blood." And he would have thrown The Flame
over, too, just as Sam Spade does with Brigid O'Shaughnessy in
The Maltese Falcon, if she hadn't managed to flee down a convenient fire escape.

With a few exceptions, there was not quite so much relentless
vigilantism in other private eye novels of the thirties and forties. Most writers seemed to prefer the freewheeling, wisecracking style which evolved in the pulps, to no small degree because
of a consistent misunderstanding that the wisecrack was an
integral factor in the success of such writers as Hammett and
Chandler, and of why those writers used the occasional flip
remark in the first place. In Chandler's work especially, wisecracks helped mask Philip Marlowe's emotions; they gave him
time to think and they helped him put people off their guard.
They are a distinct character trait, like picking one's nose in
public or drinking four quarts of whiskey a day—not a delib-

erate attempt on the part of the author to inject either toughness or humor.

As a result of this misunderstanding, too many private eyes
became what can only be called smart-asses, an annoying con-
vention which unhappily continues in the work of some contemporary writers. Among the first wave of thirties smart-asses
was one named Tip O'Neil, who stars in James Edward Grant's
The Green Shadow (1935).

According to a biographical sketch at the back of the book,
Grant was the son of the Chief Investigator for the State Attorney of Illinois, a former prizefighter, the manager of boxers and
a "toe dancer", and the author of a syndicated newspaper column out of Chicago called "It's a Racket," which "led him into
a personal acquaintance with most of Chicago's boom-boom
boys" and "caused such a stir in the Chicago underworld that
several prominent mobsters left town."

The plot of *The Green Shadow* can more or less be summed up
by quoting the jacket blurb: "The Harding Case was no pushov-
er—even for Tip O'Neil. He could see that the minute he arrived
on the scene, for the whole family was screwy from the poker-
playing, Scotch-soaked, maiden-aunt Amelia down to Nancy of
the round heels, the amateur tart who tried to seduce her
father's own investigators while they fought to break the case.
Corinne, the other daughter, was the only really normal one of
the lot—and she vanished from a crowded city street in broad
daylight. Leland, her lover, stacked up all right, or seemed to,
till Tip O'Neil got ideas and manhandled his own private skeleton out of the closet. And Paul himself—well, any man who
can sit and watch the exquisite torture of another's body and
never bat an eye, then roar with laughter when the victim's
legs are broken, ought to qualify as patient in a crime clinic,
hands down. Tip's right bower, Lilly—and don't get the idea he
was one—had it right when he said: 'The whole thing's a cockeyed maze.'"

Here is Tip O'Neil being a smart-ass:

> "This is Senator Wafflepoop," I said, "here's a tip.
> There's a couple of New York—or New Jersey—mob-
> bies hanging around the Senate. One fellow is about
> six foot and a hundred and ninety. . . . Got it?"
> He said: "Yes. By the way, who is this calling?"

"Philo Vance," I confessed. "The other clown is around five-eight . . . blue eyes, black hair slicked with bear-grease and a mouth that looks like it was cut-in with a ham slicer. Got it?"

He said: "Just a minute till I get a pencil. Who is this speaking?"

"Bishop Cannon," I said. "Tell your dummies to watch the little yegg. He's wearing loose, pleated pants which probably means he's got a zipper front and one of those crotch guns. Or don't you hicks keep up with the times?"

"Who is this?" he asked again.

"Huey Long," I told him and hung up.

A second notable quality of the O'Neil/James Edward Grant combo is the fashion in which O'Neil figures his way out of the "cockeyed maze"—the old "bolt of lightning" method refined to an art:

I shrugged, we shook hands and I left. Just walking around my car to get in a passing cab sloshed a tidal wave of water into my face. As I wiped it away, *the whole picture became clear and as usual when a case breaks I began to curse myself for dumbness.*

Then I climbed in and went home to make my pinch. (Italics Grant's.)

And so it was with the private-detective novel until the late forties, when two completely different writers added new elements to the mystique and produced a pair of original characters. The most important of these writers was, of course, Frank Morrison "Mickey" Spillane, whose first Mike Hammer novel, *I, the Jury,* appeared in 1947. Spillane's own peculiar brand of sex, sadism, and the private eye as avenging angel and self-appointed guardian of democracy struck a responsive chord in a segment of the population already stirred up by the first of the great Communist witch-hunts in 1946. Mike Hammer is Race Williams refined, updated, libidinalized. He is the ultimate vigilante, a warped symbol of rugged individualism and law and order at the point of a gun. There are no wisecracks in Mike Hammer, no nonsense of any kind; when he has a job to do he goes out and does it—relentlessly, implacably. If he was not in love with his secretary, Velda, his one weakness, he would be the perfect killing machine.

The character of Mike Hammer is nowhere better demonstrated than in *One Lonely Night* (1951), Spillane's nastiest novel, which pits Hammer against the Red Menace in a bloody paean to "Tailgunner Joe" McCarthy and his ilk. The book begins with Hammer futilely trying to save the life of a frightened woman on a rain-swept bridge ("Maybe you can smack a dame around all you want and make her life as miserable as hell, but nobody has the right to scare the daylights out of any woman") and ends with Hammer rescuing Velda, who has been strung up naked and who is in the process of being tortured, from an MVD stronghold. The way he rescues her is to use a tommy gun to slaughter a roomful of Commies who "slobbered with lust and pleasure . . . even drooled with the passion that was death made slow in the fulfillment of the philosophy that lived under a red flag!" His rationale for the slaughter would be laughable if it were not so terrifying: *"I lived only to kill the scum and the lice that wanted to kill themselves. I lived to kill so that others could live. I lived to kill because my soul was a hardened thing that reveled in the thought of taking the blood of the bastards who made murder their business . . . I was the evil that opposed other evil, leaving the good and the meek in the middle to live and inherit the earth!"* (Italics Spillane's.)

As William Ruehlmann says in *Saint with a Gun: The Unlawful American Private Eye:* "World without end, amen."

I, the Jury, probably Spillane's most widely read novel, is also an alternative classic. A blood-spattered tale of revenge in which Hammer sets out to find the killer of his best friend, it is riddled with such lines as "Living alone with one maid, a few rooms was all that was necessary" and "It gave me ideas, which I quickly ignored," and amply illustrates Spillane's dubious plotting technique. Two of the murders, for example, take place in a brothel that Hammer has under observation; both the murderess, a woman named Charlotte, and one of the victims are well known to Hammer, and neither has any idea he is watching the brothel; yet both manage to enter by the front door without Hammer seeing either of them. Another murder takes place at a society party with 250 guests; afterward, Hammer dismisses all 250 as suspects because, he says, they *all* have alibis for the time of the killing. In the final slaying—that is, the final one before Hammer pumps a .45 slug into Charlotte on the last page—Charlotte shoots another woman, Myrna, who is wearing Charlotte's coat; removes the coat, finds Myrna's own coat, shoots a hole through it in exactly the right spot to correspond with the hole in Myrna, and puts the coat on the body; conceals the bullethole in her own coat (how is not explained), as well as keeps the gun and its silencer on her person while the police are on the scene; and later manages to get coat, gun, and silencer off the premises under Hammer's allegedly gimlet eye.

The best summary of *I, the Jury,* as critic Francis M. Nevins has pointed out, is by Spillane himself when he has Hammer go to a detective film in Chapter 12 and subsequently call it "A fantastic murder mystery that had more holes in it than a piece of Swiss cheese."

Spillane's enormous success in the fifties—his first seven novels are among the top fiction bestsellers of all time—spawned a host of imitators. One of these was Jimmy Shannon, whose only book, *The Devil's Passkey,* was published in 1952. The hero of this remarkable work is one Ruff Morgan, who, like Mike Hammer, operates out of New York City. If he is not the least intelligent detective in private eyedom—alongside Morgan, Race Williams is a genius—he must surely be a close runner-up.

To give you an idea of what "Ruff Boy" is like, this is how the novel opens:

> It's only a fool who doesn't know his own strength, and last night was my night to prove it. I'd just walked into Dave's Place. A dame was sitting by the hat-check counter. When she saw me she got up and said, "Mr. Morgan?"
>
> I had my mouth open to answer, "Yes," when a big lug staggers out of the phone booth and slams into me.
>
> "Look where you're going, Buster," I say, brushing him off. But he comes back and tries to use me for a lamppost, whereupon I get a little resentful and touch him one—kinda sharp.

That's when he jammed my left eye so far back in my head that it went to work with the brains department.

What transpires after that is a chaotic scramble (the dust jacket calls it "a terrifying, action-packed thriller by an exciting new talent in the suspense field") involving a professor named Magnus Crocker, who has invented a formula for a cheap narcotic called Trilium; a bunch of "malignant czars of crime and vice" who are out to steal the formula; and dead bodies all over the place, most of them having been shot in a hail of bullets. ("Next thing I knew, lead was being slung from one side of the lab to the other. Bullets like a splattering of hail. Men crying out as the hail struck. Hell's hail it was! I saw them dying all around me.")

There is some sadism, as may be inferred from the foregoing, though Morgan is no Mike Hammer in the teeth-kicking, gutshooting game. And plenty of sex, too, after a fashion.

Here, Miss Jerry Selbridge turned on the sprinkler system—something I wasn't prepared for at all. If there'e one thing in the world that turns me into a lump of sog it's a woman who cries. I knew only one way to deal with it. Take the gal into your arms. Pat her. Maybe give her a fatherly kiss.

Somehow, I hadn't thought this one was the kind you *could* kiss. She and her incompatibility. Silly boy! She began to lean and I found out she had what for to lean on. When our lips met, as the fiction writers say, my temperature was hitting 99° and going up!

Now I'm not prudish or old-fashioned and I think it's the bunk that business and pleasure can't mix, but—I just wasn't in the mood. Maybe it was the mouse on my glimmer. Maybe I didn't want to take off my dark glasses.

"Warm for April," I cracked and got up to pour us two slugs of sherry.

"How do you like *my* version of the Dance of the Nile, Ruff?" she whispered in my ear.

"More!" I said.

Dames! Out here with seventy people using you for a pushball, they'll do anything! But get 'em in a closed room!

Kathy's curves went round and round, and I began to think—maybe this was going to be *my* Midnight on the Ganges with Kathy in my arms.

"Um . . . mmm," Kathy hummed in my ear. "You smell so good, Ruff Boy. You smell like a fondant with perfume inside."

"More!" says I going into a trance.

"You taste yummy too."

"What flavor?"

"Nut chocolate bar."

"Tell me more . . ." I murmur in a golden daze.

A much more accomplished Spillane imitator was John B. West, whose private eye Rocky Steele blasted his way through six novels from 1959 to 1961, all of which were published by Spillane's paperback house, New American Library. Steele, too, is a New York City op and considerably more intelligent and sobersided than Ruff Morgan; neither was he inclined to moon sentimentally over a well-turned ankle or any other well-turned part of the female anatomy. He tended to regard women with a more cynical eye:

"Private detective Rocky Steele," the cat at the reception desk meowed at me. She sounded like a cat on a back fence at three in the morning, and looked like the same cat twenty-four hours later. Her mug would have soured cream at twenty paces. (*Never Kill a Cop*)

She was beautifully undressed in a transparent blue thing she called a negligee, and brother, was it negligent when it came to hiding what she had! From the top of her spun-gold head to the tips of her ruby-red toenails, was pure gold—twenty-four carat gold. I knew she could be a twenty-four carat bitch, too, when she wanted to be, and so did everybody else that knew her, but right then, I loved every one of her carats, gold or bitch. (*Bullets are My Business*)

* * *

Of course, the prospect of imminent sex did make Steele eloquent on occasion.

> Eliko stood there just inside the door, holding it ajar, and she was clad only in a gossamer thing as light and airy as moonbeams, her platinum hair falling in shining cascades around her rose-pink shoulders and sparkling through the moonbeams where a woman's hair should sparkle. She was all platinum, from stem to stern. Those two peaches thrust out from her chest like they were trying to push their way through the moonbeams, and I gave 'em some help. (*Cobra Venom*)

That is a fair sampling of West's prose—nothing spectacular, a serviceable imitation of the Daly/Spillane style. His plots involve various and sundry gangsters, treacherous "frails," sympathetic and unsympathetic policemen, wicked government agents, a butler who *does* do it, and a great deal of violent action and death. His characters are moderately well drawn examples of the type found in dozens of other private-eye novels of the period, including Spillane's; they neither say nor do anything outside the norm and concern themselves not at all with philosophical or sociological matters. All of which might make the Rocky Steele series only mildly interesting if it were not for one fact.

John B. West was black.

With the exception of the last title in the series, *Death on the Rocks* (published posthumously, as were two others; West died in 1960), there are no black characters in the Steele novels. The setting of *Death on the Rocks* is West Africa, and a black African policeman figures prominently in the action; some attention is also paid to black customs and habits. But the emphasis is on death and destruction as it pertains to Steele and the other white characters.

This is even more curious in light of West's background. According to a blurb on the back cover of *An Eye for an Eye* (1959), he "was born in Washington, D.C., and educated at Howard University and Harvard University. He holds five academic degrees. Dr. West is a specialist in the prevention and treatment of tropical diseases, and he has a general practice in

Liberia, Africa. He also owns and operates the Liberian Broadcasting Company, is President of the National Manufacturing Company and President of the Liberian Hotel and Restaurant Corporation."

It is true that black writers were not exactly popular in the fifties, and black detectives were few and far between. There were only three of note in those pre-Virgil Tibbs days: Coffin Ed Johnson and Gravedigger Jones, a pair of Harlem cops invented by expatriate black writer Chester Himes; and Touissant Moore, hero of the Edgar-winning *Room to Swing* (1957) by Ed Lacy, who was white but who had been married to a black woman for a number of years. Yet West made no real attempt to hide the fact of his race. His publishers surely knew he was not a Caucasian. Why such an educated and successful black doctor would want to write slavish, lily-white imitations of Spillane instead of more serious work remains one of mystery fiction's unsolved mysteries.

The second private eye phenomenon born in the late forties was Shell Scott, a 6-foot-2 inch 200-pound Los Angeles detective with bristly white hair that sticks straight up on his scalp. The new wrinkle that Scott's creator, native Californian Richard S. Prather, added to the mystique is in one sense the antithesis of that wrought by Spillane. Which is not to say that a certain amount of lusty sex and violence, replete with corpses in bunches, cannot be found in each and every Scott caper; the hard-boiled school's influence on Prather is not minute. But whereas Mike Hammer is a cold, hard, humorless individual—a walking time bomb looking for a place to explode—Shell Scott is a happy-go-lucky sort, full of cheer, virility, and what folks used to call piss and vinegar. Prather's gift to the literature of the private investigator is that of "comic vitality," as Larry N. Landrum puts it in his essay on Prather for *Twentieth Century Crime and Mystery Writers*—meaning broad, farcical humor and plenty of it. With emphasis on sex, and plenty of that, too.

A Scott caper abounds in wisecracks, double entendres, and quite a bit of what is known as bathroom comedy; but there are also occasionally hilarious plot devices, plus enough *reductio ad absurdum* scenes to delight the satirical minded. Testimony to the fact that Prather's brand of humor tickled funny bones in the fifties and sixties (and into the seventies) is an aggregate of some forty million books sold. Of course, not everyone thinks Prather is funny—intentionally or otherwise. One person's guffaw is another's yawn. You can reach your own verdict by considering, first of all, the openings to several Scott escapades:

> She yanked the door open with a crash and said, "Gran—" but then she stopped and stared at me. She was nude as a noodle.
> I stared right back at her.
> "Oh!" she squealed. "*You're* not Grandma!"
> "No," I said, "I'm Shell Scott, and you're not Grandma, either."
> She slammed the door in my face.
> Yep, I thought, this is the right house. (*The Wailing Frail*)

> She had a seventy-eight-inch bust, forty-six-inch waist, and seventy-two-inch hips—measurements that were exactly right, I thought, for her height of eleven feet, four inches.
> The scarlet bikini which had covered a minimum of those eye-popping curves lay crumpled on the floor at her feet, and my eyes focussed on her as glassily as did the dead man's. He was dead, all right. He had been shot, poisoned, stabbed, and strangled.
> Either somebody had really had it in for him or four people had killed him. Or else it was the cleverest suicide I'd ever heard of. (*Take a Murder, Darling*)

> The Rand Brothers Mortuary was so beautiful it almost made you want to die. (*Dig That Crazy Grave*)

> I was as confused as a sterile rabbit, primarily because I couldn't make up my mind where to look. The little blonde that everybody here at the party called Dot was doing an impromptu can-can, and even if she wasn't dressed for that kind of dance, she

sure had the equipment for it. At the same time, over
in the far corner of the living room, was a long-
limbed lovely built like something designed by a sex
fiend. (*Way of a Wanton*)

This was a party that Cholly Knickerbocker, in
tomorrow's Los Angeles *Examiner,* would describe as
"a gathering of the Smart Set," and if this was the
Smart Set I was glad I belonged to the Stupid Set.
(*Strip for Murder*)

Consider also such plot gimmicks as this one from *Strip for
Murder* (1955): Scott, investigating a murder (and other things)
in a nudist camp, is chased by thugs and manages to escape
naked in a hot-air balloon, which then carries him on the pre-
vailing winds over Los Angeles and smack up against City Hall,
where a secretary leans out a window and recognizes him by
peering at a part of his anatomy other than his face. Or this one
from *Way of a Wanton* (1952): Scott, investigating a murder
(and other things) on a movie set for a B film called *Jungle Girl,*
is chased by thugs after a nude swim with an actress and manages to escape by swinging Tarzan-like through the trees on a
vine, only to come crashing down in the middle of a hundred
people who are in the process of filming a burning-at-the-stake
scene; the girl tied to the stake takes one look at Scott and says
"Aaaahhhh!" After which she bursts her bonds and runs
away.

And consider lastly the following scene from *The Cockeyed
Corpse* (1964), in which Scott, investigating a murder (and other things) on a movie set for a B Western called *The Wild West,*
disguises himself as a papier mâché rock so he can sneak up on
the thugs' hideout, which is out in the middle of a desert area.
Owing to circumstances beyond his control, he is armed at the
time only with a rifle that shoots tranquilizer darts. (He is not,
however, nude.) One of the hoods comes outside, sees the rock-
draped Scott moving from one spot to another, blinks in amazement, turns around to shout for his pals inside the house, and—

Then he bent over and put his face in his hands.
Bent way over. And that, of course, was asking for it.
Even using a bean-blower, from this distance I

couldn't have missed the vast, magnificent target he presented—magnificent, naturally, only when considered as a target.

I thrust my rifle through the [peep] hole, sighted quickly, and pulled the trigger. There was a little *spat,* and the projectile went straight and true. . . .

Farmer came running out, gun in his hand. "What in the hell is comin' off?" he yelped. . . .

Dodo had turned to face me and was pointing at me with a quivering finger, and with the other hand he started banging Farmer on the shoulder, in a high state of excitement. "You won't believe this," he said. "But that rock just shot me in the ass!"

It was only natural, given the popularity of Shell Scott, that Prather, too, would have his imitators. The most notable of these is a husband-and-wife team, Skip and Gloria Fickling, who happened to be close friends of Prather's in the fifties. But the Ficklings were not merely imitators; they took their version of Shell Scott one innovative step further: they made him a woman. And they called her Honey West.

A good many people are aware of Honey West, but not so much through the series of novels in which she is featured as through the medium of television. Honey first appeared as a character on the old *Burke's Law* series starring Gene Barry and later had her own show for a couple of seasons, with Anne Francis playing the title role. The reason for her modest success, both in books and on TV, was the fact that she was a female private eye. The idea of a lady op was not exactly new in 1957, when the Ficklings (whose only other claim to distinction is that they once appeared on the Groucho Marx TV quiz, *You Bet Your Life*) decided to become authors. A book by James Rubel called *No Business for a Lady* had appeared from Gold Medal (Prather's publishers) several years earlier; Carter Brown had already published, in Australia, the first few titles in his series about Mavis Seidlitz; and there had been other isolated efforts at establishing lady PIs, mainly in the pulps. But no one had a handle on how to do such a character commercially until the Ficklings came along.

Their Honey West formula is simple: tell the stories in the first person, put Honey in all sorts of oddball situations in which her virtue as well as her life is threatened, throw in plenty of sexual innuendo—but under no circumstances have her go to bed with anybody, not even Mark Storm, the cop she supposedly has a yen for. This is what is known as the Big Tease. Is Honey a closet virgin or isn't she? Will she get laid or won't she? The male reader becomes hot and bothered by such speculation, it is presumed, and therefore is more than willing to come back for more of the same in the next book. That there is some validity in this sort of "hard sell" is evident from Honey's longevity on the private-eye scene.

Jokes, wisecracks, and bathroom humor are plentiful in Honey's adventures, of course. The Ficklings's favorite method of adding chuckles was that old Prather standby, the double entendre:

> "I was a chorus girl at the Dreamdust Hotel in Vegas," she said, a touch of triumph in her husky voice. "Mr. Lawrence took a vote of the show's director and backstage crew. Out of thirty girls they picked me as the most outstanding." (*Honey in the Flesh*)

> "You're going to love this party, baby," Hel said. "Of course, a lot of my pictures have to be censored before they hit the magazines. You know what artists' balls are like!"
> "I can imagine." (*A Gun for Honey*)

Honey gets herself embroiled in Scott-like plots, too, such as the Miss Twentieth Century Beauty Pageant (*Honey in the Flesh,* 1959), in which she is injected with a sex stimulant ("It's tearing me to pieces," she says, and "Have you ever sat on a hot oven until you thought your bottom would burn off?"), and for a while it looks as if the impenetrable is finally going to be penetrated. But only for a while. Then there is the case of the "kissing killer" (*A Gun for Honey,* 1958), in which two beautiful women have been smothered to death in bizarre circumstances. The explanation for this, unearthed by Honey, is that a third woman, who was a close friend of the two dead ones, isn't really a woman at all but a transvestite (shades of Spillane's *Vengeance Is Mine*); even though he went around masquerading as a woman, this individual was seized with normal male desires, and when he couldn't stand the pressure any longer, he "exploded from under all his makeup and mascara" and attacked his first victim, a woman named Helena. (And no wonder he picked Helena. As Mark Storm notes, she "was an exotic woman even lying on a slab.") When he grabbed Helena, and she saw him trying to pull his dress *up* at the same time he was trying to pull her *down,* she quite naturally started to scream—and so he was forced to jam his mouth over hers to cut off the noise. Presumably he also pinched her nostrils shut; in any case, he wound up kissing poor Helena until she expired. The second victim was later dispatched in the same oral fashion.

Another notable writer of private-eye fiction who began his career in the fifties and who continues to produce novels and short stories to the present is Michael Avallone, a.k.a. "The Fastest Typewriter in the East," a.k.a. "King of the Paperbacks." These sobriquets are self-given but are nonetheless reasonably accurate. Avallone has published some 190 novels in the past four decades, nearly all of them paperback originals: PI tales, Gothics, TV and film novelizations, juveniles, soft-core porn, espionage thrillers. He is also the holder of unconventional opinions on any number of topics, a zealous old-movie buff, a tireless self-promoter and letter writer, and his own greatest fan. Francis M. Nevins, in his profile of Avallone in *Twentieth Century Crime and Mystery Writers,* calls him "a true *auteur,* with a unique personality discernible throughout his work," and goes on to state, "Whatever else might be said about Avallone, one must say what Caspar Gutman said to Spade in *The Maltese Falcon:* 'By Gad, sir, you're a character, that you are!'"

Avallone's fictional "eye," Ed Noon, has appeared in more than thirty novels since his first recorded case in 1953. On the one hand, Noon is a standard tough, wisecracking op with a taste for copious bloodletting and a Spillane-type hatred of Communists, dissidents, hippies, pacifists, militant blacks, liberated women, and anyone or anything else of a liberal cant. On the other hand, he is a distinctly if eccentrically drawn character who loves baseball, old movies, and dumb jokes, and who gets himself mixed up with some of the most improbable individuals ever committed to paper. For instance, a 6-foot-4-inch ex-circus performer named Tall Dolores, "the Shapliest Amazon in the World"—"a Glamazon, a regular Empire State Building of female feminine dame. And all woman besides" (*The Tall Dolores*). And a 440-pound female mattress tester, who leads him into mayhem and a Chinese restaurant that dispenses "wanton soup," among other savory items (*The Case of the Bouncing Betty*). And a gold-toothed, beret-wearing villain named Dean, who is on the trail of a statue called the *Violent Virgin*, "The Number One Nude," and who says things like "Your precipitous exodus from serene sanctuary propels me toward Brobdingnagian measures. Spider and I mourn for your misdemeanors but your palpitating perignations [sic] induce no termination of our grief" (*The Case of the Violent Virgin*).

Noon's wildest caper, though, is probably *Shoot It Again, Sam!* (1972), which Francis Nevins, the compleat Noon-watcher, sums up as follows in *Twentieth Century Crime and Mystery Writers:* "The President [of the United States, for whom Noon is working at the time as a special investigator] orders Noon to accompany a dead Hollywood star's body on a transcontinental train ride. While the 'corpse' sits up in its coffin, Chinese agents raid the train, kidnap Noon, and use brainwashers made up to look like Gable, Cagney, and Lorre to convince Noon that he is none other than Sam Spade (as portrayed by Bogart of course). It's all part of the screwiest assassination plot ever concocted by a movie maniac."

But, as is the case with so many writers of alternative masterpieces, it is Avallone's lurid, ungrammatical, and often hilarious prose style that distinguishes him and Ed Noon. Nevins again: "[Avallone] makes the language do flipflops, mangles the metaphors like a trash compactor." Noonisms, as they have come to be called among discerning aficionados, abound in each and every Noon title; indeed, in each and every Avallone title. One of these days, it is to be hoped, someone will publish a collection of Noonisms; there are certainly enough to fill a substantial volume. But until that happens, a sampling here of the more memorable will have to suffice.

> The next day dawned bright and clear on my empty stomach. (*Meanwhile Back at the Morgue*)

> The whites of his eyes came up in their sockets like

moons over an oasis lined with palm trees. (*The Voodoo Murders*)

My body felt as abnormal as a tuxedo in a hobo jungle. (*The Crazy Mixed-Up Corpse*)

His thin mustache was neatly placed between a peaked nose and two eyes like black marbles. (*Assassins Don't Die in Bed*)

My stunned intellect, the one that found death in his own backyard with him standing only feet away, hard to swallow in a hurry, found the answer. (*The Horrible Man*)

The door chimes were still disturbing Beethoven in his grave when I rushed to meet him. (*The Crazy Mixed-Up Corpse*)

His freshest laurel wreath was his recent interpretation of such tough aces like Stravinsky and Shostakovich; rendering their works on violin strings was like pushing peanuts up Mount Everest with your nose. (*Killer on the Keys*)

Her hips were beautifully arched and her breasts were like proud flags waving triumphantly. She carried them high and mighty. (*The Case of the Violent Virgin*)

She . . . unearthed one of her fantastic breasts from the folds of her sheath skirt. (*The Horrible Man*)

Her breasts and hips would put a scenic railway to shame. Or maybe make an artist drown himself in his fixative. (*The Crazy Mixed-Up Corpse*)

Holly Hill's figure didn't take your breath away. It just never gave it back. . . . Her breasts weren't only round and full. They pulsed and throbbed like living perfections. The deep well of her stomach fell away to the superb convex leading gracefully to

strong, starkly rendered thighs that were as firm and
full as sixteen-inch guns. (*The Crazy Mixed-Up
Corpse*)

Her breasts were twin mounds of female muscle that
quivered and hung and quivered and hung again. The
pale red of her nipples were two twinkling eyes that
said Go, Man, Go. (*The Crazy Mixed-Up Corpse*)

If her eyes were like baseballs, her breasts took you
from sporting goods to something like ripe cantel-
oupes. (*The Case of the Violent Virgin*)

"I've done a stupid thing, Ed," Opal Trace musi-
caled. (*The Case of the Violent Virgin*)

"Opal . . ." she hoarsed. (*The Case of the Violent
Virgin*)

"Obviously!" she crackled, laying a whip across me
and then turning with a sexy flounce she vanished
through the glass doors, dragging her hatbox and
portmanteau behind her. And my mind. (*Shoot It
Again, Sam!*)

I looked at the knife. . . . One half the blade was
soaked with drying blood. Benny's blood. *It was red,
like anybody else's blood.* (*The Voodoo Murders*)

Dolores came around the bed with the speed of a
big ape. . . . She descended on me like a tree full of
the same apes she looked like. (*The Tall Dolores*)

It had been a journey into the absurd.
A trip into Darkness.
And maybe a one-way ticket to Hell.
And whatever lays [sic] beyond that.
(*Shoot It Again, Sam!*)

In the sixties and seventies, the plots of private-detective novels began to grow increasingly sophisticated. To be sure, there
were—and still are—a few around with Ed Noonish premises;

but a number of serious (and pretentious) writers began to emulate what Ross Macdonald had been doing for years: using the PI novel as a vehicle for salient commentary on all sorts of social, political, racial, sexual, ecological, and psychological topics. A certain percentage of these writers have achieved critical acclaim and widespread popularity—despite the fact that, almost to a man, they are unabashed imitators of one or all of the so-called Big Three of Hammett, Chandler, and Macdonald. Their books are riddled with conventional cops, conventional wisecracks, conventional toughness, conventional violence, and conventional relationships with conventional female characters. They take their detectives as seriously as they take their subject matter, never admitting for a moment that what they are writing is pure and simple pastiche. They have, in short, brought nothing new to the form, the mystique, the Eye.

Only one writer has brought anything new to the Eye in the past thirty years.

His name is Ross H. Spencer.

His detective's name is Chance Perdue.

The first Chance Perdue novel was published in 1978.

Under the title *The Dada Caper.*

It is full of wisecracks and other conventions.

But it is still unique.

It is unique because Spencer has a gimmick.

Or rather three gimmicks.

His first gimmick is that every sentence is a separate paragraph.

His second gimmick is that he doesn't use quotation marks or commas.

Betsy said did she drink a lot?

I said was Hitler a Nazi a lot?

That is how Spencer writes dialogue.

It is supposed to be funny dialogue.

Sometimes it is.

The Dada Caper is supposed to be a spoof.

Sometimes it is.

She said why you lying cheating philandering casanova romeo gigolo any old port in the storm man about town.

That is how Spencer writes sentences without using commas not even to set off clauses like this one or long strings of pithy pointed keen witted right on target adjectives.

His third gimmick is that each chapter begins with an epigraph after the fashion of Mark Twain in *Pudd'nhead Wilson.*

These epigraphs are supposedly written by Monroe D. Underwood.

Who is also known as Old Dad Underwood.

Some of Old Dad Underwood's epigraphs are funny.

. . . going to bed with a good woman can relax a man . . . going to bed with a bad woman can relax a man twicet . . . iffen he is a good man . . .

That's a funny one.

But some of Old Dad Underwood's epigraphs are not funny.

. . . oncet I knowed a feller what smuggled a ham into a synagogue . . . only man what ever got circumcized twenty-two times . . .

That's not a funny one.

All three of Spencer's gimmicks are clever.

One reason they are clever is that they allow him to write a complete novel in less than twenty-five thousand words.

Most writers need a minimum of fifty thousand words to write a novel.

Another reason they are clever is that Spencer doesn't have to spend very much time on plotting.

There is very little plot in *The Dada Caper.*

It is about a Soviet-inspired DADA conspiracy.

DADA means Destroy America, Destroy America.

Anyhow Spencer knew a good thing when he saw it.

So he made Chance Perdue into a series character.

Other novels have followed and more are to come.

But not a lot more.

The problem with gimmicks like this is that they tend to lose their novelty after a while.

Pretty soon readers will start looking for a two-sentence paragraph.

Or a set of quotation marks.

Or a comma.

Or a plot.

And when they don't find any—

. . . oncet I knowed a feller throwed a book across the room . . . I heered him say that's your last chance Perdue.

Old Dad Underwood didn't write that one.

I wrote that one.

It may not be an epigraph either.

It may be an epitaph for an Eye.

3. Cheez It, The Cops!

"Been a long day, sir," I said briskly. "But I'm still hard at it."

"Insulting people?" he growled. . . . "Can't you ever be polite to somebody, Wheeler? Anybody?"

"If I'd known I was supposed to be polite," I told him, "I never would have become a cop in the first place."

–Carter Brown,
The Victim

"You remember that Wall Street philanthropist who was killed by a can of sauerkraut thrown at his head. . . . What a pickle the police were in that day!"

–Elsa Barker,
The C.I.D. of Dexter Drake

The policeman (cop, copper, bobbie, nabber, fuzz, pig—choose your favorite slang term) has generally been accorded more respect in Europe than in the United States. This is especially true among fiction writers, who have been inclined to venerate the actions of the professional manhunter over there and to sneer at them over here. Which is why, until the recent upsurge of interest in the American police procedural novel, far more British, French, and Scandinavian mysteries featured police detectives than did American mysteries. And why many crime stories written by Americans have had as their protagonists European police detectives. (John Dickson Carr's Henri Bencolin is just one of the more well known examples.)

Part of the reason for this dichotomy is that the modern police agency is European in origin: the French Sûreté was formed in 1811, the London metropolitan police force was organized by Sir Robert Peel in 1829. These agencies were not only well established before similar operations were begun here but also highly romanticized in popular writings. The adventures of François Eugène Vidocq, the reformed thief and forger who became the first chief of the Sûreté and later wrote a much-glamourized autobiography called, in the United States, *Vidocq, The French Police Spy,* were famous on both sides of the Atlantic in the mid-1800s and had a profound influence on early writers of crime fiction, beginning with Poe himself, who more or less modeled C. Auguste Dupin on Vidocq. This influence, as Julian Symons points out in his excellent critical history, *Mortal Consequences,* was not because of any deductive skill on Vidocq's part; during his tenure at the Sûreté, he began a card-index system and took impressions of footprints, and made such observations as that many criminals appeared to be bowlegged; but these were the limit of his contributions to police procedural methods. "Vidocq's importance," Symons says, "rested in his nature as the archetypal ambiguous figure of the criminal who is also a hero. The interpenetrations of police with criminals, and the doubt about whether a particular character is hero or villain, is an essential feature of the crime story."

Nonetheless, an aura of mystery is not the chief reason the European policeman became such a popular figure here and abroad in the twentieth century. The chief reason, conversely, is the European—and in particular, British—esteem for representatives of law, order, and the preservation of existing social and moral attitudes. Beginning with the rise of the middle class and the age of Dickens, such representatives, by their very election or appointment to lofty positions, were considered to possess any number of virtues, not the least of which was an acute intelligence. This attitude persisted until the general disillusionment that followed (or preceded, depending on your point of view) the Second World War in Europe. When a detective-story writer introduced a police detective, it was automatically assumed by the reader that he was a man of intellect and keen capabilities.

The same is not true in this country. Rampant police corruption in the cities, Western peace officers of the Wyatt Earp ilk who were little better than outlaws themselves, the pioneer spirit of self-reliance and personal rather than public code of ethics, and story weeklies and dime novels that mostly painted law-enforcement officers in unfavorable colors all combined in the late nineteenth century to create a wholly different police image in American minds. By the time the twentieth century arrived, the police were symbols of authority to be feared, scorned, or at best tolerated, but seldom to be revered. Mystery writers, naturally, reflected this attitude in their work; private investigators and gifted amateurs were much preferred to hard-working, honest cops as detective heroes. It became standard practice to depict the police as bumbling comic figures or as sadistic halfwits whose primary function was to be outsmarted and made fools of by the private individual. To some extent, the stereotypical dumb cop, with his penchant for ungrammatical sentences and the third degree, has survived in mystery fiction to the present.

Most bad mysteries treat the police in this fashion—sometimes unconsciously, in those books in which a cop is supposed to be the hero. The authors, by their very ineptitude, imbue their police detectives with all the negative and/or chucklesome traits of those who are treated as anti- or nonheroes in other mysteries and thus achieve the exact same effect of ridicule.

A case in point is Cortland Fitzsimmons's *70,000 Witnesses* (1931), which features a cop named Kethridge. Fitzsimmons wrote a number of sports mysteries in the thirties and forties, utilizing hockey, baseball, and football, among other sports, as background; *70,000 Witnesses* is the first of these. It deals with college football as it was played in 1930, a markedly different variety of football from the one we know a half-century later. Teams quick-kicked on first down, for example, even with good field position; they also *received* the kickoff after scoring a touchdown. Even more interesting are behind-the-scenes differences: coaches admitting to paying for the services of some players and seeming proud of the fact; players openly gambling on the outcome of games, sometimes even betting on their opponents to win, without anybody becoming upset or even wondering if these players might not decide purposely to miss a tackle of two or maybe commit a convenient fumble if the score got too close. Fitzsimmons implies that no one is concerned about the gambling because "college boys will be college boys," and besides, none of America's fine young manhood would dream of doing anything illegal on or off the field.

The action centers around a showdown match between two undefeated teams, University and State, whose campuses are twenty-five miles apart in an unnamed but presumably small state. A twenty-two-page radio broadcast opens the novel, most of it play-by-play of the first half of the game, with color commentary, a half-time "analysis" by a sports writer, and station breaks included, all for verisimilitude. Here are two examples of this stirring reportage:

> "The University band is coming out now. They are a snappy-looking bunch of boys and they can play too. Hear them? They are playing 'University Forever.' University's mascot is an old goat lovingly called 'American Can' but I don't see him. It is just possible that the University boys were afraid State would get their goat."

> "The timekeeper is ready, the gun is in the air. There it goes. Did you hear it? The game is on. Oh my! Butch Schupe's toe has driven the pigskin deep into University's territory. What a kick! For a moment it looked as if it had taken off permanently. It's down now. Number twenty-nine, that's Jorgenson, has taken the oval and has cut in following his interference which has begun to function quickly and efficiently. Look at him go. Ten. Fifteen. Twenty-five. They've got him. He's down but it was a good run back. The referee has dived into that swirling mass of legs and arms and is pulling them off. I might say I've never seen a referee go at a pile of men the way Collins gets into them."

* * *

So much for verisimilitude.

At the start of the second half, State's star player, an all-American boy named Walter Demuth, takes a single-wing snap and breaks through the line on a long run down the sidelines. There is no one near him as he approaches the goal line; but then he staggers and slows down as if suddenly exhausted, stumbles on the five-yard stripe, and collapses just after he crosses into the end zone for a touchdown.

The narrative switches to the third person at this point, and we learn that Demuth is dead of what may or may not be a heart attack. Both coaches decide that the game must go on in spite of the tragedy, because, as one of them says, "If we call the game, we will have to make some explanation. We can't say that he was killed, that might start a panic and a panic out there would be pretty terrible. You never know what 70,000 people will do under such circumstances. They have had a very exciting afternoon with a great play of emotion. They are curious now and upset. They are wondering what has happened and pretty soon they will begin to churn. They might go loco. It wouldn't need more than three or four screaming, fainting women to start something pretty bad."

So much for logic.

The game continues, and University wins, 27–13. And the following day, the coroner determines that Demuth died of an "explosion of the brain," in which all the small blood vessels were destroyed in the manner of apoplexy. But he suspects foul play nonetheless and calls in the homicide boys. Enter Kethridge.

Kethridge is the quintessential thirties detective: taciturn, hard-boiled, prone to the wisecrack and the sharp retort. He is also about as realistically portrayed as Fleming Stone and not half as intelligent.

He questions Demuth's sister Dorothy and Demuth's best friend Ranny, who is in love with Dorothy, and manages to find out that Demuth died on his twenty-first birthday, after having inherited a rather large fortune; Kethridge also finds out that Demuth willed half of this fortune to Ranny, because the two of them were such close chums. (The reader has known all this for some time before Kethridge learns it; Fitzsimmons was fond of imparting relevant information to the reader first, perhaps as a courtesy. It may also be through courtesy that the reader is allowed to guess the identity of the murderer on page

15, despite there being twenty-one other suspects. But that is of little import; the real joy of *70,000 Witnesses* is in trying to figure out *how* Demuth was killed—and in watching Kethridge make a fool of himself.) He also questions Harry Collins, the referee in the big game, who was once Demuth's tutor and who, like Ranny, is in love with Dorothy. And he questions various members of the State team, some of whom have minor motives for wanting Demuth out of the way, as well as selected members of the University team.

But does he have the State locker room searched for possible poisonous or otherwise deadly agents? He does not. Does he have the field searched for similar agents, or question grounds keepers, ushers, or the other officials? He does not. Does he think to investigate the uniform Demuth was wearing at the time of his demise? Yes, but only after the youth's clothes are stolen and, we later learn, destroyed by the murderer.

While Kethridge continues his bumbling investigation, Dorothy is forced to choose between Ranny and Harry when Ranny impulsively proposes to her.

> "What about these women you get in messes with? Walter isn't here now to protect you or me."
>
> A fleeting smile passed across Ranny's face. "You dear, adorable, wonderful girl, that was over a year ago and was just a mad thing that I got into and wanted to get out of and didn't know how. . . . It didn't mean anything and there has been no girl and never will be any other girl but you. You must believe me. Don't you?" he teased. "Say you love me," he went on. "Please say it. Repeat after me, 'Ranny, I love you.'"
>
> Her head dropped down on his shoulder and she started to cry broken-heartedly.
>
> "Oh, my darling, please. There, there, sweetheart. I didn't want to make you cry." He crooned over her and his own eyes glistened.
>
> "I—I—" she snuggled closer, burrowing her face into his neck so that her words were smothered. "I do, Ranny, I do and I am happy but I don't feel happy."
>
> "I know, dear, and I feel the same way."

* * *

Ranny feels even less happy when O'Brien, a uniform cop assigned to the State campus beat and Kethridge's nominal partner in the murder investigation, finds part of Demuth's missing uniform—a torn stocking—among Ranny's effects. Kethridge asks Ranny some more questions, after first advising him of his rights. (" 'You need not speak if you prefer to keep still as I must warn you that anything you say can and will be used against you.' Kethridge smiled as he repeated the trite phrase so common in criminal circles.") But he doesn't learn much; Ranny claims not to know how the stocking came to be among his belongings.

Dorothy is then recruited to pretend to believe Ranny is guilty, a ploy which Kethridge tells her might prove the boy's guilt or innocence. It does neither; all it does is upset Dorothy and Ranny both. So Kethridge then takes Ranny to a showing of newsreel footage of Demuth's fatal touchdown run. Neither he nor the reader learns much from that, either. Nevertheless, Kethridge decides he has enough of a case against Ranny to confine him to jail for the night, and this is done. Ranny takes his incarceration manfully. Of course, he *does* lie awake most of the night, tossing and turning, asking himself rhetorical questions; but then "because sleep had been a habit with him for so many years he finally slept and forgot."

The next morning Ranny is released, reunited with Dorothy, and subsequently taken to the football stadium. The reason for this is that Kethridge has had another brainstorm: he has ordered that Demuth's fatal run be restaged, along with several of the plays leading up to it, by the teams from State and University. By doing this, he says with dubious logic, maybe a new clue will come to light.

Before the re-creation begins, we are privy to several exchanges of dialogue among State's players in their locker room. It becomes obvious that two players, Cannero and Greenwood, have been withholding information from the police for reasons of their own. Greenwood is asked to play the part of Demuth in the restaging, but he refuses on the grounds that the same thing will happen to him that happened to Demuth. Cannero is given the role instead.

And to everyone's surprise (except the reader's), the same thing happens to him that happened to Demuth when the fateful touchdown run is re-created.

There is a good deal of anguish and confusion after that.

Greenwood, who is not your typical football player, swoons. The team doctor pronounces Cannero dead. Kethridge, baffled, asks several ineffectual questions and finally orders the corpse taken back to the State locker room. The doctor and the State coach do the honors; but once inside, they accidentally drop Cannero on the table instead of setting him down in a gentler fashion. The result is a tremendous explosion: "the blanket-covered body rose abruptly from the table and seemed to hang in mid air for a moment." Then there is a second explosion, which turns everyone topsy-turvy and topples the long row of lockers. No one is seriously hurt in these blowups except for Greenwood, who is found pinned and near death underneath the lockers. But he hasn't been crushed or injured by flying objects; he is near death because the same thing that happened to Demuth and Cannero *has* happened to him, after all.

Blamed by both his chief and the newspapers for this latest carnage (rightfully so), Kethridge at last begins to ask the right questions. He learns from Ranny that Greenwood was a chemistry nut, always trying experiments, and that an explosion the previous year had almost wrecked a laboratory he had set up in a rented shack. Kethridge then goes to Greenwood's chemistry professor, from whom the answer to the puzzle is forthcoming.

It seems that one of Greenwood's experiments was the manufacture of nitroglycerin. And nitroglycerin, as the professor tells him, "in small doses has a powerful heart reaction. Men, particularly when they are new at making it, often have severe reactions. They are seized with terrific headaches and often keel over." People get it on their hands and clothes, we then learn, and take it into their systems by absorption.

As for the explosion—well, everyone knows that nitroglycerin is a volatile substance and can explode at any time. When the body of Cannero was dropped on the locker-room table . . . boom! The second explosion was of a vial of nitro hidden away in one of the lockers, touched off by the concussion of the first blast.

How did the nitro get inside the uniforms of Demuth, Cannero, and Greenwood? Kethridge deduces that none of the football players could have carried it onto the field in a hidden vial, because football is a contact sport and the first time a vial-carrying player smacked into the line . . . boom! Who else was on the field? Why, the officials, of course. And which official was not only in love with Dorothy but had made a ten-thousand-dollar bet against State and regularly dived into pileups and pulled the players apart? Why, the referee, Harry Collins, of course. He had the vial of nitro inside his shirt, having gotten it from Greenwood, who turns out to have been his nephew. (The cowardly Greenwood knew too much, which is why he had to die. Cannero had seen Collins destroying Demuth's uniform; that was why *he* had to die.) And even though twenty-two football players and five other officials were in close proximity, not to mention seventy thousand other witnesses during the big game and eagle-eye Kethridge at the re-creation, Collins managed somehow to pull out the vial surreptitiously and empty the contents down each of the murdered players' backs. He did this, it is inferred, during the play before the long touchdown runs—though how he knew beforehand that Demuth was going to break away for a long touchdown run is never explained. For if Demuth had been piled up at the line of scrimmage . . . boom! No more line of scrimmage.

So much for plausibility, the great Kethridge, and *70,000 Witnesses.*

Another fictional cop whose talents, if not personality, parallel Kethridge's is Lieutenant Price Price of the San Francisco Homicide Squad, narrator and hero of Knight Rhoades's *She Died on the Stairway* (1947). Price may also be a bumbler, but he's neither taciturn nor a loner; he has a beautiful wife named Nikky (who taps out "SOS" in Morse code with her fingertips when she's thinking hard), is an expert on rabbit culture, enjoys listening to himself talk, and, like Race Williams, is fond of confiding his thoughts and opinions to the reader. He also has another unusual talent.

> Oswald [was] a symbol of battle and murder and sudden death. If a dwarf white rabbit with a pink nose and pink ears can be said to be a harbinger of crime, Oswald is it.
> Maybe you don't get the idea.
> You see, I put myself through U.C. by doing magic tricks. I always did them well, even as a kid. I had to do some choosing when it came right down to it, as to

whether I'd go on with the crime-solving, or take up
the legerdemain professionally. The crime stuff won
by a hair.

One day, when I was a rookie and trying to break
down a tough suspect, unconsciously I started doing
magic stuff. Making my handkerchief disappear.
Changing a dollar into a dime. Elementary junk like
that. The suspect got jittery and lost his nerve. I
cracked him—and the case. That gave me an idea.
I'm known as the Sleight-Of-Hand Cop, and Oswald is
my trump card.

Price Price, as may be surmised, is as unique among cops as
his name. He professes to be tough and hard-boiled, but we
know that this is only a pose; the author (who internal evidence suggests was a woman hiding behind a masculine pseudonym) allows him to slip from time to time and reveal a somewhat more delicate nature. What truly tough homicide cop,
after all, would say, "Oh, dear me, yes," to himself, and refer to
a vicious three-time killer as "Mr. Murderer"?

The case in which Price, Nikky, and Oswald become involved
is a bizarre one indeed. It seems someone is trying to poison
Abigail Winship, matriarch of the Winship family and present
owner of Winship's Folly, an architectural nightmare built on
an isolated cliff "down Monterey way." Abigail's husband, old
Kirk Winship, had decided he didn't need an architect when he
built his house and thus built it all wrong to start with; then it
became a sort of game with him and he continued to build it all
wrong; then a gypsy fortune-teller told him that he would die
the day the house was completed, so he kept right on building it
all wrong; then he stopped building it all wrong, because Abigail was tired of carpenters and plasterers hanging around all
the time, and that very day the gypsy's prophecy came true and
a falling beam whacked old Kirk into the Hereafter.

When Price, Nikky, and Oswald arrive at Winship's Folly,
they find that the house is painted slate gray, with parts of it
that are stone or brick showing through the paint "as if the
house broke out in places with a sort of ugly rash." They also
find chimneys jutting out at unusual angles; staircases that lead
nowhere; hallways with unexpected jogs; four kitchens with
bright red furnishings, poppy-yellow walls, and bright blue

floors; a red-haired Chinese butler named Wyatt; a tortoiseshell
cat that laps up cocktails before dinner; a dead parrot named
Persis; assorted members of the Winship clan, including one
named Philo; a girl plasterer; an apparent ghost; and a howling
storm that washes out the only access bridge and isolates them
from the outside world. What transpires then are three murders by poison, two disappearing bodies, a poisoned bouquet of
roses meant for Price and Nikky, some not very brilliant detective work, some clumsy legerdemain that has no relation to the
plot, no help whatsoever from Oswald, a final confrontation
during which the murderer blurts out his guilt on the strength
of a minor bit of evidence, a thrilling chase that culminates
with a falling beam crushing out the killer's life just as it
crushed out poor old Kirk's (this is what is known as
i*r*o*n*y, or maybe p*o*e*t*i*c j*u*s*t*i*c*e), and last but
certainly not least such memorable passages as:

> "I judge a man by his wife," she snapped. "If your
> wife had been a fluff or a horse, I should have asked
> you both to leave."

> "I haven't quite made up my mind," said Abigail.
> "But I think I will leave my entire fortune to Cyn-
> thia. She enjoys life the most."
> Lucy bit her lips. "All right," she shrilled. "Go
> ahead. I'm afraid for my own life. I'd rather be alive
> and poor, than dead and wealthy."
> Which was sort of obscure.

> I was picking up my handkerchief and laying it
> down on the table. Only when I laid it down, it
> wasn't anything remotely resembling a handker-
> chief. It was a little bottle!
> I keep quite a lot of "props" in my clothes. A small
> blackjack, a miniature revolver, a bottle marked
> "Poison" in big red letters. I use whichever one fits
> the crime. Do you see? In this case, I thought the tiny
> poison bottle might break them down a bit.

> Aha! I figured. So! There is somebody around up
> here! Somebody our dear friend Kirk wants to warn

of our approach. Dollars to doughnuts it's the ghost of Uncle Peter! But who the heck is this ghost in real life? Maybe the girl plasterer Nikky saw?

I didn't think that was very logical.

"Then you don't think Dr. Hugo stole the cyanide out of your locked poison cabinet and administered the same to your beautiful cousin, Cynthia, with lethal intent?"

So! He was going to play ball. The hatchet was buried. The pipe of peace was being readied. Hail, hail, the gang's all here!

Darlings!
It was such fun playing cyanide-dead, that I'm going to do a real job of it and jump into the sea from Lucy's window. I want to see what is on the Other Side, and I cannot wait to find out. Don't grieve for me, my pets.
Everything is going to be such fun. Barring those few seconds it will take to cross from one world to the other!
With all my love,
Cynthia

. . . I wondered why the would-be murderer had hidden the cyanide in the chair. Of course it was a fine opportunity, with the [fabric] slashed by a child's wanton use of scissors. But why not throw the extra cyanide away after he'd pulled off the trick with the teacup?

I decided the murderer *had* thrown his extra cyanide away!

If he'd had any.

Still another different kind of police detective is Steve Conway, who narrates Earle Basinsky's 1955 tale of murder and sadistic violence, *The Big Steal*. Anthony Boucher in his June 26, 1955, column in the *New York Times Book Review*, had this to say about the Basinsky opus: "Earle Basinsky's *The Big*

Steal . . . has a jacket inscription, 'Mickey Spillane says "The kind of book I go for," ' and a dedication, 'For Mickey Spillane who insisted * * * and for Nathan Jr. who suffered.' Those should serve as a better guide to your choice than any review; personally, I'm on Nathan Jr.'s side."

Basinsky was not the only friend or acquaintance of Spillane to receive an endorsement from the begatter of Mike Hammer in the fifties or to attempt to capitalize on Spillane's phenomenal record; at least two other writers, Charlie Wells and David J. Gerrity ("Garrity"), were also touted by the Mick and returned the favor with book dedications. Neither Gerrity, who continues to produce an occasional paperback original, nor Wells, who disappeared from the mystery scene after two novels, had the Spillane knack for raw and stomach-churning violence; Basinsky, however, did. He also had a knack for clichés, a narrative style that only approximates literacy, and a shameless desire to wax poetic every now and then, as in the following "miniprologue" which opens *The Big Steal*:

> I am caught between the past and the future like a wriggling worm in a vise. Seen through shimmering quicksilver.
>
> The present is nonexistent, the here and now is never.
>
> I either exist in the past in memory or base my future on what the past has been. But this is useless.
>
> For there are X factors over which I have no control and I cannot foresee the future even dimly, much as one would try to see the bottom of a stream through muddy swirling water.
>
> Yet I live in the future.
>
> Trapped there by what has happened in the past knowing nothing of the present.
>
> This is the story.

The story involves the theft of $400,000 in ransom money, which the police have recovered after killing a kidnapper (who had previously murdered his kidnap victim), but which mysteriously disappears en route to the police station. Conway, in charge of the suitcase in which the money was supposed to have been placed, is accused of the theft. Ostracized by his police cohorts, deserted by his wife and friends, he sets out on a personal odyssey to retrieve the missing money and find the person or persons who framed him.

The opening chapter depicts Conway being viciously beaten with a rubber hose by his former police buddies, who are not only willing to believe him guilty on the basis of circumstantial evidence but who take delight in whipping hell out of him; the final chapter depicts Conway deliberately shooting a wounded man in the belly and watching him die because the man butchered Conway's dog. In between, there are various beatings, shootings, and slashings, a beautiful dope addict with whom Conway falls in love, a variety of thugs, some crooked cops, and such dialogue as:

> As the drapes swirled close behind him, the man with the bandage turned and jammed a gun in my stomach. "Okay, let's have it pal."
> "Have what?"
> "The heater, pal. The one you use so well without squeezing the trigger. This time I wanta make sure. My face still feels like it was caught in a revolving door . . ."
> "That's right, chum, a gun can be mighty rough even without bullets. . . . And another thing . . . with you this close I could make you eat your own gun and you wouldn't even know what happened."
> He moved back two steps. "Okay, you go first. This time *I* got a itchy trigger finger."

Which brings us to a fourth kind of cop—the wisecracking type who, like his private-eye counterparts, spends more time pursuing horny females than murderous felons. And it also brings us to a phenomenon almost as impressive as Mickey Spillane himself: an Australian named Alan G. Yates, better known as Carter Brown.

Spillane, of course, is the bestselling mystery writer of all time, with close to 100 million copies sold of a mere 20 novels and 6 collections. Second place is a toss-up between Erle Stanley Gardner and Yates, whose 200-plus novels under the Carter Brown pen name have sold in excess of 60 million copies in the

English-speaking world. "Inspired" by the success of Spillane, or so he once claimed in a television interview, Yates began publishing mysteries in 1953, after a not very sparkling career as a salesman, publicity writer, and film technician; his first 50 or so books appeared only in Australia, first from Transport and then, in late 1954, from Horwitz Publications of Sydney, which continues to the present as his primary publisher. It was not until 1958 that the Carter Brown novels crossed the Pacific to the United States, when a package deal was arranged with New American Library (Signet Books). Brown was an instant success in the booming paperback market of the time, and from 1958 until the mid-1970s, he amassed the bulk of his impressive sales figures from among the American audience.

Yates created a number of series characters in the fifties and sixties, the first of these being the well-endowed private eye with the unlikely name of Mavis Seidlitz. Other of his heroes include a private cop, Rick Holman, who operates out of Hollywood; a randy San Francisco lawyer with the appropriate name of Randy Roberts; and a Hollywood scriptwriter, Larry Baker, and his besotted partner Boris Slivka. But Yates's most successful creation, the detective whose escapades first interested NAL in Carter Brown, is Al Wheeler, a lieutenant with the sheriff's office of Pine City County, an obviously fictional locale in southern California.

One of the reasons for Wheeler's success here is that he is an American character operating in a more or less recognizable American setting. (The same is true, to a lesser extent, for the success of Mavis Seidlitz et al.) Foreign writers have not often managed to create believable American characters or to capture an authentic American flavor in dialogue, action, and background; but with the exception of a dubious command of American slang, Yates has shown a remarkable facility for Americanizing his books. Frequent trips to this country no doubt helped, as did an uncanny ability to, as he put it in the aforementioned television interview, "think like an American."

An uncanny ability to think sophomorically hasn't hurt, either.

The key to an evaluation and appreciation of the Carter Brown novels is that word "sophomoric." Everything about them may be described with the same adjective—sophomoric plots (of the type television viewers have been treated to regularly on such shows as *Charlie's Angels*), sophomoric humor, sophomoric dialogue, sophomoric sex, and even sophomoric violence (reckoning from the point of view, say, of a Spillane addict). The books are all quite short—of less than fifty thousand words—and so fast-paced and formularized that they can be read in less than half an hour. After which they will promptly be forgotten. Anyone who has read more than one Carter Brown novel will be hard-pressed to synopsize the plot of any of them.

Sex, to be sure, is the main ingredient of each and every Brown title—no more so than in the Al Wheeler series. Wheeler is a *very* horny cop. He is forever bantering with beautiful women, ogling their breasts, leering at their behinds, pawing at their clothing and bare flesh, and/or thinking about rolling them in the hay. Sometimes he attains that primary objective; sometimes he doesn't. In that respect, at least, the series is true to life.

This is Wheeler about to make a conquest:

> I lay back against the cushions as her arms tightened around my neck and that nuclear fission started again as her lips met mine. I didn't know how long that clinch lasted—who puts a stopwatch on ecstasy? But finally, she wasn't kissing me any more.
>
> I knew how she felt. Sometimes you just have to stop for a moment and take a deep breath. I slid further down onto the couch and waited patiently. "You may kiss me again, honey-chile," I murmured. "Let me drink the magnolia-blossom from your lips!" (*The Victim*)

And this is Wheeler bantering about sex:

> "Appearances can be deceptive, you know that? I mean, you look very virile indeed, Al, but maybe it's all a big fake?"
>
> "I'll prove it, if you like," I said determinedly. "Give me a cracker, and I'll break it with my bare hands!"
>
> "There has to be a more interesting way of proving

it," she said throatily. "Like, if I took you upstairs to
my room, as soon as we've finished this drink?"

I shook my head regretfully. "I'm not allowed to
make love to any suspect in a homicide case. It's a
rule." (*Burden of Guilt*)

Wheeler doesn't spend *all* his time dealing, or trying to deal,
with sex. He does attend to business now and then:

"Yes?" The word exploded out of him like I had
just punched him in the solar plexus.

"I'm Lieutenant Wheeler, from the sheriff's office,"
I told him.

"Only a lieutenant?" He sounded bitterly disap-
pointed. "Is that the best they could do?"

"This is Pine City County," I snarled, "and here,
with a homicide, you get me. If you don't like the
idea, you can always take your corpse some place else
and start over." (*Burden of Guilt*)

"Haven't found your murderer yet?" she asked.

"I was just figuring," I said. "Maybe it's an inside
job, one of those least-probable-suspect capers. You
get around much in a sarong, carrying a blowpipe in
your dainty little hand?"

"Maybe it's high fashion in Waikiki," she said
sweetly, "but in li'l ole Virginny where I come from,
they'd figure right off a girl was ailing and feed her
hot molasses until she started wearing white cotton
dresses again."

"They could blame it on the hot sun," I said absent-
ly. "The sudden heat—hey! That gives me an idea!"

"Hang onto it quick, honey-chile," she said excitedly. "With you, this doesn't happen very often."

"I'm going to make like that li'l ole sun," I said,
"and turn on some heat." (*The Brazen*)

"I keep on getting this recurring symptom," I said,
"every time I listen to you run off at the mouth. It
starts with a feeling of great restlessness and impa-
tience. After awhile . . . comes this almost irresisti-

ble impulse to smack you in the mouth. You figure
I'm sickening for something?"

"Moronic egotisis," he said promptly. "It's a common disease among morons such as yourself. . . ."

"How come you're a doctor and still know nothing?" I asked in a wondering voice.

"It wasn't easy," he said. "For the first three years
I kept on wondering why everybody figured I was a
chiropodist, then I realized I'd hung my shingle
upside-down."

"When can you do the autopsy?" I asked, because I
know when I'm licked.

"Later this morning," he said. "It looks like a nice
day for it."

"You ever look in a mirror and find you're not
there?" I muttered.

"And I drink Bloody Marys, with real blood," he
said happily. "It's a fun profession, medicine. . . ."

"So why don't you just flap your wings and fly
away?" I suggested. (*Wheeler Fortune*)

Wheeler isn't exactly a lone-wolf cop, nor does he do all his
bantering with women, male suspects, and coroners. He is forever at odds with Sheriff Lavers, his superior, who doesn't care
for Wheeler's decorum. And in his early capers, he is forever
exchanging quips with a sometime partner named Sergeant Pol-
nik, who just may be the stupidest cop in the history of the
roman policier. (Yates must have felt sorry for poor dumb Pol-
nik along about 1970; in *Burden of Guilt*, published that year,
he mercifully killed him off.)

Here is a typical Wheeler/Polnik exchange from a 1963 novel:

"Since when did you get around to using all those
two-syllable words?"

"So that's what they were?" he said in a respectful
voice. "I didn't know, even, the doctor was talking
dirty." He edged closer toward me and lowered his
voice to a confidential roar. "Say, Lieutenant? What
does that 'gamut' mean, exactly?"

"I'd like to explain but I don't think you're old
enough, Sergeant," I said quickly. . . .

"Lieutenant, how come you know what it means and you got to be at least ten years younger than me?"

"I had a lousy home life," I said. . . . "I want you to stay here, Sergeant. Check the guards on the gate. Find out who was on duty through the night and if they heard or saw anything unusual. Then check the records on Nina Ross. . . ."

"Sure, Lieutenant." The muscles in his jaw stiffened dutifully. "I got just one question. Who is Nina Ross?"

"The girl who was murdered!" I tried hard but I couldn't keep a note of shrill hysteria out of my voice.

"Cheez! You sure had me worried there, Lieutenant. I figured it was maybe the nurse at the reception desk. You know, the old bat who figured 'nut' was a dirty word?"

"Well," I said desperately, "if she gets out of line you can fix her real good—just say 'gamut!' right in her face." (*The Girl Who Was Possessed*)

And this, finally, is Wheeler in action:

"Drop it, Lieutenant!" he said tensely.

I figured if I did drop it, it probably wouldn't make any difference, he'd still shoot me. So I didn't drop it. He pulled the trigger and a split second later the room exploded in front of my eyes.

My reflexes got to work belatedly, and I pressed the trigger of my own gun; then pressed it twice more. . . .

Williams still leaned against the door, but his gun was on the floor. [He] was dying, and dying fast.

I felt the top of my head and my fingers got wet. I explored cautiously and decided the slug from his gun had ploughed a furrow across the top of my scalp. Close enough to hurt, but no more than that. One inch lower, and I would have been a bad verse on a chunk of granite. (*The Victim*)

Thus Al Wheeler.

Add him up with Kethridge, Price Price, and Steve Conway, and you have a composite of the American cop as portrayed by crime writers in the United States over the past fifty-odd years. It is a composite that gives one pause to reflect.

Is it any wonder police officers tend to get upset when you ask them if they read mystery novels?

4. The Saga of the Risen Phoenix

Norma Goold was the most beautiful corpse Allen Starke had ever beheld. When he had seen her, lithe and young and magnetically compelling, doing her number at The Gayety burlesque house a few hours previously, he had understood his friend Paul Cloud's infatuation with her. And even in death the power she had over men continued.

Paul Cloud, and his whole family with him, was drawn into the net of suspicion spread as a result of Norma's violent demise. So was Paul's fiancée, and the playboy backer of The Gayety, and an Italian gambler who had known La Goold when her name had been plain Marcella Cadorna. And before it all ended, Allen wished he had never left Kentucky's peaceful blue grass for New Orleans.

—Jacket blurb for
Death for the Lady,
by Stewart Vanderveer, Phoenix Press

Once upon a time, in the kingdom of New York, there was a publishing company called Phoenix Press.

Like many others born during the Great Depression, Phoenix

was a lending-library publisher, which is to say that it grew up in a very tough and competitive neighborhood and was often forced to fight for survival with other lending-library publishers—Godwin, Greenberg, Arcadia—that operated in the same ghetto. Phoenix's parentage is unknown. Perhaps it had no parentage in the conventional sense; perhaps it simply sprang from the ashes of some defunct flapper-era publisher, youthfully alive and functional, ready to do battle in the marketplace. Such is the stuff of legends and fairy tales.

But Phoenix Press was stronger and more dedicated than the other lending-library publishers, and soon it surpassed them all to become the strongest in the kingdom. Guided by the keen eyes and iron hearts of its two chief editorial wizards, Emmanuel Wartels and Alice Sachs, it produced more mysteries, Westerns, and light romances during the thirties and forties than any other house. It was surely the monarch of all lending-library publishers everywhere.

This, however, was not its greatest distinction. Rather, it is the fact that in less than twenty years, Phoenix published almost as many wonderfully bad novels as *all* the other publishers combined.

The reason behind this remarkable achievement was an unstinting devotion to the principles of capitalistic free enterprise. Or to put it another way, it was a matter of greed. Phoenix published a large quantity of books and yet paid absolute minimum royalties to its writers. In an article for the *Writer's 1941 Year Book,* novelist and screenwriter Steve Fisher says that he received the handsome sum of $125 for all rights to his first novel, *Spend the Night,* in 1935. Rates escalated dramatically to $300 for all rights—and even to $500 for some of Phoenix's more prolific contributors—in the late thirties; where they remained for many years to come. This policy of paying rock-bottom prices allowed Phoenix to buy manuscripts that had been rejected by the major publishers and by some of the other lending-library outfits as well. And the preponderance of these manuscripts were, to put it in charitable terms, only marginally publishable by most standards. Thus, by a combination of design and accident, were so many classics given life in the kingdom.

Perhaps providentially, the reign of the Phoenix was fated to be short. It had barely reached the age of legal majority—

eighteen—when rising printing costs, the paperback boom of the early fifties, and the closing of a substantial percentage of small lending-library outlets toppled the Phoenix empire into the ashes from whence it came. This is not to say that it died; it was denied the noble end of death. Instead it was consolidated with Arcadia House, one of its archrivals, under the Arcadia imprint in 1952. Even its primary editorial wizard, Alice Sachs, was absorbed in the merger and assumed command of Arcadia's line of Westerns and (increasingly fewer) mysteries until the early sixties. Ms. Sachs even managed to survive an outright sale of the firm at that time, when it underwent another metamorphosis into Lenox Hill Press; she rather amazingly continues to the time of this writing as Lenox Hill's senior editor, holding forth at the same old Phoenix address in New York City, 419 Fourth Avenue, and still buying light romance fiction. (Lenox Hill—not to be confused, incidentally, with the academic publisher of the same name—has never published a regular mystery line and abandoned its long-standing series of Westerns in 1975. Still, the company manages to survive as the last link to a vanished era and a vanished publishing kingdom—the sole heir to what was once a lending-library fortune.)

Be all of this as it may, the Phoenix legacy—and the Phoenix mystique—of the thirties and forties is still with us today: the books themselves. Even though an average of only two thousand copies of each title were printed, and most surviving books have library date stamps; card pockets; borrowers' signatures; coffee and other, stranger stains; dog-eared pages; pages defaced by scatological graffiti disguised as readers' comments; or any combination of these, copies of most titles turn up fairly often in secondhand bookstores and on mail-order book dealers' lists. As do the cheap but durable paperback reprint editions of several Phoenix titles published just prior to and during World War II by such ephemeral outfits as Atlas, Black Cat, Bleak House, Hangman's House, Tech House, and Novel Selections, Inc. (which published Mystery Novel Classic, Mystery Novel of the Month, Western Novel of the Month, Adventure Novel of the Month).

Phoenix books were surprisingly well packaged. Dust jackets sported attractive artwork, the paper was of good quality, and there were relatively few typographical errors. In their early years, they even used a distinctive colophon for their mysteries, which depicted a smiling Grim Reaper carrying a large scythe cleverly drawn so that it was also a question mark. To read irony into this by speculating that Alice Sachs and her cohorts knew just what sort of books they were unleashing on an unsuspecting public would seem to be a misinterpretation. Such matters as colophon and editorial selection appear to have been guileless.

The total number of novels to appear under the Phoenix imprint probably approaches one thousand, with a full third of those being mysteries. Not all of that third can properly be termed alternative classics; even Phoenix Press was not *that* awesome. But the number that do achieve classic status are quite high—and there are a great many near-misses.

Most Phoenix mysteries, classic and nonclassic alike, were written by unknowns; a high percentage, in fact, are first novels. Consider this glittering partial array of heretofore unrecognized talent: M. G. MacKnutt, E. Spence de Puy, and Virginia van Urk—no doubt pseudonyms adopted by writers who had read other Phoenix books; Arville Nonweiler, K. Alison La Roche, H. Donald Spatz, Helen Joan Hultman, Kelliher Secrist, Oliver Keystone, H. W. Sandberg, M. W. Glidden, L. Morningstar, Gilbert Eldredge, Stewart Vanderveer, Saul Levinson, Addison Simmons, Amelia Reynolds Long, Paul H. Dobbins, Wallace Reed, Minna Bardon, and Robert Portner Koehler.

At least two Phoenix "discoveries" did go on to make names for themselves, in and out of the genre. Soft-cover spy novelist Edward S. Aarons sold his first three mysteries here, under his Edward Ronns pen name—the only three of his early novels he refused to allow to be reissued in modern paperback; he evidently did not want to answer to his public for such youthful sins as *The Corpse Hangs High* and *Murder Money*. And well-known editor, publisher, author, and bibliophile William Targ published his only novel with Phoenix, a collaboration with Lewis Herman entitled *The Case of Mr. Cassidy* (1939).

Established writers were also permitted in the Phoenix stable, of course, always provided that they came cheap. Among this group are:

Robert Leslie Bellem, whose highly idiomatic pulp work was immortalized in an article by humorist S. J. Perelman and who is being given further recognition later in these pages; his only hard-cover novel, *Blue Murder,* was a 1938 Phoenix selection.

Harry Stephen Keeler, the once-popular "wild man" of the mystery, who seems to have been cheerfully daft and whose plots defy logic and the suspension of *anyone's* disbelief; several of his later novels found a proper home at 419 Fourth Avenue.

Noel Loomis, Mack Reynolds, and William McLeod Raine, each with a single criminous book. Their efforts are testimony to the fact that writers of some prominence in other genres are not always well advised to try the mystery form.

Another interesting facet of Phoenix mysteries was their unique and enticing titles. For example, we have *The Case of the Little Green Men, The Case of the 16 Beans, The Case of the Barking Clock, The Case of the Six Bullets,* and *The Case of the Deadly Drops.* Then we have *Corpse in the Wind, The Corpse Came Calling, The Corpse Came Back, The Corpse at the Quill Club,* and *The Corpse With Knee-Action.* Next we have *Murder Goes to Press, Murder Goes South, Murder Is a Gamble, Murder Is an Art, Murder on Beacon Hill, Murder in the Stratosphere, Murder at Pirate's Head, Murder at Horsethief, Murder at Coney Island, Red-Hot Murder, The House Cried Murder, The Hooded Vulture Murders,* and the provocative *Murder Does Light Housekeeping.* And finally we have *Death After Lunch, Death in the Night, Death in the Dunes, Death on the Cuff, Death Paints a Picture, Death Gets a Head, Death ala King, Death Walks Softly,* and *Tread Gently, Death.*

No one has come across it yet, but there *has* to be a Phoenix book somewhere called *The Case of the Corpse Who Was Murdered to Death.*

Are there truly memorable detectives, professional and amateur, in Phoenix mysteries? Yes indeed. Nowhere else in crime fiction will you find such heroic figures as:

Duke Pizzatello, a roscoe-packing, gasper-puffing private dick known to friends and enemies alike as "the wop," who enjoys getting next to dames almost as much as he enjoys knocking off gunsels with a roscoe that stutters: *"Chud-chud-chud-chud!"* (*Blue Murder,* by Robert Leslie Bellem)

Paul Plush, a Latin professor in a girls' school, who stumbles on some poison-pen letters and is nearly poisoned by a murderer, not to mention the poison pen of the author. (Oliver Keystone's *Arsenic for the Teacher)*

Blackie White, a 5-foot-2-inch private detective "with a body like a tank and the eyes of a baby," who says things like "Holy suffering mother-in-laws!" when he's excited. (Philip Johnson's *Hung Until Dead*)

Sheila Coates, a redheaded taxi dancer who is visited by a corpse and subsequently finds true love—not, fortunately, with the corpse. (Clinton Bestor's *The Corpse Came Calling*)

Bill King of the San Francisco *Times,* who wisecracks his way to the solution of the murder-by-the-severing-of-an-artery-in-the-victim's-leg. Why such an odd method of murder? The author doesn't explain it adequately, perhaps because he was something of a knee-jerk writer. (*The Corpse with Knee-Action,* by B. J. Maylon)

Thibault Parew, amateur sleuth and authority on international affairs, archeology, aviation, science, criminology, music, painting, drama, liquor, women, counterespionage, and the well-turned phrase. His favorite saying is "By the shades of the sorrowing Aphrodite!" He also says "Deuced pretty take-off," and "You're beauteous, my dear, and extremely lovely," while solving a couple of impossible (*very* impossible) murders in a locked airplane. (*Murder in the Stratosphere,* by Gilbert Eldredge)

The Ramsay twins, Dee and Jon, "a pair of willful romanticists," who get to the bottom of some murders in Wisconsin and run afoul of such personages as Body-Finder Gillicuddy and Mr. Doppner, who has "wet macaroni for a backbone." Dee is a housewife of considerable Gothic idiocy; Jon is a university professor whose master's thesis was called *Stuttering & Tics.* (Arville Nonweiler's *Murder on the Pike*)

Margaret Annister, who gets involved with such characters as political boss Criocan Mulqueeny, Chinese xylophonist Ichabod Tsung, gang leader "Gorilla" Svenson, obstetrician Dr. Feredaigh Ovenu, and a monster with "a common evolutionary organ" we later discover to be his little finger—and still manages, unlike the reader, to emerge unshaken by her experiences. (*The Case of the Mysterious Moll,* by Harry Stephen Keeler)

The plots of Phoenix mysteries, too, are unusually interesting. Take the following, for instance:

Robert D. Abrahams's *Death in 1-2-3.* Murder strikes the New York consulate of a small South American republic, and there develops such inspired stuff as secret societies and daggers with coded numbers engraved on them. The story is narrated in the present tense by a private eye who has all the wit and charm of Calvin Coolidge, and that nobody leaves the consulate for more than three pages at a time or does much except talk only adds to the fun. In no other mystery can you read until page 73, skip to page 203, and feel that you haven't missed a single plot thread.

Louis Trimble's *Murder Trouble.* A slam-doozy (as they used to say) about headless corpses, corpseless heads, a hero who prefers to spend his wedding night digging up dead people, a dynamited outhouse on a snowy winter's eve (*I* wouldn't take that sitting down), and the smuggling of nylon stockings across the Washington state border from Canada.

Murder with Long Hair, by one-time radio writer H. Donald Spatz. All that needs to be said about this one is to quote the dust-jacket blurb: "Steve Daniels and his beautiful blonde bride attended a summer stock performance in the Poconos starring Jessica Sanford and were invited by Jessica's friend, editor Edison Cushing, to join his house party, where Jessica was found drowned in the lily pond."

The Case of Mr. Cassidy, by William Targ and Lewis Herman. In which amateur criminologist and "connoisseur of incunabula" Hugh Morris becomes enmeshed with bibliophiles (one of whom is renowned writer and Sherlockian Vincent Starrett), a first edition of Poe's *Tamerlane,* and a "notorious and uncaptured Chicago throat-cutter" called the Fiend. As detective Morris says about the atmosphere of a certain nightclub: "It's an illusion, like the slowed-up speed in a marijuana dream. It's all an enormous hashheesh hallucination, blossoming with gorgeous non-existent blossoms, fragrant with odors unknown to any perfumer, sonant with the crashing, melodic chords of a thousand piece orchestra, peopled with moon-breasted houris reclining languorously on cloud-quilted divans." It certainly is.

Robert Portner Koehler's *Murder Expert.* A gaggle of mystery writers, including the female narrator (males without the talent of a Cornell Woolrich should *never* try to write first-person females), are gathered at a party, and some of them are subsequently murdered in various ways. It is not so stated, but one gets the impression that each of the victims wrote for Phoenix Press.

The Purple Pony Murders, by Sidney E. Porcelain. Characters with such names as Breeze, Clay, and Kite populate this thrilling racetrack yarn, which has a little bit of everything, including French lessons (" *'Oui.* Always eet waz Martini and Creme Yvette een ze leetle ponee *avec biscuits.'* ") and a couple of the most improbable horse races ever run ("Murder is like a horse race. You start out with a lot of suspects, you look into their records, but you never are sure which one of them is the winner, or as it happens, the murderer. A dark horse you didn't think of might be the one who crosses the line!")

Murder Goes South, by Amelia Reynolds Long. Woman mystery writer Peter Piper solves a series of antebellum slaughters in Louisiana and in the process, uncovers more misinformation than you ever wanted to know about voodoo and cypress swamps. This is so full of Stepin Fetchit blacks and thinly veiled racism that it easily wins the Most Objectionable Phoenix Mystery award.

The Case of the Little Green Men, by Mack Reynolds. In which members of a science-fiction fan club are being terrorized and/or murdered by—it is alleged—little green men who have landed on earth. The hero, a jaded private eye, takes the case, reads a little science fiction to acquaint himself with the background, becomes hooked, and—it is inferred—immediately subscribes to every magazine in the field. He also solves the case, and it should surprise no one to learn that it was not little green men after all but a cunning human being who perpetrated the crimes.

Carl Shannon's *Lady, That's My Skull.* The opening paragraphs of this one reads as follows: "The desk calendar said March twenty-fourth. It could have said any other day and the same thing might have happened. That is, I could have become mixed up with the painted skull. Still, if I had just skipped March twenty-fourth—say been on a big party and not sobered up—maybe I would have missed a lot of unpleasant things. Well, I didn't miss March twenty-fourth, so I didn't miss the damned skull or the trail of violence along which it gyrated." What happens after that involves the skull, which the lawyer-narrator finds in a pawnshop and which bears not only the letters of his old fraternity but the fingerprints of a gangster supposedly dead for years; a murder, a twenty-thousand-dollar necklace, a Chinese valet named Chan, and a watering hole called the Donkey Room (wherein the hero makes an ass of himself—naturally).

All the Phoenix mysteries heretofore discussed are either minor classics or near-misses; none quite achieves the unqualified classic status of two others, both published in 1941: *Murder at Horsethief* by James O'Hanlon and *Death Down East* by Hayden Norwood. These two mysteries are totally unlike each other, and yet each in its own way epitomizes the Phoenix mystique.

The first, *Murder at Horsethief,* is the masterwork of former Hollywood scriptwriter and self-styled humorist O'Hanlon. It took him four other novels (three for Phoenix Press, one of which deals with a racehorse named Disaster that eats potted geraniums) to reach the lofty heights of *Murder at Horsethief.* It may be conjectured that the reason O'Hanlon wrote no more mystery novels after this one is that he knew he had reached the limit of his talent and would be unable to surpass himself. Few writers can lay claim, after all, to more than one classic in a lifetime.

Set in an Arizona desert town near which gold has been discovered (again) in 1940, it concerns itself with a crooked saloon owner who was once a mobster in Los Angeles, a group of entertainers known as Frankie Sparrow and his Seven Canaries, a Mexican who is almost hanged by a group of drunken miners after being falsely accused of murder, a tribe of Malooga Indians who live in the nearby mountains and say clever things like "How" and "Ugh," a group of vigilantes who wear floursack hoods and call themselves the Haunts of Horsethief, and the inimitable detective team of Jason and Pat Cordry, who were once extras in Hollywood but who are full-fledged stars in the firmament of southern California lunatics.

The plot (or lack of one) is only one of the reasons that *Murder at Horsethief* is a tour de force. Another is that what O'Hanlon considers funny generally isn't, but most everything else *is.* O'Hanlon, you see, delighted in concocting phonetic and idiomatic dialogue. Everybody, including Jason and Pat, drops his *g*'s and says "ain't" and butchers the English language in all sorts of fascinating ways.

Some sample Western-miner dialogue: "In a coupla minnuts, Gents, yer gonna see with yer own eyes whut brand o' law we tends t' practice in Horsethief! Whut happens t' this heah Mex is gonna happen t' any white-livered coyote who gits notions 'bout ashootin' decent citizens in anythin' but a faih and squaih fight!"

Some sample Indian dialogue: "Come catchum smoke. Chetterfiel ceegret. Come back byeumbye aftah braves makum pow-wow wit' Lomitaha."

Some sample mobster dialogue: "Dey calls dis a funeril! Say, boss, remember the one we give t' Snuffy Dolin, back in Chi? Now dere was a send-off!"

Some sample Western-preacher dialogue: "Brethern . . . and sistern . . . we are gathered heah t' give decent burial t' our departed friend an' brothah, Doc Thayah. Y'all knowed Doc t' be a mighty good man, which is more'n we kin say fer the murderin' skunk what plugged him! The Good Book sez 'Fergive us our trespissis like we fergives them what trespissis ag'in us.' By the way, lambs o' the flock," the gentleman deviated, "come Sunday, Ah'm preachin' a powerful pregnant sermon on thet subjeck of trespissin', in the Hossthief Theater, an' Ah wan's y'all t' be theah! Brothah Herman's Happy Harbor is mah new name fer the place, an' in it Ah inten's t' do a lotta soul-patchin'!"

Some sample Jason Cordry dialogue: "Oo wanna make popsie-wopsie fweel very sad an' sowwy? Tell popsie-wopsie oo fwogives him, or popsie-wopsie cwie!"

Some sample Pat Cordry dialogue, 1: "Momsey do no want popsie-wopsie to cwie. Momsy fwogives popsy-wopsie an' fwows him a biig kissie-wissie!"

Some sample Pat Cordry dialogue, 2 (after she and Jason have heard strange music being played): "It ain't swing!" Pat popped. "Sounds like their [sic] cutting a rug to wrap a corpse in. . . ."

O'Hanlon's descriptive prose is brilliant, too:

> Pat was horrified. Her stomach became a fun-house of activity and her lower lip went into motion seconds before she was able to squeeze a sound past her lips.

> Jason's stomach slapped against his backbone. Beside him, Pat had become one hundred and four pounds of concentrated gloom.

* * *

A moon, from which some heavenly force had taken a huge bite, and to which a faraway coyote was paying wailing tribute, hung over Horsethief.

A sudden thought bounced her heart to her larynx.

About ten yards away, seated atop a horse beneath a large, solitary tree, Pat's bulging eyes located the gentleman for whom the "party" was being thrown.

Murder at Horsethief, it may be said, is one of those cheerful romps, full of chuckles and guffaws and a malooga or two. Hayden Norwood's *Death Down East,* on the other hand, is a considerably more sober, if no less stunning, effort.

Norwood's novel—he also wrote the equally stultifying *They Met at Mrs. Bloxon's*—is set in a place called Hallowdale, Maine, and among its plot components are a bloody ax, a dead chicken, a wicked lady named Mrs. Ciccone (all people with Italian and other ethnic names are wicked in Phoenix Press books, except maybe for Duke Pizzatello), a missing minister, a missing town drunk, and a "hero" who goes by the name of Macbeth Archer.

These elements do not have a great deal to do with the book's classic status, though. What makes *it* a tour de force is the fact that in its entire 256 pages, nothing happens.

Nothing.

Happens.

There is no plot development, there is no characterization, there is no mystery (except why Norwood wanted to write it in the first place). Reading it, one keeps waiting for *something* to happen; one expects some sort of action, excitement, maybe even a "hell" or "damn" to liven things up; one thinks that perhaps he will be surprised or at least titillated by the ending. Nothing. The most exciting occurrence in the book is Macbeth finding the dead chicken. There is one other scene that has potential: Macbeth goes to confront Mrs. Ciccone, and she makes a vague pass at him; but he is clearly asexual, if not a eunuch, and he goes away from her shaking his head in a puzzled fashion.

Here are some examples of Norwood's artful prose:

> "The train's late," observed Macbeth. He drew out
> his watch. "Three minutes past six. Three minutes
> late. How's that for close observation, Oscar?"
> "You should of been a detective," said Waddell,
> "instead of a soda jerk."

> Penny was waiting just inside the door, and her
> arms were around him suddenly, startling him.
> "Did I frighten you, Mac?"
> "No. I involuntarily jump like that every now and
> then. Maybe it's because my mother tied up my
> thumb when I was a baby to keep me from sucking
> it."

> "I'm sorry I burst in this way," said Macbeth, "but
> axes with blood on them don't turn up every day. I
> wanted to ask Sheriff Redburn what to do about it.
> You see, there's human blood on the axe."
> "Is that any concern of mine?" asked Dr. Ashcraft
> curtly. "Is it any concern of the sick man here? Don't
> you realize that you've been made deputy sheriff to
> handle infringements of law and order, and not to
> make a nuisance of yourself? A bloody axe, did you
> say? It doesn't appear to me that that's a matter of
> any importance."
> "I'm sorry," said Macbeth. He went to the door.

> Foreboding gnawed like a cancer in Penny's bos-
> om, and when she went to bed that night she was sure
> she wouldn't get a wink of sleep.
> But she did fall asleep, soundly, almost immediate-
> ly upon resting her cheek upon the pillow. She was
> astonished to open her eyes and see the light of
> day.

> Macbeth entered his mother's house by the back
> door. He could hear his mother and Penny in the par-
> lor talking.
> He went down into the cellar and brought up the

head of the Leghorn hen as well as the carcass. He heard his mother say in a frightened voice, "There's somebody in the kitchen!"

Mrs. Archer and Penny stood in the doorway, staring at him.

"Heavens, Mac!" cried his mother. . . .

Macbeth grinned. "Say, this chicken is perfectly preserved," he said, "in spite of the fact that it's been dead for almost a week. Speaks well for the coolness of your cellar, Mama—and with cold weather coming on, it wouldn't surprise me if the carcass and head last for months without beginning to smell."

Phoenix Press, I love you!

5. The Goonbarrow and Other Jolly Old Corpses

Before we realised their plan the door was pulled to, the hasp of the padlock clicked, and we were alone in the hut.

I seethed. Tolefree . . . burst into laughter. "The old heroes!" he said. "The Lloyd blood's boiling."

"It's a damned outrage!" I cried.

"He who plays bowls must expect rubbers," said Tolefree. "Tit-for-tat, Farrar—and one up to Wales. I daresay you might have bowled 'em over, but I intensely dislike a rough house."

"Tchah!" said I.

—R.A.J. Walling,
A Corpse by Any Other Name

"Beastly mess the place seems to be in," grumbled Sir Arthur Penn-Moreton, looking round the room with a disgusted air.

"Well, if you will give balls you have to put up with the aftermath," said Dicky, his younger brother, screwing his monocle in his left eye as he spoke.

—Annie Haynes,
Who Killed Charmian Karslake?

RIDDLE: What do sex and the British mystery novel have in common?

ANSWER: When they're good they're terrific, and when they're bad they're still terrific.

This is an absolute truism. There is a certain civilized quality to British mysteries, particularly those published prior to 1960, that makes them a consistent pleasure to read. Murder may strike, all sorts of nefarious things may happen, but the reader knows from the outset that justice and order will prevail in the end. No matter how much blood is spilled in the buildings and byways of London, on isolated and legend-filled moors, in the wilds of Scotland, in stately and quite proper country homes, the essence of jolly old England remains inviolate—the last bastion of reason and tradition in a chaotic world. Even in the dark early days of World War II, when a German invasion and takeover of Great Britain seemed probable, there was little panic and no sense of defeatism; the mysteries of the period reflect a general atmosphere of hope, stiff upper lip, and business as usual. The lads at Number 10 Downing Street would sooner or later outwit the lunatic führer and restore the rational, time-honored way of life. The brilliant detective would sooner or later outwit the clever murderer and see him imprisoned or executed for his crimes. This is the way it *must* be, ergo this is the way it *will* be.

All of which tends to make the reader of English mysteries comfortable, if not downright complacent. Whether a particular book was written in 1900 or half a century or more later, he knows exactly what he holds in his hands. It is predictable without being predictable, which is not a paradoxical statement at all. If the book is a good mystery, he will sense it before he has read ten pages. If it is a bad mystery, he will also sense it before he has read ten pages, but seldom will it make a whit of difference to him. Chances are he will finish it straight through to the last page and be as satisfied with it (in the sense of time well spent) as if it were *The Hound of the Baskervilles* or *Murder on the Orient Express.* No one ever cursed a British mystery out loud and hurled it across the room in disgust. Absolutely not. It just isn't done, you know.

Until recent years and a not altogether beneficial American influence, the emphasis in the British mystery was on detection. Spy novels had their share of detection; so did thrillers

Not often do you find a pre-1960 English crime novel without a detective of some sort—policeman, private inquiry agent, gifted amateur, secret agent. Crimes were not only supposed to be solved, they were supposed to be solved by someone who knew his or her business; even amateur detectives had to have an extensive interest in criminology or at the very least in crime fiction and puzzle solving. Rogues such as The Saint were allowed to withhold evidence or information from the police because they *were* rogues. Few other nonprofessionals were granted this privilege during the course of their investigations—unless, of course, they were working hand-in-glove with Scotland Yard and withholding evidence or information served a specific purpose; then it was permissible. With apologies.

Little-old-lady sleuths have always been among the most popular of British ADs. Agatha Christie's Miss Marple is no doubt the most famous of these, but another of some renown is Beatrice Adela Lestrange Bradley, more generally known as Mrs. Bradley (in her early adventures) and Dame Beatrice (in her later ones)—the invention of schoolteacher and folklorist Gladys Mitchell.

There are those who would argue that Miss Mitchell's work is comparable in quality to some, if not all, of Mrs. Christie's and has no place in a critical study of this nature. Perhaps. Every author has followers, and there is no question that a small cult of Mitchell devotees has evolved both here and in her native England. At least two critics—Patricia Craig and Mary Cadogan, co-authors of an expert study of women detectives and spies in fiction, *The Lady Investigates* (1981)—feel that Miss Mitchell is a satirist of considerable skill bent on ridiculing various conventions of mystery fiction and that Mrs. Bradley is one of the wittiest detectives in the genre.

Still, Mitchell's prose is of the eccentric variety, to put it mildly—something of a cross between Christie and P. G. Wodehouse, with a dollop or two of Saki, or maybe John Collier, thrown in—and, like garlic and rutabagas, is an acquired taste. Those who acquire it place Mitchell in the first rank of mystery novelists; those who can't acquire it put her somewhere slightly above the likes of R.A.J. Walling. Indeed, she may be the only mystery writer on either continent to be praised as a creator of classics simultaneously at opposite ends of the genre.

Gladys Mitchell began her career in 1929 with a book called *Speedy Death,* in which Mrs. Bradley herself commits a murder (a la The Saint in at least one early exploit) and in which a red-blooded male explorer turns out to be a woman. Intermittently over the past fifty years, Mitchell has produced some sixty additional mysteries, all featuring Mrs. Bradley and many with supernatural and/or folkloric elements. One of these, even more interesting than *Speedy Death,* is *The Mystery of a Butcher's Shop* (1930), which has nothing much to do with a butcher's shop but does concern the dismemberment of a man killed on a Druidic sacrificial stone, so the title is more or less valid. This particular novel alone (*pace* Craig and Cadogan and the other Mitchell admirers) qualifies Miss Mitchell for inclusion in these pages.

The Mystery of a Butcher's Shop is *very* English. That is, it is peopled with characters who say things like "Mater, dash it all," and "greasy bounder," and "the chap's off his chump," as well as use such obscure British slang expressions as "How twiggee he isn't a padre?" and who run around extricating themselves from not-very sticky situations in a manner that might have delighted Jeeves and Bertie Wooster. It is also chock full of such passages as:

> "Really, James!" his aunt protested frigidly. "You are a most offensive-looking object, most! You are *perspiring,* boy!"
> "Sorry! Yes, I know," gasped Jim. "Beastly hot weather. Damned well out of training! Had to run the hell of a way after you! Came to tell you—came to tell you—" he rolled his eyes wildly and racked his brains. *What* had he come to tell them? Must think of something. Something feasible. Must think of something quickly. "Came to tell you—" A wave of relief flooded over him. "Tea-time!" he shouted triumphantly. "Came to tell you it's tea-time! Tea-time, you know. Hate you to miss your tea. So beastly, you know—so—er—so beastly disappointing, you know, to miss your tea. I mean to say—tea. What is life without a nice cup of hot tea? Cold tea, you see, such beastly stuff. I mean to say, cold tea—well you feel as though you've put your shirt on the hundred to eight winner and the bookie's caught the fast boat to Ostend. No? Yes?"

* * *

To say that the pace is leisurely would be to commit premeditated understatement. The pace is nonexistent. People talk a great deal, either in drolleries or in the fashion of James as just quoted, and hold endless discussions about bird watching, alpine plants, relatives, church matters (" 'Father hasn't any morals. He's a clergyman.' "), money, and such macabre topics as sacrifices and missing skulls. The book's one homicide turns out not to be a murder after all but an accidental death; the dismemberment was by a different person than the one responsible for the accident—"that poor dago"—who had planned to kill the victim. The poor dago, a monomaniac, cut up the body because that was what he'd intended to do in the first place and "his fetish seems to be exactitude and laborious attention to correctness of detail." So he whacked off the dead man's head and went into hiding with it; then, later, he returned to where he had left the trunk of the body and dragged it off to his butcher's shop to make steaks and chops out of it. The person who caused the victim's death is turned loose by Mrs. Bradley because she has an "aunt-like affection" for him. The poor dago jumps out a hospital window and kills himself.

Justice triumphs again.

Another kind of amateur detective, although less prevalent in the British mystery than the series sleuth, is the "one-shot"—a person who becomes involved in a single mystery and must solve it in order to save his/her life/good name or the life/good name of someone he/she cares for. An example is one George Fenchurch (an alias), who joins forces with an undercover agent and romps through the pages of Edward Woodward's *The House of Terror* (1930) en route to the solution of a murder involving a deadly gas. The story stutters back and forth between the Yorkshire moors and northern Spain, is populated with a variety of unbelievable characters, and features homicide and attempted homicide by means of feathered darts tipped with an exotic Malay poison and propelled through a blowgun.

The real genius of the novel, though, lies in Woodward's portrait of a psychotic dwarf. No other mystery, British or otherwise, can boast of the likes of the "hidden terror of Cleeson Manor"—a drooling, blowgun-wielding, hunchbacked little villain named Pedmore, servant to old man Dykeminster, who "had picked him out of the stews of Shanghai, and, learning

secrets, had kicked him into submission." Sprinkled throughout the narrative are such masterful descriptions as these:

> For a second, before his eyes became accustomed to
> the dim light the dwarf stood bent forward in an atti-
> tude of alterness [sic], the huge hump on his twisted
> back looking like a heavy load, his long arms and
> great hands hanging a little forward as though pre-
> pared to grasp and crush anyone who challenged
> him.
> Then he saw Alicia, and a maniacal snarl of rage
> came from the red cave of his mouth, whilst a glare of
> diabolical fury blazed in his eyes. . . . He made a
> staggering step forward, and, as Alicia, her volition
> returning, started to her feet, he hovered and a mali-
> cious leer came into his expression as his hand crept
> into one of the side pockets of his coat.
> "So you think you have trapped me, do you?" he
> grated. "Think you have Pedmore, the dirty dwarf,
> by the heels at last, do you. . . . Ha-ha-ha!. . . Pret-
> ty Miss. Rich young lady, take a dainty step towards
> me and see what happens to your beauty. . . ."

> Spinning round, his brain and judgment shaken,
> Lattimer saw Pedmore standing, openly laughing at
> him, his ungainly body shaking with amusement, his
> great head lolling sideways in his malicious mirth.
> The coat he had discarded . . . was evidently the
> only garment he had worn over his shoulders, for
> now he was stripped to the waist, and Lattimer saw
> the sun playing on his great biceps and massive, hair-
> y torso.
> In his transports of vainglorious mirth at his own
> agility Pedmore was for a moment off his guard, and
> seizing his chance, Lattimer rushed forward, hoping
> to get a sure shot at the little swine before he could
> lift the long blow-pipe he carried, to his mouth. He
> had covered a dozen yards before the dwarf saw his
> intention, and then as Lattimer fired, he ducked and
> jumped sideways; and with the speed of a darting
> swallow, zig-zagged away.

* * *

But the most memorable passage in the book is this one:

> Fury had come to the dwarf's face; saliva gleamed
> on his heavy underlip, and his eyes under their black
> pent-house brows, were red-rimmed and fierce.
> "He comes here to-night, master," he croaked. "I've
> had word."
> A crafty expression glimmered across Dykemins-
> ter's face.
> "Then he'll get what he deserves as soon as he
> passes the lodge-gates," he said with a gross chuck-
> le.
> Pedmore hopped from one mis-shapen foot to the
> other; and again he tapped Dykeminster's arm with
> the fractious gesture of a petulant child.
> "But the warning, master! . . . The letter! Don't
> forget that! I feel it in my hump that something is
> going to happen!"

The most popular of all detectives in British mysteries seems
to be the police official—either a member of Scotland Yard or a
local constable of some repute. One such heroic copper is Detec-
tive-Inspector Frederick Jubilee "Jumper" Cross of the CID,
who, with his sergeant Johnny Lamb, investigates and solves
several late-thirties and early-forties mysteries by John Donavan (a pseudonym of Nigel Morland, a prolific crime writer and
creator of Miss Pym). One of Jumper and Johnny's more notable adventures is *Case of the Violet Smoke,* published in the
United States in 1940 by the ever-reliable Mystery House (a
division of Phoenix Press's lending-library rival, Arcadia
House).

The novel opens with a cloud of "villainous violet haze,
writhing uneasily like some heavy smoke," which undulates
across London. The police trace the origin of this "colored
wind" to an old and apparently empty mansion, on one floor of
which they discover a violet-hued corpse and on another floor
of which is a chemical laboratory. Jumper and Johnny are
called in and proceed to uncover a plot that centers around
what the jacket blurb calls "a fascinating piece of industrial
espionage." This translates to mean an underhanded struggle
for control of a major chemical company.

The unraveling of events, like those in one of Mrs. Bradley's cases, can most charitably be described as plodding. *Case of the Violet Smoke* may, in fact, be prototypical in its dull dialogue, not-very-thrilling police procedure explained in minute detail, and final explanations that go on for pages in the following fashion:

> "Now then, sir: we had that red stuff tested at Hendon. Their report stated it was a double salt of antimonious iodide and an alkali iodide, which at that moment they hadn't identified. It's not material. There are two points about that. The behavior of antimonious iodide—or antimony iodide—is not very fully discussed in ordinary chemistry books. The knowledge of it, therefore, would not be in the possession of the ordinary man with chemical inclinations. Its alleged unimportance is shown by the fact that in one textbook described as a textbook for a degree course in chemistry, all that's said is that antimony combines readily with the halogens. Iodine is one of them. Antimonious iodide is a compound of antimony and iodine."
>
> "This looks interesting." Cross's attention was being aroused.

Cross's, maybe, but not that of most readers.

The private investigator in British crime fiction tends to follow one of two patterns: Sherlock Holmes, with emphasis on deduction, or a bastardized version of Philip Marlowe and/or Mike Hammer, with emphasis on sex, violence, and the ill-chosen wisecrack. Most proponents of the latter school read like bad British imitations of bad American imitations, but without any special qualities to elevate this or that book to the status of even a minor classic. The practitioners of the former school are much more intriguing. Take, for instance, R.A.J. Walling, the father of that inimitable investigator Philip Tolefree.

Walling, a British journalist and newspaper editor who began writing mysteries as a hobby in his late fifties, was a popular writer during his time. (His first book was published in

1927, his last posthumously in 1949.) He was not only popular in England but in the United States, where he received a certain amount of critical acclaim. The *New York Times* stated in 1936 that Walling had considerable skill in weaving mystery plots; the *Saturday Review of Literature* decided that he wrote suavely baffling stories; the eminent critic Will Cuppy rhapsodized about one of the early Tolefree stories, "We don't wish to seem pontifical, but if we were asked for an elegant example of modern bafflement, we'd name *The Corpse with the Floating Foot* on six or seven counts, such as style, suspense, general interest, and miscellaneous. Absolutely required reading."

One can't help but wonder, after reading this and other of Walling's literary endeavors, at the levels of mystery reviewing and popular taste a generation ago. Walling may have concocted mildly diverting plots (sometimes), but the effort required to read far enough to unravel them seems prohibitive in most cases. The fact of the matter is that R.A.J. Walling wrote some of the dullest mystries ever committed to paper—far duller than those of Gladys Mitchell and John Donavan. It may even be said that he elevated dullness to a fine art. No greater soporific has been invented by the pharmaceutical companies than ten or fifteen pages of a Philip Tolefree opus.

In the first place, Tolefree is a twit. Detectives who are twits are not uncommon in British mysteries, or in American mysteries, either; but a *private detective* who is a twit is uncommon. And Tolefree is a twit of gargantuan proportions.

This is how he talks:

> "You're a vandal, Pierce," said Tolefree. "You've feloniously broken and entered my ivory tower. Never mind. I'd have been bored in another half hour. How'd you find me out? Sit down, my dear fellow. Cigarette? Pipe? Well, carry on. What's the trouble now? Or did you come for the sake of my beautiful eyes?" (*The Corpse Without a Clue*)

And this is how he thinks:

> "Money, money, money!" Tolefree found the refrain echoing in his head when . . . the train slid alongside the platform at Paddington; "*plures pecu-*

nia strangulat—I wonder, now!" (*The Corpse with the Blue Cravat*)

A remarkable girl, thought Tolefree, while he rubbed up his small talk. (*By Hook or Crook*)

And this is how he acts:

Careful to disturb nothing, he crouched, sniffing at the face and the clothes [of the dead man]. He put a finger on the sleeve of the coat. He lifted it off the grass a little. He took a magnifying glass to examine the wound. He walked around peering at the ground. . . . (*The Corpse With the Eerie Eye*)

Tolefree is also inordinately fond of quoting obscure Latin phrases, usually without benefit of translation for those of us plebeians who either did not study Latin in school or did study it but failed to make it a second language.

"I've always found candor a good card, Mr. Quigley," said Tolefree, falling into step beside him.
"Ah?" said the young man. He looked down quizzically upon him. "You haven't read Tacitus on Vitellius."
"Haven't I? Let me see—but yes, I have." Tolefree mused. "You mean, '*Inerat tamen simplicitas ac liberalitas*'—gosh! that's a good come-back!" (*The Corpse in the Coppice*)

Other of Tolefree's traits include the pseudo self-deprecating remark:

"It's very serious indeed," said Tolefree. "And if I'm not Public Jackass Number One, it'll be more serious yet." (*The Corpse With the Grimy Glove*)

And the pointed homily:

"A politician's unlike other people—he's got to

keep away from wet tar if he wants to stick to his seat." (*The Corpse With the Grimy Glove*)

And exchanging clichéd similes and metaphors with other characters:

> "Very well. You'll be as happy as a fisherman in the Mayfly season, won't you? But I think you've hooked a sunken log, Tolefree."
> "Never mind, sir. It's not the kill that counts but the cast." (*The Corpse Without a Clue*)

> ". . . What's biting you?"
> "A nasty little insect of the hunch species."
> "Very well—produce the beast. I suppose, by the way, its family name isn't Raleigh bug, is it?" (*The Corpse Without a Clue*)

Although Tolefree operates out of a London apartment, most of his cases seem to take him into the countryside, to places like Goonbarrow Downs (*The Corpse With the Eerie Eye*), where he becomes embroiled in the murder of a man with horrible gray eyes that "failed to betray the astonishment commonly seen in people who met violent death. They were eerie. The pupils seemed scarcely larger than pin-heads. . . ." He solves this and other cases in the accepted Sherlockian manner of detection and deduction, plus an inexhaustible fund of knowledge both esoteric and ephemeral. Another of the reasons he is so successful at unmasking murderers may be traced to a familiarity with such matters and motives as skeletons in closets, hidden relationships, peculiar wills, strange disappearances, and Nazi infiltrators, since nearly all his investigations seem to uncover one or any combination of these.

On some detective sojourns, he is accompanied by a Watson named Farrar, who is inclined to drool over Tolefree's brilliance. In other books, the narrative is presented in the third person, in which event everyone (including Tolefree) is inclined to drool over Tolefree's brilliance. These other characters all have names like Garstang, Blenkinsop, Snagley, Grazebrook, Cornwood, Calderstone, Mapperley, Horridge, Quigley, Limpenny, Treglohan, Clodgey, Coverdale, Pugsley, and Sir Benjamin

Hex—and are generally upper-class folk who own large estates, play croquet, enjoy killing animals for sport, mistreat their servants, and bore each other (and the reader) with stuffy observations on politics, history, tradition, and moral decay.

Plodding though Walling's prose may be, it is not devoid of an occasional bit of flare. Every now and then a sentence or a passage of dialogue will appear that makes one sit up and take notice, as if by design on the author's part, to ensure that his readers stay awake.

> "Just a moment," said he and frowned like a man trying to find the lady's nose in a jig-saw puzzle. (*The Corpse With the Floating Foot*)

> Tolefree heard the car door bang, a deep voice exploring the soles of its owner's boots, and footsteps in the hall. (*The Late Unlamented*)

> A hint of excitement hovered about Miss Kane, looking well in an afternoon frock and explaining that she had obtained a weekend leave and was looking forward to the party. (*The Corpse Without a Clue*)

> "In plain English, Patterson," said Pye, "nix on the gats!" (*The Corpse With the Floating Foot*)

> "Lowell had nothing to do with the shooting of Beresford or the placing of his corpse on the Goonbarrow. You think Lowell had a strong motive for killing Beresford because the scoundrel was blackmailing his wife as a bigamist and playing off his daughter against him."
> "Good God!" cried Mapperley. "Have you got as deep as that?" (*The Corpse With the Eerie Eye*)

Over the past twenty years, the British mystery has shown signs of evolving into something quite different from what it had been since Sherlock Holmes made his first bow. There are those writers (Gladys Mitchell is one) who continue to cling to the traditional approach: genteel, civilized, appealing more to the intellect than to the emotions. But their numbers seem fewer with each passing year. More and more English crime novelists appear eager to emulate their American counterparts in the selection of sensational plotlines. Politics, terrorism, high finance, drugs, rock music, the sexual revolution—all these and more have replaced the traditional tale of domestic murder and/or commercial skullduggery. Concomitantly, detection has given way to action as the primary ingredient, with a keen emphasis on matters sexual and psychological.

A new kind of amateur detective has emerged. No longer do we have Dr. Fells and Miss Marples; now we have the likes of Sam North, self-styled author and hero of *209 Thriller Road* (1979), who operates The Novel Shop in downtown London:

> Here it is folks, 209 Thriller Road, step right in, transform your life into an adventure, thrill your friends with a trip to Africa or Luna 5. . . . Buy your way into the elite, the Starfleet? And I don't care if you want to be Bogie in *Casablanca,* in love with a girl on the lam and no place to hide or a reluctant hero from *Apocalypse Now.* Camelot or weeping romance, all yours for you and your friends to enjoy, written by the king of ghost writers. No more will he hide his bushel under the likes of a happy hooker or (I survived) the comeback story of a Hollywood alcoholic mother of three, no more will he suffer, now it is ghosting for the people, by the people; the ghost has gone public!

Sam's first novel-shop writing assignment is to ghost a book for Danny Plant, scrap king and mobster—a thriller in which Danny himself will be the villain and get away with his (unspecified to Sam) crime. But before Sam can get started, Danny turns up dead; and North finds himself mixed up in a wild and woolly adventure blending gangsters, a corporation worth seventeen million pounds sterling, a precocious five-year-old kid, assorted chases, some kinky sex, and a plethora of what the jacket blurb calls "fiendish" humor—all of it told in North's divergent style, replete with eccentric grammar and punctuation, plus asides to the reader.

* * *

I had never heard of such a lot of impossible coincidences. I bet even you find it hard to swallow. But there was bound to be some logic somewhere. Lord Kirk Fawcett. An English absentee landlord. Therefore an income to sustain the fabulous house near Regent's Park. . . . So would it be reasonable to assume that the absentee landlord assisted Danny in his conquest of the City underworld and money fiddles? Or . . . my brain was doing incredible twists and turns, Lord Kirk lost out on the Irish land to Danny and because of his own problems was in hock to Danny, now that he was dead, Lord Kirk was after getting everything back.

"What sort of book are you looking for?"

"Teach yourself private eye," I replied.

"Oh deary, you're in the wrong section. You've got a lot to learn about crime," the four ladies said at once.

"Which section should it be then?" I asked, disconcerted by their unison speech and eyes.

"Maps," they said.

"Maps?" Christ, did I have a lot to learn.

"Teach yourself always appears by the maps," one explained.

"It's in the nature of exploring you see ducks."

"I see," I replied. But I didn't really.

"Is there a book on teach-yourself crime?" one asked another.

"No, it's *Teach Yourself Private Detection* or something like that."

"Well you're in luck young man."

"He's out of luck Ethel, all the Teach-Yourself Crime books have been stolen. Shoplifting. It's shocking."

"So do you have a *Teach Yourself Private Detection*?" I asked stiffly.

"No. But we do have a *So You Want to be a Gumshoe.*"

"I'll take it," I said.

"We'd rather you paid for it ducks," she said.

* * *

"Hello," I said, "I'm Sam."

"Sam what?"

"Sam North."

"Hello, Sam North."

Whatever she was, she had a voice that could melt
Ice Nine.

"You're Lindy."

"Lucky me," she said.

"May I come in?"

"If you're a friend of Danny's . . ."

"I'm not exactly a friend. I'm what you might call
his posthumous biographer."

"And you want me for the index?"

"Let's say, an appendix."

"I wasn't figuring on an operation."

"Actually I came about a little list of names."

"Well, you can come inside but leave your jokes
out there."

A new kind of British policeman is emerging, too—tough,
hard-bitten, lusty; the kind who would laugh derisively at the
proper and plodding methods of old-fashioned coppers like
Jumper Cross and Johnny Lamb; the kind who take as their
role models such real American cops as Serpico, such fictional
ones as Starsky and Hutch. One of this new breed is Jack
Regan, a member of Scotland Yard's Flying Squad, who fights,
cusses, and screws his way through a series of books by novelist
and British TV writer Ian Kennedy Martin. Notable is *The
Manhattan File* (1976), the second of the Regan novels, which
finds the "Sweeney" dick in New York, hot on the trail of $200
million in missing American military hardware and pitted
against the Mafia, the FBI, and some deadly African politicos.
Kennedy's style—and that of an increasing number of British
mystery novelists—is of the following variety:

"*The* killers. The ones who are killing all of us, you
shit hawk, everyone in the deal! They're wiping us
out one by one because you sold that fucking letter!
And you know something, we don't know who the
fuck these killers are—" The guy stopped there sud-

denly, an instant decision, suddenly realizing his explanation to Regan was redundant and unnecessary as he proposed to kill the English cop shortly. "Okay, bastard, one last question."

As Tolefree might have said: *O tempora! O mores!* O England!

6. Dogs, Swine, Skunks, and Assorted Asses

A giant ray from the searchlight to the right of the laboratory flashed vividly across the night sky. It searched here and there and at last picked up an object which . . . looked no bigger than a silver cigar.

"There she is!" cried Vivanti, pointing. "The greatest airship the world has ever known—and soon to be in my power. Now for the V-ray!"

Rushing to his switchboard, he directed the pointer of a machine and pulled down a switch. The effect was uncanny, for out of the void a vivid green ray shot up and joined the white beam of the searchlight. What occurred was not only spectacular but sensational: instantly the sound of the [zeppelin's] engines stopped.

". . . The 'Sky King' is now a derelict; she is moving forward only by her own impetus. And now, Kuhnreich, for my masterpiece. I've winged my bird and I'm going to bring her to subjection. Behold, my giant aero magnet!"

—Sydney Horler,
Lord of Terror

It may safely be said that the first spy novel in the English language was written by an American—James Fenimore Cooper's *The Spy* (1821). But as Julian Symons writes in *Mortal Consequences,* the development of the spy story as we know it today "was directly linked to the inventions that came in the wake of the Industrial Revolution. As the breech-loading rifle replaced the muzzle-loader, and the quick-firing mitrailleuse, Gatling, and Maxim guns seemed to threaten the effectiveness of many other weapons, and naval power increased with the development of dreadnoughts and submarines, and airplanes turned from dream into possibility and then reality, a genuine threat was implied in the theft or copying of secret plans and documents. The highly developed industrial countries were those with most inventions to uncover, and this was the primary reason why the spy story had its origins in Europe, and particularly in Britain."

The tradition of the British tale of espionage is a long and distinguished one, beginning with the stories of William Le Queux in the 1890s and extending to the present day through the works of John Buchan, Graham Greene, Eric Ambler, the redoubtable Ian Fleming, Len Deighton, and John Le Carré. This country has had a few moderately successful spy novelists, mostly in paperback original—Donald Hamilton, Edward S. Aarons, and James Grady are among the more well known— but they pale to insignificance in comparison with the giants across the water. What both countries do seem to have had in more or less equal shares is the number of spy novels of dubious repute published during the twentieth century. This may be a bit unfair, in that England has *all* the good ones, but there is nothing to be done about that.

The first of the spy writers of interest here, ironically enough, was the first of the modern developers: William Le Queux. A journalist by training and a Secret Service agent himself before and during World War I, Le Queux spent a good part of his life on the French Riviera, and many of his novels, both spy and mystery romances, are set in and around Monte Carlo, with side trips to England and the Continent. The settings appear to be authentic, as do the military and political backgrounds of his spy fiction; what makes Le Queux a classicist are his often-farfetched plots, his ability to pad them out interminably with description and repetitive conversation, and his unsurpassed ear for stilted dialogue.

A case in point is *The Mystery of the Green Ray* (1915), which is set not in Monte Carlo but in Scotland at the outbreak of the First World War. The novel chronicles the adventures of a young man named Ronald Ewart, who journeys from London to Scotland to tell his lady love, Myra McLeod, that he can't marry her as planned because he is going to enlist in the army. While Ronnie and Myra are out fishing (the one thing they seem most to enjoy doing together), she is inexplicably stricken blind. Later on, her dog, Sholto, is also stricken blind and then dognapped. Why steal a blind dog? As one of the other characters says, "It seems to me that the man who steals a blind dog steals him because, for some reason or other, he wants a blind dog—that very one, probably."

With the aid of an occulist named Garnesk and a chum called Dennis, Ronnie sets out to find Sholto and to discover what "fiend of hell" made Myra blind. And of course he succeeds. As the jacket blurb puts it, he "solves the mystery of the Highland loch, recovers his girl's sight for her, captures for the British NID the wonderful installation of the Green Ray, upsets the devilish and deep-laid schemes of as cunning a pair of spies as ever Mr. Le Queux's fertile brain invented."

The cunning spies turn out to be Germans, naturally, the leader of which, "a brilliant physicist who has done some big things with electricity and light," has been masquerading as an American named Hilderman. The Green Ray turns out to be a device "formed by passing violet and orange rays through tourmaline and quartz respectively. The accident to Miss Leod was their first intimation of its blinding properties. . . . When the two rays are switched on simultaneously the air does not become de-oxygenised, but when you put the violet ray first it does, and it remains so until the orange ray is applied. The effect that Hilderman imagined, and succeeded in producing, was a ray of light which should so alter the relative density of the air as to act as a telescope."

Both Myra and Sholto are cured of their blindness by being outfitted with specially made motor goggles (in which Sholto looks "incredibly wise"—for a dog, that is). Those same motor goggles also help protect the eyes of the crew of a British

destroyer the German spies assault with the Green Ray before
Ronnie and Dennis and the ever-loyal and incredibly wise Sholto do them in. (Sholto was dognapped, you see, so the villains
could practice vivi-section and thus determine just why their
Green Ray made animals and humans blind in the first
place.)

Here are some examples of Le Queux dialogue, a great deal of
which the reader is assaulted with along the way:

> "Am I very heavy, Ron, dear?" she asked pres-
> ently. . . .
> "You're as light as a feather, dearest," I protested,
> "and, as far as that goes, I'd rather carry you at any
> time."
> "I'm glad you were here when it happened, dear,"
> she whispered.
> "Tell me, darling, how did it happen?" I asked. "I
> mean, what did it seem like? Did things gradually
> grow duller and duller, or what?"
> "No," she answered; "that was the extraordinary
> part of it. Quite suddenly I saw everything green for
> a second, and then everything went out in a green
> flash. It was a wonderful, liquid green, like the sea
> over a sandbank. It was just a long flash, very quick
> and sharp, and then I found I could see nothing at all.
> Everything is black now, the black of an intense
> green. I thought I'd been struck by lightning. Wasn't
> it silly of me?"
> "My poor, brave little woman," I murmured. "Tell
> me, where were you then?"
> "Just where you found me, on the Chemist's Rock.
> I call it the Chemist's Rock because it's shaped like a
> cough-lozenge."
>
> "Drink this, old chap," he said.
> "What is it?" I asked suspiciously. "I don't want
> any fancy pick-me-ups. They only make you worse
> afterwards."
> "That was prescribed by Doctor Common Sense,"
> he answered lightly.

* * *

"You see you could not possibly live for a second in electrically produced atmosphere which was so thick that you couldn't hear yourself speak. Death would be instantaneous. . . . Imagine what would happen if this had occurred in a city, in a crowded street. Hundreds would have been stricken blind, then hundreds would have suffocated. Vehicles would have run amok, and the result would have been an indescribable chaos of the maimed, mangled, and distraught. A flash like this green ray . . . at the mouth of a harbour, say, the entrance to a great port—Liverpool, London, or Glasgow—would be responsible for untold loss of life. If this terrible phenomenon spread, Ewart, it would paralyse the industry of the world in twenty-four hours. If it spread still farther the face of the globe would become the playing-fields of Bedlam in a moment. Think of the result of this everywhere! Some suffocated, some blinded, and millions probably gone mad and sightless, stumbling over the bodies of the dead to cut each other's throats in a frenzy of sudden imbecility."

For the most part, and despite their melodramatic aspects, Le Queux's books are restrained and civilized—a reflection, as are most works of fiction, of the author's outlook on life. In comparison, or more properly, in direct opposition, we have the lurid, opinionated, sometimes nasty prose of Sydney Horler—also an accurate reflection of the author.

Himself a journalist until his early thirties, Horler began publishing "shockers" in 1925 and went on to produce well over a hundred, most in the same sensational vein, until his death in 1954. He was considered heir to the prolific Edgar Wallace, and in fact adopted some of Wallace's self-promotional methods (as well as purchased Wallace's desk and Dictophone at auction after E.W.'s death in 1932, and later hired Wallace's personal secretary). That Horler was successful at this is evidenced by the fact that several of his early novels were modest bestsellers in England. He created a ménage of series characters, most of them Secret Service agents of one kind or another, including Bunny Chipstead, "The Ace," Nighthawk, Sir Brian Fording-

hame, and that animal among men, Tiger Standish. The Standish books—*Tiger Standish Steps On It* (1940) is a representative title in more ways than one—were especially popular with
Horler's readership.

In the thirties, some British and American editions of Horler's novels carried the logo "Horler for Excitement." The slo-
gan might better have read "Horler for Racism." Or "Horler for
Priggishness." He excoriated Jews, "Huns," "dagoes" (that is,
the Portuguese and Spanish), and "stinking Italianos" (a.k.a.
"wops," "macaronis," and "the hyena-race") and saw to it that
his fictional heroes, Tiger Standish in particular, expressed a
similar viewpoint. But it is in his nonfiction works—a pair of
diaries, *Strictly Personal* and *More Strictly Personal*; an informal (and surprisingly astute) commentary on popular fiction of
the early thirties, *Writing for Money*; his "impudent autobiography," *Excitement*; and a vicious World War II diatribe,
Now Let Us Hate—that he most vividly stated his prejudices.

He considered the Americans absurd, the French dishonest,
the Swiss avaricious, the Armenians a race of rug peddlers, and
the English the only civilized people on earth. An outspoken
male chauvinist, he thought that women possessed "the herd-
mind," that "the inanity of nine females out of ten is mainly
responsible for many of their husbands going completely off the
rails," and that "the majority [of 'mentally sadistic sex-novel
readers'] are women; very few men read the unhealthy novel."
He also found most females unattractive: "Of how many women
can it truly be said that they are worthy of their underclothes?"
He believed that explicit mention of sex was degenerate and
homosexuals ought to be incinerated; that male cigarette smok-
ers were emasculated because they didn't smoke pipes instead;
and that D. H. Lawrence was "a pathological case, a consump-
tive who was driven by his disease to write about sex." As for
detective fiction, he was of the opinion that the work of
Dashiell Hammett was "crude to the point of mental disgust"
and the plot of *The Thin Man* "verminous". His most memorable comment on the genre, however, is this one: "I know I hav-
en't the brains to write a proper detective novel, but there is no
class of literature for which I feel a deeper personal loathing."

It would be an understatement to say that Horler, in addition
to his charming personal views, was a writer of meretricious

spy thrillers. (LeRoy L. Panek, in a chapter on Horler in his study *The Special Branch: The British Spy Novel, 1890–1980*, calls him "an egregiously bad writer even by the less than exacting standards of the popular novel.") No other author produced more alternatively memorable novels of any type than Horler. He was *sui generis*. An entire book of the nature of this one could, and probably should, be written on his work alone.

Horler's greatest literary attribute was his imagination, which may be described as weedily fertile. His favorite antagonists were fanatical Germans and Fu Manchu-type megalomaniacs, many of whom were given sobriquets such as "The Disguiser," "The Colossus," "The Mutilator," "The Master of Venom," and "The Voice of Ice"; but he also contrived a number of other evildoers to match wits with his heroes—an impressive list of them that includes mad scientists, American gangsters, vampires, giant apes, ape-men from Borneo, venal dwarfs, slavering "Things," a man born with the head of a wolf, and—his crowning achievement—a blood-sucking, man-eating bush.

> Then came something that almost turned the watchers sick with horror. Practically the whole space in the greenhouse was occupied by a huge ugly bush about fourteen feet high that had innumerable long creeper-like tendrils of dull reddish-brown springing out in all directions from its trunk. These tendrils, covered with coarse red hair . . . might have been the suckers of a gigantic octopus—only they appeared infinitely more terrifying because of their infinitude. . . . [They] closed like a gigantic cocoon on every exposed part of the doomed man's flesh. ("The Red-Haired Death," a novelette in *The Destroyer, and The Red-Haired Death*)

A typical Horler novel is *The Curse of Doone*, originally published in England in 1928 and reprinted here in 1930 by The Mystery League, an outfit that seemed to specialize in terrible mysteries during the brief three years of its existence. It is inspired nonsense about a Secret Service agent named Ian Heath; a virgin in distress; a friend of Heath's, Jerry, who worries about "the primrose path to perdition"; a couple of incredible coincidences (another Horler stock-in-trade); a secluded mansion on Dartmoor; the "Vampire of Doone Hall" and monstrous vampire bats; a pair of bloody murders; hidden caves, secret panels and caches; a Prussian villain who became a homicidal maniac because he couldn't cope with his sudden baldness; and a newly invented "war machine" that can force enemy aircraft out of the air by means of wireless waves and stop a motor car from five miles away.

In this case, a "logical" explanation for the apparent presence of supernatural creatures is given at the denouement. The vampire, we are told, was just an ordinary spy dressed up in black clothing and wearing a mask, who used various means to create the illusion of Dracula-style killings. As for the monstrous vampire bats—

> "Inside the cave I found a tiny monoplane, a make corresponding to the new British Tiger. It was so small that it might almost have been mistaken for a toy, and was painted a dull, gun-metal gray. But an examination of the engine showed that it was a Victory sixty h.p. which would probably allow a machine of that kind to travel at one hundred and eighty miles an hour. A machine like this, flying slowly round a house at night, with the wheels tucked up inside the fuselage, would look very much like what one would imagine a vampire—"
>
> "Sounds far-fetched, old chap," cut in Morrison. "What about the sound of the engine?"
>
> "The engine was fitted with a silencer. Any more questions?"

As the foregoing demonstrates, Horler, unlike Le Queux, had a serviceable ear for and a deft touch with dialogue. His specialty was epithets. He could be positively brilliant when it came to inventing the unusual curse and the sharp retort:

> "My dear old cock-eyed ass, I was waiting for you to be Christian enough to offer me a drink!"
>
> "Having no whisky of your own—as usual!"
>
> "You heathen without bowels, do you think I

would ever cross your doorstep if I had sufficient
dough to buy a drink for myself? Hang you and your
fusel-oil whisky! May it rot you and all your descen-
dants!"

"You scraggy-haired swine, keep a civil tongue,
can't you?"

"Let me be boiled in linseed oil if I ever saw such a
perishing fool!" he declared passionately. "Let me tell
you this, you stale suet-pudding; you're coming down
to my cottage on Dartmoor if I have to carry you
there. Isn't it just the place for a sick man? Isn't it so
lonely that no one could possibly find you, even
granted that they were mugs enough to be still looking for you? And supposing this blight or blighters,
as the case may be, *should* happen to strike the right
bridle-path, am I such a useless hulk that I couldn't
put forward a blow for St. George and the Right?
Strike me a greenish-yellow heliotrope, if ever I saw
such an ass as you!"

A second Horler novel of note, *Lord of Terror* (1937), pits Sir
Brian Fordinghame, Chief of Y. 1, British Intelligence, against
Dr. Paul Vivanti, one of Horler's megalomaniacal supercrimi-
nals. Once a respected neurologist and author of several medical
textbooks, Vivanti abruptly turned to a life of crime for no
evident reason. Fordinghame's personal view is that Vivanti
"had suddenly developed an unsuspected criminal kink." In
any case, the doctor has "set himself the colossal task of endeav-
ouring to bring about the ruin of the country which up to this
time had presented him not merely with wealth but with personal honour. Mad? Undoubtedly—but his madness was of a
highly dangerous type."

One of the ways in which Vivanti previously attempted to
bring about the ruin of England was by poisoning the reser-
voirs that feed London its water, so as to murder the city's
entire population (*Vivanti Returns*, 1931); Fordinghame had
thwarted that effort at the last possible second. The Lord of
Terror's present "gigantic coup" is to throw in with Kuhnreich,
dictator of Ronstadt—thin disguises for Hitler and Nazi Germany—and render all British aircraft useless by means of a "V-

ray" machine and a "giant aero-magnet," thus allowing Ronstadt to invade and seize control of England. For the use of his
evil genius, he demands ten million pounds sterling and the
complete annihilation of the English populace. As a dry run to
prove to Kuhnreich that his V-ray and his giant aero-magnet
work as advertised, he proceeds to use these devices to capture
the *Sky King*, Britain's most advanced passenger zeppelin, and
along with it, several prominent British citizens who happen to
be on their way across the Atlantic to New York.

Fordinghame is one of those who helps foil Vivanti's plot, but
he is only an incidental figure; the novel's primary "hero" is
one Johnny Cardell, a newspaperman by trade and one of Horler's more obnoxious protagonists by construction. Cardell
insults menials, shows marked racist tendencies ("The convic-
tion that this odd-looking Scandinavian swine was possibly at
the back of the threatening letter Mary had received roused
him to a state of insensate fury."), and marked priggish tendencies ("Girls were flinging their legs about, indifferent to the
amount of underwear—elegant or otherwise—they showed.
They were asking to be kissed, and they were being
kissed. . . . It was all rather disgusting and stupid. Johnny
suddenly felt ashamed of it.").

Lord of Terror is distinguished for the aforementioned reasons of plot and characterization, and also for the overall idio-
syncrasy of Horler's prose. The novel fairly bulges with such
singular passages as:

> Johnny Cardell spoke his last words in the office
> where he had worked for the past nine months with
> acknowledged brilliance. They were memorable
> words—destined to be quoted for weeks (which is a
> long time in Fleet Street newspaper offices) by the
> incoming and outgoing staff of the Daily Whim.
> "Go and fry your filthy fish!"

> Dr. McFee frowned a second time.
> "This is verra, verra serious," he said, lapsing into
> his native tongue.

> Vivanti looked at her before speaking like a pur-
> ring animal.

"There are means of eliciting information, let me remind you—for instance, hot irons to the soles of the feet, or the more primitive thumbscrew—but perhaps in your case I should prefer a little trick I learned from the Chinese—"

"You swine!" broke out Sinclair. "Torturing a woman!"

"I am a firm believer in the absolute equality of the sexes," returned Vivanti.

He dashed to the lamp in front of the chair and was about to pick it up when a crashing sound was heard. A man jumped in through a window, the iron shutters of which were not closed. His face was ghastly; blood flowed from his chest, but he had a revolver in his hand.

"*Johnny!*" cried Mary. "Oh, *JOHNNY!*"

"Just a minute, my dear. I've got a spot of business to see to first. Where's that swine Vivanti? Ah!" catching sight of him. "Here you are! Thought I was dead, you hound, didn't you? Get back against that wall or I'll plug you!"

A considerably grimmer, if no less typical, Horler espionage tale is *Dark Danger*, published in the United States by Mystery House in 1945. It seems never to have appeared in England, which fact, if true, is not surprising; Horler is at his most vituperative in these pages, loudly beating the drums of war, railing against Prime Minister Chamberlain, the British press, the British intelligence network and Foreign Office, American isolationist tendencies, and "ballyhoo religionists preaching general defeatism and submission to Hitler" (meaning Father Coughlin and also the Fascist Christian Front—called Stanford Circle in the novel—of Father Curran in the late 1930s). The time at which the book is set is obviously not 1945 but late 1938 or early 1939, when Chamberlain was still prime minister of England and Germany had not yet declared war on the British Commonwealth. This, along with other internal evidence, suggests that the novel was written in 1938/1939 and rejected everywhere before winding up at Mystery House. Little wonder, too. This is not a novel so much as an inflammatory pro-war tract.

The underlying premise is that Nazi spies and saboteurs have infiltrated the British Secret Service and are working from within to undermine it and to steal the "Red Book," a complete list of all British espionage agents working at home and abroad. Pitted against the forces of evil are a pair of close friends named Arthur Wentworth, who is British, and John Widdemar, who is American (a rather heavy-handed attempt to demonstrate the necessity and importance of a British/U.S. alliance against "the Huns"; Horler had evidently decided by this time, in the face of creeping Nazism, that Americans weren't quite so absurd after all). Neither Wentworth nor Widdemar is a Secret Service chap, although Wentworth once held a position with the diplomatic service and had been assigned to the Berlin embassy; they are adventurous young men just back from a hunting expedition in Africa (where they shot lions, elephants, and "ever so many other things!"). They are also superpatriots, and when they uncover the Nazi infiltration plot, they decide to destroy the organization all by themselves. Just a couple of likable young fellows, doing their duty according to Horler. Witness this exchange after Widdemar has rescued a kidnapped Wentworth and Wentworth has tossed one of the Nazi thugs off a roof:

> "We had a scrap; he nearly got me, but I saved myself in time—and over he went. What was that noise I heard?"
> "The people in the street looking at his dead body, I expect; how are you feeling now, Wentworth? We ought to be away from here, you know."
> "I'm ready," was the reply: "where's this fire escape you were talking about? I want to get home; I feel hungry."
> The American laughed.
> "You've just killed a man and all you say is that you feel hungry! And this is the crowd Hitler thinks he's going to beat—what a hope!"

Joining these two jolly comrades in their quest is Hargreaves, Wentworth's "man"—the "Perfect Servant," the "Admirable One." (Horler, in most of his later books, longs for the good old days, when all the minorities were in their proper place and good domestic help was easy to find. Of course, his heroes always manage to have good domestic help in spite of the changing times.) Hargreaves, the Admirable One, fought in World War I as a machine gunner and developed such a hatred of Germans that "nothing would give me greater pleasure than removing a few more of the pests in this war." He means it, too. When informed that Wentworth had been forced to kill a Nazi, he says with a twinkle, "I'm sure that the master did it very effectively."

Horler has an abundance of theories about the Huns. All Germans have fanatical eyes, gaping mouths, and twitching lips; a fanatical devotion to the "God-sent" Hitler and the principles of the Third Reich; and nothing but contempt for England, America, and all other nations. Any person who is half-British and half-German, or any British or American citizen who happens to fall in love with and marry a German, is certain to have been corrupted and thus has become a traitor. ("Forbes-Thompson's face was a cold, repellent mask, the man's good looks adding to the impression that he was a person who would stop at nothing to achieve his ambition.") All German agents, in and out of the Fatherland, are bound to perform terrible acts of torture on helpless victims, such as applying lighted matches and burning cigarette ends to the soles of the feet, an activity Horler considers barbaric and which he angrily deplores. He does think it's all right, though, for British Intelligence to torture German spies when the shoe is off the other foot.

All Nazi thugs speak in the same fashion in this and other Horler novels of the period, saying such things as "American dog!" and "English swine!" and "Open your mouth, and I'll blast your liver to blazes!" The only exception is the Chief Thug (so designated), who is prone to propaganda-style rhetoric: "The time is coming, my friend, when England will be in the state which you Americans call 'through'—in other words, finished."

The British characters always speak proper English, naturally (except when those of "the working-class type" are brought onstage; *they* speak in exaggerated Cockney accents). The American characters—Widdemar, his fiancée Helen George, and Jonathan Grantley, the weak and evil leader of Stanford Circle—speak a curious mixture of British and American slang. Widdemar, for example, says to one of the Nazis, "You skunk! You rotten swine of a skunk!" And later he confides to his fiancée, "I'm beginning to think that way myself, honey, but as for being afraid of him, I'd be just about as afraid of a mangy cow who stood a good distance away and started yapping."

The plot of *Dark Danger* is a beautifully conceived mishmash of disconnected scenes and improbable situations. The heroes and heroine are gassed in the backseats of taxis and then abducted, or clumsy attempts are made on their lives on public streets. The head of the Foreign Office, Sir Richard Chandler, is kidnapped, and a German actor is made up to look like him and installed in his place. Helen George is spirited away from the theater where she is starring in a play, held for hours under the guardianship of a lesbian Nazi sympathizer (" 'You don't know how tempting you are, dearie' "), threatened with a whip, and then summarily released in time to make her evening performance. Grantley convinces Helen that the only way to save Widdemar, who (like everyone else) has been abducted, is to spend the night with him; he takes her to a secluded inn, but before he can subject her to this fate worse than death, Grantley himself is abducted by the Chief Thug, who, it turns out, also has a letch for Helen (" *I am here to take Mr. Grantley's place!* "). Helen is saved not by Widdemar and Wentworth but by the owner of the inn, who has no other plot function; and Widdemar and Wentworth are saved not by their own guile or ingenuity but by the fortunate intervention of a rescue squad of British Secret Service agents.

The writing of all this is handled with Horler's usual élan, as already demonstrated. Here are two additional examples:

> The permanent Under-Secretary looked as though he was about to lose his reason.
>
> "The Red Book!" he shrieked.
>
> "Yes, Sir Richard," replied the frightened Peel [Sir Richard's longtime secretary].
>
> "You'll leave the Red Book where it is," said Wentworth, taking charge of the situation. "And get out! I've told you I want to speak to this creature"—he motioned toward the toothache victim—"alone. And if you don't clear out, I'll chuck you out!"
>
> "Creature!" gasped Peel. . . .
>
> "And now, Mister Masquerader, I'll deal with you!" stated Wentworth.

"Masquerader!" choked the other.

"Yes, masquerader: if Peel wasn't so short-sighted, and scatterbrained as well, he would have seen through you himself; that faked toothache wasn't bad, but unfortunately from your point of view, it hasn't worked."

". . . You have played your game, Basil Forbes-Thompson, but you have lost the final trick. In other words, your association with the Wilhelmstrasse has been discovered, and you won't send any more valuable information, you bloody traitor. It's no good to shoot; there are six men outside, all picked fellows, and you wouldn't stand a ghost of a chance against this gang of my private execution-squad."

The other managed to gasp: "Who *are* you?"

"Call me 'Nemesis,' " was the reply.

Another prolific British spy novelist of the thirties and forties (and through the fifties into the sixties) was Bernard Newman, a member of the Civil Service, a staff lecturer with the Ministry of Information during World War II, a traveler and travel-book writer, and an amateur spy-watcher. Although Newman was not nearly as lurid or sensational a writer as Sydney Horler, he nonetheless managed to produce at least one novel of enduring status. This is *The Mussolini Murder Plot,* published here in 1939.

The jacket blurb for the American edition reads as follows:

"On October 3rd, 1935, Italian troops marched into Abyssinia. I wonder if Mussolini knows how near he stood to death on that eventful day? And I wonder if he realizes that he has me to thank for his escape? Mussolini is admittedly a nuisance, but as Saint Benito he would be insufferable! Yet, many times I have wondered if I were right in saving him from the sudden death which threatened him."

With this opening bombshell, Captain Newman plunges into the narration of a wildly exciting mystery which utilizes fact in the manner of fiction and fiction in the manner of fact.

The League of International Amity, early in 1935,

gave formal warning to the world that any states-
man who led his nation into war would be tried and,
if condemned, executed. The Abyssinian venture
proved that the organization was not jesting. Mussolini was duly condemned to death, and the sentence
came within an ace of being carried out.

The novel purports to deal with the events leading up to this
mythical assassination attempt by the mythical League of
International Amity. Newman himself is the narrator and,
more or less, hero of the piece, referred to by name. Inspector
Marshall, of the "Special Branch of Scotland Yard," also plays
a fairly large role in the story.

What is the League of International Amity? A right-wing
nut group, we are told, full of good intentions and misguided
methods of accomplishing them. As Marshall explains to Newman at one point:

"Of course, every organization is liable to become
freak on the slightest provocation. Their ideas are
often excellent in their own sphere, but enthusiasts
gradually assume that their pet theory will solve all
the world's problems. The Nudists, for example,
claim that their cult would ease our problems by
abolishing clothes, which causes complexes. Other
people want compulsory free love. One brainy fellow
devised a new religion to be ruled by a priestess, to be
chosen as 'Queen of Hearts,' as an 'object of worship,'
because of her feminine build—she was to have a
wide pelvis, and so on. The choice of the lady was to
be effected by 'detached scientists, with a tape-meas-
ure and a pair of dividers.' I should think the scientists would have to be *very* detached! Imagine choos-
ing a girl as a sort of unofficial goddess just because
she's got a bulgy behind!"

The scene of action shifts frenetically from England (where
Marshall also lectures on the methods by which Scotland Yard
solves crimes: "Anonymous letters and squeaking are the detective's stand-bys") to Venice, to Sarajevo, to the Slovene Mountains, to Rome, back to England, back to Rome, to Corsica,
through the Italian countryside back to Rome. Along the way

there are two kidnappings, some poisoned bullets, fights on narrow ledges, a character crawling out on the wing of an airplane
in flight to repair "a control wire," secret coded messages, villains who say things like "I thought we were foolproof . . . I
read up all similar cases in the Crime Club books," a couple of
chases (car and airplane), a miraculous escape by Newman
(" 'One of the arts you learn in my business is to write in the
dark—or in your pocket'"), and many footnotes to make sure
that the reader is paying attention. The thrilling climax
involves a race against time to stop the final Mussolini assassination attempt—and a deucedly clever attempt it is, as Newman might say, utilizing a rifle mounted on the roof of a building, with a string tied to the trigger and the string then dropped
down through a water pipe to the street, so the killer can stand
below and pull both string and trigger at just the right moment.
The attempt fails, of course, because Newman and his troops
arrive in the nick of time. *C'est la guerre.*

As a heroic figure, Newman leaves something to be desired.
Like Horler's protagonists, he is a class-conscious prig, though
not nearly so shrill or obnoxious. And when it comes to wom-
en . . . well, women are just not Newman's forte. He knows
very little about them. In fact, he may know less about women
than any other hero in crime and espionage fiction.

> I felt a sudden grip at my arm, heard a little half-
> strangled cry, and there she was lying on the floor
> beside me, once again in a dead faint! This was a sit-
> uation to which I was scarcely accustomed. My life
> has been planned along somewhat sterner lines than
> the succouring of distressed ladies. However, it was
> obviously no time for finesse. I picked her up and car-
> ried her to the bed again. I stripped off her skirt and
> coat, for I had the impression that the proper thing to
> do in the case of a severe faint was to remove a lady's
> corsets. However, apparently this girl wore none.
> Again I resorted to the time-honored method of bend-
> ing her double, flooding the brain with blood.

Whatever else you can say about James Bond, *he* knew what
to do when he had a woman on a bed with her skirt off. And it
wasn't to bend her double so blood would flood her brain.
The involvement of the United States in World War II

spawned a surfeit of American spy novels, some of which were the equal of anything Horler, Newman, and others were turning out in England. Nearly all of these dealt with home-front espionage—the threat of Nazi spies and saboteurs in the large cities, in and around defense plants and military installations. Outstanding among them is Frank Diamond's *Murder Rides a Rocket* (1946), featuring the breezy escapades of Vicky Gaines (a.k.a. "the Dish") and counterespionage agent Ransome V. Dragoon (a.k.a. "Drag," not inappropriately).

The scene is Manhattan, where Drag and the Dish mix it up with German spies, French spies, Russian Army Intelligence, the FBI, assorted vamps, a couple of horny but good-hearted naval officers, a couple of murders, and the model of a "new form of compact one-man hand rocket weapon," similar to a bazooka, which contains three "sausages" (i.e., rockets) and has an interchangeable barrel and magazine of "the ordinary Tommygun type." The Dish is fun to watch in action because she's cute and cuddly and kissable and wily and is always doing something unpredictable, like Lucille Ball in *I Love Lucy*. Drag is fun to watch because he has an amazing repertoire of clever expressions, including (but not limited to): "Great murderous mastodons!", "Dangle my remains from a tree," "Well, rack-and-thumbscrew me," "Burn me for an infidel!", and, best of all, "Great whistling wheels of the Pit!"

But the real charm of *Murder Rides a Rocket* lies in its breezy style. William Le Queux may have been a master of padding, but Frank Diamond was no slouch in his own right; where Le Queux's method was to use description and repetitive dialogue, Diamond's favorite tool was an endless stream of devastatingly simpleminded humor. This novel (and its forerunner, *Murder in Five Columns*, also starring Drag and the Dish) fairly bulges with wisecracks, atrocious puns, snappy one-liners, B-movie patter, and Bowery Boys routines—sort of like the joke book for a stand-up comic on the forties burlesque circuit.

Just a few samples:

> "I want a lawyer," Vicky said instantly. "Get me Danglewrit and Loophole. On second thought, get Dragoon. He's better than a lawyer."
>
> "Did Dragoon put you up to this stunt?" demanded Petersen.
>
> "Why don't you ask him?"

"Don't worry, I will! Where is he?"

"He said something about going on a USO tour, but he ought to be back by now. He wasn't in good voice, you see."

"You mean I'm a desperado?" said Vicky in delight. "Shall I start going around with a six-gun on each hip?"

"No, the hips themselves are quite dangerous enough!"

"And here I slave over a hot tommygun all day!"

"Who lives up in yon hedonistic penthouse?"

"The owner of the building," Vicky said. "He's a highly successful playwright, name of Ian Waldo Craig. In private life, Paddy Hoolahan."

"I wonder if Ian Waldo, né Hoolahan, would object if we nimbly scaled his terrace and browsed about up there?"

"He wouldn't even hear you. . . . When he writes plays, believe me, he lives 'em. Right now he's working on a play about Olde Englande."

"Odds boddikins!" exclaimed Dragoon. "I hope he doesn't decide to sink a clothyard shaft into my midriff. . . ."

The clicking of a typewriter ceased abruptly, and was followed by a loud and eerie clanking. From a desk in the corner a figure reared up. It was presumably Ian Waldo, but it could have been anybody, because it was encased from head to foot in a brightly burnished suit of medieval armor. The apparition jerked a broadsword from its sheath with a spine-chilling zing, and approached threateningly. Perceiving Vicky, he stopped, and dramatically stuck the broadsword into the floor. "Ah!" bellowed a muffled voice. " 'Tis the Gaines wench!"

"Sire, I bring with me the Duke of Dragoon!"

"Avaunt!" thundered Ian Waldo, wrenching the sword from the floor. "Let me cleave this king's man to the navel!"

* * *

"You monster!" Vicky accused. "You put me to bed with my clothes on!"

"Must you use one of my men as your calling card?" snapped Petersen.

"It's a sort of barometer," Dragoon explained, coming in and looking down with a friendly grin at Carter. "When I can't handle one of your buckos, Pete, I intend to retire and open a fish shop. I see myself now, in a white apron, behind a carefully weighted scale—"

"Breakisdamneck!" groaned Carter from the carpet.

"You realize you've assaulted a federal officer?" said Petersen.

"My dear lovable Pete, he assaulted me! By the way, here's his gun." Dragoon grinned mockingly. . . .

"Knockisbrainsout!" growled Carter, finally able to sit up.

"There's nothing so restful as slab after slab of cool, complacent fish!" Dragoon rhapsodized. "And when Pete comes snooping around, I can always wrap one around his neck. Fascinating!"

Yes it is. A veritable laff riot.

Or, as Drag says hilariously to one of the Russian characters, " 'Da, da! Ja opororzghenil nie odnou boutilkou s Semonom Vasilievim!' " And you can't argue with that, now can you?

No study of the good spy novel would be complete, certainly, without mention of James Bond; similarly, no examination of the bad spy novel would be complete without mention of some of the James Bond imitators. There have been dozens on both sides of the Atlantic since Fleming and Bond achieved international fame in the early sixties, but the two worst are American. The first of these is Sean O'Shea's rollicking and heavily erotic adventures of Valentine Flynn, a spy of sorts whose specialty is cases of industrial espionage. An oddball mixture of Bond, The Saint, Ted Mark, and Shell Scott, Flynn owns a

Ph.D. and sports a "Doctor" in front of his name. Which is appropriate, because playing doctor is what Flynn most likes to do, with bevys of beautiful and willing ladies as his "patients."

The foremost Flynn caper is *What a Way to Go!* (1966), which takes place in the Grand Bahamas and other parts of the Caribbean. The plot is undistinguished, but the writing is alternatively brilliant. Classic lines abound, the most notable of which, not coincidentally, are of a sexual nature.

> I looked at her naked figure and felt my pulse beginning to race through my veins.

> While I had now made up my mind to be clinical about my lovemaking with her, I found it somewhat difficult to remain professional in my approach. It was too hard for that.

> She frowned and kissed me again, playfully tickling me. She poked a fingernail into my navel and something stung me. When she withdrew her fingernail she was holding something up between her thumb and forefinger. "Whatever is this, Val?"
>
> I sat up and blinked in amazement. "So *that's* how the baroness was able to trail me everywhere I went! And that's why my pants' belt had been tighter than usual when I came to after she chloroformed me!"
>
> "Chloroformed *you?*" Yvette gasped.
>
> "Never mind how I got chloroformed. The point is . . . she bugged my belly button!"

The most slavish Bond imitation is the venerable Nick Carter. Like Sexton Blake, the British detective who became an unsuccessful Bondian spy for a time before his 1963 demise, Carter's roots are imbedded in the nineteenth-century dime novel. Though born a master detective in Street & Smith's Nick Carter weekly in 1886, Carter underwent several character changes in the next seventy or so years, including that of hard-boiled pulp hero and gadget-oriented radio detective in the thirties, before evolving into the master spy (and sexual acrobat) we know and love today.

The new series of Nick Carter "Killmaster N3, agent of AXE" spy stories began in 1964, the brainchild of Lyle Kenyon Engle, who arranged for merchandising rights to the Carter name and who has gone on to become a millionaire packager of paperback originals. There have been nearly a hundred titles in the Kill-master series, perpetrated by at least a score of writers; some are told in the first person and some in the third person, but all are carefully crafted in the Bond mold. Such reviews of this modern Carter as "the man who inherited the mantle of James Bond" (*Film Daily*) and "the superspy who out-Bonds James Bond, mixing espionage, mayhem, mystery and loving in equal doses" (Buffalo *News*) are testimony to the fact that Engle's troops have learned their lessons well.

As does Bond, Carter works for a top-secret espionage net-work, goes about well armed (among his accouterments are a 9-mm stripped-down Luger named Wilhelmina and an Italian stiletto named Hugo), has access to all sorts of esoteric weapons and escape gadgets, and is well schooled in karate and other methods of killing enemies in hand-to-hand combat. As is Bond, Carter is a rogue with the ladies—many of whom are summari-ly disposed of by villains after bedding down with Nick. And as is Bond, Carter is sent on assignments of vital importance to national and international security and pitted against a wide assortment of archfiends, lunatics, beasts, machines, and weap-onry.

(One of the few differences between the two superspies is that in the Carter books, violence, particularly when it involves copious bloodshed, is described in great and loving detail—a paean, one supposes, to the current marketability of mayhem. Sixteen million copies of the Carter adventures have been sold in this country alone, which makes an eloquent, if not very pleasing, statement in favor of gore.)

The wildly improbable plots of such Bond novels as *Goldfin-ger* seem downright sedate when compared to some in the Car-ter saga. In *Ice Trap Terror,* Carter goes head to head against a mad Mexican scientist named Zembla, who has invented a machine that can create mountains; "that is, simulate one with radio waves, projecting all the symptoms of a mountain into the air currents of the troposphere." With this device, Zembla intends to alter radically the weather in Mexico and Central America, creating arctic conditions and a new Ice Age that will destroy the economy, topple governments, elevate him to power, and thus establish "the Third Mayan Empire." In *The Weapon of Night,* Nick joins forces with three other spies—his sometime sexual companion, Julia Barron; a jolly Russian peasant woman "built like a tank but [with] a heart as big and warm as the sun"; and a cross-eyed Egyptian criminologist—to foil a Red Chinese plot to seize control of the free world through nationwide blackouts, clouds of poisonous smog, and mass hysteria. In *Hour of the Wolf,* Nick is sent to Yugoslavia to recover a deadly nuclear secret buried beneath the pelt of a semisavage white wolf and soon runs afoul of an evil genius named Karac, who keeps a small garrison of slaves trained as gladiators; Carter is forced into gladiatorial combat against these men, as well as against a pack of ravening wolves. (The reason he is forced into this combat is that he refuses to tell Karac what and where the nuclear secret is and in fact insults the great man by making reference to a goat. "Your family's goat, Karac," he says. "Too bad your mother didn't fit it with contraceptives.") In *The 13th Spy,* he travels to Moscow, becomes involved with a ballerina from the Bolshoi Ballet, and eventually forms an alliance with Smirnov, "legendary dean of Russian Intelligence," and the vicious Comrade Ludmilla in order to foil another insidious Chinese plot, this one designed to "explode World War III." This novel has a little bit of everything alternative, including inspired similes ("he's going to be about as unobtrusive as a can-can dancer in Lenin's mausoleum"), mixed metaphors ("A great rock of a hand reached out and slammed down on the top of the man's head like a pole-axe wielded by a giant"), garbled sentences ("Nick caught a glimpse of a machine gun and the man behind it, spitting death from the edge of the sidewalk up ahead and then saw Volgin clutch his chest and kicked out convulsively"), and not a little lyrical sex ("For long, melting moments of absolute dissolution they clung to each other on a high, hot peak of passion; as one, they soared with breathtaking happiness . . . and then slowly glided down to an earth that seemed carpeted with velvet clouds").

In all his adventures, Carter of course escapes at the end with his hide and his suavity intact. He does not, however, always escape with his dignity intact. The final few paragraphs of a recent entry in the series, *The Day of the Dingo* (1980), are a case in point—and in fact offer a much more pithy "last word" to this chapter than any I might come up with.

* * *

As we stood scanning the skies a big civilian Sikorsky appeared over a rise and headed for us. I ran back down the passageway with Yoshida, opened the doors at the top of the stairs and stood there waiting while the chopper disgorged Hawk [Carter's AXE superior]. He came over and offered his hand.

"Everything under control, Carter?"

"It was touch and go for a while, sir, but there are no more problems to concern us, now."

He started to usher Yoshida and me toward the chopper.

"I hope I wasn't interrupting a romantic interlude . . ."

"Sir?"

"I just wondered," he said. "Your zipper is still open."

7. "C-H-I-N-K-S!"

"Hell would be sweet compared to it! You—you
see, Andy, I—I have already seen the thing we must
face. It's going to be maddening—starved octopi, mad
for blood and flesh and coming—coming out of a well
with sea-water in the bottom to keep them alive!"
Her voice was rising hysterically. "Coming! Trained
by hunger to come, to leave the water. Rising up like
old stumps thrusting themselves out of the ground by
their roots! Oh! *Oh!* I—I know I can't, *can't* stand it,
Andy! *Oh-o-o-o!*"

—Tom Roan,
The Dragon Strikes Back

The evil Oriental villain, as typified by Sax Rohmer's Dr. Fu
Manchu, was a favorite of a small but prolific group of mystery
and thriller writers who flourished between the two world
wars. So much was written during that period of fiendish devil-
doctors and "yellow hordes" bent on world domination, of
secret passageways and underground lairs, of fearful opium
dens and exotic Chinese tortures, that a folkloric belief in these
things became widespread—and is still believed in in some
quarters to this day. Yet nearly all of it is spurious sensation-

alism, concocted out of ignorance and the racist attitudes of the first half of this century. As Colin Watson says of the Fu Manchu novels in his study of English crime stories and their audience, *Snobbery With Violence* (1971): "Their only clear message was one of racial vituperation. Had there not existed in the minds of many thousands of people an innate fear or dislike of foreigners—Oriental foreigners, in particular—Sax Rohmer never would have become a bestselling author."

Rohmer, a journalist whose real name was Arthur Sarsfield Ward, was certainly the foremost practitioner of the "Chinese archfiend" school, and Dr. Fu Manchu the character on whom most other Oriental villains were based. There is no question that the Fu Manchu stories are bad, full as they are of coincidence, incredible motivation, stilted dialogue, the superhuman powers of Fu Manchu himself, and such fantastic inventions as the laboratory-created Hairless Man whose trunk and limbs "glistened moistly like the skin of an earthworm" and the giant flying bubonic plague flea produced by cross-breeding with the African tsetse fly. But there is also no question that they have terrific narrative drive, an intensity that not only grips the reader but totally involves him in the action. Anyone who can suspend disbelief for one chapter of Rohmer will likely find himself hooked until the last chapter.

But the most important thing about the Fu Manchu series is that Rohmer *believed* in his creation. The insidious doctor was not just a character in Rohmer's eyes; he was a living, breathing human being, his own personal bogeyman. In a BBC radio broadcast in the early thirties (later included in a 1935 book, *Meet the Detectives),* Rohmer concocted a wholly serious dialogue between himself and Fu Manchu and closed with the words, "Perhaps one day he may conquer the world. It would be a queer world, but I am not sure that it would be any worse or any better than the world we live in." This belief, this fearful fascination, is evident on every page of every Fu Manchu novel. And it is the one quality, more than any other of the series's positives, that keeps Rohmer and his creation from being laughable today.

The same cannot be said for his imitators, however.

Like most imitators, they lacked the commitment of Rohmer; they didn't believe—or if they did, not deeply enough—in their characters and their story lines. They also lacked Rohmer's

imagination, his sense of place and pace, and his ability to portray "Satan incarnate" in a convincing fashion. The best of
these imitators produced pallid reproductions of Fu Manchu.
The worst of them produced hilarity.

Take, to begin with, the Mr. Chang series written by A. E.
Apple. Stories featuring this "slant-eyed Chinaman" first
appeared in *Detective Story Magazine,* a fairly well thought of
pulp, in 1919 and continued until 1931—a total of some thirty
tales. Several of these stories were spliced together into a pair of
episodic novels published by Chelsea House: *Mr. Chang of Scotland Yard* (1926) and *Mr. Chang's Crime Ray* (1928). Both these
remarkable books must be read to be disbelieved.

(Robert Sampson, in an article on the Mr. Chang series for a
fan magazine, postulates that Apple was basically a satirist.
"The trick in this series," he says, "is to pull the reader's leg,
gently, gently, and gently, gently, let the reader know it." If
this is so, Apple was one of the most gently inept satirists ever
to take pen in hand. He may have realized this himself in later
years; his literary career came to an end when he took his own
life in 1933.)

It should be pointed out first of all that Mr. Chang is no Fu
Manchu. He neither thinks nor acts nor talks like Fu Manchu;
about all they have in common is grandiose venality. How can
one tremble in the presence of a master criminal who says such
things as, "I am enjoying your company quite too much to per-
mit you to desert me. Stick around, old boy! In a few minutes
we are going to open a can of sardines and make merry." How
can one hate an archvillain who is billed as having the most
cunning of minds but who, at the beginning of *Mr. Chang's
Crime Ray,* has been captured in his Montreal headquarters by
a Scotland Yard detective named Lontana because Mr. Chang
"had made the fatal blunder of hiding himself in a room that
had only one exit. He had reasoned that if his secret room had
two entrances instead of one, it would double the chance of his
being reached and captured."

So much for the wily brain of Mr. Chang.

This novel continues in the same vein. Mr. Chang is taken
aboard a train bound for Toronto, where he is to be tried for
murder; but Lontana is not a very smart detective, and he
accepts a cigarette from the evildoer, which turns out to have
been "doped with a powerful drug." When Lontana falls uncon-

scious to the floor, Mr. Chang takes the key to his handcuffs and unlocks them. Then "his arm crept inside his shirt. The jade dagger, his emergency weapon, which had been overlooked when he was frisked, flashed into view."

At which point Mr. Chang turns Lontana's head and prepares to cut his throat. But instead he pauses—

"The jade dagger," he reflected, "is a killer reserved for royalty or for taking my own life in final emergency. It would be sacrilege to contaminate it with the foul blood of a Caucasian inferior."

The green blade slowly was returned to its concealed sheath.

Should he strangle Lontana? Would it be more judicious merely to knock him on the head? Mr. Chang meditated. After all, he decided, little could be gained by killing him.

So he doesn't kill Lontana after all. Elaborated reason: "Another would-be Nemesis would take Lontana's place—possibly one who would be more difficult to outwit."

Mr. Chang then escapes from the train by jumping off when it slows down for a curve and makes his way through a heavy fog to a nearby farmhouse. As he approaches, he is attacked by a large dog, which he proceeds to shoot with Lontana's gun. Lights go on in the house, and the resident demands to know what is going on. Mr. Chang tells him to stay where he is; then he cuts the telephone wires and enters the barn, where he finds a locked car. After determining that the owner probably has the keys in the house, he "wired around the lock [and] started the engine."

But before he can drive away, he hears the sound of someone opening the kitchen door of the house. He promptly fires in the direction of the sound and a frightened squeal reaches his ears, along with the "clatter of a shotgun dropped precipitately on a stone walk." Does Mr. Chang go to see if the farmer is dead or wounded? Of course not. Does he drive away in the car? Not just yet. Instead—

Leaving the engine running, he darted back into the barn.

In a stall he had noticed a horse, the oldest means
of pursuit. While a horse could not overtake this
auto, it could get the householder to a neighbor's telephone more quickly than he could go afoot.
Mr. Chang was in no mood to take chances.
He shot the horse through the head.

The book overflows with this sort of hilarious logic. It also
overflows with insane coincidences, incredible situations, a crazy quilt of plot devices, Abbott and Costello characters, and a
cathode-ray device "resembling a three-circuit nonregenerative
radio" that is capable of killing people at thirty feet, can be
strapped on the back and used portably as long as the wearer
carries a very long electrical cord with him, and is known
among other appellations as the Crime Ray, the Death Ray, and
the Murder Machine.

Mr. Chang is intent on stealing the Murder Machine, which
has been invented by a man named Professor Farrada (one of
whose idiosyncrasies is studying dead bodies through very
large magnifying glasses). To help him in this nefarious pursuit, Mr. Chang kidnaps a messenger boy named Ned and
recruits him into his gang. He also enlists the aid of evil Dr.
Yat, an "aged and half-mummified Malay witch doctor" who
keeps various items under his voluminous robes, not the least of
which is a baby boa constrictor. At one point, Dr. Yat produces
the snake and tells Mr. Chang, "I shall train it, developing in its
diminutive brain an obsession for wrapping itself around the
most convenient human throat. You would find it invaluable—
a time saver in your profession, doing your strangling for
you."

Pitted against Mr. Chang is a Chinese detective, Dr. Ling,
"famed trapper of men whose souls have been ousted from their
bodies by jungle beasts," who has been summoned by a powerful
tong of right-thinking Chinese who wish to put an end to Mr.
Chang's villainous ways. The fact that Dr. Ling is the hero of
the piece is kept cleverly concealed until midway through the
book. At first, we are led to believe the hero is Lontana, but
after his brush with death on the train, we never hear of him
again. Then we are led to believe the hero is Ned, Mr. Chang's
young recruit, who is only pretending to be on the master criminal's team because he yearns to be a detective and has an

adventurous spirit; *he* disappears from the narrative at about
the same time as Dr. Ling shows up, not long after witnessing
the effects of the Death Ray and then collapsing in Mr. Chang's
headquarters. (Mr. Chang asks Dr. Yat if the boy is dead. The
old fiend shakes his head. "A youth like this, my magnificent
friend," he says, "has such vitality that he could scarcely be
killed with a club. The boy has merely fainted from the over-
excitement of narrating his tale. In a matter of seconds he will
be restored to consciousness. I shall hasten his return from the
black realm of suspended time by administering a sedative.")

Any attempt to summarize the plot in detail would result in
several pages approximating gibberish. Suffice it to say that
Mr. Chang manages to steal the Murder Machine, in the process
disposing of Dr. Farrada, but all for naught, because the device
is "out of order," owing to the fact that one of six colored bulbs
has been cracked in transport and "there escaped a gas that was
the vital link of this mechanism." Mr. Chang attempts to hoax
Dr. Ling into believing the Crime Ray is still operational, but
Dr. Ling refuses to fall for the trick. So Mr. Chang, after a series
of incidents concerning hunchbacked coolies, opium dens, and
chases through underground tunnels, attempts to invade the
tong house where Dr. Ling has *his* headquarters. His twofold
purpose is to assassinate the good doctor and steal the $250,000
the tong has put up for Mr. Chang's capture.

But Dr. Ling is wise to this plan, too, and creates a carefully
concealed trap in the room where the money is being kept in
plain sight. And Mr. Chang walks right into it.

> He took a quick step forward, and another. Close to
> the table now, his long and tapering fingers of a born
> strangler clutched greedily for the plunder.
> The cloth-covered flooring sagged underfoot as his
> weight descended on it. . . . *Clang!* A metallic sound
> came loudly from the rear.
> Mr. Chang whirled, pistol in each hand, ready to
> shoot an intruder.
> "*Hoila!*" he whispered, meaning, "I am frus-
> trated."

And indeed he is. For, "responding to an electrical contact
effected by the sagging of the floor," a latticework door of

heavy steel bars shoots forth from the wall at his right and locks itself on the other side. Mr. Chang rips up the floor covering, tears down tapestries, and discovers steel bars everywhere: the room is a cleverly concealed giant cage in which he is trapped.

After a gas knocks Mr. Chang out, Dr. Ling appears and notes that the cages—and Mr. Chang—will soon be on a Chinese ship bound for China. Then, "in undisguised awe," he says, "Thus ends the career of the notorious Mr. Chang"—a fact for which we should all be properly grateful.

If Mr. Chang leaves something to be desired as an Oriental villain, the same cannot be said for Whang Sut Soon, the archfiend of Tom Roan's *The Dragon Strikes Back* (1936). Whang is pure Fu Manchu. There are no Western-style incongruities in *his* speech; he is every bit the "satanic Chinaman" and he damned well talks like one. Especially when he has a beautiful white woman in his clutches.

> "Before you are an hour older you will be on your knees to me. Begging, my little white flower. Begging with all your heart. With one blow I am going to crush you. All your pride and fire I will wipe away with but the lifting of my hand. I will show you but one thing, but one spectacle. It will not be a spectacle for the eyes of children or old women, or even men with weak stomachs. . . . But know, white flower, as you view this morning's event that I am your master; that I am the master of horror."

As bad as the Mr. Chang stories are, A. E. Apple's prose is for the most part pedestrian and rather dull. There is nothing pedestrian or dull about the prose of Tom Roan. On the contrary, it is some of the more lurid and inflammatory writing ever committed to paper—in spots outrivaling Sydney Horler at his absurd and sensational worst.

Roan was first and foremost a pulp writer. And a pulp writer of the old school, at that: flamboyant, opinionated, toughminded, bigoted, and slightly cracked. In short, a character. (Damon Knight, in his collection of critical essays on science fiction, *In Search of Wonder,* mentions that Roan made occasional visits to editorial offices wearing a ten-gallon hat and cussing like a muleskinner.) A former peace officer who grew up in a lawless section of Alabama, where the towns had names like Slick Lizard Ridge and Bloody Beat 22, Roan was primarily a writer of Westerns, among them such sensitive tales of the old frontier as "Here's Lead in Your Guts!" Although some of his Western and adventure pulp stories are populated by villainous Chinese, *The Dragon Strikes Back* is his only Fu Manchu pastiche and his only mystery novel; it may or may not have first appeared as a pulp serial prior to book publication. Unlike the crate of rotten Apple previously examined, one has the perverse wish that Roan had gone on to write several more "serious comedies" in the criminous field.

The Dragon Strikes Back opens with a news report of the sinking of a Japanese ship bound from Nagasaki to the United States with a dozen high-ranking Japanese government officials on board. A submarine flying the American flag is responsible, having fired two torpedoes that struck the Japanese vessel amidships. The Nippon government is naturally peeved at this and makes an official protest. In San Francisco, where the novel is set, a Japanese admiral named Takemura and "the Japanese consulate, Takahasha" [*sic*], visit a US vessel commanded by Vice-Admiral Beauregard Blunt and threaten that Japan will declare war unless a satisfactory explanation for the torpedoing is immediately forthcoming.

Blunt does not take too kindly to threats from "little brown Japs." He denies American involvement and tells Takemura and Takahasha that "we have been to war before, and if you have read your history, then surely you must know that we have shown that we, too, have teeth in our mouths and fighting guts in our bellies." After which he has them thrown off his ship.

Meanwhile, the novel's two protagonists are talking things over in San Francisco's Federal Building. One is "Old Eternity Bill" Mandell, an enormously fat man who has spent forty years in the US Secret Service and whom nothing seems to bother; he has "the ability to chuckle under the most trying circumstances," a Teddy Roosevelt-like fondness for the word "Bully!", and an appetite for eye-popping amounts of food and drink; and he takes a trenchant delight in thumbing his nose at his superiors in Washington. His assistant, on the other hand, is an excitable young man named Andrew Lee, son of "Hell-on-Wheels Charley" Lee and a cavalry captain on loan to the Secret Service from the army. Lee is the hotheaded type, always rushing around looking for trouble; Old Eternity Bill is forever counseling patience to him. He also thinks Andy ought to get married. "Think of it!" he says. "A pretty girl to cuddle up to on cold nights and her shirt-tail to keep your feet warm. Bully, my boy, bully! Maybe a couple of little dingy-dingies coming along to call you 'papa.' "

Old Eternity Bill is convinced that someone is trying to start a war between the United States and Japan; he just doesn't know who yet. He is even more convinced, and more mystified, the following day when Admiral Takemura is found slain. That is, Admiral Takemura's skeleton is found—"fully dressed and leaning nonchalantly against a lamppost in the fog settled about the corners of Jones and California streets on Russian Hill." The bones have been drilled and wired together, with thin strips of steel reinforcing them, and one of the admiral's cigars has been placed in the skeleton's "mouth." "With that cigar gripped so jauntily between his teeth, Admiral Takemura had looked like some gay-dog of a ghost from a graveyard who had been out making a night of it and, tired from his long prowl, had stopped to rest there against the lamp-post where dawn had overtaken him with his leering grin and the empty holes of his skull looking down over an awakening city."

Dr. Rodin Lafferty, the police surgeon, takes charge of the skeleton and determines that "a number of bones about the head and torso had been broken, as if crushed in the powerful embrace of some wild animal or monster." There are also strange, bill-like markings on the bones, indicating that the flesh had been devoured.

This startling new development fails to ruffle Old Eternity Bill's composure, though the Japanese are again up in arms. He and Andy Lee go out to see Vice-Admiral Blunt aboard his ship. While they are with the admiral, Blunt's daughter, Holly, "almost shockingly pretty," arrives to see her father. ("Good morning, Admiral Beauregard Blunt! Is the old pressure up or down?' ") As soon as he sets eyes on her, Captain Lee is smitten. The attraction proves to be mutual, as we discover a short while later when Andy and Holly ride back to shore together in "the Admiral's barge."

* * *

"Your eyes are green," he told her. "Green! A magnificent green! I have never seen a pair like them! And your name is Holly, and holly is green. Green like your eyes! Please, Holly, may I call you *Holly?*"

"Yes, Captain—"

"Andy!" he corrected. "Just *Andy*—"

"In private, perhaps," she nodded, "but you know the Service. Always climbing, the title always changing. . . . Some day you will go back—to the Army. Then it will be 'Major' Lee, then 'Colonel' Lee, then, I hope, 'General' Lee. Sounds beautiful, doesn't it?"

"Yes, Holly! But—you are so beautiful—"

"Not a bad-looking fellow yourself, Andy!"

"Oh, hell! I'm *serious,* Holly!"

"Well?"

"I mean it, Holly!" he seized her hands. "Honest, I do!"

"Hell-on-Wheels Charley!" she smiled. "They say he was a fast one, Andy."

"Don't you believe me, Holly?"

"Oh, of course I do, Andy! When I first looked at you, I said to myself, 'Glory be, what a handsome droll fellow!"

"Holly!"

"Yes, Andy?"

"Are you *never* serious a moment?"

"Yes, Andy, you poor, too-serious *gal-loot!* If you must know—honestly, truly and no foolin'—I have always liked the cavalry."

"Holly!"

Silence, the motor *chug-chug*-ing. A minute passed, then two—three. There was a gasp, a long-drawn sigh.

"Why, Andy, you've kissed the admiral's daughter!"

Later that night, after "the Army kissed the Navy good-bye in the hallway of Admiral Blunt's old brown-stone," Holly is kidnapped by what is alleged to be "two damned, slant-eyed Japs." The admiral calls Old Eternity Bill, who, along with a

distraught Captain Lee, hurries to the admiral's house. There
they are told that Holly's mother has been severely beaten and
is now in the care of the family doctor, whom Blunt called
immediately.

> ". . . I started looking then for our house-boy, Wu
> Fong Sam. He is in the basement, bound and gagged,
> and tied to the main drain pipe. He had blood on his
> face—"
> "You didn't release him, admiral?"
> "No. I haven't even touched him—"
> "Splendid!" nodded Mandell. "I wish everybody
> had your foresight in such things."

Lest you think Old Eternity Bill a cold-hearted racist, he has
a perfectly good reason for wanting Wu Fong Sam left trussed
up and bleeding: he wishes to examine the ropes that bind the
man and the gag stuffed in his mouth for possible clues. Of
course, Old Eternity does take time out before releasing Wu to
eat a couple of slices of cake, some cheese, three cold pig knuck-
les, and to wash it all down with three bottles of beer. But he
may be forgiven for that, too; a detective needs "physical stim-
ulation," as he points out to Andy Lee, and "a man must keep
up his strength."

When he finally does get around to Wu Fong Sam, we are
treated to such dialogue as: "Missee Hollee no likee blooey
lound losee timee." (Which makes no sense no matter how
many times you look at it.) And "Maybe so slun plochee. Me no
suree." (Likewise.) And "Everything go darkee, no see. Allee
blackee." Old Eternity Bill seems to understand, though—so
well, in fact, that he determines to have Wu watched.

The scene shifts to the underground lair of Whang Sut Soon,
deep in the bowels of Chinatown, where Holly Blunt is being
held captive. (The place is outfitted with Japanese trappings,
however, in an effort to fool Holly into believing the Japanese
are responsible for her abduction.) First we meet Cherry Blossom, Whang's subjugated mistress, also outfitted as a Japanese;
she is being kept by Whang against her will, we learn later,
and is really a good person who takes pity on Holly. Then we
meet Whang himself, who has a heart of stone and takes pity
on no one. When Holly refuses to write a note that would

"arouse her father," Whang makes his vow to show her a spectacle "not for the eyes of children or old women, or even men with weak stomachs." Whereupon Holly, good heroine that she is, promptly faints.

Upon awakening, she realizes she has been carried into a damp chamber of some sort and leaned against a yard-square pane of heavy plate glass, through which she can see a stone-walled room that is "exactly like an old-fashioned, dome-shaped beehive." In its center is a well capped with a brass dome. This "den of horror" smells of "sea-water and death, of rotting fish and flesh, the empty shells of crabs and gnawed bones." And "atop all of that ungodly filth of broken shells and scattered bones on the wet floor, two human skeletons lay grinning in the murky light."

But that's not all. Cowering against the inner side of the room is a naked, terrified Japanese; "his heavy shock of wild black hair seemed to be standing on end." A moment later Holly discovers the source of his terror.

> A finger had appeared on the well curbing—a dark and slimy finger nervously feeling. Another joined it, then another. Slowly, a dark, elongated head started to rise, a monstrosity, all ugly head and tentacles. Two wicked, bloodshot little eyes seemed to take stock of the room. The thing slipped over the curbing with alarming swiftness. It came down with a clatter on the bones and broken shells. A shapeless, rapidly moving mass, it coiled, curled and jerked its way to the other side of the room, and settled down to a dark, furiously watching lump.
>
> It was a twenty-pound octopus. . . .

No sooner does the octopus settle its slimy form against the wall than a second appears. And a third, a fourth, a fifth, a sixth, all about the same size, all "quick as light." Confronted by them, the naked Japanese becomes "a cringing, shaking thing who seemed robbed of all his blood." But the worst horror is yet to appear.

> From the well now came a short, pig-like grunting. A shiny thing, like the black head of a torpedo,

started taking shape, rising. Longer, stronger tentacles were gripping the curbing. Two reddish eyes
studied the cringing man against the wall. A low
grunting and smacking made itself known.

A wail of terror came from the man. . . . That
ungodly thing in front of him seemed to fill the well.
Like a giant diver from the depths, it was waiting.
Suddenly, a tentacle, as large around at the butt as
the calf of a man's leg, shot forward. Like a giant
feeler it tapped the man on the shoulder. . . .

Exit the naked Japanese.

Badly shaken by this experience, Holly agrees to write the
note to her father. But she's a stout-hearted and clever young
woman, in spite of her penchant for swooning, and manages to
bear down on certain letters in the note, thus creating a kind of
message that Old Eternity Bill deciphers. The message reads
"C-H-I-N-K-S!" This confirms Mandell's suspicions that Chinese
villains are behind both the kidnapping and the effort to pro-
voke war between the United States and Japan—suspicions
born because of some dubious detective work involving Wu
Fong Sam. As he says to Admiral Blunt, "Even if Holly hadn't
been born in China, so that she knew a Chinaman from a Jap
immediately, we were progressing on this case. Yes, sir!"

From this point onward, events come fast and furious. Wu
Fong Sam disappears from the Blunt house; but Old Eternity
Bill has had men watching the house on all sides and they
swear that he never left the premises. When Old Eternity and
Captain Lee investigate, they discover a hidden manhole in the
cellar, opening into an old abandoned sewer that Mandell spec-
ulates must predate the 1906 earthquake. Hotheaded Lee determines to go exploring in the sewer, since this must not only be
the means by which Wu Fong escaped the house but the means
by which Holly was spirited away. Old Eternity Bill is too fat
to fit through the manhole; Lee enters the sewer alone.

After some futile searching, he is set upon by a "huge Chinaman, well over six feet tall—a one-eyed, noseless beast of a
thing with his ears trimmed and sharpened devil fashion." Lee
subdues the giant, after which he turns the man over to a pair
of Mandell's house-watching crew who have followed Lee into
the labyrinth of underground passages. Then the captain continues alone on his quest for Holly.

He finds her in short order, after wading through "soup-thick" water like the "soft, rot-jellied belly of some slimy dead monster." She is having nasty things said to her by Whang Sut Soon. (" 'By the blood of the Great White Cock, you are a fool, my pale flower! Would you have your own slender bones grace a fire-hydrant or lean with a leering grin against a lamp-post?' ") The reason for this harangue is that Whang wants her to write another inflammatory letter to her father, and Holly keeps refusing. "You are a monster," she says to him, "oh, a laughing, sneering monster, whose every pore reeks with the stench of dead men's blood."

Overhearing this, Andy Lee is compelled to act. He is about to break down the door that separates him from Holly and Whang when Wu Fong Sam, the traitorous houseboy, appears with a nickel-plated revolver gleaming in his hand. Lee is quicker on the shoot, however; he puts a bullet squarely between Wu's eyes. But before he can get through the door, he is amazed to see the noseless beast of the sewer whom he had fought earlier and who must have somehow escaped from Mandell's men. The noseless beast smacks Lee on the head with a brick. Unconscious, Lee doesn't see him clap "his sticky hands together like a suddenly happy gorilla" or hear him laugh in "a strong, far-reaching *yah! yah! yah!* that was exactly like the braying of a wild ass."

When Lee wakes up, he is in the chamber of Whang's cohort, Yang Po-liang, the All-Seeing, All-Omnipotent Imperial Master of the Seventh Temple of Yama, the King of Hell. Lee and Yang Po-liang, a little old man who looks as if he might be a thousand years old, trade racial insults (" 'You white fools kill quickly when you kill!' " " 'No faster than you Chinks!' ") Then Yang beats on a gong, and Holly is brought in. She pretends not to know who Lee is, but the All-Omnipotent sees through her protective ruse and decrees that they must both be tossed naked into the octopus pit at midnight.

Just then they all hear a great booming explosion from somewhere outside the underground lair—and in that moment, another man, a white man this time, enters the chamber. Captain Lee is shocked when he recognizes the man as "none other than Dr. Rodin Lafferty, surgeon extraordinary of Police Headquarters!"

Old Eternity Bill, meanwhile, learns that one of his men has been killed by Lee's adversary, the noseless beast of the sewer.

Reluctantly he calls in the local police and then once more attempts to wedge his bulk through the manhole in the Blunts' cellar, this time after stripping off all his clothes. He is stuck halfway through, naked, when a bunch of reporters come in and take photographs of him. This so unnerves Mandell that he lets out a roar and slides the rest of the way through into the sewer.

While he's down there, dressed again and searching with the coppers, he too hears the tremendous explosion. The head of the police contingent, Captain Shade, telephones headquarters and learns that the mysterious submarine is responsible. It has surfaced in San Francisco Bay, discharged three torpedoes at the place where a Japanese man-of-war had been berthed (why the Japanese man-of-war has been allowed to berth in San Francisco Bay is never explained), and then "streaked" for the open sea. But it so happens that a heavy fog was blanketing the bay at this time, and "the submarine's murder-crazed commanders" were unable to see that the Japanese ship had left a short while before and that the berth was then occupied by an American freighter. The freighter has been sunk with all hands.

This latest act of villainy mobilizes Secret Service, police, and the navy into a single fighting-mad unit. Ignoring orders from Washington, ignoring property rights and the efforts of "swarms of shyster lawyers, politicians, and bandy-legged judges," they begin a systematic sack of Chinatown. ("Old Eternity Bill and Admiral Beauregard Blunt were going *through* Chinatown with the ruthlessness of cannon-balls splattering holes in the roofs of shingled houses.")

As all this is going on, Andy and Holly are trussed up together in a tiny room, awaiting the octopi. Holly breaks down into tears after telling him about watching the monster devour the naked Japanese. But then, "woman-like, with that ever gallant fighting spirit that had made woman the goddess-supreme and the queen of courage and sympathy mother-comforter of all the earth," she tries to console *him* a short time later.

Enter Dr. Rodin Lafferty, who turns out to be something of a megalomaniac, not to mention a raving lunatic. ("He was like a ghoul blown out of shape through a briar thicket by a harsh wind.") He had thrown in with Whang and Yang because of a lust for wealth and because there has always been a strain of evil in his family. He offers Andy a choice: join forces with him and Whang and Yang, which would spare both his life and Holly's, or face the octopi, as earlier decreed. He leaves them alone to think it over, but outside the room, he and Whang eavesdrop at a small earhole.

But Andy has previously discovered the earhole, and he and Holly put on an act for the villains' benefit, with Lee pretending to want to accept Lafferty's offer and Holly pretending to be horrified. Whang and Lafferty fall for this, mainly because their minds are on other matters, such as which of them will get to deflower Holly (" 'The white man loves the flesh—' " " 'No more than the yellow man, my good doctor!' ").

When Whang and Lafferty leave, Andy and Holly set about freeing themselves from their bonds. "Gnawing away beaver-like" with his teeth, Lee chews through the cords around Holly's wrists. Then she unties him. A little while later, Lafferty and Whang reappear and, lulled by what they overheard earlier, walk into the room without caution. Lee leaps to his feet and belts the surgeon on the chin, "jerking the doctor off his feet, lifting him, curving him backward, and sending him driving head-on against that solid concrete wall." Some punch. Then he hits Whang in the throat, grabs Lafferty's gun, and flees with Holly.

A dizzying chase ensues. Andy and Holly encounter Cherry Blossom, Whang's unwilling mistress, and she endeavors to help them escape. But before they can, the noseless beast appears. Lee shoots the man, but the noseless one falls on top of him and Lee's head bangs into the concrete floor, knocking him unconscious. Holly is also recaptured.

Elsewhere in this honeycomb of passageways, Old Eternity Bill, Admiral Blunt, and a swarm of navy bluejackets finally, after much blundering about, discover the entrance to Whang's lair. But Whang is gone by this time, along with Holly, Andy, and Lafferty; they have all been dispatched by Yang Po-liang to "the big house on the headland." What Old Eternity and the boys *do* find, first, is Cherry Blossom, unconscious from a pin-prick tapping of veins in both her arms—Whang's punishment for her "treason." The second thing they find is the pit full of octopi.

"Sounds came from it—a deep, pig-like grunting and a fiendishly delighted squealing." Four sailors have blundered into the chamber and been attacked by "a loathsome, gripping monster, alive with cold, anticipating intelligence, and moving as swiftly as a swallow." As Old Eternity and Admiral Blunt look on in horror, one of the sailors empties a navy pistol into the thing's "knotting and reknotting mass of pulpy body."

> But an octopus has no feeling. It has but one vital spot, and that is the devil-brain or heart in the back of what should be the monster's neck. It is a voracious, sack-like ball of body, a body as elastic as rubber, one that can stretch and expand into a snake. It is the world's most awful bundle of awfulness, a writhing, squirming mass of hell-fury, attaching itself to its victim with four hundred vacuum cups on its eight snaky legs. It is the ocean's most crafty thug, a killer and eater of sharks, and—at times—a fighting, darting villain that can put a sperm whale, their only natural enemy, to rout. A sharp knife will cut through it like butter, and yet it is an almost impossible thing to kill, for its strength is beyond measure. It is as soft as jelly, and yet as tough as a wire cable. In short, it is the monster-supreme of earth or sea or Hell.
>
> Squirting ink and grumbling, a master-devil grunting, smacking and squealing with the sheer joy of an opportunity to fight, the thing was rapidly drawing one of its victims to its mouth. And such a mouth! It was but a gaping pocket, soft and fleshy, yet just within lurked its big, horny beak, opened exactly like a parrot's bill to receive its first taste of the sailor's blood.

Admiral Blunt and Old Eternity Bill plunge forward, "yelling like madmen." Blunt picks up a pick-axe one of the sailors dropped and whacks off a tentacle that shoots forward and curls around his ankle. "No blood came from that severed tentacle; there were just a few drops of blue ooze." Another tentacle tries to clutch Old Eternity Bill, but he rams his .38 "straight between the monster's slant eyes" and fires seven shots, at least one of which penetrates a vital spot and causes the giant octopus to sink back into the well. Then the blue-jackets wade in with axes, crow-bars, and pinch-bars and hack the mother and her smaller offspring into "stringy strings."

Not long after this battle of battles, Old Eternity and his men find Yang Po-liang holed up in his Seventh Temple of Yama. ("God of gods," Mandell says, "this looks like the king dodo bird of them all.") They bully the old man, trying to get information about Holly and Andy out of him, but he refuses to say anything more than "Do not lay your hands upon me, vermin of the goat!" A group of sailors take axes and start to chop up the great statue of Yama which looms nearby, trying to "get to the bottom of the secrets of this hell-hole of torture." The great statue tilts forward like a cut tree about to fall, its jade eyes leering. Yang screeches and rushes forward, and of course the statue falls on him and crushes him flat under a ton of wreckage.

The scene then switches to "the big house on the headland," an isolated place two hours north of San Francisco, flanked by a large lagoon that opens into the sea, where Holly and Andy are being held captive along with the "Japanese consulate," Mr. Takahasha. It is here that we meet the murder-crazed commanders of the mysterious submarine—"the three vons"—and here that the thrilling climax takes place.

The three vons are German U-boat officers from World War I, who have become pirates and mercenaries of the sea and who, because they relish the thought of another war, have thrown in with Whang and Yang. The idea is to foment a global conflict that will wipe out the major powers of the time—the United States, England, Japan, even Germany—and thus leave world domination to the Chinese and their allies. The head von is Captain Felix von Zeigler, who speaks with "an affected Oxford whang" and who says things like "They tell me you are a deucedly clever scamp when it comes to making a bit of trouble." The other two vons are Lieutenant Friedrich von Rheim, who speaks broken English (" 'It vass dangerous pizness!' "), and Lieutenant Bruno von Schiller, who speaks with an American accent (" 'You have about as many brains as an empty bottle, my friend' ").

The three vons want Takahasha to write a note that will "accidentally" fall into the hands of the US President, a note that is supposed to be top secret and that says that Japan is preparing to declare war on the United States. Takahasha refuses, which prompts von Zeigler to perform a torturing trick with a cigarette. After Lee intervenes on the Japanese's behalf, von Zeigler decides the prisoners need some time alone; besides, it is past time for the three vons to begin their nightly drunken bacchanal.

Lee and Holly and Takahasha are taken into an underground passage that leads past four huge yellow guard dogs named Hans, Fritz, Katje, and Ada and into a mammoth cavern "like an awesome amphitheatre, a hundred and fifty feet high to the coral-red ceiling." In this cavern is a pool of saltwater, and in the pool is the mysterious submarine. It seems there is a great hole in the outer wall, underwater, which opens into the sea, and so the submarine can glide in and out at the will of the vons.

The prisoners are put on board the submarine, under guard of a motley crew of Germans, South Americans, and Chinese. The three vons get drunk together. Dr. Lafferty worries that they ought to get out of there. Whang Sut Soon doesn't do much of anything. Then, after dark that night, Lafferty looks out to sea "and screeche[s] with terror" when he sees the starboard lights of fighting ships—US destroyers.

The conspirators head for the submarine. But by this time, Lee, using his wiles and plenty of oil ("Submarines sweat oil . . . from every ladder rung . . . from every bulkhead"), has managed to slide off the chain binding his left wrist. He uses that length of chain to knock out a couple of the guards and then goes running around searching for weapons. In the torpedo compartment, he finds cases of hand grenades and removes three. He is helping Holly and Takahasha up into the conning tower when he hears Whang, Lafferty, and the three vons approaching.

Lee whips out a grenade, yells for the villains to stop or "I'll blow you all to hell!" Lafferty and Whang stop, but the three vons are too drunk to be intimidated. A Luger pistol appears in Felix von Zeigler's hand; he sings a couple of lines of "Deutschland, Deutschland über alles," and then starts shooting. Which leaves Lee no choice except to hurl his grenades and blow Whang, Lafferty, and the three vons to hell as promised.

Some time later, Old Eternity Bill arrives, having been told the location of the ʰideout by Cherry Blossom (whose real name turns out to be Dark Flower). Old Eternity says he is retiring, adopting Dark Flower and taking her east because "she'll be a lot of company for an old bat like me." Mr. Takahasha breaks down and pleads undying loyalty to the United States. And Lee kneels beside Holly, "her tears like a cooling rain against his cheek." One has the distinct impression that they will live happily ever after, and there will be lots of dingy-dingies to call him Papa.

And there you have *The Dragon Strikes Back,* an alternative classic with a little bit of everything—a truly wonderful piece of work. The brain of Tom Roan must have been marvelous to behold.

The brain of Pronzini boggleth to consider it.

8. The Vanishing Cracksman, the Norman Conquest, and the Death Merchant

"Anything you like, Theo," said Drummond. "I'm perfectly happy talking about you. How the devil do you do it?" He sat up and stared at the other man with genuine wonder on his face. "Eyes different—nose—voice—figure—everything different. You're a marvel—but for that one small failing of yours."

"You interest me profoundly," said the clergyman. "What is this one small failing that makes you think I am other than what I profess to be?"

Drummond laughed genially.

"Good heavens, don't you know what it is? It's that dainty little trick of yours of tickling the left ear with the right big toe that marks you every time. No man can do that, Theo, and blush unseen."

—"Sapper,"
The Black Gang

Gentleman rogues, as any aficionado of detective fiction knows, were popular long before their uncouth cousins, the violence-oriented antiheroes, came into vogue in the second half of this century. The British in particular have always had a special fondness for the outlaw (or reformed outlaw), providing he is

well-bred, witty, urbane, gallant, and given to a certain senti-
mentalism when it comes to the poor and the downtrodden.
Such an outlaw, of course, is the modern version of Robin
Hood—the anti-Establishment hero tilting at authority, mock-
ing its representatives, lusting after adventure and embracing
danger with both hands, but ever ready to lay down his life for
a proper cause.

The first of these fictional rogues was sportsman and thief A.
J. Raffles, the creation of Sir Arthur Conan Doyle's brother-
in-law, E. W. Hornung. Raffles (and his Boswell—or, if you
prefer, his Watson—Bunny) made his debut in *The Amateur
Cracksman* (1899) and carried on his life of crime until Hornung's death in 1921. But that was not the end of his career;
Philip Atkey, under his pseudonym of Barry Perowne, revived
the character in the 1930s, reformed him (he no longer steals
for thrill or gain but to help others, in the true Robin Hood
fashion), and has kept him alive to the present in a series of
short stories.

The early success of Hornung's Raffles inspired other writers
to try their hand at a gentleman rogue: Maurice Leblanc's
Arsene Lupin, Frank L. Packard's Jimmy Dale, "The Gray
Seal," and Thomas W. Hanshew's Hamilton Cleek. For our purposes here, Hanshew and Cleek are by far the most interesting
of these.

Thomas Hanshew was an American dime novelist who had
worked on the Nick Carter series, among others, for Street &
Smith, and who came to admire the "pure" detective story
form. Dissatisfied with his lot as an uncredited purveyor of
obscure sensationalism, he decided to purvey a brand of sensationalism that was neither obscure nor uncredited and that
would garner him a legitimate reputation as a detective-story
writer. Thus he begat Hamilton Cleek, "the man of Forty
Faces," a.k.a. "the Prince of Mauravania," a.k.a "the Vanishing Cracksman."

Cleek is something of a unique character for several reasons.
The first is that despite Hanshew's American heritage, Cleek is
British and operates for the most part in London and environs.
His compatriots are also British (or French), and the manner in
which he solves his cases is a mixture of Sherlock Holmes, Raffles, and Nick Carter. Except for a tendency on Hanshew's part
to have his English characters speak like Teddy Roosevelt,

whom Hanshew obviously admired ("Bully boy! Bully boy!"), it might be difficult for anyone unfamiliar with the author's background to determine that he was not himself a British subject.

The second unique quality about Cleek is that he possesses a curious ability to disguise himself at a moment's notice, which is why he is known as "the man with the Forty Faces." Unlike other masters of disguise, however, such as Nick Carter, Cleek does not need makeup, false whiskers and hair, or other theatrical trappings. He has been blessed with extreme mobility of features as well as a kind of rubber-textured skin and is therefore able to twist his face into unrecognizable features or into a lookalike image of someone else. This amazing talent is particularly handy when he infiltrates the lairs of his archenemies; even up close, as Messrs. Barzun and Taylor point out in *A Catalogue of Crime,* none can "tell a hawk from a Hanshew."

In the early stages of his career, Cleek is a master thief who taunts the police with cryptic notes informing them of what he will steal next and then disguises himself and proceeds to steal the item from under their very noses. In the opening "chapter" of *Cleek, The Master Detective*—a 1918 collection of short stories masquerading as an episodic novel—we are told that Cleek "was the biggest and the boldest criminal the police had ever had to cope with, the almost supernatural genius of crime, who defied all systems, laughed at all laws, mocked at all the Vidocqs, the Lupins, and Sherlock Holmeses, whether amateur or professional, French or English, German or American, that ever had or ever could be pitted against him, and who, for sheer devilry, for diabolical ingenuity, and for colossal impudence, as well as for a nature-bestowed power that was simply amazing, had not his match in all the universe."

A rogue among rogues, you will admit.

But then a strange thing happens: Cleek falls in love. The object of his affection is not Margot, his beautiful accomplice in crime and leader of a band of French Apaches, but a well-born Englishwoman named Ailsa Lorne. When an "almost supernatural genius of crime" falls, he falls hard; Cleek's passion for Ailsa is of such monumental proportions that, to the disbelief of everyone (including the reader), he returns to Superintendent Narkom of Scotland Yard half of a fortune in jewels stolen from the daughter of Ailsa's uncle, Sir Horace Wyvern. And with the jewels he includes a letter:

There's some good in even the devil, I suppose, if one but knows how to reach it and stir it up.

I have lived a life of crime from my very boyhood because I couldn't help it, because it appealed to me, because I glory in risks and revel in dangers. I never knew, I never thought, never cared, where it would lead me, but I looked into the gateway of heaven last night, and I can't go down the path to hell any more. . . .

The letter goes on to say that if Narkom and Wyvern will agree to a meeting with Cleek, he'll return the other half of the jewels and convert a useless life into a useful one by making the Vanishing Cracksman disappear forever. Narkom and Wyvern are only too willing to meet with Cleek. On his arrival, he hands over the rest of the jewels, tells them he has broken with Margot and the Apaches, and says, "I want to know if it is my fault that I am what I am, and if it is myself I have to fight in the future or the devil that lives within me. I'm tired of wallowing in the mire. A woman's eyes have lit the way to heaven for me. I want to climb up to her, to win her, to be worthy of her, and to stand beside her in the light." Then he asks Sir Horace to examine him and to let him know "if I or Fate's to blame for what I am."

"Absolutely Fate," Sir Horace said. "It is the criminal brain fully developed, horribly pronounced. God help you, my poor fellow; but a man simply could not be other than a thief and a criminal with an organ like that. There's no hope for you to escape your natural bent except by death. You can't be honest. You can't rise. You never will rise; it's useless to fight against it!"

"I will fight against it! I will rise! I will! I will! I will!" he cried out vehemently. "There is a way to put such craft and cunning to account; a way to fight the devil with his own weapons and crush him under the weight of his own gifts, and that way I'll take!

"Mr. Narkom"—he whirled and walked toward the superintendent, his hand outstretched, his eager face aglow—"Mr. Narkom, help me! Take me under

your wing. Give me a start, give me a chance, give me
a lift on the way up!"

"Good heavens, man, you—you don't mean—?"

"I do. I do. So help me Heaven, I do. All my life I've
fought against the law, now let me switch over and
fight with it. I'm tired of being Cleek, the thief; Cleek,
the burglar. Make me Cleek, the detective, and let us
work together, hand in hand, for a common cause
and for the public good. Will you, Mr. Narkom? Will
you?"

"Will I? Won't I!" said Narkom, springing forward and gripping his hand. "Jove! what a detective
you will make. Bully boy! Bully boy!"

The result of this stirring scene is that Cleek does become a
sort of roguish detective—an unofficial free-lancer to whom
Narkom brings a variety of baffling and bizarre cases (or riddles, as Cleek prefers to call them) involving locked rooms, mysterious monsters, black magic, espionage, and other Victorian
melodramatics. In addition to Narkom, recurring characters
include Ailsa Lorne (naturally), a vindictive Margot and her
Apaches (naturally), and Dollops, Cleek's devoted henchman—
"a youth he had picked up out of the streets of London and
given a home, and whose especial virtues were a dog-like devotion to his employer, a facility for eating without ever seeming
to get filled, and fighting without ever seeming to get tired."
Another of Dollops's virtues is an inventive turn of mind; one of
his inventions is a "man-trap," made of heavy brown paper cut
into squares and thickly smeared over with "a viscid, varnish-
like substance that adhered to the feet of anybody incautiously
stepping upon it, and so interfered with flight that it was an
absolute necessity to stop and tear the papers away before running with any sort of ease and swiftness was possible." Dollops
never travels anywhere without a full supply of ready-cut
papers and a "big collapsible tube" of the viscid, ropy glue. He is
so proud of this invention of his that he even has a name for it.
He calls it his Tickle Tootsies.

Perhaps Cleek's most remarkable case is "The Problem of the
Red Crawl," which also appears in *Cleek, The Master Detective.*
Summoned by an anonymous letter to Superintendent Narkom,
Cleek travels to an abandoned house in Paris and there, to his

amazement, finds Ailsa Lorne, who tells him that she has been living in the nearby Chateau Larouge with a friend named Athalie and Athalie's father, the baron de Carjorac. Cleek says, "Baron de Carjorac? Do you mean the French minister of the interior, the president of the Board of National Defences, Miss Lorne, that enthusiastic old patriot, that rabid old spitfire whose one dream is the wresting back of Alsace-Lorraine, the driving of the hated Germans into the sea? Do you mean that ripping old firebrand?"

Ailsa says, "Yes."

She goes on to say that all sorts of terrible things have been happening at the Chateau Larouge, which the baron moved into after a mysterious fire destroyed his villa. (Cleek recalls, from his past experiences with the French Apaches, that there is an underground passage at the Chateau Larouge that connects with the Paris sewers. Hmmm . . .) A man named Merode wants to marry Athalie; his sister, madame la comtesse de la Tour, owns the chateau; they were the ones who insisted that Athalie and the baron move into the house after the mysterious fire. ("Oho!" Cleek says. "I think I begin to smell the toasting of the cheese!") After she and Athalie and the baron arrived, Ailsa continues, madame la comtesse told them that Chateau Larouge was haunted by "a sort of family ghost, a dreadful visitant known as 'The Red Crawl.' " And what is the Red Crawl? "A hideous and loathsome creature," Ailsa explains. "It was neither spider nor octopus, but horribly resembled both and was supposed to 'appear' at intervals in the middle of the night and, like the fabled giants of fairy tales, carry off 'lovely maidens and devour them.' "

Her story becomes even more bizarre. The baron de Carjorac is terrified of spiders, a fact that Merode and madame la comtesse are well aware of; the Red Crawl has been visiting the baron during the night, had even touched him on one occasion. It was "a horrible, hideous red reptile," Ailsa says, "with squirming tentacles, a huge, glowing body, and eyes like flame. It had crept upon him out of the darkness, he knew not from where. It had seized him, resisted all his wild efforts to tear loose from it, and when he finally sank, overcome and fainting, upon the floor, his last conscious recollection was of the loathsome thing settling down upon his breast and running its squirming 'feelers' up and down his body."

Cleek ponders for a moment. Then, with his usual *nonpareil* logic, he says, "There's something decidedly German about that fabulous 'monster' and that haunted Chateau, Miss Lorne. They are clever and careful schemers, those German Johnnies." After which he postulates that Germany wants to attack England by way of France, needs to know the number, location, and manner of France's secret defenses, and has decided to send agents to obtain the information through Baron de Carjorac. Furthermore, Cleek says, the Red Crawl must have lifted some important document from the baron during his nocturnal groping; otherwise the baron, with his congenital loathing of all crawling things, would have departed the chateau immediately.

Ailsa is thrilled by such brilliant deduction and tells him so. Then she admits to having seen the Red Crawl herself (" 'It was like a blood-red spider, with the eyes, the hooked beak, and the writhing tentacles of an octopus.' ") and to having overheard a conversation between Merode and madame la comtesse, during which he called her Margot and gave her an emphatically unbrotherly kiss. The true identity and motivations of madame la comtesse are obvious to Cleek right away: his old girl friend Margot has gone to work for the Germans to spite the Vanishing Cracksman. He also identifies the name Clodoche, which Ailsa overheard Merode mention; "Clodoche is a renegade Alsatian," he says, "a spy in the pay of the German government, and an old habitue of 'The Inn of the Twisted Arm,' where the Queen of the Apaches and her pals hold their frequent revels."

Armed with all this information, and with the blessings of his beloved Ailsa, Cleek heads for the chateau Larouge. That night, after Ailsa has explained to the baron about Cleek and the baron has agreed to cooperate, Cleek impersonates the French minister. In the dark of Baron de Carjorac's bedroom, the Cracksman then encounters the Red Crawl: "It slid first one tentacle and then another over his knees and up toward his breast, and still he made no movement; then as it rose until its hideous beaked countenance was close to his own, his hands flashed upward and clamped together like a vise—clamped on a palpitating human throat."

The Red Crawl, it develops, not very surprisingly, is only a man dressed up in a costume and mask—an Apache named Serpice, whom Cleek recognizes. There is a tremendous fight, dur-

ing which Cleek tries to force Serpice to tell him the password
that Clodoche must give to Margot at The Twisted Arm in order
for her to relinquish the stolen document. But to no avail. Serpice manages to make enough noise to summon Merode, which
leaves Cleek no choice except to flee. And where he flees is
through the trapdoor, into the secret passage that leads to the
lair of the Apaches.

The scene shifts to The Twisted Arm, where Margot and her
band are engaged in the night's revelry. Soon, as they are in the
midst of their bacchanal, "there rolled up suddenly a voice crying, as from the bowels of the earth, 'Hola! Hola! La! la! loi!' the
cry of the Apache to his kind." And Cleek enters, but not as
Cleek; he has rearrranged his face so that now he looks like
Clodoche.

He asks Margot if she has the document; she says she does,
"tenderly shielded," and taps the bodice of her dress. Cleek
demands the paper so it can be taken to one Count von Hetzler,
a German spy waiting outside. She tells him he must first give
her the password. Cleek makes an incorrect guess and then
remembers that there is only one phrase ever used for a password among the Kaiser's people: "To the day!" And of course
that's it.

> "Bravo!" she said, with a little hiccough, for the
> absinthe, of which she had imbibed so freely tonight,
> was beginning to take hold of her. "A pretty conspi-
> rator to forget how to open the door he himself
> locked! It is well I know thee; it is well it was our
> word in the beginning, or I had been suspicious, silly!
> Wait but a moment"—putting her hand to her breast
> and beginning to unfasten her bodice—"wait but a
> moment, Monsieur Twitching-Fingers, and the thing
> shall be in your hand."

But Margot, in her drunken state, takes too long to open up
her dress. Dollops, whom Cleek has positioned in the sewers to
act as a lookout, gives a warning blast on a whistle: the real
Clodoche is on his way into The Twisted Arm. Instead of put-
ting his hand inside Margot's bodice, where he had presumably
had it on numerous occasions in the old days, and removing the
document himself, Cleek continues to wait for her to fumble it

out herself. This ill-advised sense of propriety almost results in his capture, for Merode suddenly breaks into the room, followed by Serpice, and shouts, "That devil, that renegade, that fury, Cleek, the Cracksman, is here. He came to the rescue out of the very skies and all but killed Serpice!"

Nevertheless, Cleek manages to leap over the bar, shut off the gaslights, throw a chair through the window, and escape the room. The crowd of Apaches converges on the bar and then streams out in hot pursuit. Before long they see "a lithe, thin figure, dressed as one of their own kind, spring up in the path of that other figure, jump on it, grip it, clap a huge square of sticky brown paper [one of Dollops's Tickle Tootsies] over the howling mouth, and bear it, struggling and kicking, to the ground." The Apaches, thinking the howling figure is Cleek, swarm over it and hack away at it with their dirks. When they drag the body inside, however, they are astonished to discover that the man they have killed is not Cleek but Clodoche.

And when the gas lamps are lit again, they also discover that "there on the floor, her limp hands turned palms upward, a chloroformed cloth folded over her mouth and nose, lay the figure of Margot, her bodice torn wide open and the paper forever gone!"

Before going on to solve other riddles, the Cracksman, the Man of Forty Faces, has a final message for Count von Hetzler in the shadows outside: "Herr Count," he says from within a car that drifts by. "A positively infallible recipe for the invasion of England: Wait until the Channel freezes and then skate over. Goodnight!"

Cleek, Raffles, Lupin, and the other early outlaws had their fair share of readers during the first two decades of the century, but the real heyday of the rogues was the period between the two world wars. Those twenty years from 1919 to 1939 saw the birth and rise of such internationally renowned rascals as Leslie Charteris's Saint, Bruce Graeme's Blackshirt, John Creasey's Toff, Berkeley Gray's Norman Conquest, even "Sapper's" Bulldog Drummond. (Drummond was not a rogue in the strict sense of the term; nor was he a cracksman, nor a rascally Robin Hood. But he did have a band of merry men and he did take it upon himself to function outside the limits of the law in his righteous struggle with the forces of evil. In *The Black Gang*

[1922], for example, he establishes his own private island con-
centration camp for captured Bolshevik spies and installs as
commander an ex-sergeant-major of the guards who is wont to
bellow at his prisoners, "In this 'ere island there ain't no ruling
classes, and there ain't no money, and there's dam' little love, so
go and plant more potatoes, you lop-eared sons of Beelzebub."
You can't get much more roguish than *that*.)

At their best, the desperadoes of the twenties and thirties
were swashbuckling, romantic types who exhibited amazing
deductive abilities—all except Bulldog Drummond, that is, who
was a man of action and seldom bothered to think, much less
deduce—while pursuing happy resolutions to their adventures.
At their worst, these rogues displayed the exact same qualities.
How a particular adventure may rate in quality depends not on
the antics of the outlaw but on the plot, or lack of one, and on a
variety of intangible factors.

The exploits of Norman Conquest, for instance, are always
entertaining; in the fashion of the Saint stories, they succeed on
the strength of pure exuberance. William Vivian Butler, in his
critical history of the popular rogues, *The Durable Desperadoes*
(1973), says that of the several thousand thrillers of all types,
genres, and eras he has read during his lifetime, he has never
come across any that matched "the sheer high-spirited gusto" of
the first three Conquest books, *Mr. Mortimer Gets the Jitters,
Vultures Ltd.* and *Miss Dynamite.* The reason for this, Butler
postulates, is that Conquest was the last of the major outlaws to
appear (*Mr. Mortimer Gets the Jitters* was published in 1938, a
full ten years after The Saint made his debut), and the author,
whose real name was Edwy Searles Brooks and who had spent
the previous nineteen years writing for the British pulp market, had channeled all his experience and energy into creating a
character to compete head-to-head with the established rogues.
That he succeeded is unquestionable; the Norman Conquest
series lasted for more than twenty-five years and fifty novels.

But Gray/Brooks had a tendency to revert to his pulp origins
from time to time, partly because he wrote very fast and was
too prolific—it is estimated that he published in excess of 36
million words in a forty-five-year career—to take much time
with plotting or polishing. Further evidence of this was a cheerful tendency toward self-plagiarism; Butler points out that
nearly all the Norman Conquest novels in the 1940s were thinly

rewritten versions of Gray/Brooks's "Waldo the Wonder Man" novellas for the *Union Jack* a decade or two earlier.

One of these forties novels is *The Spot Marked X* (1948), in which Conquest sets out with his wife Joy to save a friend from the clutches of a "Crooks' Union" that operates out of a country estate and deals in diamond smuggling. There is virtually no plot; scenes of action and peril are strung together, most of them improbable, until Conquest forces the Head Crook into a public confession of guilt by having a "corpse" sit up and accuse him. There are also innumerable passages of the following sort: " 'If this car wasn't standing here last night, I'm a chunk of *Lemna polyrhiza*,' " and " 'I mean that we've got half an hour to cook up a nice little cauldron of hell-brew for these gentlemen . . . half an hour of complete freedom. They won't move out of the library until the end of that time, and they'll be guzzling whisky solidly to keep their peckers up.' "

Some of the fifties Conquest novels are even pulpier than the rewritten pulp novellas. *Conquest Goes West* (1954) is one—another action-filled romp in which Conquest agrees to steal a compromising photograph of a young film starlet, instead winds up stealing one of the most valuable diamonds in Europe (diamonds figure prominently in several Conquest novels), and gets himself entangled with a gang of murderous thieves, a "haunted" house on the Cornish coast, a secret passageway that leads from the house to a hidden sea cave, and an electric motorboat, used to transport stolen goods across the Channel to France, which operates on batteries recharged by virtue of a very long electrical cord extending from the house down the passageway and into the cave.

Conquest is his usual jovial self in both novels, defying his old police adversary, "Sweet William"; bantering with his wife (whom he calls young Pixie and old thing, among other endearments); writing his trademark number "1066" on crooks' foreheads with indelible ink; and generally engaging in all sorts of roguish behavior. His most interesting trait, though, manifest in both books, is the contemptuous way in which he talks to villains once he gets the drop on them.

Now it is true that several British thriller writers of the twenties, thirties, and forties were fond of having their heroes bad-mouth the enemy. Sydney Horler was one of the most proficient at this, as we've already seen; another notable exponent was "Sapper," who put all sorts of slangy invective into the mouths of Bulldog Drummond and his pals. But none approached the art of name calling with more verve and scorn than Berkeley Gray and Norman Conquest, as these examples from *The Spot Marked X* and *Conquest Goes West* will demonstrate:

"Better make up your mind, you slimy toad! Make this confession and I'll get you out of this jam."

"If you're arrested, and the case goes for trial, you'll be booked for the gallows as sure as you're a double-crossing hellhound."

"There are a lot of things you don't know, reptile."

"Save it, wriggler," interrupted Conquest with such contempt in his voice that Sir Mark winced.

"Reach, slugs!" he said calmly.

"Less talk, Useless, and more action."

"You, disease, are the man who was known in the early part of the late war as the Kensington Fiend."

"It's a shame that a chunk of hellspawn like you should be one of the throng."

"Say that again, filth, and my trigger finger will give a very nasty jerk."

"I enjoy mucking about with the law, I confess, but I make a point of having no truck with vultures and buzzards. It's not my business to hand vermin over to the cops, but you're different."

"I've told you before, foulness, that I don't make deals with buzzards of your type."

* * *

The gay, free-spirited life-style of the twenties and thirties came to an abrupt end with the advent of World War II, and along with everyone else, the gentlemen rogues were forced to adopt a more serious demeanor for the duration. Some of that sobersidedness carried over into the postwar years; none of the desperadoes was ever quite the same jolly, devil-may-care character he was in his salad days. But his popularity, in every case, nonetheless continued unchecked through the ensuing decades, partly because of film and television incarnations, partly because of nostalgia, partly because of a faithful readership and the talents of the individual author—and still continues today in the case of The Saint, who has already passed his golden anniversary and who remains the titular king of the rogues.

Despite the ongoing popularity of the gentleman rascal, however, a different kind of outlaw began to develop in the fifties: the antihero, the avenging angel who works outside the law because he considers it to be weak and ineffectual, and who dispenses his own brand of deadly justice; the Mike Hammer syndrome. For a decade after Mickey Spillane's meteoric rise, rogue private eyes, rogue cops, and rogue amateurs bulled their way through countless blood-spattered pages, killing black-hearted gangsters and other evildoers with guns, knives, bombs, bare hands, automobiles, and impunity. And always, of course, in as much graphic detail as possible. The postwar public, especially in the United States, had a taste for blood and violence, and Spillane and his imitators were only too eager to pander to it.

In the sixties, still another type of antihero evolved—a combination of Mike Hammer and an updated and downgraded A. J. Raffles; the true outlaw, the professional thief and professional killer. The most successful of these characters was Parker, the laconic and coldblooded gunman who appears in some fifteen novels by Richard Stark (Donald E. Westlake) published between 1962 and 1974. Parker and others of his type are hardly Robin Hood figures; they steal for personal gain and would ridicule (or shoot) any of their number who suggested giving all or part of the spoils to someone else. Their only redeeming quality is that they seldom steal from or murder anyone in the mainstream of society; that is, their victims are for the most part other criminals, usually of a much nastier variety than they. They have a certain code and they operate within its boundaries. The crooks they plunder and destroy have no code at all and are in fact the same type of vicious cutthroats that Mike Hammer was bent on eliminating.

One of the more interesting Parker imitations is a man also known only by his last name—Sand, the protagonist of a number of novels by Ennis Willie. An ex-Organization man, Sand spends most of his time traveling around the country murdering hoods and avenging past wrongs—an odyssey Don Pendleton and others would make highly fashionable a decade later. Sand's escapades are short, tersely written, full of sex and graphic violence, and would probably have won him a legion of fans if Willie had not chosen to publish his books with a Chicago-based soft-core-porn outfit called Camerarts, whose chief claim to fame was an erratic distribution network. For the most part, Willie's prose has a certain rough lyric quality ("He had been many places many times, and he had never been a tourist"). Plots, however, were not Willie's long suit. It may even be said that plots were not his *short* suit.

To illustrate, we have *The Case of the Loaded Garter Holster* (1964). Sand embarks on a trip to Miami to avenge the death of a Cuban woman named Carmen Sanchez, who has died of a brain hemorrhage. But Sand suspects (and rightly so) that the hemorrhage was induced by outside forces. When he finally determines what those forces were, we are given what may be the most unique, not to mention most bizarre, murder method in the history of the genre:

> ". . . The guy who killed Carmen Sanchez is a very clever fellow, diabolically speaking."
> "You know how—"
> "The fire extinguishers. There are two of them on the floor. They stuck a gag in her mouth to keep her from screaming, stuck a nozzle in each ear while they held her down and turned the extinguishers on. The report called it a massive brain hemorrhage induced by some outside force. Well, there's your outside force and that's just what it would induce."

True enough. But one is left wondering why the police and/or coroner failed to notice that Carmen's ears were full of either dry chemicals or foam. Or, if the fire extinguishers contained carbon dioxide, why there were no traces of frostbite. Or, even if the hoods cleaned out the ears, why no traces of any kind showed up under forensic scrutiny. But Sand doesn't seem to worry about this, so why should we?

The antihero of the seventies, it may be said, took a somewhat regressive and deviant turn into the realm of sadistic violence for the sake of sadistic violence. The Mike Hammer syndrome allowed for plenty of sadism, to be sure, but in small doses and with sex receiving equal, if not greater, consideration. The new, supermacho style is to eliminate, or at least to sublimate, the sexual aspects and concentrate on unabashed bloodletting and general mangling of human tissue. The outlaws of this ilk are not private or police detectives, nor are they professional criminals; they are one-man armies, soldiers-of-fortune-cum-fanatics embarked on a personal crusade to destroy the Mafia, the "Communist conspiracy," or similar organizations/ideologies in the name of justice and/or democracy, and by whatever means necessary.

The pioneer rogue of this type is Mack Bolan, the Executioner, who was born in the typewriter of Don Pendleton and the publishing offices of Pinnacle Books in 1969. Bolan's one-man war is against the Mafia, a local branch of which has murdered several members of his family; in more than thirty novels, he travels all over the United States (often in a 26-foot GMC motor home known as the Warwagon and outfitted with electronic intelligence-gathering equipment and a variety of "firepower"), and through most of Europe as well, slaughtering hundreds of Mafia criminals and somehow managing to elude law-enforcement agencies of every sort.

The amazing success of the Executioner series (several million copies sold) naturally spawned the usual bunch of imitators, some of whom enjoyed a certain dubious success of their own. The standout among them is Richard Camellion, the Death Merchant, created by Joseph Rosenberger and also published by Pinnacle Books. Camellion is a sort of rogues' version of James Bond, in that he is primarily occupied in eradicating threats to the free world arranged by Communist forces or members of an organization called Spider. He, too, travels all over the world; the only difference between Camellion and Bolan is that the folks *he* slaughters are usually foreign "boobs" of one nationality or another.

It has been said that the Death Merchant series is of such style and quality that it is not pastiche but parody and that Rosenberger has unappreciated comic talents. There is no internal (or external) evidence to support this theory. The truth would appear to be that the Death Merchant *is* pure pastiche, and that Rosenberger, after his own fashion and by intent if not always by effect, is a "serious" rather than a comic writer.

This is how he puts words and sentences together to create his own inimitable style:

> Vende looked sicker than a Bible salesman on a cheap shot to nowhere when he found himself staring into the big blackness of an Auto Mag muzzle. The Indian's face twisted like a pretzel! Camellion could see that he was sorting through the metal junkpile of his mind, desperately searching for the right answers.
>
> "Drop the HK and pretend you're trying to grab a couple of clouds from the sky," Camellion said lazily. "NOW!"
>
> Surprise and confusion flickered over the faces of the other men. Dr. Panduhabaya looked as depressed as a sailor who had hoped for love but had been forced to settle for a pint of cheap booze and mechanical sex with a cheap slut. (*The Death Merchant #20: Hell in Hindu Land*)

> Keeping in a low crouch, Richard ran to the end of a row of boxes marked "Musical Panda Dolls" and peeked around the corner. Thirty feet away was the door that led to the outside. There was more than that! The gate guard had heard the gunfire and now was looking around the edge of the doorframe. He didn't like what he saw! Seeing Camellion with a pistol in his hand, the guard snapped off a shot with his MAB auto, then slammed the door. The slug missed Richard and whizzed into one of the crates, striking one of the panda dolls and somehow setting off the mechanism that controlled the music. Immediately, the tinny tune of the "Marseillaise" began issuing from the toy panda.
>
> The Death Merchant shook his head in disgust.

> *The vicissitudes of a capricious fate are indeed incon-*
> *sistent and incommensurable! Damn it! (The Death*
> *Merchant #6: The Albanian Connection*; italics Pend-
> leton's)

Richard slammed one in the face with a Magnum
barrel, chuckling when he heard the breaking teeth
and jawbone, almost laughing out loud as, dodging a
knife thrust, he twist-kicked the imbecile in the balls.
The man let out a great *"Owwwwwwwwwwww!"*
and sank to his knees, while the third barmy-brained
boob resorted to a trench knife underhanded belly
thrust which Camellion swept aside with a Korean
karate sidesweep. Even in the almost darkness, he
could see the look of absolute horror on the block-
head's face as he finished him off with a middle knife-
hand spear-thrust to the solar plexus. (*The Death*
Merchant #9: The Laser War)

Camellion is a master of karate, and one of his favorite moves
is the "twist-kick" just mentioned—otherwise known as the
"Goju-Ryu karate ball-of-the-foot *koga geri* groin kick," which
he uses whenever he is engaged in hand-to-hand combat. There
are several references to "killers with inflamed balls" throughout the series.

As can also be seen from the last quoted passage, Rosenberger
takes a jovial pleasure in describing breaking bones and teeth
(spurting blood, too). But it should be noted that he is not lacking a certain sense of humor, despite the serious intent of his
work, and that he likes to sprinkle his narratives with jokes.
Here is one such rib-tickler, from *The Laser War*:

"The Republicans are thinking of changing the
Republican Party emblem from an elephant to a con-
dom, because it stands for inflation, halts production,
and gives a false sense of security while one is being
screwed!"

The rise of the Death Merchant—as with the Executioner,
over thirty titles have been published to date—inspired Rosenberger to begin another series in the early seventies, chroni-

cling the adventures of the Murder Master. This one failed after only a few titles, perhaps because of poor distribution by the publisher, Manor Books. A second series for Manor, featuring a kung-fu expert and written under the pen name of Lee Chang, fared somewhat better; the following excerpts from *Kung-Fu: The Year of the Tiger* (1973) again demonstrate the distinctive Rosenberger touch.

> Tuskanni stood in the open doorway at the top of the stairs, a .38 Colt automatic in his hand, watching as the burly drivers tried to bring down the two brothers—their efforts making as much sense as the termite who was a conscientious objector and went around trying to eat up draft boards!

> All in the same motion, he snap-kicked the man in the right armpit! The knife clattered to the floor as Mace finished the slob off with a mule-kick to his scrotum. Looking like a goof who had just discovered that ice-cream cones are hollow, the man sagged to the floor.

And if those two passages aren't the essence of alternative literature, I don't know what is.

9. "In the Name of God—*Whose Hand?*"

Several women were looking at themselves in the mirrored panels, inserted the entire width of the dance floor, and one of them in shimmering green which displayed a lot of tanned shoulders, and considerably more underneath the shoulders where they begin to swell out and mean something if you like them that way, stopped in front of the table.
—Darwin and Hildegarde Teilhet,
The Feather Cloak Murders

With one of those queer kinks common to all lunatics, Damian was not homicidally inclined towards his victim. He might kill him, but it would be a pure inadvertence. He might kill millions of others, maliciously, but Windermaine was required for another and far greater end.
—Austin J. Small,
The Avenging Ray

The novel of suspense—or thriller, as the British call it—has historically been almost as popular among mystery-fiction

addicts as the *roman policier* or the whodunit. Its antecedents
are the Gothic novel and the supernatural horror story; in its
early years, such writers as Joseph Sheridan Le Fanu, Arthur
Conan Doyle, and Eden Phillpotts mixed qualities of both with
the traditional tale of mystery and detection to create the basic
hybrid.

H. Douglas Thomson, in *Masters of Mystery* (1931), the first
book in the English language to assess crime fiction critically
and historically, offers a succinct definition of the thriller and a
"recipe" of its three basic ingredients. Thomson's opinions are
not always to be trusted, nor are his historical facts; he makes
the following gaffe-strewn dismissal of Hammett and Sam
Spade, for instance: "Sam Spade, the ex-Pinkerton man of Mr.
Dashiell Hammett's *The Maltese Falcon, The Dain Curse,* and
Red Harvest, is an honest-to-goodness, 100 percent American
detective. There does not appear to be much more than this to
commend him." But Thomson's comments on the tale of suspense are nonetheless valid.

The main attraction of the thriller, he says, is "derived from
the excitement of the action, from a primitive and pugilistic
romance. The first, second and third virtues . . . are, like the
orator's, Action. Human life is cheaper in the thriller. The connoisseur has to bear with the 'copious effusion of blood.'" Con-
tinuing, Thomson lists the thriller's three ingredients:

1. Careful attention to creating "the nerve-wracking
   atmosphere. Otherwise, there will be no catharsis, and
   at the best we will be mildly amused."
2. A brisk simple narrative, "unvarnished save with horror."
3. Exploitation of the dramatic effect. "Forlorn hopes, narrow shaves, last-minute rescues, 'tense' situations, all
   the frills and furbelows of sensation come under this
   heading."

Thomson goes on to document four plots "which the thriller
shows a reluctance to abandon"; that may have been true fifty
years ago, but contemporary thriller writers *have* abandoned
such gambits as "the daughter of a murdered man determines to
avenge her father's murder," and "the rescue of a beautiful girl
who has got into the clutches of a criminal gang." Or, at least,

the writers of good thrillers have abandoned them. The writers of bad thrillers, like sentimentalists and packrats, never abandon anything they can still get a little use out of.

One of the favorite ploys of early thriller authors good and bad, which Thomson neglects to mention, is the invention of a supercriminal to terrify the populace, baffle the police, flaunt his villainous ways, perform feats of iniquitous derring-do, and generally make a nuisance of himself. In the 1920s, the most famous of these devilish desperadoes was the Bat—the somewhat deformed offspring of the then-queen of Gothic thrillers, Mary Roberts Rinehart.

The Bat was first conceived by Mrs. Rinehart as a play in 1918, based on her novel *The Circular Staircase;* but by her own testimony, in her autobiography *My Story* (1931), she was worried about her sons who were fighting in World War I and did not have her heart in the creation of bats and archfiends. With two acts completed, she turned the play over to her friend Avery Hopwood, who supplied the third and final act. *The Bat* was produced in 1920 and ran successfully on Broadway and in road versions for a number of years thereafter. Some audiences howled with laughter when they saw it, Mrs. Rinehart notes, and not just during the moments of planned comic relief. This seems to have mildly depressed her; the play was, after all, conceived as an amusing thriller, not a farce.

Farce, however, is what it is.

And farce is what the novel version is, too.

Published in 1926 and written by Mrs. Rinehart alone, although Hopwood is given a joint byline, *The Bat* has the rare distinction of being a novel based on a play based on a novel. The stage version bears little resemblance to *The Circular Staircase,* which evidently persuaded Mrs. Rinehart (or her publishers) that the play could be novelized, changing the character names, without subsequent cries of self-plagiarism. And she was right; judging from sales figures, her audience appears to have welcomed *The Bat* with open wings.

What elevates the novel to classic status is its consistently maintained high pitch of melodrama. Reading it, one does not envision a play; one envisions a Pearl White silent-movie serial, replete with actors heavily made up and mugging at the camera, the villain in cape and mask and sinister pose, outdoor shots of a howling storm, indoor shots of shadows on walls that resemble bats, hidden rooms, clutching hands, sudden black-outs, and fast and furious action. You can almost hear the cree-py organ music playing in the background, full of crescendos. Whatever else may be said about Mrs. Rinehart's literary abil-ities, she was indeed masterful at the concoction of Gothic mel-odrama in its purest form.

The Bat opens with a lengthy commentary on the super-crook's crimes—jewel robberies, bank robberies, six known murders—and the police department's frustrated efforts to put an end to his reign of terror. Among the more feverish descrip-tive passages, we have:

> "Get him—get him—get him—*get* him!" From a thousand sources now the clamor rose—press, police and public alike crying out for the capture of the mas-ter-criminal of a century—lost voices hounding a specter down the alleyways of the wind. And still the meshes broke and the quarry slipped away before the hounds were well on the scent—leaving behind a trail of shattered safes and rifled jewel cases—while ever the clamor rose higher to "Get him—get him—get—"
>
> Get whom, in God's name—get what? Beast, man or devil? A specter—a flying shadow—the shadow of a Bat
>
> The Bat—they called him the Bat. Like a bat he chose the night hours for his work of rapine—like a bat he struck and vanished, pouncingly, noiseless-ly—like a bat he never showed himself to the face of the day. He'd never been in stir—the bulls had never mugged him—he didn't run with a mob—he played a lone hand and fenced his stuff so that even Ikey the Fence couldn't swear he knew his face. Most lone wolves had a moll at any rate—women were their ruin—but if the Bat had a moll, not even the grape-vine telegraph could locate her.
>
> Columnists took him up—played with the name and the terror—used the name and the terror as a starting-point from which to exhibit their own par-

ticular opinions on everything from the immortality
of the soul to the merits or demerits of the Lucy Stone
League. Ministers mentioned him in sermons—
cranks wrote fanatic letters denouncing him as one
of the seven-headed beasts of the Apocalypse and a
forerunner of the end of the world—a popular revue
put on a special Bat number wherein eighteen beautiful chorus-girls appeared masked and black-winged
in costumes of Brazilian bat-fur—there were Bat club
sandwiches, Bat cigarettes and a new shade of silk
hosiery called simply and succinctly "Bat." He
became a fad—a catchword—a national figure. And
yet—he was walking Death—cold—remorseless. But
Death itself has become a toy of Publicity in these
days of limelight and jazz.

(If you conclude from the above that Mrs. Rinehart's favorite
form of punctuation was the dash, you are correct. *The Bat*
contains more dashes per page than even a Carolyn Wells novel—no small achievement—to be sure.)

Next we are introduced to some of the lead players in the
melodrama. First we meet Detective Anderson, one of the
chief's best men, who has been working on another case and
thus hasn't been able to go bat hunting until the present. Then
we meet the "indomitable" Miss Cornelia Van Gorder—sixty-
five, longing for some adventure at the end of a quiet, discreet
life; Miss Cornelia's comic-relief Irish maid, Lizzie (" 'I'm not
going to bed! Do you think I want to wake up in the morning
with my throat cut?' "); Miss Cornelia's Japanese butler, Billy
(" 'She no take nap. She out in srubbery shotting.' "); and Miss
Cornelia's favorite niece, Dale Ogden, who has recently fallen
in love with someone.

Miss Cornelia has rented a country house belonging to Courtleigh Fleming, president of the Union Bank, which has just
failed because the cashier, a young man named Jack Bailey, has
allegedly absconded with most of the funds. Fleming, meanwhile, is reported to have fled to Colorado; his son, Richard,
was the one who rented the house to Miss Cornelia.

She and Lizzie and Billy arrive at the house, which is "two
miles from the nearest railroad" and otherwise isolated. No
sooner do they settle in than strange things begin to happen:

Miss Cornelia receives a note warning her to leave immediately or she'll be killed; prowlers are seen on the premises; Miss Cornelia's Ouija board spells out "BAT," further terrifying the superstitious Lizzie. But Miss Cornelia refuses to be intimidated; the excitement of the mystery appeals to her. She has in her possession a revolver, which for unexplained reasons she purchased two years previously, and proceeds to take some target practice with it. Which is what she is doing when Dale arrives from the city. ("'Good heavens, child! I might have shot you like a rabbit,' and, overcome with emotion, she sat down on the ground and started to fan herself mechanically with a cartridge.")

Enter the rest of the principals. First there is Brooks, who purports to be a gardener but who thinks urticaria, rubeola, and alopecia are types of shrubbery ("'Young man, urticaria is *hives*—rubeola is *measles*—alopecia is *baldness!*' "). Then Detective Anderson shows up, having been summoned from the city by Miss Cornelia, who evidently has friends in high places. Then comes Dr. Wells, a local physician who acts in a decidedly peculiar fashion when nobody is paying attention to him; Richard Fleming, Courtleigh's son; a young lawyer friend of Richard's named Beresford; and a bloodied Unknown who has a penchant for turning up at odd moments.

One of these men, of course, is the Bat.

And why is the Bat flying around this particular old country house? Because he knows that somewhere inside it is hidden a fortune in cash—the very money Jack Bailey was accused of stealing from Courtleigh Fleming's failed bank, but which Fleming himself stole and hid in the house. How the Bat knows this is uncertain; how *we* know it is because Mrs. Rinehart has revealed that Brooks isn't really a gardener, or named Brooks, but instead is Jack Bailey, who happens to be the man Dale Ogden fell in love with and who has been brought to the house by Dale in order to protect him from the police and also so he can search for the missing money, which he is convinced is hidden inside a hidden room.

Clear?

"'Listen, honey,'" Bailey says to Dale at one point, "'it's like this. Here's the house that Courtleigh Fleming built—here, somewhere, is the Hidden Room in the house that Courtleigh Fleming built—and here—somewhere—pray Heaven—is the money—in the Hidden Room—in the house that Courtleigh Fleming built. When you're low in your mind, just say that over!' "

" 'I've forgotten it already,' " Dale says, drooping.

More strange and exciting things happen. A second warning note is thrown through one of the French windows, tied around a rock. The lights go out unexpectedly, and a sinister figure slips inside the house and up the rear staircase. Lizzie spies the figure and gives vent to "a piercing shriek that would have shamed the siren of a fire-engine." When Miss Cornelia rushes in, accompanied by Detective Anderson, she accidentally spills hot coffee on Lizzie's foot, causing the maid to dance up and down and squeal hysterically, "Oh, my foot—my foot!"

> Miss Cornelia tried to shake her back to her senses.
>
> "My patience! Did you yell like that because you stubbed your toe?"
>
> "You scalded it!" cried Lizzie, wildly. "It went up the staircase!"
>
> "Your *toe* went up the staircase?"
>
> "No, no! An eye—an eye as big as a saucer! It ran right up the staircase—"

The action at this point becomes frenetic. Richard Fleming, unaware of the hidden room until Dale blurts out Jack Bailey's suspicion that there is one, locates the blueprints of the house, struggles over them with Dale, tosses into the fire all but a portion that reveals the location of the hidden room, and is then mysteriously shot to death for his trouble. Dale hides the blueprint portion inside a dinner roll to keep Detective Anderson from finding it. The image of a bat appears inside a flashlight beam that somebody shines through one of the windows. A dead bat turns up on one of the doorknobs. The telephone line goes dead, yet someone seems to make a call on it a little while later. The Japanese butler uses some jujitsu on Beresford, who has been lurking around outside. And, unobserved by anyone,

> a Hand stole through the broken pane of the shattered French window behind their backs and fumbled

for the knob which unlocked the window-door. It found the catch—unlocked it—the window-door swung open, noiselessly—just enough to admit a crouching figure, that cramped itself uncomfortably behind the settee which Dale and the Doctor had placed to barricade those very doors. When it had settled itself, unperceived, in its lurking place—the Hand stole out again—closed the window-door, re-locked it.

Hand or claw? Hand of man or woman or paw of beast? In the name of God—*whose hand?*

Well, it turns out to be the hand of the bloody Unknown, who makes his first up-front appearance a short while later . . . after the hidden room has been found, the lights have gone out again, Miss Cornelia and some of the others have been locked in the living room, the Bat (complete with mask and cape) has climbed up a ladder from outside and stolen the money that was hidden inside the hidden room, and there has been a fight between Anderson and Dr. Wells. The bloody Unknown knocks on the front door, and when Billy opens it, he falls wounded inside. He had been hit on the head earlier in the garage, that much he remembers; but he hasn't regained all his faculties yet and doesn't know who he is or what he's doing there. This is why he has been stumbling and lurking about the place, hiding behind furniture and flashing his hand.

Detective Anderson says the bloody Unknown must be the murderer of Richard Fleming and that he must have hidden the stolen money somewhere on the grounds; a few minutes alone with the man, he says grimly, and he'll have the truth. At this point Miss Cornelia cries out that somebody just went through the skylight and out onto the roof, which creates a good deal of excitement and a lengthy offstage chase. Meanwhile, the Unknown remains near Miss Cornelia and regains enough of his senses to filch her revolver when she isn't looking.

Jack Bailey returns from the chase first, and Miss Cornelia confesses that she didn't really see anyone go through the skylight onto the roof. She believes the stolen money is still inside the house and wanted Detective Anderson outside so she'd have freedom to search. She and Jack and Dale and Lizzie begin to prowl the upstairs, where they find a second body in one of the closets. This corpse is that of Courtleigh Fleming, who did not die after all in Colorado; that was just a ruse concocted by Fleming and his cohort, Dr. Wells, so Fleming could return to the house on the QT, retrieve the stolen money—*he* stole it in the first place, you see—and exit for South America or some other exotic port of call. (Wells, we are told, somehow hauled another body up to Colorado to substitute it for Fleming and thereby complete the death ruse. Ingenuity, thy name is Wells.)

But who killed the Flemings, *père et fils?* Jack Bailey theorizes that Courtleigh shot his son and was in turn murdered by Dr. Wells, who wanted the money all for himself. Miss Cornelia has other ideas. Before she tells what they are, however, she wants to search for the missing money.

In a clothes hamper, they find some books (*Little Rosebud's Lover, or the Cruel Revenge* is one) and unsoiled clothing that belong to Lizzie. These things were in Lizzie's satchel, meaning that somebody dumped them in order to put something else in the satchel. "Isn't that your satchel, Lizzie?" Miss Cornelia asks, indicating a battered bag she happens to notice "in a dark corner of shadows above the window." And indeed it is. Inside it, of course, is the missing money.

Lizzie then looks out the window and notes that the barn is on fire. "Fire!" she screams. But before they can all rush out, the bloody Unknown blocks their way and throws down on them with Miss Cornelia's revolver. "Not a sound if you value your lives!" he says. "In a moment or two, a man will come into this room, either through the door or by that window—the man who started the fire to draw you out of the house."

The suspense, lest it become too great for the reader's heart, is not allowed to linger. The ladder, up which the Bat climbed earlier, is still propped outside the window, and a black bulk appears atop it and stands outlined against the glow of the fire. "The Bat, masked and sinister on his last foray!" As soon as the Bat enters the room, the Unknown and Jack Bailey jump him and take his gun away. Then Bailey rips off the black silk handkerchief that hides the master crook's face—

A simultaneous gasp went up from Dale and Miss Cornelia.

It was Anderson, the detective! And he was—the Bat!

"It's Mr. Anderson!" stuttered Dale, aghast at the discovery.

The Unknown gloated over his captive.

"*I'm* Anderson," he said. "This man has been impersonating me. You're a good actor, Bat, for a fellow that's such a *bad* actor!" he taunted.

There is one more brief flurry of action when the Bat, in spite of handcuffs, jerks the revolver away from the real Anderson and throws down on everybody. But Miss Cornelia heroically disobeys his order to put up her hands and tells him that she took the bullets out of the gun two hours ago. Whereupon the Bat flings the revolver at her and tries to flee, but Anderson gets the drop on him with the Bat's own weapon. Miss Cornelia then reveals that the gun really is loaded after all: she breaks it open and lets five shells fall to the floor. "You see," she says, "I too have a little imagination."

In the final wrap-up, we learn that the Bat "had probably trailed the real detective all the way from town," knocked him unconscious, and stole his identity papers. How did the Bat find out about the money hidden inside the house by Courtleigh Fleming? We are never told, although there is an inference that he somehow managed to tap the telephone wires to police headquarters. Who is the Bat? Where did he come from? Why did he keep running around with his Bat costume on, when he could have accomplished more with less trouble in his guise as a detective? Mrs. Rinehart chose neither to divulge nor infer the answers to these and several other questions. And perhaps she knew best.

Why clutter a perfectly bad melodrama with logic and plausibility?

Logic and plausibility—of a sort—*are* present in another perfectly bad melodrama of the same period, *The Invisible Host* (1930), by Gwen Bristow and Bruce Manning. So is a different kind of supercriminal: the brilliantly cunning madman. *The Invisible Host* was also produced as a play, under the title *The Ninth Guest* (which was what Popular Library called its paperback reprint of the novel in 1975), though in this case the book came first. It was the maiden effort, in fact, of the Bristow and Manning team—they having been husband and wife at the time, despite the different surnames; they perpetrated three additional mysteries in 1931 and 1932, all published by the redoubtable Mystery League, none of the same tour-de-force proportions of *The Invisible Host*. Bristow went on to write a successful string of historical novels bearing such titles as *Calico Palace* and *Jubilee Trail*. It is not generally known what Manning went on to do.

Just one of the many remarkable things about *The Invisible Host* is the fact that its plot is quite similar to Agatha Christie's *Ten Little Niggers* (also published as *Ten Little Indians* and *And Then There Were None*). This is made even more remarkable by the added fact that the Bristow/Manning opus was published nine years *before* the Christie. Dame Agatha is certainly above reproach and doubtless was unaware of the existence of, much less had read, *The Invisible Host* when she conceived her masterpiece; writers of her stature do not look elsewhere for inspiration. The truly fascinating point is that a team of young American writers and the British grand dame should have come up with essentially the same plot nine years apart and have made of it a pair of classic novels, one at each end of the mystery spectrum.

The Invisible Host is set in New Orleans, among the café society of the French Quarter fifty years ago. Eight telegrams are sent to eight individuals, men and women, all of whom are acquainted with each other; each telegram reads as follows: CONGRATULATIONS STOP PLANS AFOOT FOR SMALL SURPRISE PARTY IN YOUR HONOR BIENVILLE PENTHOUSE NEXT SATURDAY EIGHT OCLOCK STOP ALL SUB ROSA BIG SURPRISE STOP MAINTAIN SECRECY STOP PROMISE YOU MOST ORIGINAL PARTY EVER STAGED IN NEW ORLEANS. And each one is signed YOUR HOST.

The eight recipients each think a different person sent the telegram, for a different reason. Thus, a clever ploy to introduce each character in turn. The eight are: Margaret Chisholm, a snooty dowager; Dr. Murray Chambers Reid, a hard-hearted university dean; Peter Daly, playwright and nominal hero; Sylvia Inglesby, "an admirable lawyer, logical and coldly inspired"; Henry Abbott, also known "in the lopsided familiarity of the Quarter" as Hank, an intellectual who has been tossed off the university faculty for preaching subversive social theories; Jean Trent, a "beautiful, misty, diaphanous" movie star who has come home to New Orleans on a holiday; Jason Osgood, a pompous philanthropist; and Tim Slamon, a local politician whose main characteristic is that he never chews his cigars in public.

When the principals gather in the Bienville penthouse on Saturday night, none of them admits to being the host. The consensus is that the host hasn't yet arrived. While they wait for him or her, the guests engage in much gay party talk as well as some barbed exchanges and not a little philosophizing about death.

> "But—" Jean hesitated. "Maybe it's a trick party. Maybe he'll come in costume, or drop through the ceiling, or come up the dumbwaiter—"
>
> "Jean's been to Hollywood, Hollywood, Hollywood," sang out Jason Osgood, waving his cigar in the air to mark time.
>
> "Be still," ordered Margaret, spanking his cheeks with her fan.

> "Age is heartbreaking to contemplate," agreed Tim. "I dread growing old."
>
> Peter almost shuddered. "Who wants to grow old— sitting huddled in an armchair clutching at the withered dry cord that he feels slowly being drawn away from him—"
>
> "Exactly," said Hank, "until at last Death, the great housewife, sweeps one's puzzled moldiness into the dustbin."

Suddenly a large console radio crackles to life. "This is Station WITS broadcasting," a strange, flat voice says. "I trust you have enjoyed the first part of the evening's entertainment. You are listening, ladies and gentlemen, to the voice of your host."

The voice goes on to tell them that they are about to play an amusing intellectual game—a very different game from any they have ever played before, for they "must be tired of gatherings at which you hear only the soft bubbling of elegant effervescence." This game pits the host against the eight guests in an ultimate battle of wits, with the prize being death. "If I should win," the voice of the host tells them, "it is my privilege to inform you that you will all be dead—before morning."

The guests are horrified, of course. And even more so when the host informs them that they are trapped in the penthouse, for "retreat constitutes a violation of the rules." The only exit is the door by which they entered and the doors in the patio wall, and all are "charged with electricity sufficient to kill ten men." The host then does a little more philosophizing on the subject of mortality:

> "Death has too long been a portentous affair, solemn, sedate and distinctly annoying. With your kind permission I shall introduce to you tonight death in a new guise, amusing, nonchalant and clever; death, in fact, presented as a social divertissement. . . . Choice diversion, carefully planned to amuse the eight most exacting guests in macabre New Orleans. Tonight you shall learn to laugh with death, the bogey man of the ages. . . . [For] death should be flippant, the last snap of the fingers at a bungling stage manager. Death ought to be the playful unicorn forever teasing the edges of life."

After the host signs off, the guests frantically explore the penthouse. The butler and waitresses who served drinks earlier are discovered in the kitchen, unconscious from having drunk drugged wine with their dinner. The voice of the host comes back over the radio, to taunt the guests with comments about each, proving that he knows them well, and with explanations of his cleverness in rigging his little penthouse game. There are high-tension wires strung atop the patio wall, so they can't climb up and signal for help; they can't start a fire to draw attention because the fire-sprinkler system is "provided tonight not with water for the extinguishing of fire, but with lethal gas for the extinguishing of the flame of life"; they can't flood the apartment so that water will drip through the ceiling because the supply has been cut off at the kitchen and bathroom taps; the electrified patio gates can't be battered down with a piece of nonconductive furniture because they are sufficiently strong to withstand any sort of battering ram.

But, the host says, he has also made other preparations to

assure them of a pleasant evening: liquor, cigarettes, cigars, and other items have been provided in copious quantities. He mentions the favorite drink of each guest, prompting Peter to say that the host must be "a bartender running berserk." And he announces that Jason Osgood will be the first to die.

When he signs off again, the guests split up to conduct a more intensive search of the penthouse in an attempt to find out where the host is hidden. All except Jason Osgood, that is. Osgood slips back inside the front room and "hisses in a sibilant whisper" at the radio; after which he offers the host three million dollars to spare his, Osgood's, life. No answer from the radio. Osgood then offers to be the host's partner in the murder plot; he'll help kill all the others in exchange for his life. Still no answer. But Osgood is a man possessed; his cowardice drives him to mix eight cocktails, seven of which he laces with the contents of a silver flask the host has told them is prussic acid (should any of them want to commit suicide instead of playing his game). Osgood puts the cocktails on a tray, carries them in to the others. But before any of them can drink, the host's voice warns them not to. And suddenly, without warning, Osgood drops his glass and slumps across a chair, dead.

> "I knew it!" Tim almost shouted. "I knew it—when we saw those coffins . . ."
>
> "Coffins?" Margaret repeated. "Tim—what coffins?"
>
> "On the patio," he answered, sinking back into his chair. "Eight coffins."
>
> "Heaven's mercy," whispered Sylvia.
>
> "My friends," said the voice of the host.
>
> "You mad squeaking devil!" cried Tim. . . .
>
> Margaret covered her face with her hands. "I think I am going to die before he can kill me," she said.

The question of how Jason Osgood was murdered is soon answered by the host. "The flask was prepared to give double assurance of suicide in the event that one of you sought that method of escape. Its grape-topped cap spurts tetraethyl lead through a cleverly constructed hypodermic. The cap fits close, and in the effort to unscrew it he pricked his hand in several places and the pressure sent the poison into his blood." The "cleverly constructed hypodermic" must also have injected instant-acting novocaine, since Osgood did not seem to feel any of the needle pricks. But then, why quibble with genius?

The others, out of terror, begin to turn on each other and make accusations that this or that person is responsible for Osgood's death—at the same time dragging before the reader all sorts of past indiscretions that (a) make each of them a likely target for homicide, and (b) give each of them a motive for homicide. The host has told them that if he hasn't claimed a second victim by midnight, they will have won the game and will be allowed to go free; so when twelve o'clock comes and they all seem still to be alive, they become jubilant. Then they discover that Margaret, who hasn't spoken for some time, *isn't* alive. The voice of the host comes over the radio again to tell them how he accomplished her death.

> "If you will lift the cushions in the chair occupied by Mrs. Chisholm, you will find hidden just where her head rested a thin black rubber object that looks like a double foot rule, joined with three clasps. This is a receiver connected with this radio by a wire which runs through the leg of the chair and under the floor. When the chair is resting on a particular spot the connection is made. . . . While you were engaged in your entertaining conversation, I whispered into Mrs. Chisholm's ear and what she heard was a secret so terrible that Mrs. Chisholm, weighing it, preferred to die rather than to face the world again; for I told her that in five minutes you would all hear what she was hearing. So she died."

Masterful stuff. Except for the fire-extinguisher ploy of Ennis Willie, can there be any more ingenious method of murder in all of mysterydom?

The voice goes on to reveal what it was he whispered in Margaret's ear that made her heart stop beating: She was a bigamist, by virtue of a first husband whom she had thought dead turning up alive after she had married her current, and very wealthy, spouse. Enough to make any reputable café-society matron die on the spot, to be sure.

The next victim turns out to be the Irish politician, Tim Slamon. He gets his while sitting in a particular chair that has
rococo carving in which is concealed "a little knob at the front
of each arm, and another on each of the front legs. These, if
pressed with the finger, will release four needles, each capable
of injecting into the blood a sufficient quantity of tetraethyl
lead to cause quick cessation of life. When the lights clicked off
a few moments ago, Mr. Slamon, already under a nervous
strain caused by his having received word that his death was
imminent, started and gripped the arms of the chair, and with a
characteristic convulsive motion curled his legs about the front
legs of his chair."

The host goes on to give further evidence of his ingenuity:

> " . . . Perhaps Miss Sylvia Inglesby will be able
> to explain why in all her dealings with Mr. Slamon,
> she was never able to make him overcome the effects
> of his lowly origin? . . . If Miss Inglesby had taken
> a little while from her so-called legal practice to out-
> line to Mr. Slamon the elements of good taste, he
> might still have been among us. . . . How did I
> know Mr. Slamon would select the chair prepared for
> him? Because, ladies and gentlemen, that chair was
> included in the furnishings of this apartment with
> the purpose of attracting Mr. Slamon's approval. Mr.
> Slamon, you will observe, had elected to sit in the
> only chair in the room which is in thoroughly bad
> taste."

In the face of such an overwhelming indictment against her,
Sylvia loses control of herself and tries to flee through the front
door. And gets herself electrically fried for her tacky display of
panic.

A few minutes later, the lights go out again, slowly, causing
darkness to gather "like the creep of shameless abominations."
Then there is a pistol shot and the sound of breaking glass.
When the lights come back on, Peter and Jean find Hank
Abbott slightly wounded and a bullethole in one of the windows opening onto the penthouse terrace. They also find Dr. Reid
dead, shot in the chest. "The bullet that killed Dr. Reid," Peter
observes, "was fired from above Hank's head. It took a down-

ward course. The hole in the glass is just above the back of
Hank's chair. The bullet came in there, grazed the side of
Hank's head, and struck Dr. Reid's heart, which was lower
still."

Sound deductive reasoning. But not accurate, as we soon discover.

Peter and Hank go into the bathroom, ostensibly to bandage
Hank's wound; instead, Peter knocks Hank down and proceeds
to wrap him up mummy-fashion with adhesive tape. When
Jean enters, Peter tells her that Hank is the madman. Hank, in
turn, says that Peter is the madman, which causes Peter to tell
him to "stop your grinning, you ghastly death hound!"

The result of the verbal battle that ensues is that Jean sides
with Peter—she has had a yen for him ever since they were
kids—and Hank, still mummified and helpless, shrugs and confesses his guilt. He claims to have had cause, real or imagined,
to hate every one of his victims and to want each of them dead.
"Don't you know who they were, that crew I've mercifully
reduced to the elements? The epitome of narrowness, dishonesty
and crookedness—in their heyday they've cost New Orleans
more in broken hearts and misspent cash than the town can
recover from in a decade."

Hank then claims to have swallowed a slow-acting poison
while Peter was trussing him up, because he had vowed that he
will never meet the hangman. Before he dies, though, he says,
he'll willingly dictate a confession that will exonerate Peter
and Jean of any complicity in the murders and not incidentally
allow them to explain all those corpses scattered around the
penthouse. This is his explanation for the mysterious voice of
the host:

> "Under the name of Roger Calvert—chosen at ran-
> dom from a tombstone—I had taken the suite direct-
> ly under the penthouse and had placed there the
> phonographs on which my records were to be played.
> You who read this may play the records again if you
> like. You'll find there three microphones in a circle of
> talking machines. Each machine is controlled by a
> switch in this penthouse, and will change its own
> records. One of the microphones is in action. The oth-
> ers are strung for emergency.

". . . Each record [was] designed to follow the other in perfect sequence as the crime developed. For in planning these murders I had a simple task; there was nothing more intricate than arranging the lines in the same fashion that a playwright arranges them."

And this is his explanation for the murder of Dr. Reid:

". . . I turned off the lights and took a pair of target pistols from a recess behind the chair I was occupying, where I had hidden them. In the darkness, with a pistol in each hand, I pointed one at Dr. Reid and the other toward the window behind me, and I fired both at the same time.

"Both pistols were equipped with Maxim silencers. Both had long barrels that smothered the flash. One had an aluminum bullet with a light charge of powder. Synchronizing my touch, I had placed the muzzle of the pistol in my left hand just where the aluminum bullet would graze my temple, and go through the glass of the window behind me.

"Giving the pistols a polish with my handkerchief to take away fingerprints, I dropped them back into their hiding place and turned on the light."

Yet another masterful ploy. But not the last in Hank's repertoire; he has one more, which he attempts to spring when he finishes dictating the confession. "Like a leering mummy in his bandages, rocking with uncontrollable and awful laughter," he tells Peter that he won't sign the paper and what he swallowed was not poison but a dab of talcum powder. And it is *Peter* who will be dead in thirty seconds, with a confession in his own handwriting in his hand.

This does not happen, however. Jean suddenly knocks Peter's pen to the floor, an act that enrages Hank and requires Peter to subdue him again. The reason for Jean's action is that she tumbled to Hank's final trick an instant before it would have been too late for Peter: Hank, knowing Peter always bites the top of his fountain pen when he's thinking hard, had loaded the pen with enough prussic acid to kill the proverbial horse.

In total defeat now, Hank strikes a bargain with Peter. If Peter will give him the poisoned pen, allowing him therewith to cheat the hangman, he'll tell Peter how to shut off the electrical current on the doors. Peter agrees. And the final curtain comes down as Jean and Peter leave to summon the police and Hank makes a fatal snack of the pen.

The thrillers of the forties, fifties, and sixties tend to resemble those of the earlier years in format and style, utilizing the same basic elements. But during the past dozen years or so, the suspense novel has begun to evolve in a somewhat different direction. At times, today's thriller is indistinguishable from the straight or "mainstream" novel and has sometimes been, in fact, a roman à clef. It still has the "copious effusion of blood" and the "forlorn hopes, narrow shaves, last-minute rescues, and 'tense' situations" of its ancestors, but more often than not, it also contains varying amounts of scientific extrapolation, current events, cautionary advice, and overtones of the psychological and the sociological. High-level kidnappings, terrorist attacks on public conveyances and public officials, murder in the White House, earthquakes and other natural disasters, disease epidemics, occult manifestations, doomsday conspiracies— all these and many more are the stuff of the modern thriller.

Not that contemporary writers have altogether abandoned such old standbys as the supervillain. Bestselling thrillers of recent vintage—Lawrence Sanders's *The First Deadly Sin* is one example—still focus on head-to-head match-ups between masters of venality and their opposites, the guardians of justice. Yet supervillains need not be human in today's tale of suspense, as Peter Benchley proved with *Jaws*. Since the publication of that novel, dozens of others have come along to chronicle the activities of other predatory "monsters" of the animal and insect kingdoms—everything from giant whales (*Leviathan*) to bugs (*The Hephaestus Plague*).

Perhaps the most popular of these "evil creatures" of fiction, aside from the venerable shark, has been that symbol of evil, the snake. A great many people are afraid of these crawling reptiles, particularly those of the poisonous variety; their physical appearance and their biblical history make them a natural as villains to instill fear in the hearts of readers—as John Godey's *The Snake* and a number of other books have done quite nicely, thank you.

But in no other reptilian thriller will you find a more deadly, wicked, monstrous, cunning, all-around *nasty* snake than the taipan of Michael Maryk and Brent Monahan's *Death Bite* (1979). The taipan, we are told, is an ugly, black-brown snake indigenous to Australia and New Zealand that grows to between eight and eleven feet in length at maturity, contains enough venom to kill 173,912 mice (and any human being in three minutes), and is the most aggressive and intelligent of all species. The villain of *Death Bite* is no ordinary taipan, however. It is "a giant taipan, twice as large, twice as vicious, and three times as deadly as the normal Australian taipan," and *its* native habitat is "some obscure, uninhabited island" off the coast of New Guinea.

The name of this island is Naraka-Pintu, and the monster taipan is hunted down and captured thereon by a group of native snake catchers, after which it is smuggled into the United States to be displayed at a Miami serpentarium. In San Diego, awaiting transshipment, it escapes, kills a couple of people, and then goes looking for a topography similar to its natural habitat. This quest leads it, intelligent reptile that it is, to a biology extension campus near San Diego, in which vicinity it piles up more corpses, chases a cat inside a house, and with "eyes glistening with rage," attacks a girl while she's taking a shower by trying to climb up over the shower door. (Not only is this taipan the deadliest of all snakes, it is beyond any doubt the horniest.)

Three people set out either to capture or kill the taipan— Scott Miller, the owner of the Miami serpentarium; his Asian girl friend Ioka, who thinks tangerines are called tambourines; and a biology professor named Wrightson, who helped smuggle the snake into the country. The taipan leads them a grisly chase. It goes to a punk-rock concert given by a group calling itself Sudden Death, eventually causes a panic, and murders the pet boa constrictor of lead singer Rex Flint. (" 'Bruce!' he cried in a pathetic tone, cradling the mangled body tenderly in his arms, letting the real blood ooze across his two-thousand-dollar costume. Rex looked up at the shocked revelers, still cowering on the tabletops. 'Animals!!!!' he roared at the top of his lungs, tossing back his tawny mane. 'You animals!!!!' ") Then it heads into the Mission Ridge Mountains, where it knocks off a weekend horseback rider and one member of the search party that goes in after it.

Finally Miller, Wrightson, and Ioka catch up with the taipan. Miller confronts it singlehanded, catches it, and there is a final death struggle in which Miller strangles the snake while it spits venom into his face. Some of the venom gets into facial wounds he sustained while scrambling down the face of a cliff, and "he knew then what caused the bubbly, dizzy feeling just under his hairline. A minute amount of the liquid death . . . had worked its way into . . . his nervous system." But before he expires, he manages to finish off the taipan, and "with a final, superhuman effort, he sat up, pulled the snake into a convoluted mass, and hurled it down to the base of the mound."

Finis. And not a moment too soon, either.

At an earlier point in the novel, while discussing death bites, Wrightson says to Miller, "What melodrama! What unadulterated bullshit!" An apt description of *Death Bite* itself, perhaps, although not a negative one.

What, after all, makes a good thriller but melodrama? And what helps make an alternative classic but a dollop of two of the aforementioned unadulterated substance?

10. The Idiot Heroine in the Attic

As their steps died away upstairs I shivered in spite
of the fire. The great hall seemed so gloomy, the empty House around me treasured only its past, the only
young person in it had gone off on his own business.
Was I a fool to have landed myself here?
— Ray Dorien,
The House of Dread

I know now that there must have been a touch of
madness in me that raw October night I went to
Cemetery Key and the house of horror known as
Stormhaven.
— Jennifer Hale,
Stormhaven

"A gothic," Donald Westlake once said, "is a story about a girl
who gets a house."

And so it is. Since the first Gothic novels of Horace Walpole,
Ann Radcliffe, and Matthew Lewis, written in the last decade
of the eighteenth century, the two primary ingredients of the
form have been an imperiled woman and a sinister house. In the

● ● ● 199

early days, gloomy old castles and dark monasteries or convents were the staple structures; and the beautiful heroine possessed an unblemished virtue, fainted at least a half-dozen times (especially when that unblemished virtue was threatened), and faced all sorts of natural and supernatural evil: abduction, seduction, lechery, treachery; wicked barons, monks, nuns, outlaws, and bogus lovers; ghosts, vampires, werewolves, shaggy gorillas, and other beasts.

But despite all her misadventures, the heroine almost always emerged with two things: her maidenhead intact and, through marriage or rightful inheritance, the deed to the castle. The only exceptions were those stories laid in monasteries or nunneries, which were of course purged of their venal monks and nuns and left in the hands of the righteous. The women in these stories, however, unfailingly retained their virginity; the stories themselves were all that were ever laid in a monastery.

The Gothic formula, as established by Walpole and his contemporaries and nurtured through countless shilling shockers, story papers, penny dreadfuls, dime novels, hardcover romances, pulps, and paperback originals, has remained remarkably unchanged for close to two hundred years. Gothic women are still pure and still being menaced by all manner of dreadful things, though the emphasis on the supernatural is much less today than it used to be. Despite the best efforts of the feminist movement, they still faint at moments of high melodrama and are still prone to what Lee Wright, former mystery editor at Random House, characterizes as "the idiot heroine in the attic" syndrome; that is, when they encounter a hidden room, or a locked door "that must never be opened, my dear," or some other plot device that common sense tells them is fraught with danger, they invariably enter the room, or unlock the door, or do whatever else is contrary to logic, intelligence, and the basic rules of story plotting.

In the architectural sense, the Gothic-novel house is different today from those of the nineteenth century. Monasteries and nunneries have fallen into disfavor; castles are still permissible, but only in special European settings. The gloomy old country house, of the type popularized by the Brontë sisters and Jane Austen, continues to be a favorite, particularly if it is situated on a barren cliff overlooking the sea. Houses on islands, in swamps, on mountaintops, in jungles, or perched forbiddingly on crags high above isolated valleys are also acceptable.

The rest of the formula is *de rigueur.* The woman goes to the house as a servant or tutor, or because she is summoned by a relative, or because she marries or becomes betrothed to its owner. She faces her peril and does her "idiot heroine in the attic" number. She escapes all attempts on her life and sexual charms. She lives happily ever after with the handsome man of her dreams (not necessarily her husband or betrothed, who may turn out to be the villain of the piece). And, most important of all, she gets the house.

The Gothic novel has been popular in this country for most of its two-hundred-year history, but never more so, perhaps, than in the past three decades. The paperback boom of the sixties and seventies, when half of all soft-cover novels seemed to carry such titles as *Bride of Menace, The Secret of Devil's Cave,* and *Brooding Mansion* and had cover illustrations depicting a dark house with one lighted window and a woman fleeing from it in the foreground (also *de rigueur*), brought thousands of neo-Gothics to a predominantly female and evidently insatiable readership. Some of these rose above the average—those of Phyllis Whitney, Victoria Holt, Dorothy Eden, and Willo Davis Roberts, for instance. Most, however, were contemporary pastiches of *The Miseries of Miranda; or, The Cavern of Horror* and other shilling shockers of the early 1800s.

There is an infallible method for separating the classic from the median Gothic suspense novel. This is known as the first-paragraph test. Not all bad Gothics have commensurate opening paragraphs, but those that do are always and without fail bad Gothics.

Some examples:

> Through all that queer business at Shadow Lodge, those days of accumulating excitement and terror, I was kept as much as possible in the dark. It seems to me now, looking back on it all, that if they hadn't treated me like a Peeping Tom, I would not have been half so curious, so intent on finding out the meaning of it all. I could have helped Dad more, I am sure, if he had told me of his suspicions and his fears, of his dealings with Eudora the medium, with Squint the spy, and the other complications of that summer. . . .
>
> Authors, I suppose, must hover for a trying yet fascinating period on the brink of their books, deciding

just where to jump in. I'd like to take time to dress up my adventures and make myself out the fearless and efficient heroine of this story, but the real truth is I've lived through such strange things that I can't write in cold blood about them. (Gertrude Knevels, *Out of the Dark*)

Two murders would probably have gone unsuspected during the last year if Eunice Hale had not eaten a chicken croquette of questionable virtue. . . . (Jean Lilly, *Death Thumbs a Ride*)

The old woman's breasts were balanced over her folded hands like the loaded scales of justice waiting for her final judgment. (Leslie Paige, *Queen of Hearts*)

Does the ghost of that thing we fear most hang with us always, peering over our shoulder like an omnipotent, though fallen, guardian angel? (Grace Corren, *Mansion of Deadly Dreams*)

It had always frightened her to be in the woods at night alone. But now she was not alone, and it was this realization that sent little shivers of fear dancing up and down the back of her neck. (Jan Alexander, *The Wolves of Craywood*)

Catkins shivered in the cold spring wind that blew bitter round Camilla Forest's ankles. Shivering too, she pulled her light shawl more closely round her and wished for the warm pelisse that lay in her box. (Jane Aiken Hodge, *Marry in Haste*)

The silver light of the storm shifted perceptibly as though a black velvet curtain had fallen over the mountains, enclosing the girl in the small car into a cube of impersonal aloneness without destination. The morning's May sunshine, which had turned the sea to azured splendor, might have been a dream or one of those glazed picture postcards which traveling friends and relatives send from Cannes or Venice or, for that matter, Santa Barbara in California. (Ruth McCarthy Sears, *Wind in the Cypress*)

Anne Gunther stopped her Volkswagen after a particularly bad pothole had jarred her against the car's roof for the third time since she had left the village of Allen's Grove. . . . Anne rubbed the top of her head, surprised to not find on it her own mountain range of lumps. She reached out and patted the instrument panel of the little car.

"Patience, old car," she said aloud. "We'll make it yet, if we both have to walk." (Grace Corren, *The Darkest Room*)

The house talked. (Barbara Michaels, *The Dark on the Other Side*)

Other Gothics must be dipped into a bit to uncover their true colors. The way to do this is to look for descriptive passages of the following sort:

She nodded and they relapsed into a long silence, as though the immense soundlessness of the place muffled them under a pall. She began searching the sky for a bird flying, anything to take the curse off the emptiness, and for this reason missed the first sight of Drachensgrab—dense dark boxwood hedges rearing up seven or eight feet. When she came to, they were running over the abrupt thunder of a short bridge that spanned the remains of a moat, and approaching the most sinister medieval gateway she had ever seen in her life. Awful, cruel and menacing, it bulked astoundingly before them. . . . In the pale hot sunlight its ancient stones had a splotched silvery cast, leprous. . . . (Evelyn Berckman, *The Evil of Time*)

A lightning blast awoke her. She lay in bed, drenched with sweat, the sheets tangled about her body, one corner twisted completely around her

neck, and tied in a knot in her fist. One of the two
pillows was over her head. . . .

A nightmare? A dream?

Selina could taste the scream in her throat, its
afterlife still raw across her vocal tissues. (Grace Corren, *A Place on Dark Island*)

Wrapped in a clean cloth and covered neatly with
a branch of white spirea, she found a chicken sand-
wich and one small, cold sausage beside a vial of
milk. O ambrosia! O manna from heaven! The sweet
remains of the dear old man's lunch, which he had
saved to share with her. *God bless him!* Trembling
with hunger and felicity at the joy to come, she
buried the food under her arm and shrank into the
shadows of the grape arbor out of sight, wolfing the
food like a starved alley cat. (Ruth McCarthy Sears,
Wind in the Cypress)

One can also examine passages of dialogue. Curiously enough,
those beginning with the word "no" seem the most fruitful:

"No," she said in full retreat, reviling herself for
her weak surrender to the joys of premature tongue-
wagging. (Evelyn Berckman, *The Evil of Time*)

"No," I replied coldly, as I glimpsed through the
broad windows out over the back drive, the white
panel truck driving up, with *Bockstein's* written in
fancy script on the side. I said firmly, "Dolly will lay
the table, if you've finished with the silver and crys-
tal." (Ann Forman Barron, *Bride of Menace*)

"No!" If he felt less angry, his young vis-a-vis
looked more antagonistic than ever, if that was possible. (Charlotte Hunt, *The Cup of Chanatos*)

Yet another way to separate the chaff from the wheat, as it
were, is to carefully read the publisher's jacket or cover blurbs.
The choice items will almost always be advertised in the fashion of Jeanne Hines' *Bride of Terror* (1976):

* * *

Her Honeymoon Heaven Turned Into a Flaming Hell

From the moment Devon saw the Casa del Cielo—the "House of the Sky"—she fell in love with it. This ancient Spanish-built castle, high on an almost inaccessible Mexican mountain, was to be her new home as she began her life as wife to Drake Janeway . . . Already she felt as if she had loved Drake forever, and that the Casa del Cielo had been made for them alone.

Little did Devon realize that but a few nights later she would stand beside her husband and watch flames licking around the towers. Little did she suspect the truth about this man who had captured her heart. Little did she dream how soon after her wedding night her nightmare would begin. . . .

Bride of Terror is an interesting specimen—an alternative giant of the Gothic genre that also, heretically, breaks many of the form's cardinal rules. But it does start off typically enough:

Devon Layne stood at the top of the Pyramid of the Sun at Teotihuacán, grasping desperately at the floppy straw hat with the wide yellow band that mingled, wind-whipped, with her bright yellow hair that fell like a shining shawl over her slim shoulders. That same wind, she told herself, had ruffled the manes of the conquistadores' horses and glanced off their bright armor as they marched on Moctezuma's Palace.

After which Devon meets Drake, a mysterious but compelling figure. It is, of course, love at first sight.

His arm slipped easily around her shoulders and she felt her heart constrict. The scent of the roses on her lap was almost overpowering. *If he kisses me,* she thought, *I don't think I can stand it.*

Well, he does kiss her and she does stand it. Rather well, too. A member of the tour group Devon is with (who, incidentally, has come down with "Moctezuma's Revenge") warns her against growing too close to a man she knows so little about. But Devon ignores this advice and later, when Drake proposes, agrees to marry him. The author, like most Gothic writers of the "Had I But Known" school, is compelled to let the reader know at this point that all is not rosy in Devon's future.

> On the way back they passed a billboard advertising an airline. In the warm glow of happiness that enveloped her, the caption on the billboard did not strike her as even faintly ominous. It said, "Fly now—Pay Later."

After Devon and Drake are married, they move into the "House in the Sky" and commence their honeymoon. (This is the first of the atypical qualities: Devon loses her virginity on her wedding night.) Later, she and Drake are chased and almost caught by two hard-looking *norteamericanos;* when she questions him about their identity, he admits that they are Mafia hit men who are after him because he has something the Mafia wants—but he won't tell her what it is. (This is the second atypical quality: the Mafia generally has better things to do than run amok in Gothic suspense novels, so you almost never find them in one.)

Not only does Devon have this to worry about, but at night, Drake cries out the name of his dead first wife, Carla (one presumes not at intimate moments). And then—the unkindest cut of all—he takes to sleeping with a gun instead of Devon. Naturally she's upset and rather miffed by all this.

> On angry feet, she ran up the tile stairs. But once in the big bedroom with its tall fireplace that slanted toward the ceiling at a rakish angle, its hearth that was raised a step above but made of blue tiles exactly like the floor, its casements and its heavy carved doors—the one to the hall and the other that connected with Drake's room—she undressed quickly and crouched in bed with her arms around her knees, thinking.

Drake gets reports that the Mafia hit men are closing in on Casa del Cielo, so he decides to take Devon and flee to Mexico

City, where a friend named Siggy, who works in the German embassy, will help them hide. Before they can leave, however, the hit men show up, and there is a running gun battle. (This is the third atypical quality: there is seldom anything so plebeian as a running gun battle in a Gothic novel.) Devon is sent to a bat-infested cave to wait for Drake's arrival. When he shows up, and they then leave the cave together, Devon is horrified to see that Casa del Cielo is on fire: "She stared at the pillar of flames leaping unchecked to the sky. Their honeymoon house. A leaping hatred rose up in her against the men who would do such a thing. Mafia monsters!"

They make their escape on horseback and are soon in Mexico City, safe in Siggy's apartment. A number of other exciting things happen to Devon in the Mexican capital—she goes shopping for new clothes, for one—and matters escalate until the truth about Drake and the Mafia comes out.

It seems that Drake met his first wife, Carla, on Capri and married her in Naples, not knowing that she was the daughter of a Mafia chieftain named Lantern Jaw Jake Barberetti. The Mafia Chieftain did not take kindly to his daughter marrying somebody named Drake Janeway, so he kidnapped his daughter and ordered Drake worked over by a couple of his—Lantern Jaw Jake's—goons.

But Carla and Drake got back together anyway, after Lantern Jaw discovered that Drake wasn't the first to deflower his precious little girl, and they did some traveling around Europe together with a pair of Mafia bodyguards. Carla was very jealous and believed Drake had been seeing other women on the sly. (Devon reflects that jealousy is a consuming passion: "There'd been a woman back in Applewood who was so jealous, she stabbed her husband with a paring knife when he answered the phone—and it had turned out to be a wrong number.") A few of Drake's friends began having fatal accidents, which he attributed to Carla and her bodyguards, and so he fell out of love with her and decided to take the first plane home.

En route in New York, he learned that Lantern Jaw Jake, indicted by the Feds, had fled to Sicily and been shot to death by somebody who didn't want him to talk. Meanwhile, a woman named Ingrid, the wife of one of Drake's friends who had died in a fatal accident engineered by Carla, showed up at Kennedy Airport and told Drake she was going to kill Carla. Drake tried to talk Ingrid out of it, but she got away from him by shouting, "Oh, no, there's one of their goons now!" and then, when he turned to look, knocking him down the escalator with her suitcase.

It then developed that Ingrid murdered Carla in spite of her Mafia bodyguards, which made Lantern Jaw's right-hand man, Virelli, furious because Virelli was in love with Carla. Drake and Virelli had a terrific fight in Lantern Jaw's house in Cleveland (Drake had gone there to look for Ingrid because he knew the goons would have her there "burning designs on her stomach with cigarettes"). They knocked each other out, and when Drake regained consciousness, Virelli was gone. Accidentally—he was still groggy from the fight—Drake knocked over a bookcase, which in falling slid back part of the carpet, and underneath he discovered "this little hook-like thing in the floor." Knowing Lantern Jaw must have had a good reason for having a hook-like thing in the floor under the carpet, Drake tugged at it and was amazed to see a section of paneling slide back. Inside was a hidey-hole that contained four suitcases full of run-out money. Drake figured that since Carla and Lantern Jaw were both dead, he was the logical heir to all that loot. So he took it and later put it into secret-numbered Swiss bank accounts and a few well placed safe-deposit boxes.

And *that* was why the Mafia was after him.

Devon doesn't know what to say. But Drake is her man and she's determined to stick by him, even if he is a thief and an accessory to murder and has half the world's goons chasing after him. And there *is* all that money, of course, not that she cares very much about money. (This is the fourth atypical quality: the hero's wealth is not only ill gotten but is subsequently embraced by the heroine, which is something that is *never* supposed to happen in a Gothic.)

The novel's climax is very exciting. In a surprise twist, it is revealed that Carla isn't dead after all ("Carla! Not dead, but alive! Alive and well and living in Acapulco!"). It was Ingrid who was killed in Cleveland, which means that the postcard Drake received from Stockholm, supposedly signed by Ingrid, was a phony sent by the Mafia. So it was not only Virelli and the rest of the mob that were after Drake, it was Carla, too—because she wanted to take revenge on him for running out on her and for marrying another woman after she (Carla) was alleged to be dead.

The way Carla decides to kill both Devon and Drake is to have them jump off the terrace of a cliffside mansion into the roiling waters of Acapulco Bay below. And they do jump, just like the famed cliff divers at La Quebrada. But they aren't killed, of course; they survive the fall. Then they are almost sucked under by a riptide. They survive that, too. Then they hear a sudden roar, and a motor launch with Virelli at the wheel looms up in front of them. Also appearing, moments later, is a schooner belonging to Carla.

Devon and Drake are once again taken captive, this time aboard the schooner. But then there is another surprise: it is revealed that Virelli, in spite of his love for Carla, has been trying to take over control of the Mafia family that was rightfully hers after the death of Lantern Jaw Jake. Furious, Carla turns her gun on Virelli.

> "No, Carla Maria! No, cara mia!" Instinctively Virelli brought up his own gun to shield himself. But too late. The gun in Carla's hand discharged twice, and Virelli, a shocked look on his face, suddenly doubled up, his fingers spasmodically clutching the trigger, causing his own heavy automatic to fire, and fire again, directly into that slender red-garbed figure who swayed like a reed caught in a strong wind and crumpled to the floor before he did.

With both Carla and Virelli dead, Devon and Drake slip out through a porthole and jump into the bay again. But when they surface, they hear more gunfire and realize that another boat, a cabin cruiser, has arrived on the scene. This one is populated by good old Siggy, "who helped them aboard with one hand, his other cradling a submachine gun which raked the deck of the black-sailed motor schooner, keeping all heads down."

Siggy is a pretty cool customer, all right. In short order, he fires several flares at the schooner, and soon the whole boat is aflame. There are cries of pain and horror from the Mafia goons still trapped aboard, but Siggy is unmoved.

> "Men hate to die," observed Siggy. "Even those who enjoy killing." He pelted several more flares at the schooner, which was now a mass of flames. "And

the virtue of phosphorous," he added as someone with his shirt on fire plummeted into the water, "is that it burns quite nicely under water."

(This is the fifth atypical quality: not only are *two* running gun battles unheard of in Gothics, but so is such coldbloodedness on the part of a supposedly sympathetic character. Even Devon tacitly condones it.)

The novel ends with Devon and Drake on their way to Argentina, where they will live off his stolen Mafia money. Devon is aware that "she might have to renew her wedding vows in many countries under a variety of aliases," but that's aces with her. "As long as Drake was hers, her world would sing. . . ."

This is the sixth, final, and most amazing atypical quality of all—the one thing, more than any other, which makes *Bride of Terror* the tour de force it is.

Devon does not get Casa del Cielo, or any other *casa*.

The heroine does *not* get a house!

11. "Don't Tell Me You've Got a Heater in Your Girdle, Madam!"

> Do you believe that those who live violently rarely die in bed? Is it true that he who takes the sword ends with it?
>
> You've never given it much thought? I didn't, either, until the day Fate hung a delayed fuse on me and blasted my little world into a million pieces.
>
> —William L. Rohde,
> *Help Wanted—for Murder*

> Twice I heard the swish of that sap and one of those times it cracked my shoulder. The arm appended thereto, as they say in court, became as useless as a sarong in Siberia. . . . A purple comet with a fiery, lashing tail zoomed around the periphery of my skull and I seemed to fall from a great height . . . a floating downward into a tar pit that had been excavated to a depth just short of Hell itself.
>
> —Chester Warwick,
> *My Pal, the Killer*

The paperback original was born in the United States, along with a lot of other "illegitimate" infants, during the Second

World War. It only achieved legitimacy several years later, while in its teens, after a prosperous but much-maligned childhood that may or may not have left it permanently traumatized. And it was in its twenties before it threw off the onus of "second-class citizen." But by then it had already taken heinous revenge by fathering a couple of little bastards of its own, not the least of which were the soft-core and hard-core sex paperbacks of the sixties and seventies.

Until 1944, all book-length fiction first appeared between hard covers or as serials in magazines. (Dime novels, which flourished in the 1800s and in the early years of this century, were never books so much as pulp magazines in book form.) A large number of the more successful hard-back mysteries, Westerns, and general novels from 1920 onward were gobbled up by the budding paperback industry during the war. But none of these soft-cover publishers seemed willing to gamble on originals. It took an enterprising—and ultimately failed—New York City outfit called Green Publishing Company to break the ice.

The first of Green's line of originals, Vulcan Books, began in 1944; the second, Five-Star Mystery, commenced in 1945. A total of twenty novels was published under these two imprints before the company's demise in 1946. Each was approximately 45,000 words in length, of digest size, written by an unknown or, in the case of Kendall Foster Crossen (who later wrote the Milo March novels under his pseudonym of M. E. Chaber), on assignment, and usually of dubious merit.

Outstanding among them, from an alternative point of view, is *You'll Die Laughing,* an "impossible crime" tale by Bruce Elliott, amateur magician, free-lance writer, and men's magazine editor. Picture, if you will, a weekend house party in the mansion of a wealthy individual who likes to play practical jokes on his guests—a place called the House of Jokes. One night the guests hear a clap of thunder, then a gunshot from inside the host's bedroom, one of three adjoining bedrooms on the second floor; when they investigate, they find the room empty of habitation, the bed gone, the rug rolled against one wall, and the chairs smashed. A few moments later, they hear a noise in the second of the three rooms, and one of the guests comes out holding his head and complaining that he has been drugged. And a few moments after that, in the third room, they find the body of the host, Jesse Grimsby, shot to death. How did the body get from the first room to the third? How did the murderer disappear, and where did he go?

The answers, which are doped out by Lieutenant Brissk of the New York Homicide Squad, are based on the principle of a magician's three-compartment trick box. The box contains only two compartments, not three, which can be slid back and forth within the box's frame, thereby forming a third compartment at either end. If the two movable compartments are pushed all the way over to the left, you have the third compartment on the right; if the movable compartments are pushed all the way over to the right, the third compartment is on the left.

Now you can determine how the murder was done. The killer committed his crime in one of the movable rooms, shifted himself and the body by means of a sliding mechanism, and thus made Grimsby's "bedroom" seem empty. The chairs were broken and the rug rolled up for the following reason: "The outer box, or the house, as in our problem upstairs, had to be a trifle bigger. That leaves a space between the real wall of the house and the wall of the inner sliding rooms. In that space, the killer stuffed as much of the furniture as was possible! That's why the chairs had to be smashed! When the inner rooms were moved, the carpet and chairs fell out of their hiding place and onto the floor. You see, the outer wall of the inner room is at this moment the wall between the first and second rooms!"

As to the *raison d'être* for the sliding rooms, the device exists in the house because of Jesse Grimsby's penchant for practical jokes; at one time, he liked to shuttle his guests back and forth in the night, in order to disorient them. None of the current guests knew about this, we're told, except for the murderer—this in spite of the fact that a couple of the current guests are relatives of the deceased jokester. And as for the clap of thunder, it wasn't thunder at all; it was the noise of "the two inner rooms sliding across the real floor to its new and seemingly impossible position!"

One wonders what John Dickson Carr would have made of all this.

Elliott's character motivation is in the same league with his plotting. So is his dialogue.

> She said slowly, working it out as she spoke, "Then you were right and my nymphomania is psychical and not physiological as I thought. . . . I'm a fool.

I've been riding the whirlwind and I've reaped—
nothing. But now—the compulsion is gone. It's been
seventy hours since I've drugged myself and I'm still
sane. My mind hasn't cracked as I always thought it
would. Bread pills! Bread pills! And they did the
work just as well, because I believed they were my
nirvana. If belief can do that, belief can also mean the
end of my bondage."

Poor distribution, as well as disinterest on the part of the
reading public, put an end to Green Publishing's ambitions. But
other publishers were soon ready to take up the gamble of doing
originals in the postwar boom. The most successful, begun in
1949, was Gold Medal Books (Fawcett Publications), which
claimed dozens of million-seller titles during the ensuing
decade. Others had varying degrees of success; they included
Pyramid, Lion, Handi-Books (which had been doing reprints
since 1942), Croydon, Falcon Books, and Uni-Books (the publisher of, among other items, a science-fictional mystery by
David V. Reed called *The Thing That Made Love*). Among the
short-lived shoestring operations was an outfit known as Far-
rell Publishing Company, the perpetrator of three originals in
1951 under the "Suspense Novel" imprint. (They also published
a moribund jack-of-all-fiction magazine, *Suspense*, "inspired"
by the radio and TV show of the same title, which lasted five
issues in 1951 and 1952.)

The last of the Suspense Novels is *Naked Villainy*, by Carl G.
Hodges, and is worthy of consideration here for two reasons.
One is that it is of minor historical interest: *Naked Villainy* is
the first novel to use real members of the Mystery Writers of
America organization as characters, predating Brett Halliday's
She Woke to Darkness by three years and Edward D. Hoch's
The Shattered Raven by eighteen. One of the book's fictitious
characters is a writer of pulp whodunits, a fact that leads the
narrator, police lieutenant Wick Davis, to a meeting of the Chicago chapter of MWA. Among the more recognizable names
mentioned—recognizable, that is, to anyone who reads and col-
lects old paperback originals—are Milton K. Ozaki, W. T. Bran-
non, and Paul Fairman. (Hodges, himself a writer of pulp whodunits, was also a member of the Chicago chapter in the early
fifties.)

The second reason *Naked Villainy* is worthy of mention is the presence of such dazzling passages as:

> A fuzzy voice I'd recognize in three feet of water drifted up to me. "Lieutenant, this is Tuffy. I got a hot one for you on the radio. . . . Some dame. Somebody cracked her skull with a thundermug."
> "What?"
> "That's what I said. A thundermug. One of them things they have under the bed where there ain't no bathroom. One of them crocks with handles on both sides."
> "What will they think of next!"

> It was then I saw coagulated blood on the left temple and clotted matter that had seeped from the bullet hole into the coverlet.
> I knew the man was dead.

> Hope flared in her dark eyes as she grabbed the rope I had tossed to her drowning brain.

> Then I felt damp fresh air hit the back of my neck and I knew somebody had opened the door. Before I could see who it was, somebody stuck a red-hot poker in my ear and all my brains ran out of the hole. My bones turned into macaroni and I sank down into a gooey mass of tomato sauce that looked like blood. Then somebody began rubbing the end of my nose with sandpaper and there was a big balloon of pain tied to my ear.

The one unforgettable exchange in the book is when Wick trades some banter with a frowzy blond B-girl in a bar. In front of the blond are five empty martini glasses, each with an olive in it, and in her eyes, as the song says, is that old come-hither stare.

> I looked back at the glasses. "Five will make you dizzy."
> She stared at me. Then her red mouth gashed open

and she said, "The price is right, but my name is Daisy."

Of all the publishers doing originals in the early fifties, the one with the most impressive list of alternatives would have to be Ace and its line of Double Novels. These glorious postpulp pulp mysteries (and Westerns and science fiction) came two to a package, back to back and bound so that the half you weren't reading was upside down: "turn this book over for a second complete novel." Carl G. Hodges was one of their writers; so were such stalwarts as Michael Avallone, Frank Diamond, Chester Warwick, Russ Winterbotham ("J. Harvey Bond"), Mel Colton, Bob McKnight, Louis Trimble, and James Hadley Chase.

But Ace's single greatest achievement was the publication in 1953 of a novel entitled *Decoy*, by a writer—actually, a collaborative team of two writers—known as Michael Morgan. To read one page of this fascinating work is to marvel at the talents of its creators, C. E. "Teet" Carle and Dean M. Dorn. For they were truly blessed with genius.

According to the biographical sketch on the jacket of *Nine More Lives* (Random House, 1947), the only other full-length mystery novel by Michael Morgan, Teet and Dean were a pair of Hollywood movie flacks who began collaborating on pulp stories after the war. (At least two Michael Morgan novelettes were published in *Dime Detective* and one in *Mammoth Detective*; they, like *Nine More Lives*, are almost but not quite as bad as *Decoy*.) Teet did the writing and Dean served as a leg man (?) and gimmick creator. Dean's gimmicks are pretty wonderful, but Teet's writing is what lifts *Decoy* below the ranks of all the others. The man was a poet laureate of the absurd.

The plot of *Decoy* is both complicated and farcical and does not lend itself well to simple summary. It has to do with an unofficial Lonely-Hearts Club/gigolo/blackmail racket in Hollywood operated by a villainess called the Duchess; but another gang from the East Coast, led by a mysterious "Mr. Upstairs" who goes by the name of King Lazarr, is trying to muscle in on her crowd. In the middle of this mob warfare is one Bill Ryan, hero and narrator (of *Nine More Lives* and the Morgan pulp stories, too), who is a Hollywood stuntman. He is also a dumb cluck, by his own testimony on at least a dozen occasions throughout the book.

Also involved are several hard-boiled types colorfully named Joe Salka, Belmont Spur, Franklin Carter, Geoffrey Dare, Russell Orth, and Mr. Yegg and Mr. Thug. Plus several soft-boiled and sexy ladies called Linda Douglas, Sally Willow, Ina Andrews, and Judith Monroe.

There is quite a bit of exciting action, most of it choreographed by Dean so Bill Ryan can use his stuntman's wiles to escape the jaws of death—once by doing a neat one-and-a-half gainer out a fourth-floor hotel window into a swimming pool full of guests (and, lucky for him, full of water too). There are quite a few interesting murders as well, including one in which a minor baddie is impaled on the spine of a giant, and *very* well-endowed, cactus.

To give you an idea of the complexity of the plot, here is a passage of dialogue spoken to Bill Ryan, operating under the alias of Reynolds at the time, by the Duchess, who sounds more like Duke Wayne, or perhaps Edward G. Robinson in *Key Largo*:

> "I didn't find out your name just today, Reynolds. I knew it last Friday when you busted into the picture, claimin' you was a friend of Russell Orth's, wantin' a setup with the Andrews dame. I could of cooked your act that day. I said let you have plenty of rope. I wondered how come you said you was a friend of a guy who was already croaked. Russ was one of my pets, brother. I know about your playin' games through the Traxton halls so's you could make contact in the men's room with Salka and Spur. Right after that you tied onto Frank's tail an' followed him outside the hotel. You never came back, an' early this ayem, another of my best boys was found on the lawn— dead as a poop. Today you show up here with that dreamy-eyed blond, Judith Monroe, actin' like you was a real gee-gee. That give you an idea of what I know?"

As may be seen from the above, Teet had a positive passion for euphemism, hyperbole, and the innovative simile, all of which combine to create brilliant deadpan farce. None of the commonplace for Teet, not even where basic English is concerned. Slang and pseudoslang were among his most effective tools.

Men aren't men in *Decoy* ; they're chaps, ginks, bozos, cook-
ies, Joes, characters, and didos. Women aren't women; they're
dames, babes, skirts, tamales, dolls, floozies, chippies, and trol-
lops. Crooks aren't crooks; they're yeggs, thugs, mugs, lugs,
lunks, punks, hulks, scums, gigs, palookas, plug-uglies, rats,
buzzards, birds, baboons, monkeys, apes, and apemen. Guns
aren't guns; they're rods, heaters, six-shooters (or six-shoters),
cannons, and gats. People don't walk or run; they ankle, loll,
amble, stretch strides, or get on the speed track. Nor do they
speak much; they burp, wheeze, dribble, chirp, crackle, croak,
crisp, hulk, syrup, gruff, grunt, and gurgle.

Now then, the Pronzini bozo burped, let's get on the speed
track and open the novel to page 1.

And we find that Teet wastes no time letting the reader know
he is a writer to be reckoned with. Witness the very first sentence:

> The way she looked at me sent a craving through
> my body for a tall cold drink.

Ah. And a few sentences later:

> Her face was rounded with beauty and had two
> features which demanded complete attention. Of
> these, her eyes were most absorbing; they were two
> wide pools of darkness which exuded warmth. Then
> her lips; they rose from her face with the vivid fresh-
> ness of lovely, sparkling champagne bubbles.

One of Teet's strong points, as the foregoing demonstrates, is
description—particularly of babes. Here are a few more examples (including the single greatest sentence ever to spring from
Teet's nimble brain).

> When she moved, [her] muscles stood up individu-
> ally and made a speech. Her hair was still tousled and
> the disarray snapped at my eager fingertips.

> She wore low-heeled Oxfords, the kind made for
> walking, and the backs of firm-swelling calves of her
> legs told me she might be a chorus girl who'd turned
> somebody's moll.

* * *

Her graceful legs, swelling gradually upward to the bottom of her white swim suit, were as appealing as they'd been, sheathed in sheer hose, straddling the window of Carter's bedroom the night before.

Just as I was wondering how I could pull Ina out of this itchy situation, a Mountie came riding to our rescue. It was a female Mountie, and she was a flaming torch on top of a lithe body which swooped down on us like a kootch dancer in a waterfront dive.

Ina syruped, "Hello, Sally." The redhead laid an eye on me and started rubbing it over my bulk as though she was sizing up a rib-roast.

I sat beside her in the Traxton's Parisian Room and let the edges of my eyes siphon up the pleasure of her tall, slender figure in a blue evening gown which made a low-bridged criss-cross right above where the meat on a chicken is the whitest.

Teet's greatest sentence, of course, is the last one quoted. It may even be the single greatest bad line in the history of crime fiction. Certainly none quoted elsewhere in these pages is more ingenious, lyrical, delightful, and absurd.

Ankling right along, we discover that Teet was also adept at describing chaps, especially cop chaps:

The cops weren't long in arriving. They descended on the corridor like a blustering winter wind off the Nebraska plains. The character who apexed their flying wedge was a hunk of tough meat.

And that other of his strong points include dialogue.

"Suck back that crack, copper. That kid's strictly top of the heap, and I knew it the minute I laid eyes on her shaking down Carter's room. . . ."

"Don't tell me you carry a heater in your girdle, madam!"

* * *

And compelling introspection.

> I wanted to see the murderer of that beautiful crea-
> ture seated in the gas chamber. I wanted it so bad my
> saliva glands throbbed.

And emotional reaction.

> "What are you afraid of, Linda?"
> "Afraid?" She sucked the word clear down to her
> short ribs.

And action sequences.

> The blast of the iron fist caught me high on the
> jaw, and my guardian angel must have been astride
> my shoulder, because, surprisingly, my jaw bone
> didn't crack. I went streaking out through the dark-
> ness on the wings of pain. A tidal wave rolled up
> from Wilshire, a hundred yards away, and engulfed
> me. My jaw bounced off the back of my skull and I
> wallowed in the softness of a cloud. I groped around
> for my brain and after a couple of years it came back
> from San Francisco and said "Get up!"

And cryptic messages and reactions thereto.

> Ryan:
> The giant cactus at nine sharp. Come up path from
> Inn, whistling Yankee Doodle. Keep hands on top of
> head. Remember, you'd better be on the level.
> > Spur
> It was a little melodramatic, but that was fine with
> me. . . .

And (this is where Teet really shines) the masterful one-liner.

> Silence settled like a hen squatting on her eggs.

> He laughed once in the direction of his right ear.

> My stomach dropped out of my body.

*   *   *

My head flew off and hit the ceiling.

Her cheeks had a case of the flushes.

His eyes popped out of his pink-cake face and danced in the air.

Below his hat were enough eyebrows to stuff a pillow.

Lips seemed to be Teet's specialty, though.

His lip did a nip-up at the left end.

He puffed out his lips and they made a blooping sound.

Her lips wore smugness like a slipper.

There was interest licking his lips.

His lower lip hauled in its droop.

Unfortunately, some of Teet's one-liners don't quite make it. Following are a few examples of what might be termed "Huh?" sentences.

He ran his eyes over my silence.

My burn was going to boil soon.

She laid a hand on my arm and I knew I really had her in the palm of my hand because her face was contorted.

Judith just didn't look like a hot urge having its fling.

He put his vocalizing on arrested motion.

A choking pig couldn't have done better and I patted my inspiration on the head for the effect it had.

She went up in a puff of smoke, and a startling truth dribbled out of her explosion.

Reality cut me down six notches.

The fire from my ears, my eyes, and my throat congregated into a lump and shoved off the top of my head.

The realization of what all this meant exploded inside my head and shot me from the mouth of a cannon.

As evidenced by the foregoing, Bill Ryan (and some of the other didos and dolls) has a difficult time keeping himself together, what with his head flying off, his stomach dropping out, his brain going off to San Francisco for a couple of years, and his whole self being shot out of a cannon. But he manages somehow and is more or less whole when the moment of the exciting final chase arrives.

And it *is* exciting, make no mistake about that. In fact, it starts out as a literal cliff-hanger. By using his stuntman's wiles, Ryan escapes from a car sent hurtling over a precipice by Mr. Yegg, after which he hangs by his fingertips for a short while (about half a page) before the old S. W. come through again and he's able to scramble to safety.

But that's not all; not by any means. Next we have a car chase, which commences when Ryan commandeers a police car (with the police still in it). He's driving at 100 mph, right on the tails of the apemen, when they throw out a "spare wheel" directly into his path, causing a spin-out and allowing the palookas to escape. Ah, but not for long. Ryan and the coppers are soon back on the road and bearing down on a private airstrip where a small plane is about to take off.

Ryan notes the plane as soon as he wheels the police go-buggy inside the airstrip grounds—and notes, too, through the open cabin door, that it not only contains Mr. Upstairs, the mysterious King Lazarr, but Ryan's own lady love, Judith Monroe. Then the door closes and the plane begins to taxi down the runway. How can Ryan stop it in time?

In a flash of inspiration, he realizes the answer: *He'll have to use his Stuntman's Wiles!*

So he rockets the rattle (police car, that is) onto the runway, opens the driver's door, leaps out onto the tail of the plane, grabs the rudder, and rides the tail into the ground "like a cowboy bulldozing [*sic*] a steer."

Bravo, Dean!

Bravo, Teet!

Bravo, *Decoy!*

Between 1955 and 1970, dozens of writers wrote hundreds of private-eye, spy, and other mystery originals for Ace, Monarch, Lion, Zenith, Pyramid, Avon, Gold Medal, Popular Library, and Dell. But none of them turned out more shlock than a West Coast wordsmith named Lynton Wright Brent. If Brent's output had been confined to the mystery field, he would have to be considered one of its alternative giants; unfortunately, most of his fiction was in the Western, soft-core porn, and not-so-soft-core porn categories. (Another of his talents was a positive genius for titles. One Brent novel, a Western/porn hybrid published in 1965, carries the magnificent title of *Lust Gallops into the Desert.* Others of note include *Passionate Peril at Fort Tomahawk, The Sex Demon of Jangal,* and *Lavender Love Rumble.*)

Brent did write a trio of mysteries in 1969 for Powell Books, an ambitious but sadly inept southern California publishing concern that went out of business in 1970. One is called *Death of a Detective* and features the adventures of "that great news-scooper, Sam 'Stark-Mad' Stark" who gained his nickname by "poking his nose into the danger zone!" The danger zone he pokes it into here is a lot of interesting twaddle about a just-released ex-con who has vowed to kill Stark for sending him to the slammer, assorted good and bad cops, assorted good and bad crooks with sobriquets like Nutsie and Scrapsy, a girl named Mala (" 'H'm—Mala! Sounds like an Eskimo's daughter.' "), and Stark's enamorata, a fiesty little number called Trixie.

"What are you thinking about?" she asked bluntly.

"Us."

"Oh my, brother Stark! So—so soon?"

"I've got a trigger heart," he drawled. "It reacts at the drop of a hat."

* * *

Stark straightened up, looking as though he had just won a prize. "So! Here we have Hammond's girl friend! Now, that's a feature story!"

"Leave it lay, you beast!" Trixie growled. "If you print anything about my college roommate I'll—I'll find a way to castrate you. From your job, I mean."

"Wish I was a farmer . . . with nothing to fret about but horses, chickens, and cows."

Sam Stark grinned and grunted, simultaneously. Then he replied, "You'd be bored stiff. After one week of that kind of life you'd be . . . wishing to hell you were back in the big city where the action is."

"Really? You think it would be that bad?"

"Worse. Who but a farmer wants to listen to a cow announcing with a low and moanful moo that it's time to milk her?"

The standout among Brent's Powell mysteries, though, is *One Man's Crime*, which stars Justin Strong, an ex-matinee idol and crooner who has been reduced to doing sports promotion for the roller derby because of a scandal involving murder. As he reflects on page 2:

Ever since the newspapers had blasted his alleged drowning of a beautiful movie starlet, he had been as—nothing! *Movie dust!* A human thing consigned to a heap of discarded celebrities, for foolish people jumping to conclusions before his trial had warned movie producers that they would no longer allow their families to attend movies which starred him. It was cheap and cruel, but it was the way of the world. And so at this moment he felt out of place in a world where a man made a place for himself, or became a segment of the mud at the feet of people who counted.

The plot in this one revolves around the roller-derby circuit, some juvenile delinquents, the movie business, and an aspiring actress and all-around "plucky girl" named Macey Love (who at one point fastens a scuba tank between her breasts, floats in a swimming pool, and pretends to be dead in front of a dozen or so people, not one of them with eyesight keen enough to notice the oxygen bubbles from her breathing apparatus). The first time Justin sets eyes on Macey, he's smitten.

> Justin's glance dropped to the gracefully formed cleft which separated breasts made as stout and round as summer melons. Then he appraised the contour of her hips and legs and felt a queerness coursing through his veins—*for this was a woman!*

He knows what to say to her, too, in his charming, suave, ex-matinee-idol-and-crooner fashion. "Jeez, baby," he says. "You're really something!"

Later he sings a song to her, and she gets all excited, and they hurry off under a pier on the beach for several paragraphs of heavy breathing. The result of this is inevitable. Like Justin, Macey is hot-blooded and passionate and knows what she wants. "Oh my beloved darling!" she says softly, excitedly. "Sing to me some more!"

And so he sings to her some more. All through the book, he sings to her and sings to her. Nothing much else happens, but in no other mystery will you find half so many bedtime lullabies.

The emphasis in the paperback original of the seventies seemed to be on graphic violence, at least in the series-character category, as previously discussed. The Executioner, the Death Merchant, Nick Carter—these and carbon copies had the highest sales figures of that decade's criminous soft covers. In the mid seventies, an offshoot that likewise became popular was the occult-detective series. These forebears of today's large-scale occult thrillers were similar to the male-action sagas of Pendleton and Rosenberger in their unstinting devotion to blood and maimed flesh, the only appreciable difference being that the righteous heroes went around slaughtering vampires, werewolves, and members of satanic cults instead of gangsters and paramilitary groups.

One such series was "The Satan Sleuth," authored by the

creator of Ed Noon, Michael Avallone, and featuring the unpleasant exploits of Philip St. George, "a man with a mission . . . on the side of the angels, those sentinels of Reason and Goodness who continually must wage war against Satan and his projects."

In the first of the series, *Fallen Angel* (1974), St. George vows vengeance on all satanists when a Manson-like group of devil worshipers brutally murders his wife. This particular bunch is led by a pair of individuals who call themselves Wolfman (he has a "grotesque hump" between his shoulder blades) and Dracula, who is as "gay as a green goose when the bare asses were down." St. George methodically tracks them down and obliterates them, initiating such immortal lines in the process as " 'Geezis!' Dracula whimpered in a low, girlish voice. *'Let's get the hell out of here!'* "

One paperback publisher of the late seventies embraced the more traditional type of mystery and not incidentally followed in the footsteps of the early Ace Doubles by producing a long and impressive list of clinkers. This was Major Books, another southern California venture that was established in 1975 and that apparently went out of business in 1981. During their first few years, they published dozens of mystery, Western, Gothic, and science-fiction titles, among them the first Western novel of venerable screen cowboy Rory Calhoun, called *The Man from Padera*. It would be unfair to say that all the Major mysteries are of a breed that qualifies them for inclusion in these pages. But not by much.

A representative example is William L. Rivera's *Panic Walks Alone* (1976). This stars one Arthur "Turo" Bironico, Investigative Consultant, who works mainly for insurance companies and who has offices in San Francisco. The case he is called upon to solve concerns the murder of an insurance executive, a psychotic killer, a spate of willing women, plenty of running around (to Mexico and Europe, among other places), and a final confrontation in an "austere Presbyterian church." But the novel's main attraction is neither Bironico nor the plot; it is Rivera's own special brand of prose.

> After a few quiet minutes of window staring, Langly put his things away, donned his coat and exited his office. He had taken two steps into his secretary's

office when he felt a sharp pain just beneath his left shoulder blade. The pain quickly became searing. His breath changed from a smooth flow to quick, stunted gasps. He slowly turned to face his attacker. His assailant gave him a sterile, malevolent gaze. Their riveted eyes seemed to have suspended time and motion.

Langly, sinking rapidly now, expleted: "You!"

[Turo] normally prepared the coffee pot the night before—which was what he did last night, so he would only have to exert a minimum amount of effort until after his first cup had awakened him. Since he used the coffee cannister more than the other two, he usually placed it an inch away from the wall for easier retrieval. As he looked at the three cannisters, he noted that they were all flush against the wall.

His distress increased as alarm bells went off in his head. His lair had been transgressed upon!

It was two in the morning when the killer creeped out of his hiding place.

"Who are you investigating, our former employee, Mr. Oosting?"

The fencing had begun, thought Turo. I'll be coy too. "Yes," he said simply.

The shock of the separation with Sue permeated through Bironico's senses. He wanted to lash out at these snotty women libbers, who poisoned the atmosphere with their hysterical hostility, and just think, Sue bought that crap, he concluded. His angry thoughts roamed all over the deck. He was a casualty in this war of liberation; and Sue was a willing rifleperson. The dumb bitch!

Long live the paperback original!

12. Ante-Bellem Days; or, "My Roscoe Sneezed: *Ka-chee!*"

> A thunderous bellow flashed from Dave Donald-
> son's service .38, full at the prop man's elly-bay.
> Welch gasped like a leaky flue, hugged his punctured
> tripes, and slowly doubled over, fell flat on his smell-
> er. A bullet can give a man a terrific case of indiges-
> tion, frequently ending in a trip to the boneyard.
> —Robert Leslie Bellem,
> "Diamonds of Death"

Good things, as the saying goes, come in small packages. Take
the criminous short story, for instance. In his introduction to
The Best [English] *Detective Stories of the Year 1928,* Father
Ronald Knox said, "The short story must always take an hon-
orable place in detective fiction; it is the medium which has
given us some of the best Holmes literature, and the whole cycle
of Father Brown." Howard Haycraft, the eminent critic and
author of *Murder for Pleasure: The Life and Times of the Detective Story* (1941), is just one of the many who concur: "The
short story has often been called the perfect and ideal form of
expression for detective fiction. However that may be, it has
surely been the most influential. Think of the authors and
detective characters who have survived from an earlier day to

the present: almost without exception they have flourished in the shorter medium."

All of which, when applied inversely, turns out to be just as true. Wonderful *bad* things come in small packages, too. And some of mystery fiction's finest alternatives may be found in the short story.

When Edgar Allan Poe wrote the first detective stories in the 1840s, he could not possibly have envisioned the directions his new form would take in future generations. If he had known what Doyle, Chesterton, and others of similar talents would create, he might have approved. If he had known, on the other hand, that there lurked a vast horde of lurid-covered pulp magazines somewhere in the mists of time ahead, and that among those who would write for them was the awesome figure of Robert Leslie Bellem, he might have burned the manuscripts of "Murders in the Rue Morgue," "The Gold Bug," "The Mystery of Marie Rogêt," and "The Purloined Letter," and run screaming into the streets. Poe was not noted for his sense of humor, especially when it came to literary matters.

Those of us in the contemporary world who have read Bellem's work might also be inclined to run screaming into the streets—but with laughter, not anguish. Anyone whose sense of humor leans toward the ribald, the outrageous, the utterly absurd is liable to find himself convulsed by the antics and colloquialisms of Dan Turner, Bellem's immortal "private skulk." The list of Bellem admirers is long and distinguished and includes humorist S. J. Perelman, who, in an essay called "Somewhere a Roscoe . . ." called Turner "the apotheosis of all private detectives," and said he was "out of Ma Barker by Dashiell Hammett's Sam Spade." Heady praise, indeed.

For those readers not acquainted with the background of Robert Leslie, a short biographical sketch:

He was born in 1902, began writing for the pulps in the mid-1920s, and was soon producing over a million words a year for such magazines as *Spicy Detective, Spicy Mystery, Popular Detective,* and *Private Detective.* In 1942, he helped launch his own magazine, *Dan Turner, Hollywood Detective* (later *Hollywood Detective*), which featured at least one and sometimes several Turner capers and for which Bellem customarily wrote the entire contents under a variety of pseudonyms. In less than three decades, until the collapse of the pulp market in the early fifties, Bellem penned the staggering total of three thousand pulp stories. He also managed to find time for two novels under his own name, *Blue Murder* (1938) and *The Window of the Sleeping Nude* (1950); two collaborations with Cleve F. Adams, *The Vice-Czar Murders* (1941), as by Franklin Charles, and *No Wings on a Cop* (1950), as by Adams; and a ghosted mystery, *Half-Past Mortem* (1947), as by John A. Saxon. In the fifties and early sixties, he concentrated on teleplays and was a regular contributor to such popular TV shows as *The Lone Ranger, Superman, Perry Mason, 77 Sunset Strip,* and *The FBI.* He died in Los Angeles in 1968.

Dan Turner's first public appearance was in the June 1934 issue of *Spicy Detective,* one of a series of "Spicy" titles from a Delaware (of all places) outfit that called itself, ironically enough, Culture Publications, Inc. The Spicys featured fast action and as much sexual titilation as the law would allow in the 1930s. Mandatory in every story was mention of bare breasts, lithe hips, and alabaster thighs and the appearance of at least one hot-blooded female character. Those issues from 1934 to 1936 also contained mild descriptions of foreplay to intercourse, with the hero clasping a nude or seminude female to him and either fondling or drooling on her bosom; such "hot" scenes would then terminate in the ever-popular ellipses. Another feature of the Spicys was provocative illustrations of those same nude or seminude women, sometimes in the throes of ecstasy but more often being shot, stabbed, or tortured in a multitude of fiendish ways.

"Public decency" organizations, outraged over such moral turpitude, waged an all-out battle against the Spicys that eventually proved victorious. Pressured by these groups, the US Postal Service first required Culture Publications to tone down the sexual content of their magazines, in order to avoid a revocation of their second-class mailing privileges, and then, when this failed to satisfy the guardians of American morals, forced Culture to abolish the entire Spicy line not long after America's entry into World War II. Culture Publications, however, was nothing if not resourceful; by adopting a new series title, "Speed," and abandoning all sexual content beyond mild innuendo, they were able to reobtain second-class mailing privileges and to perpetuate their detective, Western, and adventure books until the early fifties.

Dan Turner was easily the most popular Spicy/Speed series

character, as evidenced by the success of his own magazine and the fact that he and *Hollywood Detective* were the last of Culture's stable to become extinct. Turner's appeal to readers seems to have been predicated on two factors: the wildly improbable but at the same time comfortably predictable plots Bellem concocted; and Bellem's breezy, sexy, colloquial style. Many of the Dan Turner stories deal with some aspect of Hollywood filmmaking and are populated with fast women, Bogart-style tough guys, and plenty of false glitter. (Bellem's evocation of the Hollywood milieu of the period lacks the true color and insights of the work of Raymond Chandler, Steve Fisher, and other writers who made southern California their stock-in-trade.) Corpses turn up in great quantities, most of them leaking "arterial ketchup"; there are gun battles, fistfights, and car chases galore. Bellem's prose, which may or may not have been intentionally humorous, is unlike that of any other writer in or out of the pulps, past or present. As Perelman indicated in his essay, the Bellem style can't be described; it has to be experienced.

To begin with, here is Dan Turner on various Spicy ladies:

> I tackled her, tripped her. She went down. I mashed her with my weight. She squirmed, moaned feebly. Then she pulled an unexpected stunt. She wrapped her arms around my neck; glued her crimson kisser to my lips. She fed me an osculation that sent seven thousand volts of electricity past my tonsils. ("Design for Dying")

> Of all the tamales who've come up from south of the Rio Grande, Carmen was tops in talent, looks and that quality they call yoomph. ("Coffin Frame")

> This yellow-haired wren was maybe a couple of years younger than the one with the russet coiffure, but she was just as pretty. Her plump figure was something to knock your optic out, particularly since she was garnished in a gossamer negligee that didn't leave much to the imagination. From my spot on the floor I could pipe her shapely shafts, the lilting symmetry of her thighs under the diaphanous chiffon that draped them.
> Farther up, her attributes were equally thrilling.

> Her hips had just the proper amount of lyric flare and
> her breasts reminded me of ten nights in a Turkish
> harem. But when I finally glued the glimpse on her
> piquant pan, all I saw was a cargo of misery and woe.
> There were tears brimming on her azure peepers, and
> tremulous grief twisted her kisser. ("Forgery's
> Foil")

The feminine "attribute" in which Bellem and Dan Turner
seemed most interested was the bosom.

> She swayed toward me, a sob swelling her perky
> pretty-pretties. ("Killer's Harvest")

> And the curves above were lush white melons nes-
> tling in mesh cups of a formfitting bandeau. ("Forge-
> ry's Foil")

> It [a red satin dress] clung to her slender curves
> like sprayed varnish; emphasized the lilt of her hips
> and the perky arrogance of her firm little tiddly-
> winks. ("Killer's Keepsake")

> I sneaked a downward gander at the low-slashed
> decolletage of her red evening gown where it dipped
> into the tempting valley between her creamy bon-
> bons. ("Killer's Harvest")

> Her breastworks were firm and full and erect;
> [they] possessed a voluptuous maturity that left me
> gasping like a gaffed shark. ("Bullet from No-
> where")

> The swim suit's brassiere top had cupped the nif-
> tiest set of plumply domed whatchacallems this side
> of a castaway's dream. ("Killer's Keepsake")

One may infer from all this that Turner, if not Bellem, was a
card-carrying male chauvinist. He also had a tendency toward
sadism in that he was forever smacking "frills" and "janes"
around and on occasion shooting them if he felt they deserved

it. And he was more or less inadvertently responsible for the deaths of hundreds of others: no sooner would he finish making love to this or that beauteous frill than she would turn up quite messily dead.

The typical Turner scenario begins with Dan encountering a perky set of tiddly-winks, in or out of distress, with or without a rod in evidence. He then seduces or almost seduces her, after which somebody either takes a shot at him or the woman and/ or knocks him over the head. Of course, "takes a shot at him" and "knocks him over the head" are far too pallid descriptive phrases for Bellem and Turner. These actions are described with such color and flare, and recurring frequency, and inventive variation, that they have become the Bellem trademark.

First, the roscoe:

> And then, from the doorway, a gun barked: *"Chow-chow!"* and I went drifting to dreamland. ("Design for Dying")

> The rod sneezed: *Chow! Ka-Chow!* and pushed two pills through Reggie's left thigh. ("Murder Has Four Letters")

> Against a backdrop of darkness the heater sneezed: *Ka-Chowp! Chowp! Chowp!* and sent three sparking ribbons of orange flame burning into the pillow. ("Come Die for Me")

> From the window behind her, a roscoe poked under the drawn blind. It went: *"Blooey—Blooey—Blooey!"* ("Murder on the Sound Stage")

> From the window that opened onto the roof-top sun deck a roscoe sneezed: *Ka-Chow! Chowpf!* and a red-hot hornet creased its stinger across my dome; bashed me to dreamland. ("Lake of the Left-Hand Moon")

> From the front doorway of the wigwam a roscoe stuttered: *Ka-chow! Chow! Chow!* and a red-hot slug maced me across the back of the cranium, knocked

me into the middle of nowhere. ("Killer's Keepsake")

"Ker-choob!" a cannon sneezed through the wood-
work, sent a spurt of flame and lead and wooden
splinters stabbing at the spot where I would normally have been standing. ("Killer's Keepsake")

Then Dave Donaldson's service cannon said: *"Ker-
blam! Ker-blam!"* across my shoulder. ("Death
Dubbed In")

Tension jerked me around; but even as I made the
move a rod barked: *Ka-pow!* from the doorway of the
apartment stash and the ozone alongside my left ear
was split by the passage of a pellet. Half an inch
closer and the slug would have nicked a notch out of
my favorite brain. ("Death's Blind Date")

From a bedroom a roscoe said: *"Whr-r-rang!"* and
a lead pill split the ozone past my noggin. ("Dark
Star of Death")

My roscoe sneezed: *Ka-chee!* and flashed a lethal
lump at the slithering snake. ("Focus on Death")

Then we have the blunt instrument or the blunt fist:

"Now," she drew a bead on my tripes. "We'll see if
you handcuff me."
"Ixnay!" I caterwauled. "You can't—"
She raised the roscoe, slapped me on the side of the
noggin. For a wren who didn't look hefty, she packed
a terrific wallop. I staggered, felt my knees turning to
jelly. She maced me another swat that put me down
for the count with bells jangling in my think-tank.
("Gun from Gotham")

The Murphy bozo intercepted me. "Lay off her,
Sherlock. This is none of your affair." Then he fes-
tooned an uppercut smack on my chinstrap. . . . It

rocked my conk so far back I could count the rafters
overhead. They merged into a jumble as my glimmers
went cockeyed. Then Max corked me again.

All my fuses short-circuited and I became useless.
When I woke up, I thought I was drowning. Some
dope had fetched a big red fire-bucket full of water
onto the stage and was engaged in the maniacal pas-
time of dunking my profile like a cruller. I strangled,
choked, sputtered, and snapped to my senses just as I
was going down for the third time. "Hey, what the
gloobsch is the idea?" ("Diamonds of Death")

The typical scenario continues with Turner finding a corpse
of one variety or another. These corpses are not merely dead;
they are invariably deader than (or as defunct as) "a pork
chop," "a stuffed mongoose," "fried oysters," "French fried
potatoes," "George Washington's cherry tree," "year before
last," "silent pictures," "a Confederate dollar," "the Petrified
Forest," "Hitler's conscience," "ten cents worth of canceled postage," "an iced codfish," or "six buckets of fish bait." When the
corpse is one of the beautiful women Turner has seduced, he
(being a sentimentalist) sometimes feels like "tossing his biscuits" or "flinging his pancakes"; but of course he is too tough
to let anything like that happen. Or to shed a tear for the dear
departed. Instead he gets on the telephone to his cop pal, Dave
Donaldson, to report the crime like any good citizen.

When Dave came on the line, I said, "Turner
squalling. There's been a knock-off at Ellen Ban-
croft's wikiup." I gave him the address. "The victim
was a Metromount ham named Joe Dunn, and kindly
flag yourself out here with a meat-wagon as fast as
Whozit will let you."
Donaldson's explosive voice rattled the receiver.
"The hell you yodel! Who cooled the guy?" ("Widow
by Proxy")

"Dan Turner squalling," I yeeped. "Flag your dia-
pers to Sylvia Hempstead's igloo. There's been a
croaking." ("Come Die for Me")
* * *

"Zarah Trenwick just got blasted to hellangone in her tepee at the Gayboy. Drag your underwear over here—and bring a meat-wagon." ("Killer's Harvest")

Sometimes, depending on the case, Turner waits for Donaldson's arrival; on other occasions, he rushes off "hellity-blip" or "hellity-larrup" or "lickety-boop" or "buckety-gallop" on his own, to confront this or that character.

The instant my peepers focused on [the] fantastic wordage I leaped away from the desk as if it had suddenly sprouted a nest of cobras. "You crazy dim-wit!" I yeeped. "Do you realize you've dumped me in the grease up to my dimple?"

"Why, I—wh-what do you mean?"

"I mean these!" I screamed, brandishing the letters ferninst his abashed mush. [sic] ("Murder Has Four Letters")

At some point hereabouts, Turner is certain to be bitten by a hunch in one fashion or another: "A hunch crawled up my slacks and nipped me under the hip pocket," or "A hunch needled me like a hornet on the asterisk," or "An idea spanked me in the chops." If Donaldson is present at the time, the two of them are likely to head straight for the "stash" of the "bump-off artist."

"Hell's hinges and hot buttered popcorn, goose this chariot!" I bleated in his ear. ("Come Die With Me!")

If Turner is alone in his pursuit, he'll wait until arrival at the murderer's "wikiup" before he starts to talk tough.

"A while ago you mentioned my hardboiled rep. You said I'm considered a dangerous hombre to monkey with. Okay, you're right. Now will you come along willingly or do I bunt you over the crumpet till your sneezer leaks buttermilk?" ("Murder Has Four Letters")

* * *

This is where Turner usually reveals the nature of his hunch; that is, how he arrived at the identity of the guilty party. The revelation is always in italics, lest the reader skip right over it to a bare whatchacallem or a sneezing roscoe.

> ". . . It hooked up with something Velma said in my stash when she first gandered the bauble. At the time, I thought she was exclaiming *that's a rock*. Instead her words were the excited start of the phrase *that's-a Rocco's ring!*" ("Killer's Clue")

Either before or after the explanations, the murderer is removed from the scene in one of three ways: more or less docilely by the police or Turner himself; feet first, having pulled a rod and having had his or her tripes punctured by a pill from Dave Donaldson's service .38 or Turner's own gat; or in irons, after having put up a terrific struggle in hand-to-hand combat with Turner.

> My knees turned to boiled noodles and I felt myself sliding into a tailspin. That would never do. I straightened up, reached out and grabbed the beefy beezark. . . . I got my lunchhooks on his rugged mush and shoved. I tried to feel for his eyeballs so I could gouge them.
> I missed and found his mouth instead.
> He bit me. His grinders crunched down on my fingers and the pain crawled all the way up my arm, into my shoulder. Somehow, before he gnawed my flipper off, I yanked it free. . . .
> Be a detective and get trounced every hour. Learn the snooping trade and win a badge, a license and lumps. Scar tissue thrown in for free. ("Come Die for Me!")

There is one last point that should be made about Dan Turner, private skulk. In addition to being a male chauvinist and a literal ladykiller, he is also a cheefully outspoken racist. His adventures are sprinkled with "wops," "spicks," and other ethnic characters. Bellem's favorite appears to have been "chinks," either Chinese or Japanese (neither he nor Turner seemed able to tell the difference). This is how lovable old Dan treated Orientals:

> I drove over to Argyle; parked in front of Fane Trenwick's modest stash. . . . I thumbed the bell. The door opened. A Chink houseboy gave me the slant-eyed focus. "Missa Tlenwick, him sleep. You go way, come tomollow. Too late fo' vlisito'."
> I said: "Nerts to you, Confucius," and gave him a shove on the beezer. ("Killer's Harvest")

When Bellem was not chronicling the capers of Dan Turner, he turned out hundreds of nonseries detective, weird mystery, and adventure stories for the other Culture Publications pulps as well as for Leo Margulies's Thrilling group. These tended not to be half so colloquial in style and somewhat less formularized in plotting. Which is not to say that they were any less melodramatic. Or, during the Spicy years, any less titillating. Sex and sadism reached no loftier pulp heights than in the 1934 to 1938 issues of *Spicy Mystery*, one of the leading "shudder" or "weird menace" magazines that featured both exotic and erotic methods of torture and homicide.

A representative example of Bellem's work for *Spicy Mystery* is a story called "Mesa of Madness," which appeared in February 1937. Set at an isolated archeological dig in the "Damnation Range" of Arizona—a supposedly haunted area known as Red Ghost Mesa, where the shades of ancient Indian medicine men are said to "visit weird death on interlopers"—the story features one John Brent, who comes looking for a missing archeologist named Shafter and who soon finds himself enmeshed with Shafter's beautiful daughter Margo, the naked corpse of an Indian girl, a "shining ghost" (a.k.a. "the phosphorescent specter"), and a fiendish plot to steal a deposit of radium-bearing pitchblende.

After a near sexual encounter with Margo and during a thunderstorm, Brent finds the missing archeologist in a scene that culminates with one of the unforgettable lines of pulpdom—a Bellem masterstroke to rival anything in the Dan Turner *ouevre*.

* * *

Brent realized that he was dealing with a madman, not a ghost, when he watched the way Shafter cuddled that feminine form. He knew his theory had been correct: that George Shafter, instead of dying on the mesa last year, had gone insane and had hidden from the searching party. Ever since then, the archeologist must have wandered the region, bathed in phosphorescent muck-glow and giving rise to weird superstitions about ghosts haunting the plateau. . . .

But it was not this knowledge that sent a great gout of relief surging through Brent's soul. It was something else; it was the realization that Margot was not the girl in the madman's clutch. Not Margot, but the dead Indian woman whose corpse had been spread-eagled on a knoll earlier tonight!

In horrid mockery, Shafter cuddled the body closer. Daubed with glutinous mud, the corpse emitted an eerie glow that matched Shafter's own hellish halo. Revulsion shuddered through John Brent's marrow. He lunged at the wizened maniac.

"Drop that corpse, you fool!"

One other pulp detective worth mentioning is pint-size but tough-minded Cash Wale, the hero of a series of long novelettes by Peter Paige in *Dime Detective* in the late forties. The Wale stories are a mixture of Bellem and Carroll John Daly—hardboiled, violent, slangy, brash, and full of outrageous humor. (In one, Wale is being hounded—as usual—by his nemesis, New York Homicide Inspector Anthony J. Quinn, who wants to question him about a murder. When Wale telephones Quinn to tell his side of things, Quinn orders him to give himself up immediately; otherwise, he says, he'll have every cop in the city take part in the manhunt. "Take it easy," Wale tells him soothingly. "Don't get your bulls in an uproar.") What is unique about the series, though, is that one "massacre" for which Wale and his punch-drunk, ex-pug partner Sailor Duffy are framed is not resolved in a way that proves their innocence; thus they are forced to flee New York City and become fugitives constantly on the run. At least half the stories in the saga are related in the form of "letters" from Wale to the author, Paige, and involve narrow escapes from Quinn and various local police as well as standard "kill circuses." The misadventures of Cash Wale may not have inspired the creation of the popular sixties TV show *The Fugitive*, starring David Janssen, but there *is* a certain similarity.

The most notable Wale caper is an early one, "When a Man Murders" (*Dime Detective*, March 1947), in which he and Sailor Duffy are on the trail of a fortune in missing diamonds and run afoul of such disparate types as Filipino freedom fighters, the denizens of a mental hospital, and a Caspar Gutman-type fat man named Mr. Manilla. Quinn and his police "goons" keep trying to pin the killing of a man called Morton H. Wolson on Wale, as in this exchange in the little shamus's office:

> He growled some words at me that I had to take. . . .
> "O.K.," I told him when his words ran out, "I'm a rat, a louse, my feet stink and you won't play marbles with me anymore. All I want to know is, where's your warrant?"
> "In the morgue, Shrimp."
> "Who?"
> "Wolson."
> I whistled softly. My unbidden guests eyed me hungrily. I could envision the meal for which their eyes drooled—grilled Wale a la Ossining.

The villain of the piece is Wolson, despite the fact that he is murdered in the first chapter. He is depicted as "a fleshy man in a wrinkled blue suit. His features were coarse and flaccid. Wisps of dirty blond hair sprouted from his pink scalp. Yellowed teeth showed in a gaping mouth." He is also depicted as thoroughly evil: a murderer, a thief, a lunatic. When Mr. Manilla tells Wale that Wolson murdered two patriotic Filipinos with a knife fashioned from a spoon, Wale says, "That sounds like the Wolson I knew."

The amusing thing about all of this is that Peter Paige's real name was Morton H. Wolson.

Mystery writers, it is true, are fond of inside jokes; a considerable number have been perpetrated over the years, including a couple on the typewriter with which these words are being written. But if there is another story (or novel) in which an author put tongue in cheek and made himself the villain, and such a nasty villain at that, I'm not aware of it.

With the decline of the pulps in the early fifties, the criminous short story graduated, for the most part, to the digest magazines that flourished during that decade. Between 1953 and 1956, the biggest seller was a hardboiled magazine called *Manhunt*—a showcase for tough, downbeat, violent stories "of the seamier side of life" and for the work of such important writers as James M. Cain, Ross Macdonald, John D. MacDonald, Erle Stanley Gardner, Evan Hunter, Erskine Caldwell, Ray Bradbury, and Fredric Brown. *Manhunt's* initial success spawned a host of imitators: *Accused, Hunted, Pursuit, Guilty, Trapped, Two-Fisted, Off Beat, Saturn Web, Justice, Mystery Tales*, and four from *Manhunt's* own publishing company, *Verdict, Menace, Murder!* and *Mantrap*. Only a few of this proliferation of minor titles survived the decade, and those few had all disappeared by the end of 1962.

These publications were a showcase for the work of such important alternative writers as Mickey Spillane, Michael Avallone, Richard S. Prather, and Erle Basinsky. A good many bad stories appeared in their pages, to be sure—and in the pages of such higher quality digests as *Mystery Digest, The Saint Mystery Magazine, Mike Shayne Mystery Magazine*, and *Alfred Hitchcock's Mystery Magazine*. Some, such as "Lust Be My Destiny" by Art Crockett and "Soft Arms Mean Slaughter!" by Don Unatin, both of which appeared in *Two-Fisted* in 1959, come close to being classics. Yet none quite has that special stamp of greatness that would elevate it into the Robert Leslie Bellem class.

Television, paperback books, rising printing costs, mismanagement, and inflation forced all but a handful of crime fiction magazines into extinction before 1970. *Manhunt* expired in 1967, as did *The Saint*; the only major survivors were *Ellery Queen's Mystery Magazine*—the dean of crime digests, having first begun publication in 1941, and also the best by a good margin—*Alfred Hitchcock's Mystery Magazine*, and *Mike Shayne Mystery Magazine*. A few new periodicals emerged in the late sixties, here and there throughout the seventies and in the early eighties, but nearly all these were of mediocre quality and ceased publication after only a handful of issues. At the time of this writing, only *EQMM, AHMM,* and *MSMM* remain active; they have persevered on the (relative) quality of their stories, for the most part.

Inevitably, however, an alternative classic was bound to show up sooner or later, even in one of these august publications. This happened in 1978, when Robert Twohy's story "Slime" oozed into print in the June issue of *Alfred Hitchcock's Mystery Magazine.*

The reason for the unusual title is that the protagonist's name is Slime. Slime, you see, is a private detective. And "Slime" is a spoof of private-eye stories. At least, this is what "Slime" appears to be. Given Twohy's penchant for writing strange (and quite often very good) satirical crime tales, one supposes that a spoof is what he had in mind.

The story opens with Slime sitting in his office in a "drab building in a low-grade business neighborhood in San Francisco." We know it is Slime's office because the door glass has the word "Slime" on it. Slime has been sitting there in his office for a long time; he has, in fact, been sitting there for twenty-two days, waiting for a client, because "if a man isn't in his office clients who come looking for him won't find him, because he isn't in his office."

Then the door opens and three men come in. One of them is wearing a rubber goose mask and brandishing a .45. The other two are wearing grocery bags over their heads, with eyeholes cut out of the paper; they are brandishing .22s. The goose-headed one, who is known as the Fowl, tells Slime that he and his henchmen are the kidnappers of Mortimer Feekwood (also known as Sonnyboy and Laddykins), son of "renowed [*sic*] San Francisco tycoon" Phineas Feekwood. It seems Mortimer was abducted the previous Friday on his way home from school—"a school set up by the court system for habitual drunken drivers. Mortimer was fifty-two years old. Some years before he had been in the papers, accused by the parents of numerous local debutantes of trying to establish a white-slave empire, but the jury had decided that he was misunderstood and really only paying compliments to the girls."

Slime tells the Fowl to put away the guns, he doesn't talk to clients who point guns at him. The Fowl tells Slime that he's going to act as a go-between to collect a two-million-dollar ransom for Mortimer Feekwood. Slime tells the Fowl to put away the guns, he doesn't talk to clients who point guns at him. The Fowl and his henchmen decide Slime is a very cool character—*too* cool—and so they're going to finish him off because he won't agree to their demands. Slime asks the Fowl and his henchmen to have a drink with him. The Fowl says he can't drink with his goose-head mask on. One of the henchmen says he's reformed, living a much better life now, with friends and a sense of purpose; he advises Slime to give up drinking. The other henchman says he promised his mother he wouldn't use alcohol. The Fowl tells Slime to drink his drink by himself and to hurry it up.

> They watched as Slime took a paper cup and reached for the bottle of bourbon.
> He picked up the bottle with a sudden strong yank. The three social misfits could see, for one startled instant, that a wire was attached to the base of it. The wire ran into a hole in the desk. The yank caused an instantaneous action of some gear within the desk and in the blink of an eye the front of the desk fell forward, exposing a nest in which reposed a belt-loaded machine gun on a swivel, obviously ready to fire.
> Six amazed eyes were riveted on the menacing muzzle of the gun, and three pistols drooped in three unnerved hands.
> Slime, still sitting, with one hand now out of sight behind the desk, said in his quiet way, "Drop the guns. I have in my hand a cord which, if I pull it, will fill you full of lead."

The Fowl and his three henchmen throw their guns on the floor. After which Slime calls the cops, in the person of his friend Gilhooley, who is very glad to hear from him (" 'Slime! What do you know! How've you been, Slime?' ") and even gladder to hear that Slime has the Fowl and his henchmen under the gun. Ten minutes later Gilhooley arrives and identifies the Fowl with one glance. "It's a frame," the Fowl says. "We don't know nothing," the first henchman says. "I want my mother," the second henchman says. Then Gilhooley thanks Slime profusely, picks up the front of the desk for him and hangs it to conceal the machine gun, and takes the Fowl and his henchmen away.

Slime keeps on sitting at his desk, waiting. "Thwarting the Fowl had earned him nothing. Phineas Feekwood might offer a reward but Slime didn't accept rewards. It was part of his code. He took only what he earned—his fee. Plus expenses. But he had had no expenses thwarting the Fowl. So he hadn't earned a dime."

He keeps on waiting awhile longer. Then, at five o'clock, he gets up, locks the office door, and goes out (in that order).

> Tomorrow was another day. A customer would come. If not tomorrow, the next day. Or the next. Somebody would be struck by the name in the yellow pages.
> He would wait.
> He was Slime.

The eloquence of those last three words renders any further comment superfluous.

A Postmortem

And there you have them—the unsung alternative heroes of crime fiction and the *crème de la crème,* as it were, of their efforts. Perhaps now you can understand why I was compelled to write this book. Perhaps you have even come to agree with my axiom that greatness is not necessarily predicated on a high level of quality, and with its corollary that greatness *does* exist among the ignored, the downtrodden, the forgotten, the inept, if only one will take the time and effort to seek it out.

In that spirit of seeking out greatness, I hope you will decide to hunt for some of the works discussed in these pages and to read them for yourself. Most are not difficult to find, providing a little diligence and patience are exercised; they turn up regularly in secondhand bookstores and on the sales lists of mail-order mystery-book dealers, a partial list of whom can be found, among other places, in the classified-ads section of *Ellery Queen's Mystery Magazine.* In most instances, I have only hinted at the delights to be found in these books and stories, only offered a scant few of their quotable passages. No capsule summary can do justice to a Sydney Horler novel or to those of Carter Brown, Carolyn Wells, Michael Avallone, R.A.J. Walling, Nick Carter, Joseph Rosenberger, and a host of others. They must be experienced, just as the prose of Robert Leslie Bellem must be experienced, to be fully appreciated and fully savored.

I also hope you will make an effort to seek out other alternative classics not covered here. There must certainly be dozens that have escaped my attention, that remain hidden, unread, waiting to reveal their treasures. I know *I'm* going to be looking for them. And I know, too, that I will again experience that familiar thrill every connoisseur feels at each new discovery and that I will utter once more, like the cry of "Eureka!" from a prospector who has just struck gold, the words:

"My God, that's *really* bad!"

Bibliography

NOVELS

Abrahams, Robert. *Death in 1-2-3.* New York: Phoenix Press, 1942.

Alexander, Jan. *The Wolves of Craywood.* New York: Lancer Books, 1970.

Apple, A. E. *Mr. Chang's Crime Ray.* New York: Chelsea House, 1928.

Avallone, Michael. *Assassins Don't Die in Bed.* New York: New American Library (Signet), 1968.

_____. *The Case of the Bouncing Betty.* New York: Ace Books, 1957.

_____. *The Case of the Violent Virgin.* New York: Ace Books, 1957.

_____. *The Crazy Mixed-Up Corpse.* Greenwich, Conn.: Gold Medal, 1957.

_____. *The Horrible Man.* New York: Curtis Books, 1972.

_____. *Killer on the Keys.* New York: Curtis Books, 1973.

_____. *Meanwhile Back at the Morgue.* Greenwich, Conn.: Gold Medal, 1960.

_____. *The Satan Sleuth No. 1: Fallen Angel.* New York: Warner Paperback Library, 1974.

_____. *Shoot It Again, Sam!* New York: Curtis Books, 1972.

_____. *The Tall Dolores.* New York: Henry Holt, 1953.

_____. *The Voodoo Murders.* Greenwich, Conn.: Gold Medal Books, 1957.

Barker, Elsa. *The C.I.D. of Dexter Drake.* New York: Sears, 1929.

Barron, Ann Forman. *Bride of Menace.* Greenwich, Conn.: Gold Medal, 1973.

Basinsky, Erle. *The Big Steal.* New York: E. P. Dutton, 1955.

Bellem, Robert Leslie. *Blue Murder.* New York: Phoenix Press, 1938.

Berckman, Evelyn. *The Evil of Time.* New York: Dodd, Mead, 1954.

Bestor, Clinton. *The Corpse Came Calling.* New York: Phoenix Press, 1941.

Brent, Lynton Wright. *Death of a Detective.* Reseda, Calif.: Powell Books, 1969.

_____. *One Man's Crime.* Reseda, Calif.: Powell Books, 1969.

Bristow, Gwen, and Manning, Bruce. *The Invisible Host.* New York: Mystery League, 1930.

Brown, Carter. *The Brazen.* New York: New American Library (Signet), 1960.

_____. *Burden of Guilt.* New York: New American Library (Signet), 1970.

_____. *The Girl Who Was Possessed.* New York: New American Library (Signet), 1963.

_____. *The Victim.* New York: New American Library (Signet), 1959.

_____. *Wheeler Fortune.* New York: New American Library (Signet), 1974.

Carter, Nick. *The Day of the Dingo.* New York: Charter Books, 1980.

_____. *Hour of the Wolf.* New York: Award Books, 1973.

_____. *Ice Trap Terror.* New York: Award Books, 1974.

_____. *The 13th Spy.* New York: Award Books, 1965.

_____. *The Weapon of Night.* New York: Award Books, 1967.

Chang, Lee. *Kung Fu: The Year of the Tiger.* New York: Manor Books, 1973.

Corren, Grace. *The Darkest Room.* New York: Lancer Books, 1969.

_____. *Mansion of Deadly Dreams.* New York: Popular Library, 1973.

_____. *A Place on Dark Island.* New York: Lancer Books, 1971.

Daly, Carroll John. *Murder from the East.* New York: Stokes, 1935.

_____. *The Tag Murders.* New York: E. J. Clode, 1930.

_____. *Tainted Power.* New York: E. J. Clode, 1931.

Denbow, William. *Chandler.* New York: Belmont-Tower, 1977.

Diamond, Frank. *Murder Rides a Rocket.* New York: Mystery House, 1946.

Dorien, Ray. *The House of Dread.* New York: Paperback Library, 1967.

Eldredge, Gilbert. *Murder in the Stratosphere.* New York: Phoenix Press, 1940.

Elliott, Bruce. *You'll Die Laughing.* New York: Five-Star Mystery, 1945.

Fickling, G. G. *A Gun for Honey.* New York: Pyramid Books, 1958.

_____. *Honey in the Flesh.* New York: Pyramid Books, 1957.

Fitzsimmons, Cortland. *70,000 Witnesses.* New York: McBride, 1931.

Grant, James Edward. *The Green Shadow.* New York: Hartney Press, 1935.

Gray, Berkeley. *Conquest Goes West.* London: Collins, 1954.

_____. *The Spot Marked X.* London: Collins, 1948.

Hale, Jennifer. *Stormhaven.* New York: Lancer Books, 1970.

Halliday, Brett. *The Violent World of Michael Shayne.* New York: Dell Books, 1965.

Hanshew, Thomas. *Cleek, the Master Detective.* New York: Doubleday, Page, 1918.

Haynes, Annie. *Who Killed Charmian Karslake?* New York: Dodd, Mead, 1930.

Heath, Eric. *Murder of a Mystery Writer.* New York: Arcadia House, 1955.

Hines, Jeanne. *Bride of Terror.* New York: Popular Library, 1976.

Hodge, Jane Aiken. *Marry in Haste.* New York: Doubleday, 1961.

Hodges, Carl G. *Naked Villainy.* New York: Suspense Novel No. 3, 1951.

Horler, Sydney, *The Curse of Doone*. New York: Mystery League, 1930.

_____. *Dark Danger*. New York: Mystery House, 1945.

_____. *The Destroyer, and The Red-Haired Death*. London: Hodder & Stoughton, 1938.

_____. *Lord of Terror*. New York: Hillman-Curl, 1937.

Hunt, Charlotte. *The Cup of Chanatos*. New York: Ace Books, 1968.

Johnson, Philip. *Hung Until Dead*. New York: Phoenix Press, 1940.

Keeler, Harry Stephen. *The Case of the Mysterious Moll*. New York: Phoenix Press, 1945.

Keystone, Oliver. *Arsenic for the Teacher*. New York: Phoenix Press, 1950.

Knevels, Gertrude. *Out of the Dark*. Philadelphia: Penn Publishing Co., 1932.

Koehler, Robert Portner. *Murder Expert*. New York: Phoenix Press, 1945.

Le Queux, William. *The Mystery of the Green Ray*. London: Hodder & Stoughton, 1915.

Leroux, Gaston. *The Perfume of the Lady in Black*. New York: Brentano's, 1909.

Levinrew, Will. *Murder in the Palisades*. New York: McBride, 1930.

Lilly, Jean. *Death Thumbs A Ride*. New York: E. P. Dutton, 1940.

Marlowe, Stephen. *Killers Are My Meat*. Greenwich, Conn.: Gold Medal, 1957.

Martin, Ian Kennedy. *The Manhattan File*. New York: Holt, Rinehart, 1976.

Maryk, Michael, & Monahan, Brent. *Death Bite*. New York: Andrews & McMeel, 1979.

Maylon, B. J. *The Corpse with Knee-Action*. New York: Phoenix Press, 1940.

Michaels, Barbara. *The Dark on the Other Side*. New York: Dodd, Mead, 1970.

Mitchell, Gladys. *The Mystery of a Butcher's Shop*. New York: The Dial Press, 1930.

Morgan, Michael. *Decoy*. New York: Ace Books, 1953.

Newman, Bernard. *The Mussolini Murder Plot*. New York: Hillman-Curl, 1939.

Nonweiler, Arville, *Murder on the Pike*. New York: Phoenix Press, 1944.

North, Sam. *209 Thriller Road*. New York: St. Martin's Press, 1979.

Norwood, Hayden. *Death Down East*. New York: Phoenix Press, 1941.

O'Hanlon, James. *Murder at Horsethief*. New York: Phoenix Press, 1941.

O'Shea, Sean. *What a Way to Go!* New York: Belmont Books, 1966.

Paige, Leslie. *Queen of Hearts*. New York: Belmont-Tower,1974.

Parker, Robert B. *Looking for Rachel Wallace*. New York: Delacorte, 1980.

Pinkerton, Allan. *The Expressman and the Detective*. Chicago: W. B. Keen, Cooke & Co., 1874.

Porcelain, Sidney E. *The Purple Pony Murders*. New York: Phoenix Press, 1944.

Prather, Richard S. *The Cockeyed Corpse*. Greenwich, Conn.: Gold Medal, 1964.

_____. *Dig that Crazy Grave*. Greenwich, Conn.: Gold Medal, 1961.

_____. *Strip for Murder*. Greenwich, Conn.: Gold Medal, 1955.

_____. *Take a Murder, Darling*. Greenwich, Conn.: Gold Medal, 1958.

_____. *The Wailing Frail*. Greenwich, Conn.: Gold Medal, 1956.

_____. *Way of a Wanton*. Greenwich, Conn.: Gold Medal, 1952.

Raison, Milton M. *Murder in a Lighter Vein*. Culver City, Calif.: Murray & Gee, 1947.

Reynolds, Mack. *The Case of the Little Green Men*. New York: Phoenix Press, 1951.

Rhoades, Knight. *She Died on the Stairway*. New York: Arcadia House, 1947.

Rinehart, Mary Roberts, and Hopwood, Avery. *The Bat*. New York: Geo. H. Doran, 1926.

Rivera, William L. *Panic Walks Alone*. Chatsworth, Calif.: Major Books, 1976.

Roan, Tom. *The Dragon Strikes Back*. New York: Julian Messner, 1936.

Rohde, William L. *Help Wanted—for Murder*. Greenwich, Conn.: Gold Medal, 1950.

Rosenberger, Joseph. *Death Merchant No. 6: The Albanian Connection*. New York: Pinnacle Books, 1973.

_____. *Death Merchant No. 20: Hell in Hindu Land*. New York: Pinnacle Books, 1976.

_____. *Death Merchant No. 9: The Laser War*. New York: Pinnacle Books, 1974.

"Sapper" (H. C. McNeile). *The Black Gang*. New York: Geo. H. Doran, 1922.

Sears, Ruth McCarthy. *Wind in the Cypress*. New York: Lenox Hill Press, 1974.

Shannon, Carl. *Lady, That's My Skull*. New York: Phoenix Press, 1947.

Shannon, Jimmy. *The Devil's Passkey*. New York: Appleton-Century-Crofts, 1952.

Small, Austin J. *The Avenging Ray*. New York: Doubleday Crime Club, 1930.

Spatz, H. Donald. *Murder with Long Hair*. New York: Phoenix Press, 1940.

Spencer, Ross H. *The Dada Caper*. New York: Avon Books, 1978.

Spillane, Mickey. *I, the Jury*. New York: E. P. Dutton, 1947.

_____. *One Lonely Night*. New York: E. P. Dutton, 1951.

Targ, William, and Herman, Lewis. *The Case of Mr. Cassidy*. New York: Phoenix Press, 1939.

Teilhet, Darwin, and Teilhet Hildegarde. *The Feather Cloak Murders*. New York: Doubleday Crime Club, 1936.

Trimble, Louis. *Murder Trouble*. New York: Phoenix Press, 1945.

Vanderveer, Stewart. *Death for a Lady*. New York: Phoenix Press, 1939.

Walling, R.A.J. *A Corpse by Any Other Name*. New York: Morrow, 1943.

_____. *The Corpse With the Blue Cravat*. New York: Morrow, 1938.

_____. *The Corpse in the Coppice*. New York: Morrow, 1935.

_____. *The Corpse With the Eerie Eye*. New York: Morrow, 1942.

_____. *The Corpse With the Floating Foot*. New York: Morrow, 1936.

_____. *The Corpse With the Grimy Glove.* New York: Morrow, 1938.

_____. *The Corpse Without a Clue.* New York: Morrow, 1944.

_____. *By Hook or Crook.* New York: Morrow, 1941.

_____. *The Late Unlamented.* New York: Morrow, 1948.

Warwick, Chester. *My Pal, the Killer.* New York: Ace Books, 1961.

Wells, Carolyn. *The Broken O.* Philadelphia: Lippincott, 1933.

_____. *The Man Who Fell Through the Earth.* New York: Geo. H. Doran, 1919.

_____. *The Wooden Indian.* Philadelphia: Lippincott, 1935.

West, John B. *Bullets are My Business.* New York: New American Library (Signet), 1960.

_____. *Cobra Venom.* New York: New American Library (Signet), 1959.

_____. *Death on the Rocks.* New York: New American Library (Signet), 1961.

_____. *An Eye for an Eye.* New York: New American Library (Signet), 1959.

_____. *Never Kill a Cop.* New York: New American Library (Signet), 1961.

_____. *A Taste for Blood.* New York: New American Library (Signet), 1960.

Willie, Ennis. *The Case of the Loaded Garter Holster.* Chicago: Merit Books, 1964.

Woodward, Edward. *The House of Terror.* New York: Mystery League, 1930.

Short Stories

Bellem, Robert Leslie. "Beyond Justice." *Spicy Detective*, November 1935.

_____. "Bullet from Nowhere." *Dan Turner, Hollywood Detective* No. 1 (1943).

_____. "Bund Bump." *Dan Turner, Hollywood Detective*, July 1943.

_____. "Coffin Frame." *Speed Detective*, January 1944.

_____. "Come Die for Me." *Speed Detective*, December 1946.

———. "Death's Blind Date." *Dan Turner, Hollywood Detective,* July 1943.

———. "Death's Passport." *Spicy Detective,* June 1940.

———. "Diamonds of Death." *Hollywood Detective,* August, 1950.

———. "Death Dubbed In." *Spicy Detective,* July 1940.

———. "Design for Dying." *Spicy Detective,* April 1939.

———. "Don't Go Near the Slaughter." *Hollywood Detective,* September 1947.

———. "Focus on Death." *Hollywood Detective,* January 1944.

———. "Forgery's Foil." *Spicy Detective,* August 1942.

———. "Gun from Gotham." *Rue Morgue No. 1,* edited by Rex Stout and Louis Greenfield, Creative Age Press (New York), 1946.

———. "Killer's Clue." *Hollywood Detective,* October 1944.

———. "Killer's Cue." *Spicy Detective,* April 1941.

———. "Killer's Harvest." *Spicy Detective,* July 1938.

———. "Killer's Keepsake." *Spicy Detective,* June 1942.

———. "The Lake of the Left-Hand Moon." *The Great American Detective,* edited by William Kittredge and Steven M. Krauzer, New American Library (New York), 1978.

———. "Mesa of Madness." *Spicy Mystery,* February 1937.

———. "Murder Has Four Letters." *Hollywood Detective,* February 1945.

———. "Murder on the Sound Stage." *Private Detective Stories,* June 1937.

———. "Murder's Messenger." *Dan Turner, Hollywood Detective,* No. 1 (1943).

———. "Widow by Proxy." *Hollywood Detective,* January 1944.

Paige, Peter. "When a Man Murders." *Dime Detective,* March 1947.

Twohy, Robert. "Slime." *Alfred Hitchcock's Mystery Magazine,* June 1978.

Nonfiction References

Adey, Robert. *Locked Room Murders.* London: Ferrett, 1979.

Arlo, Michael. *Penny Dreadfuls and Other Victorian Horrors.* London: Jupiter Books, 1977.

Barzun, Jacques, and Taylor, Wendell Hertig. *A Catalogue of Crime.* New York: Harper & Row, 1971.

Boucher, Anthony. "Department of Criminal Investigation" column in the August 13, 1947, San Francisco *Chronicle.*

———. *Multiplying Villainies: Selected Mystery Criticism, 1942–1968.* Privately printed, 1973.

Butler, William Vivian. *The Durable Desperadoes.* London: Macmillan, 1973.

Craig, Patricia, and Cadogan, Mary. *The Lady Investigates.* London: Gollancz, 1981.

Fisher, Steve. "The Literary Rollar Coaster." *Writers 1941 Year Book.* Cincinnati: Writer's Digest, Inc.

Goulart, Ron. *Cheap Thrills: An Informal History of the Pulp Magazines.* New Rochelle, N.Y.: Arlington House, 1972.

Haycraft, Howard. *Murder for Pleasure: The Life and Times of the Detective Story.* New York: Appleton-Century, 1941.

Horler, Sydney. *Excitement: An Impudent Autobiography.* London: Hutchinson, 1933.

———. *More Strictly Personal.* London: Rich & Cowan, 1935.

———. *Now Let Us Hate.* London: Quality Press, 1942.

———. *Strictly Personal.* London: Hutchinson, 1934.

———. *Writing for Money.* London: Nicholson & Watson, 1932.

Hubin, Allen J. *The Bibliography of Crime Fiction, 1749–1975.* Del Mar, Calif.: Publisher's Inc., 1979.

Kittredge, William, and Krauzer, Steven M. Introduction to "Lake of the Left-Hand Moon" by Robert Leslie Bellem, in *The Great American Detective.* New York: New American Library (Signet Mentor), 1978.

Knight, Damon. *In Search of Wonder.* Chicago: Advent Publishers, 1967.

McCormick, Donald. *Who's Who in Spy Fiction.* New York: Taplinger, 1977.

Nevins, Francis M. "Murder at Noon: Michael Avallone." *The New Republic,* July 22, 1978.

Nolan, William F. *Dashiell Hammett: A Casebook.* Santa Barbara, Calif.: McNally & Loftin, 1969.

———. "Pulp Pioneer of the Private Eye." *Mike Shayne Mystery Magazine,* October 1980.

Ousby, Ian. *Bloodhounds of Heaven: The Detective in English Fiction from Godwin to Doyle.* Cambridge, Mass.: Harvard University Press, 1976.

Panek, LeRoy L. *The Special Branch: The British Spy Novel, 1890–1980.* Bowling Green, Ohio: Bowling Green University Popular Press, 1981.

Perelman, S. J. "Somewhere a Roscoe. . ." *The Best of S. J. Perelman.* New York: Random House Modern Library, 1947.

Prager, Arthur. *Rascals at Large.* New York: Doubleday, 1971.

Queen, Ellery. *The Detective Short Story.* Boston: Little Brown, 1942.

Reilly, John, ed. *Twentieth Century Crime and Mystery Writers.* New York: St. Martin's Press, 1980.

Rinehart, Mary Roberts. *My Story.* New York: Farrar & Rinehart, 1931.

Ruehlmann, William. *Saint with a Gun: The Unlawful American Private Eye.* New York: New York University Press, 1974.

Sampson, Robert. "The Chang Monster." *The Science Fiction Collector No. 14* (1981).

Shaner, Carl. Interview with Joseph Rosenberger in *Skullduggery*, Spring 1981.

Sparafucile, Tony. Introduction to reissue of Carroll John Daly's *Murder from the East.* New York: International Polygonics Ltd., 1978.

Symons, Julian. *Mortal Consequences: A History from the Detective Story to the Crime Novel.* New York: Harper & Row, 1972.

Thomson, H. Douglas. *Masters of Mystery.* London: Collins, 1931 (American edition: New York: Dover Publications, 1978).

Turner, Darwin T. "The Rocky Steele Novels of John B. West." *The Armchair Detective*, August 1973.

Turner, E. S. *Boys Will Be Boys.* London: Michael Joseph, 1947.

(Various Hands). *Meet the Detective.* London: Allen & Unwin, 1935.

Watson, Colin. *Snobbery With Violence.* London: Eyre & Spottiswoode, 1971.

Wells, Carolyn. *The Technique of the Mystery Story.* Springfield, Mass.: The Home Correspondence School, 1913.

Index